BLADE'S HONOR

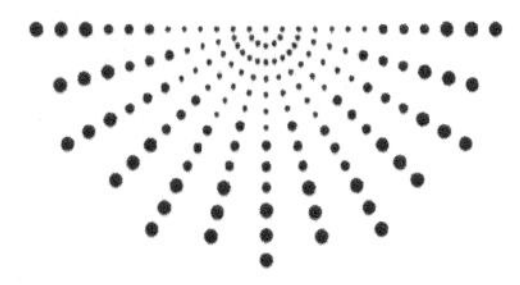

LISA BLACKWOOD

BLADE'S HONOR

ISHTAR'S LEGACY / BOOK 2

LISA BLACKWOOD

ABOUT THE BOOK

A gryphon prince. A warrior maiden. An impossible love.

Rescued from her grandfather's dungeon by the King of the Gryphons, Enkara only wishes to repay that great debt by serving as one of the elite Shadow Guards tasked with protecting the royal line. Unfortunately, the gods have other plans, for she was born with the mark of a goddess running down her spine and her destiny is far greater than that of a simple guard.

She is one of the Goddess Ishtar's Avenging Blades, born into the world when danger stalks the royal line.

While that brings far more attention than she ever wished, she is still happy to serve Crown Prince Kuwari, for he is also her closest friend, and their bond is unlike any other Blade and Prince before them.

But Ishtar isn't the only goddess with a desire to claim Enkara as her Blade and Kuwari as her King. Ereshkigal, Queen of the Underworld, is jealous of her younger sister, Ishtar, and will do all in her power to snatch them away, even if she must destroy the gryphon kingdom to do it.

BLADE'S HONOR

FREE STORIES

GET TWO FREE STORIES FROM MY BESTSELLING
SERIES WHEN YOU
SIGN UP FOR MY NEWSLETTER.

I send regular monthly newsletters with details about new releases,
    special offers, freebies, and other bookish news.
    If that's something you'd be interested in, just follow the link below.

http://lisablackwood.com/join-the-newsletter-here/

BLADE'S HONOR

PROLOGUE

Enheduana hurried down the musty corridor as she made her way to the hidden temple deep below the palace. She was running late after having to take a longer way when a servant had been cleaning the seldomly used room that housed a secret entrance to these older tunnels.

It was imperative that she hide her presence and destination from even a simple servant. Several of the king's elite Shadow Guard regularly bribed the servants for information about various nobles and to be notified of anything that looked out of place. Spies for the king could be anywhere.

After the failed coup and assassination attempt sixteen years ago, nowhere in the kingdom of New Sumer was safe for Ereshkigal's servants. But that would soon change if they stayed faithful to the cause and didn't fail the Queen of the Underworld.

When she reached the temple, at last, she found her two accomplices had already arrived ahead of her. She didn't acknowledge them, instead going to the altar and honoring Ereshkigal with a prayer.

"We're going to need far more than prayers if we have any hope of delivering Prince Kuwari to our goddess."

Enheduana turned from the altar and glowered at the speaker. She had never really liked Balathu, not his narrow-shouldered frame, not his piercing whine, or plentiful complaints. Even as he stood there just breathing, he annoyed her.

Unfortunately, he and his servant, Enusat, were the only agents of the goddess that she'd been able to bring into the city without raising suspicions.

"Balathu, there is still hope of success. We need only bide our time for a little while longer." And by the grace of Ereshkigal, avoid a disaster like what that overconfident fool Ziyatum and his equally short-sighted daughter had put into motion all those years ago.

Balathu huffed out a sound of disbelief. "Hope? What hope? The goddess's Blade has been lost—most likely discovered and killed in the fall of Kalhu. We lost so much when Ditanu and his Blade ransacked that great city-state. Then he doled out the remains of the city to those loyal to him. That blow weakened us. It will be years before we can proceed with the plan."

Enheduana glanced sidelong at Balathu and wondered yet again how one so inept could have been gifted with one of the Queen of the Underworld's most potent talents. The ability to mask one's true thoughts and motives from the King's Shadows was an exceedingly rare gift, and Balathu just happened to possess it.

There was no doubt of the strength of his talent. He tested it daily as he pretended to be one of Ishtar's own priests.

Too bad the talent hadn't gifted him with charisma or an agile mind.

Sighing, she didn't show any of her internal thoughts. "I'm quite certain Ereshkigal's Blade isn't dead."

"You think she is still alive and in hiding?"

Isn't that what I just said? Enheduana reined in the bite of annoyance and said, "Alive yes. Though not in hiding. She's been out in the open all these years."

She could see Balathu still wasn't getting her meaning. "Have you not seen the similarities between how King Ditanu protected his true mate and Blade, Iltani, by hiding her away on the training island of New Assur until she matured, and how Kuwari and his childhood friend, Enkara, are following the same path? I think they know Enkara is a Blade, and they're just waiting for her magic to wake before revealing that fact."

"It's too obvious," Balathu said as his brows scrunched.

"Only because we know there is a second Blade. None but Ereshkigal's loyal servants know there is a second. No one else would ever dream there would be more than one Blade at a time."

"I hope you're correct for I don't know how we'll ever deliver Prince Kuwari to our Queen without the Blade's help."

"I am correct. Trust in that. And if we can use the new Blade to force Kuwari's hand, all the better." She paused and looked around, spearing first Balathu and then his servant with a stern look. "But I'm not placing all my hopes on one plan. I've set into motion a secondary one that will make Prince Kuwari come with us willingly if our Blade isn't yet strong enough to do it on her own."

"Willingly?"

Was she talking to a parrot? "Yes. Kuwari will go willingly into our goddess's embrace if it's the only way to save all those he loves."

"You mean to use the plague mist?" Enusat said, speaking for the first time. Balathu's servant rarely spoke, not because he was lacking in wit—Enheduana was sure it was the opposite. He liked to think upon a topic and be confident of his footing before verbalizing his thoughts.

Not for the first time she wished that Enusat was the priest and Balathu the novice.

"I see your way of thinking," Enusat continued. "It would be much safer for all if the Blade can be brought to bear first. Releasing a plague is much riskier, too hard to control or predict where it will spread."

"Yes," Enheduana agreed. "Before we do anything, I will summon an anunnaki and have him confirm what we already suspect. Even if Enkara is Ereshkigal's Blade, we can't be certain she will fall into line with our plans without a guiding nudge."

"She might have her own agenda, you mean," Enusat speculated thoughtfully while he picked at a loose thread on his robe.

"There is that possibility. However, she will still answer to our goddess's call. Of that, I am sure. In the meantime, we will work to discover all we can about Enkara the foundling but be cautious. The King's Shadows are suspicious and even more protective after what happened sixteen years ago."

The two males agreed and then departed the temple by separate ways. Later, they would emerge in different parts of the city. For now, Enheduana knew Ereshkigal's servants must skulk in the shadows, but if they were successful with their plan, soon they would be able to worship the Queen of the Underworld openly, as their ancestors did more than five thousand years ago.

The Queen of the Underworld was patient. Enheduana reminded herself she must be as well. What was a season or even a turning of the seasons compared to thousands of years?

It was nothing in the grand scheme of creation.

CHAPTER ONE

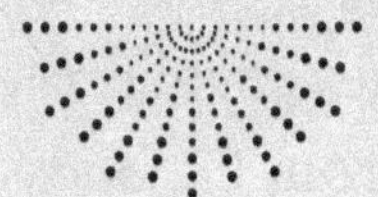

Dawn was still a far-off thought, and Enkara would have been sleeping if the softest of footsteps in the sand outside her tent hadn't stirred her to wakefulness moments before. Sleep hadn't entirely retreated, and she already had a blade in her hand. Instinct and close to four years of her mentor's most brutal training had turned her into a light sleeper.

It wouldn't be the first time either Burrukan, or one of the other instructors, had come upon her in the dead of night to test her readiness to take up her duty to protect those of the royal line.

Burrukan claimed she needed to be ready to defeat assassins at any time, even half asleep. Enkara silently freed herself from the thin blanket covering her body but kept the blade itself hidden under her pillow so the assailant wouldn't see a betraying glint in some stray moonbeam.

Not that this assailant was an actual assassin, or one of

her Shadow instructors either, for that matter. No, now that she was awake, she knew this assailant. Since an early age, Ishtar, Mother Goddess of the Gryphons and Queen of Heaven, had blessed Enkara with the gift of sensing the whereabouts of all the blood-members of the royal line. Presently, there was a gryphon of royal blood trying to sneak into her tent unseen.

She only knew one gryphon of royal blood foolish enough to sneak away from his bodyguards for a night flight to the training island of New Assur.

Enkara fought to keep her mind calm as if still deeply asleep.

The rebellious idiot. He was practically begging to get himself assassinated. Well, last time, she'd warned him if he tried such a stunt again, she'd give him a sound thrashing for his trouble. That time, he'd only laughed, saying she'd never followed through with any of her threats in the years he'd known her.

And he was correct. In the four years she'd been on the island of New Assur to complete her training to become Ishtar's Avenging Blade, he'd found ways to escape his guards no less than ten times to come visit her. Not once had she followed through on her threats when he sought her out.

Outside her tent, the footsteps had stopped. A moment later the fabric rustled as he untied the closures. She kept her eyes closed and remained still as he ducked inside the tent. More soft footsteps told her he was moving closer. When he was within striking distance, she sprang into motion, leaping from the bed and was upon him before he could react.

She twisted in the air, swiping at his lower legs with her

own. While he was off balance, she planted her hands on his shoulders and rode him to the ground. She was careful that his head didn't collide with anything on the way down. After all, she only wished to hurt his pride, not his person.

His body slammed into the rugs covering her tent's floor, and his breath escaped him in a huff of surprise. While he was still stunned, she locked her left hand around his right wrist and forced his arm above his head. Her other hand pressed the edge of her blade to his neck. She was ready to pull it away if he moved so much as a hair's breadth.

Accidentally killing the heir to the throne and her only childhood friend wasn't on today's list of activities.

She lowered her head until she was nearly nose to nose with the gryphon prince. "Kuwari, if you'd been an assassin, you'd be dead right now."

The open tent flap allowed just enough starlight into the interior to see the flash of his white teeth as he grinned up at her. "It's good I'm not an assassin, then, isn't it?"

Prince Kuwari didn't sound the least bit perturbed or mortified by his swift defeat. Hmmm. That was never good. Neither was the second flash of teeth.

"Kuwari, what are you doing here?" She tried for stern and mature, like the tone she'd heard High Priestess Kammani use on the council members when a session got out of hand.

"I missed you," he said, his voice soft and unguarded.

Her frown vanished. The four years of separation required for her training on New Assur hadn't been easy for her either. She and Kuwari had been inseparable from the day they first met in person until Burrukan had spirited her away for the final phase of her training on the remote island of New Assur where all the king's elite Shadows guards were trained.

The distance had also limited their ability to communicate through their unique mental link, forcing them to use images and emotions more than actual words like they'd done when Kuwari was still a cub.

He'd just turned sixteen when she'd been packed off to New Assur. Kuwari had taken their separation hard. But the previous four years had changed them both. During that time Kuwari had grown into a man and would soon be a fully trained governing prince, but he would always be her dearest friend.

But that didn't mean she'd go easier on him. "You are an idiot. Burrukan's going to tan your princely ass for this."

Kuwari shrugged, the small shift of his body under hers drove her earlier thoughts right out of her head. "Oh, by the Goddess—!"

"I see you've missed me, too," Kuwari said and shifted underneath her again. He couldn't move much, not with her body straddling his and her weight pinning him to the ground, but it didn't stop him from speaking. "Should I assume our Great Goddess Ishtar has finally awakened your full power? And that she wants us to perform the Sacred Marriage as our first official act?"

Enkara had only worn a light-weight shift to bed, and by the feel of Kuwari's muscular thighs trapped between her knees, he was wearing even less than her. With a curse, she rolled to her feet. She maintained her grip on Kuwari's wrist and hauled him up as well. When he was on his feet, she dropped his hand like it burned and turned her back on him.

"Why are you running around New Assur naked? If Burrukan catches you, he'll use your pale backside as a target before he tans your ass." Not that Enkara knew if Kuwari's backside was paler than the rest of his delicious olive-brown skin. After he'd grown to manhood, she'd done her best to avoid noticing Kuwari wasn't still the boy she'd grown up with. Of course, every time he'd seen her awkwardness, he'd go out of his way to make it impossible not to notice him more. Like now.

"Circumstances didn't give me time to pack a satchel before I made my escape. Besides, I fly faster without the weight of supplies."

Kuwari's laugh sounded far too intimate in the confines of her small tent. She scowled at him in the darkness, knowing he could probably see better in the gloom than she could. A full-blooded gryphon had a few tactical advantages over a half-blood with human heritage.

Her scowl deepened. Some days she highly doubted her gryphon heritage and wondered if her mother had strayed and if some unknown human man was actually her father.

By the goddess, she was twenty-four summers old and couldn't even shapeshift yet!

Enkara jerked the blanket off her bed and tossed it in Kuwari's general direction.

She was rewarded by his huff of surprise. Huh. He hadn't seen that coming. Good. A smile tugged at her lips as she made her way to a small, backless chair and grabbed the candle and striker she'd left there.

Once the candle was burning, she set it on the stool and then turned to face the younger prince. Her fists naturally planted themselves on her hips. "Naked is one thing. Weaponless is another matter altogether. Have you no care what your death would do to your parents?"

And to me?

"There was no danger," Kuwari said as he fussed with the blanket, folding it in half and then tying it at one hip all without glancing up at her.

"No danger?! There is always danger."

"Not this time." Kuwari finished securing his impromptu robe and then looked up, opened his arms wide, and waited for her to answer his silent summons.

Even while Enkara aimed a dark scowl at him, she stepped forward and into his embrace. Her own arms wrapped around him in a fierce hug—though she was still angry at him. One squeeze didn't offset that. But feeling his warmth, hearing his mighty heart and seeing his vibrant smile went a long way to soothing the sharp-edged fear that cut at her insides when she thought of the danger he put himself in just to visit her.

"You worry too much—"

She smacked him on the shoulder. "I wonder why that is?"

Kuwari had the decency to look abashed. "I knew no danger would touch me tonight."

Ah. He'd seen this visit in one of his visions. "Then you also should have expected the floor and the knife."

A sheepish look crossed his face as a pinkish hue darkened his cheeks. Her brow arched up in surprise. She couldn't ever recall him blushing. Not even the time when an overeager daughter of the nobility caught him at his bath.

But her words caused him to blush? Why?

Ah…oh! He *had* seen what would occur. He could have outmaneuvered her had he wanted. Apparently, he hadn't wanted to change that outcome.

She'd thought she had put this particular issue to rest two years ago on one of Kuwari's other unauthorized visits. Just what she could do to dissuade him without hurting his feelings was unclear.

And, if he decided to turn the full force of his charm upon her, she doubted she would fare better than any other woman would. Kuwari shared his father's looks. But he also shared his generous soul. Looks she could withstand easily enough. Bravery, kindness, and intelligence added to the mix was something else far deadlier.

Love was a seductive call, a distraction she couldn't afford. And distractions were too easily exploited by assassins.

Even though she was his Blade—a Goddess-ordained guardian of the royal line—Enkara believed Kuwari's parents would prefer if he took a mate from one of the ruling houses to help stabilize his future kingdom. Certainly, the council would expect that. The king had kept his council ignorant of Enkara's true identity for her own protection until she was fully trained, and the Goddess had claimed her and awakened her full power.

As for herself, she'd never forgotten that she was born of a disgraced house plagued with traitors. And as much as she'd loved her mother, that long-dead human woman had been a servant, not a noble lady. Only half gryphon, not able to shapeshift, and born of a traitorous line.

In no way was she a good candidate for Kuwari's future mate.

But how to persuade him that she wasn't a candidate for courtship without crushing what she loved most about him? Kuwari saved her from having to come up with an immediate solution to that problem by starting to pace in the narrow confines of her tent.

The restlessness was another trait he'd inherited from his father. A smile tugged at her lips as she remembered a sixteen-year-old Kuwari pacing and fretting like this four years ago when Burrukan had said Enkara would need to go to New Assur to finish her training as tradition dictated.

He'd survived the four years without her at his side; he'd survive having her reject any future advances on his part. She'd just have to be strong and reject Kuwari's overtures.

Might as well get it over with. "Not that I haven't missed you, but you can't keep doing this. It's not appropriate."

"I don't care about appropriate. I'm trying to avoid an unwanted future," Kuwari said as he turned. Grinning at her, he took two long paces and sat on her sleeping pallet as if it was the finest of furniture.

"That tells me absolutely nothing."

He shrugged, drawing her gaze to the flex and bunch of his broad, muscular shoulders.

Stop that, she scolded herself.

"I saw a vision of someone slipping something in my goblet during a feast. I decided since the nearest feast is my name day celebration in twelve days, it would be best to come collect my Blade and have her at my side."

A shiver of horror slithered down Enkara's spine. Before she'd thoroughly thought out a plan of action, she'd snatched up her sword and was belting the harness around her waist. "Why hasn't Burrukan come to retrieve me? I only agreed to come and train on New Assur as long as you were safe. At the first sign of trouble, Burrukan was to come immediately and deliver me back to Nineveh."

After a long pause, Kuwari cleared his throat and glanced down at his hands. "It's not that kind of danger."

"What do you mean? If you saw an assassin..." She unsheathed one of her daggers.

Kuwari chuckled. "My Blade might want to dress before she goes charging off to slay my enemies. Besides, it wasn't an assassin I saw in the jumbled-up flashes of fragmented visions. There's not going to be an attempt on my life. More like an attempt at the throne by way of becoming my mate."

Enkara's hand froze on her harness's buckle. "Are you saying someone is going to try to use the sacred fertility rite elixir to force a mating?"

While she was half human and wasn't yet sure if she would possess some of the other advantages and disadvantages that came with being a full-blooded gryphon, Kuwari was pure stock. If someone managed to drug him, there was a chance that he'd be forced to take a mate out of necessity rather than love. The council might not give him a choice. His survival was linked to the survival of all the gryphons. Whatever female was chosen to be matched to the drugged prince would become his mate and future queen.

Kuwari shrugged. "It wouldn't be the first time in the history of the gryphon kingdom that such a thing has been tried."

"By the gods! I'll hunt down and kill the ones behind this newest threat before they can get close enough to catch your scent. I'll make them regret even thinking of subverting your will. I'll—"

"You know it is never as easy as that. When it comes to the council and the ruling body of New Sumer, you never truly know friend from ambitious noble. And my vision only showed a hand pouring a liquid from a vial into my cup."

"Male or female?"

"Female. So that only leaves half the population of New Sumer." Kuwari sighed. "For once I wish the gods would just come out and clearly state what they want us to do."

Enkara grunted her agreement. Mortals, both human and gryphons, offered up too much entertainment for the gods to make things easy.

"Even if the gods showed me a clear vision of whoever is behind this attempt, there will always be someone else scheming to merge their bloodline to that of the royal line for the power and privilege."

She flopped down on the bed next to him as she realized what he said was true. She'd seen it firsthand more than once, hadn't she? Since Kuwari's first flush of manhood, nobles had been instructing their daughters on how best to catch the young prince's eye. Some had fewer scruples than others.

Kuwari wouldn't be safe until he finally fell in love and took a mate. That unknown woman would become his future queen and co-ruler, aiding with the governing of New Sumer.

"There is only one way to completely safeguard against future attempts of this nature." He glanced sidelong at her and then down at his hand where it rested on his thigh. Slowly he lifted his hand and slid it along the sleeping pallet until his fingers closed over hers.

Enkara didn't move, didn't speak, didn't even breathe, although she knew she should say something. Or do something. Stand up. Walk away. Something.

He gave her fingers a squeeze. Nothing else. Enkara drew a deep breath. "Kuwari, you should know if you're—"

"One day, far in the future when the throne comes to me, I would very much like for you to rule by my side."

"You're too young to know where your heart will lead. There's plenty of time—"

"Actually, there isn't as much time as one might think if my visions are accurate." Kuwari's tone softened. "Besides, I'm a gryphon. I know my heart already."

"Yes. Yes. But nothing is set in stone." Enkara stared at the slight flutter of the drab brown tent wall in front of her. If she didn't weaken toward Kuwari and grant him what he was asking, he'd be free to find true love and a more appropriate mate elsewhere. As for others trying to force his hand, she would see to it that no one was ever given the opportunity to trap the prince.

Not even herself.

Their bond forged out of shared childhood horrors transcended the ordinary bonds of love and friendship. She could and would love him completely—as his Blade, not his mate.

"You still have time to find a suitable mate to rule at your side. There's no rush. You're still only nineteen."

Kuwari laughed. "In twelve days, I'll turn twenty and become Crown Prince over all the city-states and receive my first true responsibilities. With that comes many demands from the Council. One of the first things they'll expect is some hint at my choice of a mate and future queen."

At the nervous thrill in his voice, Enkara glanced sidelong at him again. "The Council may have sharp teeth, but they can't force you into doing something you don't want."

"Oh, my innocent Blade," Kuwari said as he reached out to cup her cheek. "The council members always find ways to twist a situation to their liking."

"Still, they can't force a mate on you unless they try unscrupulous methods and if they do, they'll find themselves, and their ambitions, delivered swiftly to the underworld."

"A Blade's point of view is always so refreshing. Mother Iltani is the same way." Kuwari turned one of his most beguiling smiles upon her.

His look made her heart skip a beat. She steeled herself for what she sensed was coming next. She could withstand almost any opponent. But Kuwari's charm could slay a female of any age.

"Truth be told, I'd much rather savor a long, slow courtship and win your love, but I am not sure if I'll be given the time." Kuwari's hand dropped from her cheek to rest on her leg, just above the knee. "If you would agree to a year of courtship, it would do much to put my mind at ease and dissuade many of the nobles with eyes on the throne. And soon all will know you are Ishtar's Blade—my Blade."

His voice dropped at the last, coming out in a seductive purr as he gave her leg a caress. He leaned closer, closing the distance between them.

"Kuwari, no." Enkara planted a hand on his shoulder and blocked him from reaching his destination.

He froze, a chagrined look crossing his face. She hadn't missed the flash of pain that had proceeded it, either.

"I'm sorry Kuwari. I would never willingly cause you pain, but I know my duty, and it also includes protecting you from yourself." She covered his hand with hers, their fingers interlacing for a moment before she pushed his hand off her thigh and anchored it to the pallet between them so he wouldn't attempt a second touch. "That you might feel infatuated is only natural. It will fade in time."

She could still feel the phantom heat on her leg from where his palm had rested only a moment ago.

"Ah. The hard way it is, then." Wry humor touched his words and that now familiar determined look was back in his eye. "The goddess rewards those with the greatest patience."

Enkara didn't know what he was planning, but she had a few ideas, none of them good for her peace of mind.

Kuwari's chuckle filled the small tent's interior. "Besides, if I guessed the day and timing of my vision correctly, Burrukan and my guards would only have interrupted at the best part."

He'd seen something between them? Heat rushed up her

cheeks at his surprising words. As much as she really shouldn't want to know more about this vision—

"Kuwari," she growled, putting a fierce note in her voice. "You're jesting just to see if you can get a rise out of me, aren't you?"

The prince shrugged, attempting to look all innocent and blameless. Right. That was another trait he shared with his father. Those two could dupe even the most skeptical of councilors with that look.

She snorted. "I thought we didn't lie to each other?"

Kuwari grinned. "I'm not. But not all my visions come to pass. This one was weaker than most, just a distant and blurry possibility. I could share the details of this particular vision if that would help…"

"No! Thank you, my Prince, but no."

"Ah. Very well then, but don't complain later that I didn't share." He had the nerve to grin again. "But you should probably get dressed and gather your weapons. Burrukan and my bodyguards will be along shortly. You should be ready to leave. Once I tell Burrukan about the earlier vision, the one with someone slipping something into my drink, he'll agree that you should return to Nineveh with me."

"Of course, I'll come. I just wish Ishtar would awaken my mark." She rubbed at the back of her neck, feeling the slightly rough skin of her tattoo-like birthmark. The sooner she had control of her full powers, the better.

"Ishtar will wake your power soon, and we will perform the first of the blooding ceremonies within a moon's cycle." He flashed her a grin. "If Burrukan complains about your training, he can finish that on Nineveh."

Enkara nodded sharply. Her duty was to protect the prince, and she couldn't do that on New Assur.

She left Kuwari sitting on her sleeping pallet and gathered her linen shirt, leather vest and leggings. On the training island of New Assur, she wasn't required to dress in the knee-length robes that fully trained Shadows wore, nor did she have to wear the ceremonial skirt of veils that Ishtar preferred her Blades adorn themselves in—not yet at least.

She'd worry about that later. For now, she was more concerned with being presentable when her likely-to-be-livid mentor showed up with twenty equally perturbed Shadows hunting for their errant prince.

"You realize Burrukan is going to drag your royal ass down to the training fields over this stunt, right?" Enkara said as she pulled on her undergarments and leather pants. "Then he's going to bring me into the ring to reinforce his lesson."

"Won't be the first time. Besides, it will be worth it to have you in Nineveh again. These last three and a half years have been…lonely. Our mental link, letters, and a few visits aren't the same as crossing swords with you in a sand ring or sitting in front of a fire, sipping wine and discussing the newest political intrigues."

"Hmmm. The joys of court life. I've missed you, your parents, and younger sisters and brothers, and even many of the Shadows, but the council members and the rest of the nobility? Not in the least. But I have missed spending time with you just talking." Enkara turned her back on the prince and pulled her sleeping shift over her head and tossed it into a corner, then grabbed up the band of fabric she used to bind her breasts during training sessions.

She was just tucking the knot and loose ends between her cleavage when Kuwari cleared his throat. When she glanced over her shoulder, he was holding out her linen shirt and leather vest. The prince's gaze was locked on to a portion of tent wall above her head, but there was an impish slant to his lips that hadn't been there before.

Shaking her head, she pulled on the shirt and then the vest, still lacing it as she met Kuwari's gaze. "Thank you for coming and notifying me of this new danger to you."

With that she turned and ducked out of her small tent, leaving behind a flustered Kuwari, naked but for her blanket wrapped around his waist. She knew many of the noble ladies of the court would kill to be in her place. Yet nothing had happened. Nothing could ever happen. Not unless the gods claimed her and Kuwari during the spring fertility rite.

Though Ishtar and the harvest god, Tammuz, didn't bless every monarch and Blade with such a distinction. Sometimes Blades were merely there for protection and as a military leader in times of war. In other, more peaceful times, Blades were born to help a monarch govern the vast city-states.

Since Ishtar and Tammuz had King Ditanu and Queen Iltani to perform the Sacred Marriage during the spring rites, Enkara doubted they'd need her and Kuwari. If she was to go by the chaotic fragments of the future Kuwari saw in his visions and shared with her, she thought it much more likely she was his war leader. That role suited her much better.

Though, after Ditanu and Iltani put down the coup

planned by the traitorous governor of Kalhu and liberated Enkara and the other prisoners more than sixteen years ago, things had been quiet, and Kuwari might not need her as a war leader for many, many years to come, if they were lucky. Unfortunately, his visions usually offered little or no context of when they'd occur, much to the prince's displeasure.

That left helping with governance. Which, if Enkara was truthful with herself, terrified her. Since she'd spent the first nine years of her life confined in a dungeon, Kuwari's education and social skills far outstripped hers.

Even after being freed, the long days of training with Burrukan to prepare her to become a Blade hadn't left enough time for studying statecraft. She knew she hadn't mastered all the skills needed to aid in running a kingdom.

The thought of daily interactions with nobles or, goddess forbid, the council, set her heart pounding. Nine years in a cell had damaged her in ways she wasn't sure if she'd ever overcome, but she desperately needed to hide any hint of weakness from the blood-thirsty courtiers.

Even the lowest born noble lady would have a level of education Enkara lacked. At first, she'd consoled herself with the knowledge that once she was a fully trained Blade, she'd have time then to master the predator-filled waters of New Sumer's court. But after three and a half years of training, she felt no more confident with her social skills than when she'd first come to New Assur.

And if the gods happened to choose her and Kuwari for the Sacred Marriage?

She knew her duty, but the thought of one day becoming Kuwari's Queen gave her night-terrors. It had nothing to do with Kuwari, and everything to do with his title and the scrutiny that would come with it.

Secretly, if Kuwari wasn't the heir, she might have allowed him to court her and then in a few years when he'd matured enough to be sure of his own heart and mind, and she'd mastered her own fears and inadequacies, she wouldn't be averse to becoming his mate.

But that was a foolish dream. Kuwari was the Crown Prince, and she was very ill-suited to be a queen. A war leader though, that she was born for. Battle tactics, troop placement, Burrukan had drilled every bit of his knowledge into her.

Overhead the moon still rode high in the sky and dawn wasn't yet even a thought upon the eastern horizon, but she spotted ten darker shapes against the midnight blue of the sky. As they winged their way closer to the island of New Assur, Enkara instinctively reached out with her gift. It confirmed these newcomers were no threat. She'd already guessed as much but would never risk Kuwari's safety on a guess.

The identity of those about to arrive on New Assur confirmed, Enkara looked over her shoulder to see Kuwari emerging from her tent.

"That would be Regent Burrukan come to spank your royal ass."

Kuwari snorted with humor and came to stand shoulder to shoulder with her. "Burrukan is never boring at least."

CHAPTER TWO

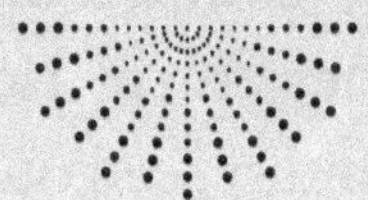

As the ten gryphons came in for a graceful landing on the sandy beach, Enkara fought to shove aside the feelings of frustration and jealousy the sight inspired. Over the last two years she'd tried not to feel embarrassed over the fact she couldn't yet shift to gryphon form. She really did.

She still lost the battle every time she saw one of her people swoop down in a graceful dive or run across the ground, their powerful muscles driving them forward and then almost effortlessly up into the air.

Her father was a gryphon. She was a Blade. In historical records, there were even mentions of fully human Blade's blessed by Ishtar and growing in power over time until they were able to take on gryphon form. Even Kuwari's second mother, Iltani, who was born without a drop of gryphon blood in her veins, had gained the power to shapeshift after several Blooding Ceremonies with King Ditanu.

There were even many other documented cases of non-Blade hybrids being able to shapeshift into gryphon form.

But not her.

Not yet. Maybe never.

Kuwari called her a late bloomer. That somehow only made the humiliation worse. She scowled as the gryphons touched down one after another. Once they'd folded their wings against their sides, their riders—other Shadows—dismounted as a group and spread out upon the beach.

They were hunting for any dangers that might be nearby. Not that there were any. Enkara certainly wouldn't let her prince remain on the beach if she'd sensed danger.

One broad-shouldered, bald-headed figure struck out from the rest and marched straight for Kuwari and Enkara's position. When Burrukan was close enough that he could address them without yelling, he glowered at the prince and started to chew him out. "Do you know how much trouble you're in? Again?"

Burrukan covered the rest of the way and came to a halt in front of them in a storm of sand and irritation, then he addressed her. "While Kuwari is completely hopeless, I'm glad to see you're ready to defend him."

His eyes narrowed. Glancing over at Kuwari, he took in the prince's mostly naked form with a frown. He turned his gaze back to Enkara. After a moment, he cleared his throat and rubbed a hand along the back of his bald head. "Did you just give in to the silver-tongued rebel?"

"Give in? Not sure I understand your meaning." She knew what he was asking, but it was entertaining to goad her mentor when the rare occasion arose.

A deep scowl darkened his expression. "Are you now mates?"

"Nothing happened."

"Huh. Too bad. The council would be irate. Would have made the next council meeting worth sitting through." He rubbed the side of his jaw thoughtfully, "You sure nothing happened? I and the other Shadows can go a little way down the beach if you and Kuwari want to retreat back to your tent for a short while…"

Enkara glowered at her mentor. "Not funny."

"Actually, it is. I never know what I'm going to find when King Ditanu sends me to retrieve his errant cub. It's possible there might be bets about the outcome of each escapade, but you didn't hear it from me."

"I'm not a cub anymore," Kuwari growled as he approached, his arms folding across his chest. "If something happened between Enkara and me, it's no one's business but our own."

"Nothing happened," Enkara clarified.

"Not for lack of trying on Kuwari's part, I imagine." Burrukan's dry reply was far closer to the truth than Enkara would willingly admit.

She folded her arms across her chest. "I wouldn't know anything about that."

"When Kuwari came sauntering over here wearing nothing but your bedding, I was sure I'd just lost the bet for the first time."

"We were just discussing how Kuwari can't keep doing this."

"Too bad. Because Kuwari in your bedding would be a

great story to get the gossip geese honking." Burrukan guided them back toward the tent while they talked. "Now tell me what's the real reason he came, if not to seduce you into becoming his future queen?"

There was no putting off Burrukan, so she told him the truth. Kuwari elaborated with details about his newest vision.

"Kuwari, stay here. Enkara, walk with me." Burrukan jerked his chin in the direction of the empty beach and then broke into a long, ground-eating gait.

She glanced once at Kuwari and shook her head when he made to follow.

"Fine," he said with an expression of disgruntlement. "I'll get it out of you later."

With that utterance, he spun around to go talk with the other Shadow guards. Enkara shook her head and marched off in pursuit of her mentor.

Once she caught up to him, he glanced sideways at her. "Kuwari doesn't know it yet, but his father has actually ordered for your return. He wouldn't tell me why, but Ditanu's gift of prophecy has reawakened of late. If I were to guess, I'd say Ditanu saw some threat to his son that he thinks you can guard against."

"Kuwari has seen something as well." Enkara briefly described what Kuwari had revealed.

Burrukan rubbed the back of his neck. There was an old scar there that he sometimes fingered when he was worried or unhappy about something.

"I was against bringing you back to Nineveh until Ishtar awoke your power, but the king overruled me." Annoyance flicked across Burrukan's expression. "You're needed back at the capital, but we still can't risk exposing you as a second Blade to our enemies."

"That's nothing new. I've been hiding what I am all my life."

"There is a new complication given what's happened in the recent past. The Council has been hounding King Ditanu to agree to a betrothal year between Kuwari and a female of proper lineage."

"That's nothing new either," Enkara stated as she stopped and folded her arms across her chest.

"No, but this time the Council was in complete agreement."

"Ha. That's a first." Enkara chuckled even though she wasn't feeling particularly humorous. The council never agreed unanimously on anything. Ever.

"Surely you and Kuwari's parents wouldn't agree to allow the council to force his hand." But even as she said it, she saw Burrukan wince. Her stomach did a little unhappy flip.

"Regent Ahassunu and High Priestess Kammani agreed with the rest of the council. They convinced King Ditanu of the merits of such an arrangement. It will halt the infighting between the different city-states once Kuwari announces his choice and the female in question accepts."

"But what about Kuwari? Doesn't he get a vote in this? It's his life after all. What if he doesn't want to court a woman yet?" She intentionally ignored Burrukan's raised eyebrow. Nothing had changed. There was no way she could agree to become 'the female' Kuwari picked.

"Kuwari doesn't actually know about the councilors'

decision yet. He escaped his guards just after dinner before the Council meeting had concluded."

Knowing what she did about Kuwari, she wasn't sure he didn't already know about the current decision regarding his future. Was that why he'd let her beat him so easily back in the tent? He'd hoped that things would develop naturally so he'd be spared the Council's interference in his life?

That was likely. It also explained his vision and why ambitious nobles would risk royal displeasure for the chance to bind a daughter to the Royal line.

It didn't make any of it right or just.

"All those in power think it's just fine to take away Kuwari's choice in a mate? You'll force him together with the female, and if she goes into heat and forges mating bonds with him, then that's just fine? It's barbaric." Enkara's blood rushed in her ears as her rage grew.

"Queen Iltani and I voted against it, but we were over-ruled." Another hint of anger touched his voice.

Enkara turned from Burrukan to watch the surf roll in. The briny scent soothed her as it had since she'd first been freed from her dungeon cell to see the beauty of the world outside.

Sighing, she turned back to her mentor. "I don't see how it affects me directly. There's nothing I can do to change the councilors' minds without revealing that I'm a Blade."

"King Ditanu expected you and Kuwari to become betrothed. As did I." Burrukan rubbed his jaw. "But you've rebuffed Kuwari more than a few times over the last two years, haven't you? If asked, you'd turn down the betrothal."

That was an entire speech coming from her closed-mouthed mentor. He deserved a truthful response.

"I love Kuwari dearly, but I couldn't accept such an overture. It's my duty to protect him from all dangers, including guarding his heart when he would give it away so freely. He needs a wise and compassionate mate, but she must also be shrewd and have a solid understanding of how to run a kingdom. I'm sure with a bit of digging he'll find a suitable mate somewhere among the nobility. But the timing should be his choice and hers."

She couldn't lie to herself. The thought of the prince finding someone else was...painfully unsettling, but that didn't negate all her earlier insecurities. She still had so much to learn and personal flaws to overcome before she'd be Kuwari's equal, and she wasn't certain if she would ever be a worthy mate to a future king.

"You make it sound easy, like there's an abundance of tolerable ladies for him to choose from," Burrukan said with a dry huff.

Enkara shrugged. "As much as I don't like the Council's heavy-handed approach to this, there's nothing I can do to change it, short of killing all the councilors."

"Hmm. The part about killing all the councilors. Hmm. That idea has some merit..." Burrukan's grin faded as his expression turned serious once more. "Kuwari is stubborn. He won't bow gracefully to the council's wishes. Even if you're determined to be as blockheaded as him, and he's forced to pick some other lady for the trial year, it doesn't mean he'll court her. Once the trial year expires, he'll be free to court whoever he wishes. At which point we can all continue as we were, a year older and wiser."

Enkara nodded in silence. A year or two from now, she might genuinely feel worthy to be both Ishtar's Blade and Kuwari's future co-ruler. And Kuwari would have matured into his role of Crown Prince. At which point, they'd be free to love each other if that's what they both still wanted.

"Nonetheless," Burrukan said, looking happy to have this particular conversation over. "I just wanted you to know what kind of situation you'll be walking into. Once Kuwari is betrothed for the trial year, no one can interfere with the couple."

"I know the rules—"

"Then you see the problem. The only humans or gryphons allowed to spend any great length of time with the newly betrothed pair are already mated couples, the King's Shadows, and Ishtar's Blade. So once Ishtar awakens your power, you'll be allowed to spend every moment shadowing him for his protection, but until that happens, Kuwari's friend, Enkara, cannot remain at his side for any length of time."

"I know. That's why I'm hoping you'll elevate me to a full Shadow shortly after we return to Nineveh."

"I elevate no one, not even you, to a full Shadow until their training is complete." His expression softened even though his tone didn't. "However, I've let drop enough comments that even the densest of nobles will think I'm training you to be my replacement. Goddess knows I'm not getting any younger, so I suppose after Ishtar claims you as her Blade, I really am going to have to start looking for an apprentice to follow in my footsteps." Burrukan shook his head sadly. "Then I'll have to start all over again."

Ah. Burrukan was correct. If he named her as his successor, her new duties would give her a legitimate reason to remain close to the heir.

"My mentor is wise," Enkara said in a somber tone, fighting back a smile. "I am most blessed to receive so many bruises."

"Mere reminders to move faster and strike down your opponent quicker."

The grin bloomed fully. "Very true. In all seriousness, I couldn't have asked for a better mentor."

"And you are one of my best students. I'd have been happy to retire and leave the Order in your hands one day," he grumbled. "Don't know why one of Ishtar's Blades can't also be leader of the Shadows."

"Because Ishtar doesn't share. Or at least that's what High Priestess Kammani once told me."

Burrukan huffed his agreement. "Well, now that that's out of the way, shall we go collect our very stubborn young prince? If we leave now and fly at top speed, we can be back to Nineveh before anyone knows the prince was missing."

Burrukan's words made sense. Unfortunately, she was still stuck on the 'flying' part.

"Do you wish me to take a boat back to Nineveh with my possessions?"

"No. You'll fly with us. I'll have one of the other students pack up your things and ship them back."

Enkara nodded sharply, hoping she didn't give away even a hint of the fear stirring in her blood. Fly. Burrukan wanted her to fly back to Nineveh. Well not actually fly, since she had yet to learn to shapeshift, but ride. He'd expect her to ride one of the other pureblood gryphons.

Goddess be merciful.

CHAPTER THREE

Kuwari fidgeted with his makeshift robe while he waited for Burrukan to finish with whatever he thought he had to tell Enkara in private. The older male was mistaken if he thought she would keep her own counsel.

Secrets were an insult to the bond he shared with his Blade. She never kept secrets from him, and he shared everything with her, even his visions. At least the ones he understood. It needed to stay that way if they had any hope of averting future threats to the crown and the kingdom of New Sumer.

He still didn't understand everything the goddess chose to show him, but sometimes he saw an event clearly, and by seeing it was able to sidestep some minor troubles. That wasn't always the case, though. Other times, he'd change one outcome only to cause more headaches, leading in turn to new visions and seeing more fragmented bits of the future.

His father always said the chaotic visions were more curse than blessing, but Kuwari disagreed, at least in part. Without his gift, he never would have been able to touch Enkara's mind when she'd been trapped in a dark cell. While he hadn't been able to free her physical body himself, he'd been able to free her mind from that dark dungeon by showing her things through his own eyes.

That same gift allowed him to know her almost as well as he knew himself. He'd watched her grow from a horribly mistreated child into a strong, fiercely loyal woman. Oh, she had many other facets to her personality and insecurities as well. But as a boy, he'd idolized the brave girl who stood up to all those who attempted to befriend him for false reasons.

Being a Blade, Enkara could read a person's intent. It was one of the first abilities Ishtar endowed upon her Blades. The talent would only grow in strength once Ishtar finally claimed Enkara as her Blade. He hoped other aspects of their relationship would grow stronger after that event.

As Kuwari watched Burrukan and Enkara stride across the sandy beach toward his location, he couldn't help but notice Ishtar had endowed her Blade with other gifts not limited to her mind.

He'd watched the dark-haired girl grow into a graceful warrior woman. She was no delicate beauty, no. His Enkara was as tall as a man, broad-shouldered and muscular, and could best him in a sword fight, matching him in brute strength while surpassing him in style and skill.

While no one would call her soft and her features might be too lean and angular for the court ideal of beauty, she still possessed enough curves no one would ever confuse her for a man. Only half consciously, his gaze slid from her face to study those enticing curves. Realizing that he'd likely be expected to shapeshift shortly, he directed his thoughts, and his eyes, to a safer location so a specific rebellious body part wouldn't betray his current line of thought.

"You," Burrukan growled as he halted before him. "Why aren't you in gryphon form already? We're leaving now."

The barked tone doused the heat rising in Kuwari's blood which was a benefit.

"You didn't ask nicely," Kuwari's grin stretched further. Actually, Burrukan hadn't asked him to return to gryphon form at all.

"I didn't ask?" Burrukan's question ended in a string of muttered curses in the ancient tongue.

Kuwari's gaze settled on Enkara in time to see her fight back a smile.

"I'll be but a moment. I just need to speak with her before we're in the air and speech becomes difficult." Kuwari snatched Enkara's hand and dragged her with him toward her tent.

Communication was limited to their mental link once he shifted to his natural form and took to the air, but he hadn't revealed to anyone how deep that bond went. Some secrets were beneficial to maintain.

Once they were far enough away that Burrukan couldn't hear, Enkara speared him with a dark look and muttered, "You just lied to Burrukan. And, yes, I'll tell you what he said later before we reach Nineveh. But what do you really want to speak to me about?"

Kuwari didn't answer her until they were almost at her

tent. "I know you can't shapeshift yet and you dread the thought of flying."

Predictably she squared her shoulders and clenched her jaw.

"I'm not afraid of flying."

"You're lying to yourself and me."

"Since when is reading minds one of your gifts?"

She was coming a little too close to the truth there. He shrugged noncommittally to throw her off. "I've known you all my life, and my father taught me to read every nuance of a person's body language. The body always tells the truth even when the owner's mouth lies."

Enkara sucked in a deep breath and then expelled it on a long sigh. "I don't like flying, but I'm not afraid of heights. It's the element of absolute trust required."

Oh, his poor Enkara. Even after being free from a dungeon cell for sixteen years, she still couldn't trust anyone, not even him, not wholly. That had to change.

She needed to trust, to learn that not everyone would betray her or die and leave her all alone like her parents had. It might take time, but flights like this one were a good exercise in mutual trust.

"I trust you with my life. Will you not offer me the same?" He held out his hand and waited. After a few uncomfortable moments, where he thought she was going to reject him, she finally rolled her eyes at him, snorted, and then placed her hand in his.

With a surge of joy, relief, and mild humor at her abrasiveness, he tugged her closer and pulled her inside the tent with him. "I'll never betray you, my Blade."

"I know." She stared at his hand where it cradled hers. "You're the only one who has never tried to lie to me, not even in the everyday way people tell small falsehoods to keep the peace or protect another person's feelings."

"And I never will. Although you might not always like what I say."

"Fair enough." Enkara sobered a moment later and looked around the small tent and then back at him. "Would you prefer I leave while you shift?"

"No," he said as he began to work loose the knot tying his impromptu blanket-robe in place. "You've seen me shift before and didn't I just say I trust you with my life?"

She nodded sharply, held his gaze for a moment, and then hastily glanced at the floor.

Hmm. Enkara never broke eye contact first. If there were more time, he'd have liked to explore this new shy and uncertain Enkara. He hoped it had something to do with her starting to see him as a man and potential mate.

If not, he'd just continue as he always had. Eventually, he'd win her as his future queen, even if it took him years.

After all, he was gryphon. His species knew how to stalk prey. He'd also been born with a natural patience most people lacked. His father said it was a good trait to have when one was playing long game politics.

However, outside he heard Burrukan stomping toward the tent. That male's patience was growing shorter by the season. A grin flashed across Kuwari's lips as he realized he was the cause of the older male's pique.

He glanced at Enkara. "Your grumpy mentor is heading this way. We're almost out of time. Will you trust me to carry you back to Nineveh? No one else need know the depth of fear surrendering control causes you. Especially not Burrukan."

Enkara swallowed and then nodded sharply. "Thank you."

Joy flicked through him as he tossed the blanket aside. Squatting, he called his power. Heat raced through his body, stretching out to his extremities until it pumped through his blood in time to the thunder of the pulse pounding in his ears. In a fierce, wild joy, the magic took him between one heartbeat and the next.

Wings erupted from his back even as his body shifted into a lion's. His vision sharpened. His sense of smell increased tenfold. With a roar, he shed the last of his human nature, rejoicing in the strength and power of his gryphon form.

He gaped his beak and dragged in a taste of Enkara's scent. Her pleasant aroma always calmed him after the rush of adrenaline caused by the shift. After he'd mastered his newly emerged predatory nature, Kuwari gathered his feet under him and stood, folding his wings tight to his back. While he was still flicking tawny feathers into perfect alignment, skilled fingers buried themselves in the thick mane running along his neck where fur and feathers merged.

As Enkara gave him a good scratch, Kuwari purred and leaned into her touch. Even his tail twitched, betraying his delight. He often wondered why Enkara would share her loving touch with him so easily while he was in gryphon form, but rarely did so when he was a man.

It must have something to do with human modesty and

morals. Or cowardice. Not that he was about to ask and ruin this delightful moment of mutual love.

He was still purring when Burrukan thrust back the tent flap and stuck his head inside.

"You've shifted, so what's the holdup?"

Kuwari snapped his beak at Burrukan and then gently bumped Enkara until she moved toward the tent flap. She gave him one more scratch before exiting.

Happy to follow her scent, he ducked under the hanging flap of fabric and squeezed from the tent. He nearly didn't fit, his broad shoulders and bulky wings stressing the tent's fabric until it tore.

"You owe me a new tent," Enkara called back to him.

He'd be happy to replace it, but then again, he didn't plan for her to need a tent anytime soon. His chambers were more than large enough for them both. And better yet, perhaps it wouldn't be long before she was sharing his bed.

But first, they needed to return to Nineveh.

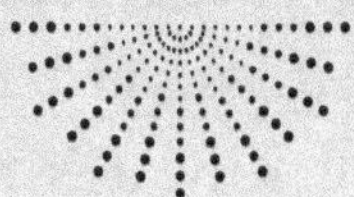

CHAPTER FOUR

As Kuwari kept pace beside her, dwarfing her with his much larger bulk, she eyed his back and wished someone had thought to bring an extra saddle harness. Bareback just made everything about flight all the more harrowing.

Though, when Burrukan gave the order for the unit to mount up, Enkara didn't hesitate, only bracing one hand on Kuwari's shoulders and the other on his powerful hindquarters. Then using her calf muscles, she leaped and swung a leg over his back.

Once she was astride, he barely gave her time to find her seat, or register the heat radiating from his lion's body. Then with a powerful bunch and flex of muscles under his fur, he moved off to join the others. Enkara leaned forward, locking her fingers in his thick mane.

"A saddle would have been nice." At her words, the big gryphon shook with deep huffing growls of laughter.

Burrukan barked out an order, and the three forward-most gryphons in line took off at a run, racing down the beach as they unfurled their broad wings and leaped toward the sky in a series of thunderous wing beats. Even before they were airborne, Kuwari and the rest of the gryphons surged forward and followed the first three into the air.

Once they were out over the water and the beach was left far behind, Enkara leaned forward, her fingers stroking the feathers and thick fur of Kuwari's mane even as her mind reached out for his. His gift flared at her touch, and suddenly his voice was in her mind, surprising her.

"You're safe with me, my Kara."

Uncomfortable with his use of the too-intimate nickname, she scrounged for something else to say. *"Your gift has grown stronger."*

"It has." He tilted his head and gave her a gryphon smirk. *"I've matured in other ways, too."*

Enkara laughed at his blatant flirting. *"I've noticed."*

But all humor aside, their special bond had grown stronger over the years, and she knew it had the potential to become so much more. But for now, his friendship was enough for her.

The flight to Nineveh was uneventful for which Enkara was heartily thankful. While she trusted Kuwari and enjoyed their closeness, she wasn't ready for stormy winds or aerial battles. Especially not without a saddle.

Luckily, they had nothing more than a gentle ocean breeze to contend with. Still, she was relieved when the great island city-state of Nineveh emerged out of the dark seas, silhouetted against the horizon.

While most of the city-state slept, torches still burned, dispelling some of the darkness and acting as a beacon against the night. As they drew nearer, she picked out guards walking on the stout walls and positioned along the wheelhouse on either side of Ishtar's Gate, the eastern entrance to the city.

Behind the massive gate, the processional way snaked through the city and led up to the multi-leveled terraced gardens surrounding Ishtar's temple and the majestic gleaming white walls of the palace. Both structures glowed in the moonlight.

Over the distance, she felt the power emanating from the tall stone figures of the eternally watchful Lamassu. Their massive bull's bodies, tightly folded wings, and regally carved human heads topped with horned crowns cut an imposing figure against the night and inspired fear in the hearts of New Sumer's enemies.

Both Lamassu and goddess-chosen Blades took their duties of protecting New Sumer, and its gryphon monarchs, very seriously. Closer now, she could sense something she'd never been able to before: the simmering power of the other stone guardians watching over the island of Nineveh. The anunnaki, with their human bodies, double sets of wings and eagle heads, might share a similar function as a Lamassu, but their power felt different...colder... when compared to a Lamassu's protective magic.

That she could now sense the anunnaki was an exciting development. Did it mean Ishtar would call her to serve soon? She hoped so.

Prince Kuwari dipped lower, and the view of the city was

obscured by Ishtar's Gate. The sentries standing guard had already taken note of Burrukan and Kuwari's return and had the portcullis lifted and the gate open wide in welcome.

As the gryphons flew through the open gate, Kuwari followed. The moment they passed through, Enkara felt the tingle of the great dome of power that protected the city.

Once inside the city, they winged their way higher and approached the palace from the north. Soon they were circling to land in one of the many courtyards. This one was guarded by a solitary Lamassu.

As soon as the group touched down the Lamassu's attention skittered over the new arrivals and then briefly settled upon her. She mentally acknowledged the ancient spirit residing in the stone statue with a small flare of her own unseen magic like she had since a child. It returned the gesture with one of its own.

Around her, the other gryphon guards halted and allowed their riders to dismount. Kuwari apparently had other ideas and prowled deeper into the palace.

"I can walk."

He flicked one feather-covered ear at her. *"And I can walk faster."*

Enkara bit her cheek and held her silence.

Before Kuwari made it five steps, Burrukan called to them. "Prince Kuwari. Throne room. First meal. Be there, or I'll hunt you down and spank you like a naughty child. Don't think I won't. Enkara that goes for you too."

Kuwari paused and flicked his tufted tail disdainfully at Burrukan. Then with a huff, he continued his slow, unhurried pace.

Once they were around the corner and out of earshot, she smacked Kuwari in the shoulder. "You run away, and I get in trouble. How's that fair?"

Her mount didn't answer, which only annoyed her more since he'd been 'talkative' on the flight home.

"Fine, you're not going to talk so I will. You can't keep rebelling against your parents. The edicts are there to protect you. Burrukan has reason to be grumpy. You'll be lucky if your father ever lets you out of his sight again."

Enkara paused in her dressing down and glanced at the tiled mosaics on the floor and the blue and golden dragon motifs on the walls.

They were approaching the royal wing where she and Kuwari had shared a suite off the nursery since they were children. Not long after she'd gone off to New Assur for her training, Kuwari had been relocated to the rooms at the end of the wing next to the nursery and all her things had been packed away into storage.

That event had led to Kuwari's first escape and night flight to New Assur. She could still see the sixteen-year-old boy yelling that they were trying to erase her from his life.

Her younger self hadn't known how to soothe the young prince, so she'd sat him down, swung an arm around his shoulders and hugged him as fiercely as she'd been able. He'd eventually calmed. King Ditanu and Queen Iltani had arrived and found them like that.

Father and son had talked and Kuwari had learned it was his biological mother, Ahassunu, who had ordered the move, saying it was time for him to become a man and leave childhood things behind. It was the first time Enkara had been certain Regent Ahassunu wanted to put some distance between her son and a girl born of a traitorous line.

Regent Ahassunu didn't hate her—Enkara would've sensed that, but Kuwari's mother didn't fully trust her either. Now that she was older, she understood the regent's thinking. Didn't mean she liked it. Back then, she hadn't liked anything or anyone who sought to separate her and Kuwari.

She still didn't like when a life situation interfered with her duties, but for now, she had other more immediate concerns. Like where was Kuwari taking her? She'd thought he was bringing her to the Shadow barracks, but they'd traveled too far into the royal wing for that. On the left of the hall were doors leading to Ahassunu and Burrukan's chambers. On the right, ones leading to King Ditanu and Queen Iltani's suite.

"Kuwari, where are you taking me? You know that side corridor six doors back? That was the way to the Shadow barracks, as well you know." She half turned, hoping to change his course. It was futile as expected.

She no longer belonged in the royal suite—not that she ever really did, but years ago, when Kuwari had still been a cub, she'd been his play companion and then loyal friend.

It seemed he still wasn't willing to be parted from her as he stomped resolutely toward his own rooms.

This wouldn't end well.

Enkara might not be able to dismount to either side with his wings folded over her legs, but there was another way off his back. It just wouldn't be fun for either of them. She braced her upper body and used her arms to shimmy backward. Every ridge of his spine abused her backside, but she slid back further until gravity took hold and pulled her weight down the slope of his heavily muscled rump. Her abdomen slammed into the protrusions of his hipbones on the way down. Wincing, she thumped heavily to the ground.

Kuwari grunted, his tail flicking in annoyance. Rubbing at her abused midsection, she glowered at him. "Next time just let me dismount and neither of us will get bruises."

Kuwari's fluffy tail tuft was suddenly in her face. She snatched it and held it in a tight grip so he couldn't get away easily. "Watch where you wave that thing, or it might get lopped off."

Kuwari attempted to twitch his tail out of her grasp as he looked over his shoulder at her disdainfully.

"Hey, if you'd just do as you're told, I wouldn't have to take liberties."

The door nearest them opened and King Ditanu's broad-shouldered profile appeared. When he spotted them, he crossed his arms and glowered at his son. Then he sighed deeply and glanced at her. "I see my son's hunt was successful. Welcome home, Enkara."

"Thank you, Your Highness," she said with all the dignity she could muster while tugging on his son's tail.

Ditanu grinned at them both and then stepped back inside and closed the door. From behind the stout wood, Enkara heard a sleepy female voice ask some question followed by King Ditanu's laughter and the mention of Kuwari's name.

"You," Enkara said as she glowered at the retreating shape of Kuwari's muscular lion's ass, "are in so much trouble."

He merely flicked an ear in her direction and continued

to his suite where two guards hurried to open the dark wood doors.

There he waited for her to proceed him. Enkara squared her shoulders and entered first, pretending she was searching the room for unseen dangers. There weren't any, of course. But it gave her a reason to ignore Kuwari since she was supposed to be annoyed with him for embarrassing her in front of his father.

A servant had left a fire in the outer chamber. She could see light flickering in the room beyond this one as well. Candles to judge by the scent of beeswax.

Glancing around, she took in the sight of two chairs by the fire and the rows of shelves lining the west wall. A table and bench sat in the middle of the room, its polished wood surface heaped with scrolls, clay tablets, and styluses as well as an assortment of other writing instruments.

Against the north wall, a large, raised sleeping platform was piled high with pillows and the most exquisite woven blankets. Multilayered fringed veils swept down from a central knot of fabric attached to the ceiling, obscuring portions of the bed. All in all, the two rooms she could see from her present location had a homey, lived-in feeling unlike the more formal parts of the Palace.

This was Kuwari's retreat from political intrigues and harassing councilors. It was his private domain. She had no right to be here, especially in the middle of the night and knowing what he wanted for their future.

"Kuwari," Enkara said as she infused steel into her tone. "I shouldn't be here."

"Why ever not?"

The sound of his voice surprised her. She hadn't expected him to vocalize an answer out loud since he'd still been in gryphon form moments ago. Her gaze traveled in the direction of the voice.

A very human and very naked Kuwari was kneeling before the fire. Her breath froze in her lungs, and her feet might as well have fused to the floor for all she could move as she drank in his masculine beauty.

Her gaze settled on the arch of his neck and followed that to the slope of his broad shoulders. Next, she studied the flex and shift of his toned biceps. One hand rested on his knee while he used the other to grab a poker and stir the dying fire.

That wasn't the only fire he stirred. He was breathtaking, but he could never be hers.

Oh, by the goddess, stop drooling over him! He's a person, not an object. Even as she berated herself, her gaze stole lower and took in the sculpted abdomen and well-muscled flank. The knee closest to the fire rested against the stone. The other was raised, preserving a bit of modesty and preventing her from seeing everything.

Which was good since she didn't possess a drop of willpower or have the courtesy to look away.

Kuwari's gaze left the fire to meet hers. His expression was full of warmth.

"Enkara, why ever not?"

She blinked at him. "Why not?"

What was he talking about? She'd allowed herself to

become so distracted, she didn't have a clue what he was talking about. *Oh, Merciful Goddess, just open the ground beneath my feet and end my humiliation.*

The gods weren't merciful and Kuwari only laughed at her confused look.

"You said, 'I shouldn't be here' and I asked, 'why ever not' at which point you seemed to become distracted by something."

His grin told her he knew exactly what she'd been so distracted by, but his comment also said he was still expecting a response.

"Now you're being intentionally obtuse." Enkara stared at a spot on the wall above the hearth. She wasn't going to look at him because she knew that devastating smile would be focused on her.

"You're the one who won't answer."

"I shouldn't have to explain it. These are your chambers. I shouldn't be here. We're not children anymore."

"I noticed that a few years back," Kuwari added helpfully. "But you're wrong. These rooms, and all that I own—all that I am—it is yours too. We made a childhood pact that we would always stay together. Are you saying you will no longer honor our pact?"

"That's not what this is about."

"Yes," his voice softened, no longer holding his earlier playfulness. "It is. I'm going to go get dressed. If you still honor our childhood pact, you'll follow me, and we'll discuss this in more detail."

True to his word, Kuwari stood and strolled away from

the hearth and meandered his way deeper into his chambers, vanishing behind the fringed curtain leading to his sleeping chambers.

She remained rooted in place.

Could she ever willingly break her pact with Kuwari?

CHAPTER FIVE

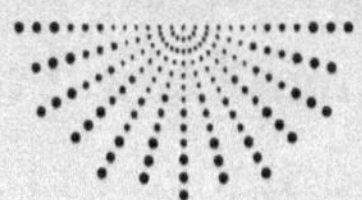

Kuwari's heart pounded in his chest, and his stomach was tying itself into knots, but he focused on the simple act of dressing. He belted on his linen robe with a force bordering on violence.

Ultimatums were never a good tactic. He knew that! His father had drilled such teachings into him along with many other valuable pieces of information. He knew better than to act so rashly and lose his composure. But Enkara's rejection had sent him into a snit.

Fool, he berated himself, *now that your Blade isn't following, what will you do?*

His father said ultimatums resulted in unfavorable outcomes half the time.

Pressing the heel of his palms against his closed lids, he rubbed them as if that could erase his drastic error in judgment.

Soft footfalls approached, then hesitated just outside his sleeping chamber. A moment later the curtain's beaded fringe rustled and that constricting pressure circling his heart loosened and he drew a deep, shaky breath.

Warm fingers came to rest on his shoulder, then Enkara stepped up behind him and wrapped her arms around his waist, her cheek pressing against his shoulder. "I could break faith with you no more than I could cut out my own heart."

He closed his eyes and sighed in relief.

"I'm sorry for being so thick-headed, my Kara. I shouldn't have questioned your devotion in such a way."

"My Prince, I'm sorry I made you doubt our bond. Never doubt that."

"Then why are you pushing me away? Tell me so I can understand."

She squeezed him tighter. "I'm afraid."

"Afraid?" Genuine surprise engulfed him. "You've never been afraid of anything in your life. How can you be afraid of me?"

"Afraid I'll never be good enough." She gave an embarrassed little chuckle. "I realize how insecure that makes me sound. I didn't say it was logical."

"Self-doubt is seldom logical, but it is very, very natural." Her warm breath puffed against his skin, and he wanted to turn and take her in his arms but retained enough reason to know that would likely drive his strangely skittish Blade far from his side for the rest of the night.

"Talk to me, Enkara," he said instead and turned his head just enough to brush his cheek against her hair.

She sighed and then dropped her arms to her sides. She

didn't bolt from him which he took as a good sign. After turning to her, he slowly reached out and took her hand. Once he had a firm grip, he tugged her farther into the room, toward the warmth of the fire and the bench that sat nearby.

While she stared into the fire, he began with a few gentle inquiries. Soon she was baring her soul to him, whispering of her deep insecurities and all the little ways she still wasn't ready to take their relationship deeper.

But not once did she say she didn't love him. He leaned forward and pressed a kiss to her hair to hide his grin. He wasn't fooled by his Blade. She couldn't lie, not to him, and she was far from indifferent.

"Do you understand why I'm not ready to commit to anything beyond friendship?"

"Yes. There is no pressure. The council can drop hints all they want, but they can't force me into a match I don't want. We'll wait until you've completed your training and have had a chance to settle in as my Blade, and then we will reopen this conversation."

That doesn't mean I'll stop courting you in the meantime.

He'd been so focused on his own plans, he'd missed the exact moment Enkara's expression had turned guarded. Now her lips compressed unhappily as she studied him, searching his face for something.

She stood straighter and then cleared her throat. "I'm afraid that's no longer entirely accurate, my Prince."

"What's not accurate?" he asked slowly, but suddenly one of his past vision fragments was beginning to make an unsettling kind of sense.

"That the council can't force your hand."

"Does this have something to do with what Burrukan wanted to speak with you about when he pulled you aside back there on the beach?"

She nodded sharply and told him everything Burrukan had told her about the Council's decision regarding the betrothal and a trial year. "So, you see, this…complicates things."

He wasn't happy about the council's heavy-handedness, but he wasn't entirely surprised by their move either. What did surprise him was how readily his parents agreed to this debacle. Why hadn't they thought to ask what he and Enkara wanted? Then he huffed. His parents and High Priestess Kammani knew how he felt about his Blade and they likely thought Enkara returned his feelings.

And she did. He was certain of that, even if Enkara didn't yet know her heart belonged to him. Perhaps if he gave her a few days and she had time to settle in, she'd realize just how much she cared. After all, with her earlier soul-baring confession, she hadn't said she didn't love him.

If he could convince her to say 'yes' to the betrothal, then he'd secure a year's time to win Enkara over. He was sure it wouldn't take her half that long to overcome her momentary misgivings and self-doubts. She was self-assured by nature, and whatever had caused this skittishness would run its course. She'd eventually know her heart and mind. And he was rather confident it was her growing awareness of him as a potential mate versus childhood friend that was the cause of her disquiet.

Kuwari tapped her on the shoulder to gain her attention. "As much as I would like to sit and talk for the rest of the night, we should get some sleep. My parents will be none too pleased with my escape. It is best I have my wits about me in the morning."

"Yes," Enkara agreed with a genuine smile.

"Though, I'd much rather talk for the rest of the night." Sighing with dramatical sadness, he started toward the back of his sleeping chamber. "There's a separate chamber off this one. I'm aware it's not as big, but that's where I put all the possessions you left behind when you went to train on New Assur. I think you'll find it tolerable."

Enkara parted her lips as she drew breath to speak, then hesitated at length before murmuring a soft 'Thank you.'

In truth, he'd expected more resistance, but Enkara strode forward, brushed aside the beaded curtain that marked the border of the two rooms and then halted just inside the threshold to survey the chamber. He followed on her heels and tried to see the room with an objective eye but failed. He'd often spent time here when Enkara's absence became intolerable but also when he wanted a place to unwind, or hide, at the end of a long day.

Along the south wall, a bed covered with the finest linens and pillows was flanked by two storage chests. A small table and large wardrobe took up most of the east wall. His eyes briefly rested on a large weapons rack that spanned the entire west wall. The remaining space was occupied by shelves laden with various stones and trinkets they'd collected as children.

At last, his eyes halted on a small fireplace with a tidy stack of wood sitting beside it.

"Did you want me to start a fire? The ocean breeze has been blowing cold this last cycle."

"I don't need the comfort of a fire," she said as she stepped further into the room.

"Comforts are never needed — that's why they are comforts, not necessities." Kuwari grinned at the familiar way she rolled her eyes at his words.

"You're growing soft, my Prince."

"Not yet home a day and already insulting me. Gods, I've missed you."

An answering grin touched her lips, and he found his gaze riveted to them. Within the year, Ishtar should claim Enkara as her Blade, and maybe even require them to perform the Sacred Marriage.

Lust heated his loins at the thought of finally taking Enkara as his mate. He cast fugitive glances at her sleeping pallet, wondering how soon and how aggressively he dare begin his courtship.

"Out!" Enkara pointed back toward his sleeping chambers.

Sometimes the special link they shared had a downside, exposing deeply personal feelings. Well, perhaps if she had no doubt of his...affections, it would help her regain her confidence around him and shorten the length of their courtship.

Kuwari grinned at that thought.

Enkara's responding glower vanquished his growing lust.

Ah. Courtship would begin later, then. A cautious, gentle courtship at that, but he'd win her in the end.

He didn't move fast enough to suit her, and she grabbed

him by the shoulder. A couple of well-aimed shoves sent him in the general direction of his chamber.

"Dawn isn't that far off, and your parents want to speak with you before first meal," she reminded him as she followed him into his chambers. "You. Bed. Now."

Kuwari laughed, a joyous sound he couldn't contain. This was his Enkara, his weapon — the commanding girl who'd grown into an equally dominant woman.

Gods, he loved her so much. He even loved the way she stood there, her arms folded across her chest as she waited for him to obey her. He savored the exact moment she realized her mistake. Then, his trap set, he bestowed her with a seductive show as he slowly walked to his bed, discarding clothing as he went.

She couldn't look away or retreat to her room without ceding the challenge to him. His warrior woman—even if she was being uncommonly skittish—wouldn't back down from a challenge.

Though, when he glanced over his shoulder at her, he noticed she was leveling her best glower at him the entire time.

He'd intentionally left all the candles burning to give Enkara a good look, showcasing what he could bring to a physical relationship. To give her credit, she stood there unmoving, her face expressionless while he arranged the pillows and blankets to his liking.

Only after he was settled did she stroll further into his room where she proceeded to blow out all the candles until just the fire in the hearth provided any light.

"May you have pleasant dreams, my Prince," Enkara said

as she padded across the thick rugs and then brushed aside the curtain before disappearing into the shadows beyond.

Kuwari grinned up at the ceiling for long moments. It wouldn't have surprised him if he was still grinning as sleep claimed him. And if he dreamed about Enkara? Why that was only natural.

CHAPTER SIX

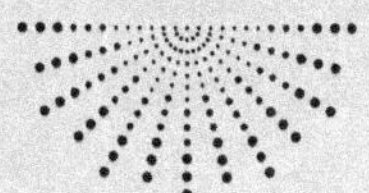

The sun was only just a hint on the horizon when they reached the throne room. Kuwari's gaze went to the south end of the large room, where four thrones sat upon a raised dais. None of the thrones were occupied. They often weren't. His parents detested all the royal trappings that went along with the crown.

Presently, his parents were sitting around a large table off to one side of the room. Potted plants and gilded screens offered some privacy. Though, no one else was presently in the throne room beside the usual guards.

"You ready for this?" Enkara asked in a whisper.

"Always," he said with a grin.

When his father's gaze landed on him and narrowed in that familiar way, Kuwari knew he had some explaining to do.

"Don't think you're getting out of punishment for

running off without your guard, but I'll give you a chance to explain yourself first."

Kuwari didn't know if his explanation about the vision with the hand pouring something into his goblet would help or hinder his defence, but he told the truth and hoped. Once finished his tale of escape, Kuwari had hoped they would be granted a reprieve from duties for the rest of the day. The gauzy curtains were pulled back from the massive archways, allowing the early dawn sunlight and playful ocean breeze to enter. It looked to be a beautiful day for walks along the beach and drinks under the shade of a palm tree.

Alas, if his father's dark expression was anything to go by, a walk along the beach wasn't in Kuwari's immediate future.

"We have other business we need to discuss," Ditanu said as if guessing his thoughts.

Ditanu wasn't the only one good at reading expressions.

"Ah, this is about the betrothal and trial year, I assume," Kuwari drawled.

Ditanu, in turn, glowered at Burrukan.

Kuwari summoned up his most disarming smile. "Ah. I see Burrukan wasn't supposed to mention that little tidbit."

"I wanted to tell you and Enkara myself."

"Hmm. Guess Burrukan saved you the trouble. I don't suppose it would have occurred to anyone that Enkara might refuse my courtship? No?" He pointedly looked at Enkara before glowering at each of his parents and then lowered his voice to a more menacing growl. "Well, she did. As is her right."

"What?" His father's appalled expression was almost humorous.

"You heard me."

"Gods above and below! Did I just force my son into a year of misery to pacify the damned Council?" Ditanu bolted upright and stormed away in a rare showing of temper. "Summon the council. I'll not stand by and allow this disaster to unfold!"

Ahassunu was taken by surprise as well, but she covered it better, her expression already turning thoughtful. "This need not be a disaster…"

King Ditanu turned his dark glower upon Ahassunu. "Kuwari loves Enkara. I was certain she loved him in return. That's the only reason I agreed to the Council's scheme."

His father's voice grew louder with each word. Kuwari picked up his goblet and sipped out of it to hide his smile. He could always tell his father that he knew Enkara's decision wasn't necessarily final, that she just needed time to come to terms with what fate had just rolled out in all its glory. But… it was always fine entertainment when the King lost his temper with his Council.

Queen Iltani stood and joined her mate. "No one is forcing Kuwari into something he doesn't want."

Ah. His second mother was always more fun than his father.

"Kuwari is young yet," Ditanu continued with his earlier line of thought. "The royal line is secure and robust for the first time in centuries. This was a foolish, unneeded ploy on the part of the meddling Council."

"I'm more than happy to cure them of this foolishness, my King." Iltani caressed the hilt of her crystalline sword.

Kuwari wondered for a moment if he was going to get to

see Iltani as Ishtar's Avenging Blade. It had been years since there'd been an assassination attempt. Her sword must be hungering for new blood.

At Iltani's less than subtle threat, Burrukan broke out into snorts of laughter. Which earned him a glare from all concerned.

"It's not foolish," Ahassunu said with a glower at Burrukan and then Ditanu.

Ditanu narrowed his eyes, looking at the two Regents. "Ahassunu, this was your idea. You can be the one to go tell the Council there will be no betrothal and deal with the consequences."

"It isn't foolish! Statecraft and alliances stabilize the relationships between all the city-states." Ahassunu rolled her eyes at Ditanu.

He scowled. "I know how statecraft works."

Kuwari was grinning into his cup when Enkara suddenly elbowed him sharply in the ribs. *"Should we say something to stop this?"*

"Nah. This is much more entertaining. Besides, my parents deserve to stew for a good long time. Maybe next time they'll consult us first before making life-altering decisions on our behalf."

She arched an eyebrow at him. *"You're terrible. And it was an honest mistake on Ditanu's part. He thought I..."*

"I know."

"Come, this might actually be a blessing from the gods," Ahassunu said, trying for diplomacy this time. Though Kuwari doubted very much that it would work on his father.

"Now Kuwari can find a noble lady of proper lineage and training to rule at his side. He's still young. I doubt my son even knows his own heart yet. I didn't at that age. And since nothing has happened between my son and his Blade, they're both free to find love elsewhere in time. A trial year will give Kuwari time to further mature and start to understand what he truly wants."

"I'm sure our son disagrees with your line of thinking," Ditanu barked out.

"Yes, at first he will, I imagine. But in time he'll see this is better."

Now his parents were talking like he wasn't even in the same room.

Ahassunu tilted her chin up, a hard look entering her eyes. "In time he'll see Enkara wasn't born to be his queen. Her strengths lay elsewhere. She would make a very poor choice."

"See? Told you," Enkara sent along their link. *"Even your mother thinks I'd be a terrible mate."*

A wave of rage rolled through Kuwari.

But his mother continued unaware. "She'll be to Kuwari what Burrukan is to you: a war councilor."

"You overstep, Mother." He didn't care if Ahassunu was his biological mother, she still didn't get to insult the woman he loved.

Enkara's fingers wrapped around his wrist, stopping him from rising and leaving the table.

"Kuwari, let it go. She didn't say one word that wasn't true, and we both know it."

Enkara's words and emotions seeped into him, but he was still too angry to acknowledge them. She sensed as much and continued after a long-suffering sigh.

"Please, Kuwari. Regent Ahassunu is correct. I'd make a terrible queen. I have no patience for the Council. I know almost nothing about ruling a kingdom. All my training has been in order to ready me to oversee your protection. I haven't lived in the city for years. Plus, if I were to become queen one day, eventually my true lineage would come to the surface and people would always question my loyalty."

"I don't care about that. I know there is none more loyal to me than my Blade."

"You should care. Even if Ereshkigal has temporarily given up destroying the gryphon royal line, and I'm not needed as a war leader, I'd still be a disastrous choice as your queen."

Kuwari fought to master the anger building inside. *"I doubt Ereshkigal has abandoned her plans, but that doesn't mean a war leader can't also be my queen. Look at Iltani. She had no desire for power, but she adapted."*

"Ha. Didn't she just offer to kill the council members if they didn't conform? Statecraft in action?"

Kuwari rolled his eyes to the ceiling and counted to ten before exhaling. *"Fine. We'll discuss this later, once we're alone."*

"Good idea," Enkara said and then looked toward King Ditanu. *"Since you need to redirect your parents' conversation before blood starts to flow."*

Kuwari silently agreed and turned to focus on his parents again. "If you are done bickering about *my* future, there's something *I'd* like to say."

Kuwari's parents fell silent with expressions of varying degrees of guilt, but it was Ditanu who cleared his throat and nodded.

"Of course, you have a say in your future." King Ditanu's

gaze slid toward Enkara. "But first I want to hear Enkara's thoughts about all this."

"My King?" Enkara inclined her head, politely conveying she didn't know what he wanted to know.

"I find it hard to believe that you turned Kuwari down. If I were to wager a guess, I'd say you love my son as much as he loves you. Are you willing to deny this before your monarchs?"

Kuwari winced. His father wasn't easily fooled and didn't mince words. He must have scented the smallest hint of deception. Queen Iltani stepped closer, her eyes hardening and her expression turning shrewd.

Enkara cleared her throat and held her hands out away from her body, unconsciously showing she didn't have anything to hide. "I have no ambitions toward the throne. And I agree that Kuwari needs a worthy and wise mate to rule at his side when he takes the throne someday, far in the future."

"Well," Iltani said with a glint of humor in her eyes. "That was a first. False truths."

Ditanu arched an eyebrow at his mate.

Iltani clarified. "Her heart and mind are not in agreement. She honestly doesn't want the throne or any of the power that goes with it, but also hates the idea of another filling the role of mate to Kuwari. She's far more than just a loyal friend to our son."

A becoming pink hue flushed Enkara's cheeks a darker color and her lips twisted as if to deny Iltani's words, but she held her tongue.

"Ah. It's as I originally thought." King Ditanu rubbed his

chin, looking much happier. "That news gives me hope that one day you and Kuwari will make each other very happy. I won't pry more into your personal feelings or judge you for whatever hang-up has you carefully skirting around each other. However, that still doesn't solve the issue with the Council. They'll be expecting a betrothal announcement within the next moon cycle."

"Then we'll give them one," Kuwari said, calmly folding his arms over his chest. "I will select a noblewoman to be my betrothed, and we will complete the trial year as the council demands, but it will be fake. Once the year is over, I plan to resume courting Enkara."

Beside him, his Blade started to choke like she'd swallowed her tongue. He thumped her on the back until she had her breath back.

King Ditanu barked out a laugh. "My son, you're underestimating the time it will take to win her over if her reaction to your declaration is anything to go by."

"I have reason to believe that isn't true," Kuwari said and winked at Enkara.

Soon after his declaration, the tension in the room lessened. There was still some back and forth between his parents as they hashed out new issues that could, and likely would arise, out of this.

Queen Iltani was still deeply unhappy, but Kuwari assured her it would be fine.

"However," he modulated his voice to carry over his parents' conversation. "I will handle this betrothal in my own way. I'll tolerate no interference." He paused to meet Ahassunu's gaze. "Is that understood?"

After a small hesitation, his mother agreed.

"I shall stay out of it as I've already interfered more than I had any right," King Ditanu said around a mouthful of fruit and speared Kuwari with a piercing look. "And since I remember what it was like at your age to be separated from the woman I loved, I'll grant you this day to spend together. But don't think you're escaping your punishment for the New Assur escapade. Tomorrow you will report here before first meal and learn what your punishment will be."

Kuwari grinned. "Enkara is worth any punishment."

"Wait until after tomorrow, and then we'll see if you still think the same." Humor gleamed in his father's eyes.

After his father's ominous warning they all returned to their meals. Kuwari found he was hungry. Even inconvenient political issues revolving around his impending betrothal and whatever 'punishment' his father had planned didn't dim his hunger.

He couldn't say the same for Enkara. She pushed her food around her plate and continued to look distressed.

Grinning, Kuwari decided the gods had put him on this earth to distress his lovely Blade.

CHAPTER SEVEN

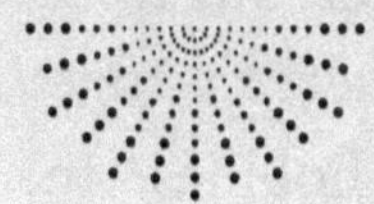

Enkara had forgotten the beauty of Nineveh's black sand beaches. But as she and Kuwari walked along the water's edge, she felt at home, as if the last four years were no time at all. Even the ten Shadows trailing along behind felt like an old routine.

While they walked, Kuwari updated her on the newest court gossip and other news, his renditions probably more humorous than actual events.

When he ran out of things to say, he started to hunt for her secrets, seeking any confessions. But she had none. The last four years were full of training and little else. And she'd never mastered his ability to talk about something mundane and make it sound interesting. He could describe bread dough rising and make it seem fascinating.

"Oh, come on. There must have been more than just training," Kuwari said at last.

"Well, you would have seen if there was. You were in my head almost every night."

Kuwari looked momentarily sheepish. "I'm sorry...I couldn't always control the link."

Enkara laughed. "You're not sorry in the least."

"No, not really." He turned serious, glancing sidelong at her and then quickly back out to the ocean. "That still left a lot of time when we weren't together even mentally. You must have had other hobbies, made friends with other Shadow trainees."

His line of questioning took her by surprise. He'd never asked any of those questions while she was away training. Why now?

"They were acquaintances, my competition. Training was our focus. While some of them became friends after a fashion, none of them are what I'd consider a close friend." Enkara continued to study his profile. "But surely you must have known that from when we linked in dreams."

"I didn't want to pry." Kuwari didn't look at her. "But if you hadn't been so focused on training, would any of them have...caught your interest?"

That's what he'd been fishing for this entire time?

"No," she answered simply before thinking better of it. *None of them were you.* "I think I'm gryphon enough to only be interested in a long-term relationship."

Kuwari's shoulders relaxed, and he breathed out a sigh of relief. "Good. I don't have to challenge any males."

"Why didn't you ask that while I was away training if it has been bothering you all this time?"

"I couldn't. If I asked and the answer was yes, I would

have had to fly to New Assur and challenge the male. That would be bound to draw attention to you. And I know how much you hate attention."

"Just because I said I hadn't met anyone doesn't mean we're destined for each other."

"We'll see," Kuwari said, his confidence returning. "If you weren't making friends or courting, what *did* you do for fun?"

"I…," Well this was going to sound pathetic. "There wasn't much time for fun. I studied. I trained. I avoided the other trainees as much as possible so I wouldn't give away that I'm a Blade."

"Well, I suppose learning to weave might not be considered fun…" The humorous glint was back in his eyes.

"Who told you about that?" But she knew a moment later. "Burrukan has developed a case of loose lips with his advanced age!"

"Can I tell him you said that? Never mind. I'm absolutely going to tell him that next time I see him."

The little brat. "Do that and you'll never see the gift I made you."

Kuwari's expression fell, and he placed a hand dramatically over his heart. "You have my solemn word that I'll never breathe a word of our conversation to your mentor."

"You better not, or I will make you regret it for years and years."

His grin grew broader. "I can't picture my fierce warrior with a hand loom across her lap."

"I couldn't either, but I wanted to make you something for your name day, so I learned to weave. My gift for you is still with my personal items. They're being shipped in from New Assur but won't arrive for a couple of days yet." She ducked her head, wiggling her toes in the hot sand. "I made a blanket for you. It isn't much."

"Tell me more." Kuwari grinned and wrapped an arm around her shoulders.

It was a blanket. What was there to tell? But she did explain how she had learned to weave, though it had taken over twenty failed attempts.

"It's far from the work of a master guildsman," she ended feeling even more embarrassed than she'd started.

"I will cherish it more than any other gift," he said solemnly.

"Don't get carried away. It's a blanket."

"Yes. And made for what?" he asked innocently.

Enkara paused before finally answering. "A coverlet for your bed in the storm season."

"Made by your hand for my bed. Covered in your scent." He wasn't openly laughing at her, but his grin was back full force, and his mirth made little bird's feet at the corners of his eyes. "It's a lovely courtship gift."

A moment later Enkara's cheeks flamed. It was all Kuwari's fault. She'd blushed more in the last day than in the previous four years combined.

"You know it's not a courtship gift!" She stumbled over her words in her rush to get them out. "I'll wash it first."

Kuwari gave her hand a squeeze, and she realized he'd been holding it for a while. Before she had a chance to free it, he steered her over to the shade of a palm tree.

Uncaring of their audience of Shadows, the Rebel Prince

walked her backward into the tree's trunk. He leaned forward, his lips brushing her ear as he spoke.

"I forbid you to wash your courtship gift. And I expect to receive it on my name day. Or before if you're so inclined."

"Why do you have to be so... so..." She stumbled to a halt realizing anything she said would only add fuel to the fire.

"Male?" Kuwari supplied in a laughing tone. "Charming? Or maybe rakish?"

"Infuriating!" Enkara braced her hands against his shoulders and gave him a firm shove. Kuwari rocked back and laughed, and then held out his hand for hers. She thought about sidestepping around him, but in the end, she reached for his hand and dragged him from under the shade to continue the walk before he could get any more ideas.

CHAPTER EIGHT

The dawn of her second morning on Nineveh, Enkara and Kuwari had reported to the throne room where they sat through a somewhat awkward meal waiting to hear what his punishment would be.

King Ditanu was in no hurry, attending to other city-state business before finally turning his attention to his son and ordering him to go aid Councilor Nakurtum in preparations for Kuwari's upcoming name day ceremony.

The prince had looked horrified and said that was traditionally a task for his siblings. Unfortunately for him, his siblings were still all with their grandfather, and Councilor Shalanum wasn't due back for half a moon, in time for Kuwari's name day celebrations.

So Enkara now found herself in the company of a very sullen Kuwari.

"You know that stupid tradition has surely resulted in more than one heir having assassins sent after them?"

Enkara mused to herself as they walked to the opposite end of the Palace complex where the Council chambers were situated.

"Which stupid tradition are you referring to?"

"The most immediate one." She rolled her eyes at him. "You know, the one where you're formally named Crown Prince on your name day and given one of the city-states to rule? That one."

"I know the one you meant," Kuwari mumbled by way of reply.

"Well, it's a stupid tradition. I'd bet my favorite sword that governors in the past have sent assassins after that poor heir in a bid to hold onto their power."

Kuwari stopped walking, forcing Enkara and their escort to halt as well.

"Your warrior's training is superb, but you're correct about the other facets of your education. I might as well start the lessons now," he said with a laugh. "The displaced governor has much to gain. Firstly, often the heir ends up betrothed or romantically involved with one of the governor's relations or another of the noble houses. Either occurrence will bring great honor to the island state. Secondly, the governor gets to advise and influence the heir. And thirdly, when the heir eventually takes the throne at some future time, that governor is likely to be elevated to a special advisor or some such."

"Hmmm. And fourthly," Enkara chuckled and punched him in the shoulder, "I don't think you could have sounded more like your mother if you tried."

He grinned. "Ugh. Didn't mean to sound so condescending."

"Seriously, I think I'd prefer assassins over lifelong political ambition and manipulations. At least physical danger can be solved with the sharp edge of a blade."

Kuwari attempted a frown but lost the battle and began to chuckle. "Gods, Enkara, you're turning into Burrukan."

She arched an eyebrow at him. "What did you expect? He's my mentor."

"I'm not sure. But not Burrukan with breasts."

"Thanks for that image. I'll be sure to mention that to my mentor the next time I see him." Enkara snorted with laughter as she walked away.

They were still joking like old times when they reached their destination.

There was only one councilwoman present when they reached the council chambers, but she was already issuing orders to harried servants who were bringing her bits of colored fabrics, wall hangings, bench cushions, various foods, and other assorted items that needed to be tested, judged, and sampled in preparation for the big festival in honor of Kuwari's name day.

Enkara had always avoided council members as much as possible, but she still recognized Councilor Nakurtum. The woman hadn't changed a bit. Mind you, it had only been four years although it felt much longer.

"Ah, Prince Kuwari, I'm so happy you've come to help oversee. I've already selected some items for your inspection and approval." The councilwoman continued like this was the most important event in three hundred years.

"Delighted to help," Kuwari said cheerily which Enkara's gift told her was a complete lie.

Enkara didn't bother to put on a pleasant face, preferring to stand at the prince's back, a silent and menacing presence, like all good Shadows. Though inwardly, she agreed with Kuwari's mental thoughts—she'd love to be just about anywhere else.

But then again, punishments weren't supposed to be fun, and this was absolutely Kuwari's punishment for escaping his guards and flying to New Assur.

"AREN'T you supposed to protect me from danger?" Kuwari whispered in her ear. "I nearly died from boredom. If she waved one more sample of scented oil in my direction, I might have expired at your feet. Then what would you have done?"

"Killed the councilor for slaying you," she said in her best inscrutable tone.

"Oh, my beautiful, bloodthirsty Enkara, have I told you how much I've missed you?"

"About three times a day." When she rolled her eyes at him, he had the nerve to wink.

"But, seriously," Kuwari asked, "who actually cares about what herbal oils are used to scent the candles as long as they burn evenly and produce a good flame?"

"Oh, come on. It wasn't that terrible."

"Death. By. Boredom."

"Fine. At least it's over now."

"Only until tomorrow. She wants me to report back in the morning." Kuwari shuddered dramatically.

"Well, you can always pull one of your vanishing acts," she said brightly and was rewarded by his pained groan.

"Don't tempt me, woman."

"Very well, *boy*, I won't."

Kuwari's sour expression transformed into a grin as he began to laugh. Once he had himself under control, he raked her with a heated look. "If you think I'm a boy, then you have very poor eyesight."

Enkara swallowed back her retort when she heard footfalls approaching. She assumed it was a servant going about their business since it was only the one person and nobles seemed to travel in packs.

Glancing behind to study the newcomer, she realized her mistake at once. By the woman's dress, she was most certainly a noble lady.

"Prince Kuwari, Shadow Enkara, forgive me for interrupting." The woman halted, bowed deeply, and then straightened in another graceful move. She hesitated a moment as if uncertain of her welcome. "I had just joined my mother when she spotted this. She said it was for you."

Kuwari took the hammered gold torc she held and gave her a regal nod in thanks.

The gregarious young man was gone, replaced by an aloof stranger. This was Prince Kuwari, future ruler of the gryphon kingdom. There was no hint of Enkara's lifelong friend in evidence.

Seeing the change was fascinating. She'd known he'd have changed in ways she hadn't yet discovered, but this was the first time she'd witnessed one of those changes. It was mildly disconcerting.

"I'm sorry to interrupt. In truth, my mother sent me in pursuit so we'd have reason for some small interaction." The young woman's rueful twist of lips suggested this was nothing new. "May I walk with you for a short while? Otherwise, my mother will just find some other reason to send me chasing after you."

The woman blushed with embarrassment, and Enkara almost felt sorry for her.

Kuwari must have as well for his posture softened and he nodded. He inclined his head in her direction. "Enkara, meet Lady Kullaa, councilor Nakurtum's oldest daughter and heir to Nippur."

Enkara bowed to Kullaa. "I am honored."

Lady Kullaa grinned, genuine joy sparkling in her eyes. "I'm glad we meet at last. Kuwari has told me many stories about your shared childhood. It's almost like I already know you."

Under normal circumstances, Enkara would have attributed the statement about spending time with the prince as a female gryphon's natural tendency to mark her territory or stake her claim to a male she fancied, but strangely she felt no accompanying hostility or jealousy radiating off this lady.

Enkara stole a glance at Kuwari. His earlier aloof mask had cracked, replaced by something humbler. Actually, he looked mildly flustered. Hmmm. Perhaps he wanted to say something but was tongue-tied? Kuwari tongue-tied?

Nope. That would never happen. Something else then.

She glanced at her oldest friend and then back to Lady Kullaa. "You and Prince Kuwari are close acquaintances?"

Lady Kullaa frowned. "Yes, whether Prince Kuwari wished it or not. You see, my mother is very manipulative. However, the prince has been kind enough not to chase me off every time my mother shoves me in his direction."

Truth. Every word dripped with honesty. Lady Kullaa didn't have one ambitious or dishonest bone in her body. The poor girl. The more ambitious, or merely cruel, members of the court would devour her alive. No wonder Kuwari had taken her under his wing.

"I don't remember you from before I left for my Shadow training on New Assur. How long have you been at court?"

"Five months. It has been very..."

Enkara could practically see the girl hunting for something polite to say. Eventually, she settled upon a satisfactory word. "Very eye-opening."

Kuwari snorted with laughter. "That's one word for it, but I can think of a few more accurate descriptors as well, though, they are better not spoken in such delicate company."

"He's definitely referring to you, not me," Enkara added for clarification.

"No doubt," Kullaa agreed, craning her neck to look at Enkara. "You're much worldlier than me. Though, even if I had your training and knowledge, I doubt I'd be much use in battle or putting down assassins."

Kuwari grinned. "Enkara is breathtaking to watch in the practice ring but let us hope she doesn't have to use her skills in a real battle anytime soon. I'm much more partial to peace than strife."

As they continued to walk, Kuwari and Kullaa enlightened her to other minor things that had changed here on Nineveh while she'd been away training. After walking one whole wing of the palace with them, Lady Kullaa sighed. "Well, that should be long enough to satisfy even my mother. Thank you for your hospitality, Prince Kuwari, Shadow Enkara. It was a pleasure, but I won't monopolize any more of your valuable time."

"You're welcome to seek us out anytime your mother becomes too overbearing," Kuwari offered.

Lady Kullaa thanked him and then bowed deeply, saying her goodbyes. Once Kuwari had excused her, she departed. Though, at a much slower pace than they'd walked before. Grinning, Enkara knew she'd walk just as slow if her destination was Councilor Nakurtum.

Once they were alone, Enkara grinned at Kuwari. "I think I just met a mythical creature."

"Yes?" he prompted.

"A noble lacking ambition."

Kuwari's expression remained neutral. "There is nothing between us."

"Don't recall saying there was." Enkara arched an eyebrow at him. While her love for her childhood friend was limitless, she knew they weren't well matched. As much as it hurt to admit, fate was showing her a way to divert his affections elsewhere. She'd thought finding a pure soul worthy of him would be hard, but perhaps it wouldn't be such a problematic hunt after all.

He would need a woman he could trust for the betrothal year, she reasoned. "You could do worse than Lady Kullaa."

"Do?" he asked, although she was sure he knew exactly what she was talking about.

"Betrothal. Marriage. Mate."

His brows furrowed. "Haven't you listened to anything I've said since I snuck into your tent night before last? Or do my words just slide off your skin? Because if you need actions instead of words, I'm happy to demonstrate my feelings for you."

The earlier glint of anger morphed into something more mischievous as he stepped toward her.

She held out her hand. "Don't do it or you'll find yourself on your ass again."

"I rather like a challenge and if you have to pin me down, all the better." Kuwari spread his arms wide and started for her only to pull up short as the sound of voices carried down the hall. His expressionless mask settled back in place, but he stepped closer so he could whisper in her ear. "This mockery of a betrothal the Council plans to force on me will be as fake as all those smiles I gave Councilor Nakurtum earlier."

Enkara rolled her eyes at him. "Fine. You'll still need someone you can trust in your fake betrothal. She seems like a good choice."

Kuwari's expression darkened further as he leaned in even closer. "If you like her so much, you marry her."

With that, Kuwari jerked straight and marched off. She'd almost caught up when he halted and turned so suddenly, she was nearly nose to nose with him.

"That's perfect," he crowed. "Why didn't I think of that sooner?"

"What's perfect?" Enkara asked, trying to figure out the inner workings of his mind.

"My idea of a fake betrothal crossed with your idea that I should betroth someone I can trust," Kuwari said, his devastating grin back in place.

Enkara's brows scrunched together. "Your thought process always makes my head hurt. Are you agreeing that Lady Kullaa would be a good match?"

"No. She has a lovely soul, but for the last time, I'm not interested in her. But I don't want to hurt her feelings or waste a year of her time. However, as you pointed out, I need a female I can trust at my side. And since you aren't ready for a real relationship with me, why not a fake one instead?"

Enkara gripped his shoulders and turned him in the direction of his quarters. "The servants will have your midday meal waiting for you, and you're clearly delirious with hunger and rambling nonsensically."

"Am not."

"Are too."

"Fine. We'll continue this in my chambers," Kuwari said with a glance around at the corridor and the Shadows standing guard. "But only because this isn't the best place to have this discussion."

Kuwari grabbed her hand and hurried back to his quarters. Once there, he did a quick check to be sure none of the servants were present. The guards could be trusted implicitly, but Kuwari's expression said he was thinking of sending them out into the hall.

After a slight hesitation, he scooped up the trays containing their midday meals and continued deeper into his chambers. He didn't stop until he was in Enkara's room.

"Kuwari, I'm not going along with whatever idea you've concocted."

He snatched a warm roll from the tray and tossed it at her. "Eat. You get grumpy when you're hungry."

She glowered but bit into the deliciously fresh, still-warm bread and nearly moaned. The food on New Assur was more along the lines of cold rations and hard, day-old bread. She took another bite. "Mmm. That's good. Fine. You talk."

Kuwari grinned and opened his mouth.

"Oh," Enkara muttered around a mouthful of bread. "You have until this roll is gone to explain your grand plan and it better make sense."

"I'm going to announce to the council that we're betrothed."

Enkara choked on her roll and Kuwari calmly thumped her on the back hard enough to clear her airways. When she could breathe again, he sat next to her and slung an arm around her shoulders. With his free hand, he held out a goblet of water.

"You said you'd give me time to settle in, for us to learn the depth of what we feel."

"Yes, and you can still have that. What I'm proposing is a fake betrothal." He grinned impishly.

Enkara scowled at him. "How's this going to be any different from a real betrothal?"

"We won't actually be courting each other. It's the best solution to our unique problems. And you have my word that I won't court you once we're in private. It will just require a little acting on both our parts when we're out in public." Kuwari started in on his own meal, devouring one of his favorite sweetcakes while he waited for her response.

She closed her eyes and debated that possibility. "But it won't be fake for you, would it?"

Goddess, of course it wouldn't. Kuwari would court her with every bit of his seductive charm. She wouldn't last a moon cycle before she gave into him.

"I won't lie. You'd sense it anyway. While it will be acting in public, I'll still want you with everything in me," he said, honesty burning in his voice.

"Gods, Kuwari. I've told you I'm not ready for a complicated relationship."

Kuwari stroked her cheek. "I know, and I respect that. I'm patient and willing to wait until our joining is free of fear and is something we both want above all else."

"Gods, you're such a romantic." That's what made it so hard for her to deny him.

He shrugged. "I'm my father's son."

Enkara could only nod. "You swear this will be fake on your part? At least in public?"

"I swear before our great goddess Ishtar, that if you agree to this, I will keep my word and not attempt true courtship until after I've gained your permission."

"That's an evasion."

"It's the closest thing you're going to get from me. I'd take it if I were you."

Sighing, she glanced sidelong at her prince, already sensing defeat looming. Besides, he looked so damned hopeful she found the words slipping out before she could stop them.

"I'm not saying no, not yet. But I do still want more time to think about this."

His boyish grin lit up his entire face.

I'm going to regret saying that, aren't I? Enkara thought to herself.

CHAPTER NINE

It couldn't possibly be dawn, her exhausted body reassured her waking mind, but a noise reached Enkara's ears, and she was instantly awake. Her eyes strained to find the threat in the darkness.

Reaching under the pillow next to her head, she eased a dagger out of its sheath and slid out of bed without so much as a rustle of fabric to betray her movement. She used the flat of her blade to shove the curtain aside. Unfortunately, there was no way to shift the curtain without setting the small beads rattling.

A soft sound of denial came again, this time accompanied by the sound of Kuwari fighting the blankets trapping him. She sensed no immediate danger or hostile intent focused on him. This wasn't a physical threat to his life. In fact, when she came to the side of the bed, it looked like he was in the grip of a nightmare. Though, she doubted this was anything as harmless as a simple dream.

Coming alongside his bed, she scanned the room once more and then laid her hand on his bare shoulder. It was cold to the touch and magic tingled against her fingers.

No, not a dream. This was a magic-induced vision.

His gift had him firmly in its grip. A soft footstep near at hand distracted her for a moment. When she confirmed it was just one of the Shadows guarding the outer chamber come to check on the prince, she nodded to the sentry. "Vision. A bad one."

The guard nodded and then vanished back the way he'd come. A moment later he spoke with one of his brethren. There must be standing orders to report all such events to the king.

Turning her attention back to Kuwari, she set her dagger on the small table beside his sleeping platform and then pressed both hands to his shoulders and closed her eyes.

His muscles twitched and shifted under her touch, and soon a chilled magic flowed from him, over her hands, and up her arms. A vision chased close on the penetrating power's heels. Enkara knew enough from previous encounters not to fight the magic or risk pulling Kuwari out of the vision before either of them could learn anything of importance.

Relaxing into his vision, she waited as a new world formed around her. She now stood in a temple. Tall columns, statues, and mosaics decorated the antechamber she found herself in. Burning torches lined the walls, providing the only source of light. She saw no windows or archways leading outside from her present location. And no visible indication where Kuwari was either.

She took a closer look at the columns and walls with their strangely familiar motifs, but these were not Ishtar's symbols. These belong to her sister, Ereshkigal, Queen of the Underworld. And this felt like no vision she'd ever experienced before.

An increasing sense of danger rolled over her like a wave, and she reached out for Kuwari. Moments later she felt his strong life force and the warmth of his mind. He was near, but somewhere in one of the upper levels of the structure.

At least her gift worked. She hesitated to converse with him using their mental link, fearing it might give away her presence to their enemies if this was more than a vision. Surprise might be the only advantage she had in this strange dream-world.

But what else might be all-too-real in this vision? Was it possible for him to come to harm here?

The antechamber had two exits, one at either end of the large, column-lined room. She headed for the closest. A scabbard bumped against her leg as she walked. Frowning down at the harness and sword, neither of which had been there a moment before, she drew forth the sword and was only a little surprised to see this was a crystalline blade of power like what Ishtar had given Queen Iltani.

She hadn't been wearing a sword when she'd sought out Kuwari, but in the way of dreams and visions, she accepted the sword for what it was: an item of protection given to her by a goddess.

Striding from the antechamber, she came to a long tunnel that opened onto a landing in the distance. Beyond, the open sky beckoned her forward. She was confident she was inside a ziggurat and looking at one of the exits which would lead her up to the next level.

With her new sword's hilt held firm, she darted down the tunnel. As she approached the exit, drums and chanting drifted to her. Human voices wove a counterpoint to the deeper tones of the drums. She couldn't be sure of the exact number of priests and priestesses worshiping close by, but there were enough that they might have been able to over-power the prince. And that wasn't counting the unknown number of guards that would undoubtedly be present.

That didn't bode well. She bolted to the archway on silent feet and was about to cross under to the landing beyond when her gift flared in recognition. Coming to a sudden halt, she sidestepped and put her back against the wall as she peered out through the opening.

Just outside, two winged anunnaki stood guard on either side of the archway. And these anunnaki weren't locked in stone. They were very much awake and on guard. Worse, they blocked the stairs she needed if she had any hope of getting up to Kuwari on the next level of the temple.

The anunnaki were fierce guardians of what they deemed worthy of protection. These two beings would battle anyone they deemed a dangerous outsider every bit as much as their kin back on Nineveh would act to protect the capital city. But they stood between her and fulfilling her duty, and she was also a fierce protector with a great power gifted to her by a goddess.

She approached them with bared blade, her power rising within her to meet this new challenge. To her surprise and great distrust, they stood at attention. A moment later, they raised their crossed spears, allowing her to pass. The male on her left was one of the bird-men variety, with the body of a human and the head of a desert eagle. In contrast, the one on the right looked entirely human if one ignored the wings.

Tilting her head to study them for any betraying shifts of muscle, she tightened her hold on her sword hilt and slid between them. The human-headed one's expression was no more scrutable than the eagle-man's.

She found their acceptance more unsettling than if she'd had to fight them. When she was past, they returned to their earlier stance, staring out ahead of them.

Outside, the music and chanting were clearer, drifting down from the top level of the ziggurat. She eyed the stairs that flanked the side of the structure. There was no cover. She'd be completely exposed, and if there were more anun-naki above, they could easily fly down in an ambush.

Lacking wings herself, she didn't look forward to a fight on the stairs where one misstep could send her tumbling two-thirds of the way down the side of the ziggurat to a painful vision-death. Above her head rose the last level of the structure and upon its flattened pinnacle loomed the temple.

Drawing in a deep, fortifying breath, she darted up the steps, only halting when she was almost even with the temple's topmost level. She crouched, studying the layout. Rows of torches lined the edge, their light reflecting against the gold-plated temple columns. In other places, polished lapis lazuli and colored plaster devoured the light, empowering the deepest shadows to hide unseen assailants.

Dancers moved in time to drum and voice, twisting and spinning gracefully between the shadow and the light. She was about to run headlong into an unknown number of enemy, but she didn't care. Kuwari was up there and needed her help.

She leaped into motion, taking the last stairs two at a time and emerged on to the floor of the temple. The dancers didn't react to her arrival as she'd expected. Instead of scattering to make way for armed guards, they shifted closer to her as they continued their graceful spinning and leaping dance. Their actions weren't at all aggressive, but rather inviting as if they'd been expecting her.

Enkara threatened any who came too close with a flick of her sword's tip. But they were unarmed and not attacking. She wouldn't kill unarmed novices, not even in a vision, but she wasn't against giving them a few cuts and bruises if they got in her way.

Easing past the dancers and between the first two rows of columns, she moved deeper into the temple. Musicians were spread out among the columns, with the greatest clustered along the front wall. Circling the central altar, priests and priestesses chanted their praises for Ereshkigal, their great queen of the underworld.

All of this only got the barest glance, her gaze locked onto Kuwari, where he was being dragged toward an altar by two powerfully built anunnaki. She rushed forward, still expecting someone to halt her, but the dancers merely drew aside as she passed. Though, again, some reached out to her, attempting to persuade her to partake in the dance with them.

She swatted away their reaching hands.

Kuwari struggled against his two anunnaki captors,

twisting and bucking and kicking out, using every trick Burrukan taught. Twice he nearly escaped their hold, only to get recaptured as three more anunnaki came forward to help.

The tallest of them, a broad-shouldered, eagle-headed anunnaki, who radiated ancient power, turned from Prince Kuwari and gestured in her direction. After a moment he said something to the prince. Kuwari froze in place. Then turning, he met her gaze but said nothing, not even over their special link. But she noted the moment he straightened from his fighter's crouch, waiting for what was coming next.

The tallest anunnaki placed a hand on Kuwari's shoulder and said something else, his head tilting back to the central altar. The prince shook his head at whatever the guardian said.

Enkara shoved her way through the dancers now clustering around her. When the large anunnaki said something else to the prince, Kuwari shook his head violently and struck at the nearest guard, taking him by surprise. He only made it a few steps before the anunnaki flared his broad wings, sweeping Kuwari's feet out from under him.

The prince rolled, using his momentum to propel himself back to his feet. Not one to be trounced, Kuwari latched on to the wing of the nearest anunnaki and darted under his opponent's outstretched arm. He gave it a wicked twist, one with enough force that it would have dislocated the joint if it had been an arm. Unfortunately, the ploy failed, the wing having much more flexibility.

Enkara shouldered aside two dancers and then ran into a group of musicians, sending them crashing to the polished stone floor when they didn't move out of her way fast enough. She resumed her sprint but was still too far away.

The anunnaki screeched out a raptor's sound of rage, then flicked his wing out of the prince's grasp and slammed a hand firmly against Kuwari's chest. Even over the distance, she felt the wave of force that slammed her prince back into the waiting arms of two more anunnaki.

She pounded closer, knocking priests and priestesses out of her way, but before she could reach Kuwari, other anunnaki converged on him, grabbing him by his arms and legs, hoisting him off his feet. They carried him bodily toward the altar.

An expanse of creamy, red-fringed feathers blocked her view of Kuwari and suddenly the tall anunnaki was confronting her. She slashed at him with her sword, and he blocked the strike with his own.

"Peace to you, honored Blade." The anunnaki's voice was deep and mellow, full of rich resonance and beautiful to hear. He didn't sound the least bit concerned.

"I thought an anunnaki couldn't lie?" she challenged in return.

"That is correct. We mean no harm to you or our King."

Our King? What did he mean by that? Not that she had time to figure it out now. Snapping her sword around, she brought the tip close to his throat and was about to see if one of his kind could bleed when her gift flared and confirmed his words were true. Her hesitation saved the anunnaki and he deflected her strike.

"Why did you bring us here?"

He snapped his beak together and his facial feathers

fluffed in a way she'd have said was humor on a gryphon. On an anunnaki, she didn't know what the expression meant.

"I didn't bring you here. Our King chose to return. You followed like any good Blade would do."

Truth again.

Why, by Ishtar's great tempers, were they calling Kuwari their king?

"Kuwari's gift might have brought him here, but it wasn't willingly. That's clear to see."

The anunnaki snapped his beak together again. "That is true. Our king is a touch confused, but once you and Kuwari perform the Sacred Marriage, Queen Ereshkigal will make everything clear to both her beloved husband and you."

"You might believe what you say, but I know Ereshkigal seeks to rob her sister of the gryphon heir and his Blade."

"I am one of the seven justices. The oldest of my kind. I do not lie. When I say Ishtar stole something very dear to Ereshkigal's heart, it is the truth."

Well, someone was lying. Kuwari wasn't meant for Ereshkigal. Enkara was damn certain of that, and as long as she drew breath, she'd make sure the Queen of the Underworld never got within touching distance of Prince Kuwari.

"Let us prepare our king for you."

"No!" She brought her crystalline blade to bear. This time there was no hesitation, and the anunnaki had to work hard to keep his head on his shoulders. Even so, the divine being didn't act concerned that she might take his head at any moment.

"There is no fighting fate, child." The anunnaki's tone

hinted that he'd had a taste of fate before and didn't much care for the lack of choice.

"Perhaps not, but this isn't our fate."

"Young one, your fate is already written. You always have been and will always be Ereshkigal's Blade."

The anunnaki grunted in surprise as her crystalline blade buried its burning length in his chest. Taking a two-handed hold on her sword's hilt, she twisted with all her strength. If he'd been mortal, he'd have dropped to his knees and swiftly bled out, but this opponent merely stumbled back, pressing a hand to the hole in his chest.

Shoving him out of her way, she leaped clear, targeting the next nearest anunnaki, one of the four holding Kuwari down upon the altar. She attacked before he had time to draw his blade.

He buffeted her with his wings, but her crystalline sword blazed bright, burning through feathers, bones, and cartilage. She slashed again, intent on dealing with this opponent swiftly, but he'd managed to draw his sword before hers completed its deadly arc, and he deflected her blow. They circled each other in a deadly dance, both seeking the other's weakness.

All the while she faced her opponent, she also tracked Kuwari. He'd managed to throw off the anunnaki holding his legs. And as she watched, he kicked up, nearly folding himself in half to land a powerful kick to the head of one of his remaining captors. His momentum carried him on over. Twisting out of the hold of the last anunnaki, Kuwari landed on his feet, one of his opponent's swords in his hand.

At which point Enkara was forced to focus on her own

fight. Her new anunnaki opponent wasn't pulling his strikes like she now realized the first one had been. While they fought, exchanging bone-jarring strikes, her gift flared again, and she felt the approach of other guardians.

Casting a swift glance skyward, she spotted dozens of winged forms descending from the star-speckled sky overhead.

Time was running out. She didn't know what would happen if they were captured by the horde of anunnaki or if Ereshkigal arrived while they were still fighting, but she wasn't waiting around to find out. They needed to escape. Now. She dived under her opponent's sword arm and sprinted the last few steps to her prince, and together they shoved their way through the surprised crowd of priests, priestesses, musicians, and dancers.

They reached the edge of the temple and glanced down the steep slope of the ziggurat's gleaming wall. Above them, the winged figures loomed large, descending fast. There was no way they'd be able to get to the stairs before the anunnaki reinforcements were upon them.

Kuwari glanced sidelong at her and reached out for her hand. "I think we've overstayed our welcome."

Enkara couldn't agree more, but they had nowhere to go unless Kuwari shifted to gryphon form, and, even then, the open sky offered no safety. Not against flying opponents.

Her crystalline sword had its own ideas, though, and flared brighter. Inside her, Ishtar's warm power flared stronger, and the dormant tattoo stamped along her spine tingled with a new warmth.

Relief washed over her only to be stolen a moment later

as a second, colder power rose up within her to battle Ishtar for control. Against her will, Enkara took a half step away from the temple's edge. Turning farther, she glanced over her shoulder to see a coldly beautiful woman standing behind them, dressed only in her fierce and glorious power.

Wings stretched out behind her, arched proudly, framing her form. In her right hand, she grasped a scepter of power. Perched on her left wrist sat a small, watchful owl. Its eyes blinked once, slowly, as it studied first Enkara and then Kuwari.

The owl's mistress made no move to come closer, but she held her arms wide in welcome. "My King and my Blade have finally come home. Welcome."

Gasping out in surprise, Enkara remained locked in place, her muscles rigid as the two powers mixed, battling for control. The warmth spiked suddenly, and Enkara's sword flared even more intensely, chasing away some of the cold.

"Sister, you should know better than to steal what is mine," Enkara said, though the words were not hers, nor was the will behind them. The warm rush of power flooding her body slowed but didn't diminish or release its hold.

"Ishtar," Ereshkigal said in acknowledgment, her earlier welcoming expression shifting into something darker and more hateful "You should heed your own words. I only take back what is rightfully mine."

"Not this day," Ishtar countered, and then Enkara turned back to Kuwari and placed a hand on his forehead. "Prince Kuwari, I order you to wake. Listen and obey, for I am Ishtar, Mother to all gryphons."

"As my goddess wishes." On the tail of Kuwari's words the temple shimmered and blurred, beginning to fade. Only Kuwari's hands wrapped around hers still felt real, warm, and alive.

He pulled her to him. Instinctively, she wrapped her arms around him. Off balance, they fell forward through an impossibly great distance.

The cold began to recede, replaced by the warmth of a human body pressed against hers. Voices drifted closer, dragging her further from the world of dreams and visions, back to warm and painful life. Enkara gasped out a surprised sound as she blinked down into Kuwari's equally startled eyes.

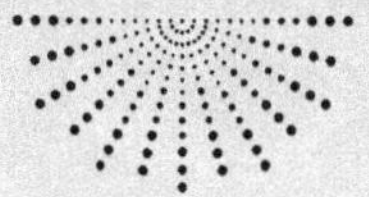

CHAPTER TEN

"That was a nasty one." Shock slowly melted from Kuwari's features as he blinked up at her. "I'm glad you were here for it."

His voice was shaky, his breathing no better. At least he had a voice. Enkara still didn't trust herself to speak even if she had any notion what to say.

Kuwari swallowed and then licked his lips. "I think you just saved me from something very unpleasant."

It took her mind far too long to process the simple fact that she was likely crushing the heir to the Gryphon Kingdom under her weight. But if she was to judge by his fierce hold on her, he didn't seem to care about that minor discomfort. His gaze was a touch wild-eyed. Hers probably was as well.

Enkara braced her hands on either side of his head and levered some of her weight off him. Voices encroached upon her awareness and her senses slowly expanded outward.

Twin weights rested on either side of her shoulders—hands, but they weren't Kuwari's. His were locked around her waist.

"You are alright, Enkara. You're safe now," said a voice that was nagging in its familiarity. "Kuwari's safe. It's over now."

One of the hands squeezed her right shoulder. Enkara turned her head enough to gaze upon Queen Iltani. The Queen was standing on the right side of the bed, her expression calm but concerned.

The bed shifted as another weight settled on the left. "It's over. Easy. Come back to us."

She glanced over her other shoulder to see King Ditanu kneeling on the edge of the bed, worry for his son still evident in his eyes. For once his King's emotionless mask was missing.

That could only mean the situation was as bad as she'd feared.

"That's it. Kuwari's safe now," the King crooned. "Let me examine my son."

Slowly, feeling returned to her body. She almost wished it hadn't. An intense throbbing ache pulsed down the length of her back. The skin along her spine felt blistered and stiff. Moving caused the red agony to flare brighter, but Kuwari's parents needed to see their son. And one didn't disobey the rulers of the ten island city-states.

There was no telling what Kuwari had suffered. He'd been under the influence of the vision-dream longer than her. She forced herself to move, trying to slowly shift off him, but she could barely move even with help. The parts of her body that didn't hurt were numb and unresponsive.

"My son, tell me what happened. Are you hurt?" Ditanu asked.

Kuwari glanced at his father, his gaze sharpening. Reluctantly he released his hold on her. "I think I'm fine, considering. I just need a moment to commit to memory all the vision showed me before the details grow hazy."

Enkara could understand needing a bit of time. Her own mind felt foggy, her senses dull and sluggish. It was only when she was lifted away by several helping hands that she realized there were others in Kuwari's quarters. Many others.

Regents Ahassunu and Burrukan were standing at the end of the sleeping platform. Behind them waited a dozen silent, unhappy Shadows. Enkara could understand their disquiet. The vision was unquestionably an attack. But how did one fight an enemy one couldn't touch with magic or edged-weapons here in the real world?

Four of her Shadow brethren helped to lift her from the bed and carefully placed her on her feet. She was still gathering her wits when her mentor came over to check on her. Burrukan grabbed her by the shoulder and turned her to face away from him while he studied her back. He made a low murmur of sympathy.

Damn. It must look just as bad as it felt to get that response from her mentor.

"Nasty. Burned right through the fabric of your night robe. Priestess Kammani is mixing something to take away the pain, but in the meantime, what, by Ishtar, just happened? When the guards woke me to say Kuwari was under the influence of a powerful dream, or some form of attack, and that you tried to aid him but then turned unresponsive yourself, I knew the gods were up to no good."

"Don't tell him anything that incriminates us. Assume everything we heard there was a lie until we discover otherwise," Kuwari whispered along their mental link without even taking his eyes off his parents. *"I don't want to share this with my parents until I know they won't separate us. I don't know what is happening, but I do know we are much stronger together."*

"Just until we get our bearings," she agreed.

She then rallied her scattered thoughts enough to answer Burrukan's question. Taking her cue from Kuwari, where he was talking with his father, she kept the details sparse until she could better understand the vision's meaning. But she did describe how she'd found the prince and merged into his vision, and then she told some of what she'd seen in the underworld. Though she skirted around what the anunnaki had said about her being Ereshkigal's blade or that the goddess had called Kuwari her husband.

Coming to the end of her tale, she said, "This vision, if that's what it was, was far stronger than any he's had before."

"That's what the guards thought as well. When I felt the magic rising off you, I had Iltani and Ditanu summoned," Burrukan explained. "Ditanu said Kuwari was trapped in a powerful vision, one he feared was real enough to cause trauma in the waking world should either of you sustain an injury in that alternate vision plane."

Enkara remained silent and Burrukan continued. "Iltani merged with you and Kuwari. She was able to focus Ishtar's magic using your tattoo and with the goddess's help, she was able to break you free of whatever spell held you trapped."

"I must thank our Queen then."

Burrukan grunted. "Iltani said you were holding your own until she got there. Clearly, there was a physical cost since your mark was dormant. You'll need to rest and heal before we continue your training, but that's a small price to pay for saving the heir."

"You did well," Queen Iltani said as she joined them. "Besides, I don't know how much I was able to help. You were doing well on your own. Kuwari is lucky to have such a fearless and loyal Blade."

Enkara wasn't so sure. If the anunnaki was to be believed, she was originally Ereshkigal's Blade before she was Ishtar's.

To focus on something other than that new fear and the growing pain throbbing along her back, Enkara glanced around the room. Ditanu's aunt, High Priestess Kammani, was approaching with a large bowl in one hand and a copper pitcher in the other.

Enkara stood while the elder poked and prodded at her back to evaluate the extent of the damage and then applied cream to the burn. More than once, only her iron will held back the pained hisses.

"The cream will numb the skin for now, but it will need a second application shortly. The first only opens the pores. I'll instruct Kuwari how to clean and dress it for the day." Kammani patted her shoulder in sympathy. "You will heal up in a day or two. Blades always recover faster than the rest of us."

A new concern entered Enkara's mind. "The damage...will it affect my ability to become a Blade later, during the Blooding Ceremony?"

What if this crippled her for life? That was one way of stopping Ereshkigal from claiming her as her Blade. But if she was crippled, how would she protect Kuwari if the Queen of the Underworld sent her anunnaki to recapture him? Because after witnessing that vision, she was sure their enemies would strike again soon.

A shudder rolled down her body at the thought of Kuwari becoming Ereshkigal's new husband.

"No need to fear," Kammani said, misreading Enkara's worry. "Any remaining damage will heal during the first Blooding Ceremony. Or if the damages are greater than what Kuwari's magic-laced blood can mend, Ishtar will heal it. What is a little burn to a goddess's power?"

She wasn't at all reassured. If Ishtar could heal such a wound with ease, so too could her sister. All Ereshkigal had to do to claim Enkara as her Blade was to heal the wound.

"I'm fine," Kuwari growled, drawing Enkara's attention. "Stop fussing and give me a moment to get dressed. I'll fill you in on the details of the vision in a bit."

"Very well," King Ditanu said as he gently cuffed his son's ear. Then he turned to the others. "We'll continue this discussion in the throne room over first meal. I'm certain Enkara and my son need some nourishment after the night they've had."

With that, King Ditanu held his arms out wide and physically herded the others from the room.

Once the room was empty except for Kuwari, Enkara braced an arm against the wall by the hearth. She swiftly changed her stance since it hurt too damn much. It took two tries before she could put words to the horror swirling in her heart and mind.

"The vision...I've never experienced one that strong before. Have there been others like it while I was away training on New Assur?"

Kuwari shook his head. "No. That was the first of that strength. They're not normally so detailed either. I'm usually an observer in the visions, not a participant."

"I don't like it."

"Can't say I'm very fond of it either." Kuwari glanced down at his folded hands for a moment and then tossed back his blankets and stood. He pulled a robe from the chest at the foot of the bed and was still belting it on when he joined her by the hearth.

"I want to see the damage for myself." Taking her by the shoulder, he gently urged her to face the fire. His hissing exclamation wasn't very reassuring.

"By the goddess! Burrukan was right. The power burned clear through the linen."

His fingers poked at the bits of fabric fluttering along her back. Then she felt his thumb brush along the blistered skin. "My poor Kara. I'm so sorry."

He left her side to retrieve the bowl, rag, and pot of cream Priestess Kammani had left for Enkara's use. When he returned to the fire, Enkara held out her hands for the supplies.

Kuwari snorted. "There's no way you can reach your own spine. At least not without making it hurt worse than it already does. Lie belly down." One long finger indicated the nearby bench.

She gave him her best 'don't be daft' look but knew what he said was true. Twisting, stretching, and straining to dress the burn would do more damage than good, but that didn't mean she was completely comfortable having the future king of the gryphons attend to her like a servant.

He set the supplies down next to the bench and picked up a finely woven blanket and placed it over one arm while he eyed the hem of her shift.

"I can undress without help."

"Only you would be stubborn enough to try." Kuwari turned her to face the fire a second time. "It'll just be easier and less painful if I do it. Trust me."

Deft fingers brushed against the back of her neck, and then the sound of tearing fabric was loud in the silence. Linen brushed against her body as it slid to the floor. Then Kuwari was wrapping the blanket around her waist, being careful he didn't touch painful burns.

She'd never been particularly modest and Kuwari's unusual seriousness was strangely comforting.

"You. Bench. Now," Kuwari ordered. She complied, and he wasted no time in dipping the rag into the bowl of water infused with healing herbs. Soon the air filled with the rich scent.

Once she was on her stomach—which was a very slow and painful process—she used her arms as a pillow and tried to ignore the throb of her back. Soon Kuwari was dripping the cool herbal water over her shoulder blades and down the length of her spine. The coolness of the water took away most of the heat and soon he was rubbing more of the herbal pain-deadening cream into her back. A numbness spread out from where his fingers brushed across her skin.

"Oh, Goddess. Thank you."

Kuwari huffed and continued to work. "I'm not sure you should be thanking any gods. They're the ones that caused this damage."

"That's sacrilege," she mumbled into her arms.

"Perhaps a bit, but it doesn't mean it's not true in this instance." He paused as if thinking. "I'm sorry I dragged you into the vision but thank you for being there for me."

"I will always come for you."

"And I, you."

As Kuwari worked, the pain faded to a more manageable level. She'd be as slow and stiff as an old woman tomorrow, but it would heal. In the interim, she'd continue to see to Kuwari's protection in other ways.

That included protecting him from herself. His vision had proven how much danger Kuwari faced, and it made it clear that she was also a threat.

Whether the anunnaki's words were true or not, it was clear Ereshkigal wanted to steal Kuwari away from Ishtar and make him her new husband. It was also abundantly clear that the Queen of the Underworld wanted to make Enkara into her Blade to perform a perversion of the Sacred Marriage.

Well, she'd just have to teach a goddess that this 'Blade' was not a tool easily mastered.

But first Kuwari would need convincing that she was a potential threat. Things had to change. She had to put emotional distance between them. A betrothal was now out of the question. It was far too risky for him to become further romantically entangled with her.

If she thought for a moment her absence would prevent Ereshkigal from hunting Kuwari, Enkara would leave, put an entire ocean between them if that's what it would take to keep him safe. But Ereshkigal would only find another way to have him, and if Enkara was far away, there'd be nothing she could do to stop the next attempt.

So, she'd stay.

Beside her Kuwari froze, an intense and unmoving presence. "Enkara, what's wrong?"

Damn. He'd read something in the tension of her body. Now that her back didn't hurt as much, she got up, wrapped the blanket around her shoulders and met his gaze.

"Kuwari, you were there. You heard Ereshkigal and the anunnaki. You heard what they wanted of us. After what I learned in that vision, I can't be your betrothed. Fake or not, completing a trial year with you would be a risk we can't afford. I might form mating bonds with you. That would make Ereshkigal's task all the earlier."

"Enkara, you're panicking. Just because the Queen of the Underworld wants an event to turn out in such a way, doesn't mean it will. Ishtar is a jealous goddess. She'll not willingly share us with her sister."

"This feels different."

Kuwari took her hand and pulled it into his lap. "Ereshkigal has been planning attacks against my family for thousands of years. She hasn't defeated us yet. I don't plan to be the first of my line to fail."

Kuwari tried to draw her closer, but she blocked his hand

from touching her face. "That doesn't mean Ishtar will win this time. Ereshkigal is just as powerful as her younger sister."

"That doesn't mean our fate is set. We can fight, avoid Ereshkigal's plans. Together we are strong."

"Not this time. As long as I draw breath, I will do everything in my power to keep you out of her clutches. And that means I must turn down your offer of betrothal."

He placed a hand on her shoulder. "Enkara please…"

"I won't change my mind. I can't." Standing, she shook off his hand and started to walk away. "I'm going to get dressed, and we're going to go tell your parents exactly what we saw in that vision. They need to know about the danger I represent to you."

Powerful fingers locked her wrist in a punishing grip. She turned and stared at the offending digits. If anyone other than Kuwari attempted such, they'd swiftly find themselves on the ground with a dislocated shoulder and their hand crushed under her boot.

He jerked her closer, surprising her. She was suddenly nose to nose, looking into his fierce eyes.

"You are *my* Blade. You will do nothing that will spur my parents to act rashly. I will not be parted from you. Our futures, our very lives, depend on the special bond we share."

"Now isn't the time for passionate speeches."

"Speeches? Passionate?" Anger edged his voice and his eyes narrowed.

Before she thought to react, he jerked her closer, his lips coming down to press hungrily against hers, demanding she acknowledge him as a male entering his prime. He stole her breath with his power and passion. With everything she was, she wanted to melt into him, to accept what he was offering.

But she knew better than to let him steal her wits. After breaking off the kiss, she shoved him and put a body's length worth of space between them.

Panting, he stared at her. Something ancient and powerful peered out at her through his eyes. "That was only the smallest shred of my passion."

Enkara didn't know how to counter that confession, but the foreign look in his eye was more concerning.

"However," he continued just as fiercely, his tone and manner almost unrecognizable. "I will concede to your wishes in one thing. I would never force you to become my betrothed. If I must complete a trial year with some other female, I shall. But it will mean nothing to me. No matter how much the Council likes to manipulate events, they can only force me to the betrothal ceremony. They cannot make me love or take to mate their choice."

"That is true." Enkara was still uncertain where this new Kuwari had come from.

"And you will not share your fears with my parents about being Ereshkigal's Blade until we have solid proof. All I saw was Ereshkigal attempting to steal what rightfully belongs to her sister. It isn't the first time the Queen of the Underworld has tried to capture one of my family line. It won't be the last."

"I'd feel better sharing this with someone."

"Do you actually believe Ishtar would have allowed you to grow up at my side if you really are Ereshkigal's Blade?" Kuwari stepped closer and tucked a loose piece of her hair behind her ear. His expression softened, the fierceness fading from his eyes until the Kuwari she knew returned. "Ishtar isn't subtle. If you are not her Blade, she'd have made her displeasure known long before now. Besides, the lamassu like you. And my other visions involving you have been far more pleasant than the one we just shared."

That all might be true, but Enkara was still going to tell his parents the truth.

"Fine. I can see I still haven't convinced you." Kuwari's nostrils flared, and he hissed out a frustrated breath. "Have you thought what will happen once you tell my parents? No? Then let me tell you! I've seen snippets in some of my visions. Although I didn't know until today what could possibly cause my parents to try to separate us."

Enkara latched onto his words, fear rising within her. "So, once I tell them, your parents will come to the same conclusion as me? That I'm a threat? It's not just my overly suspicious nature dreaming up dreadful scenarios then?"

Kuwari huffed in humor. "My Blade and my parents both dream up 'dreadful scenarios' more often than anyone should. Unfortunately, I'm both blessed and cursed with the gift to witness potential future events. Those fragments always show that nothing good comes from our separation. So, if you love me at all, you will do everything in your power to remain close."

Enkara curled her fingers into a fist. *Why does this have to be such an impossible situation?*

"If it gives you comfort, just remember you'd find it terribly difficult to protect me locked away in a dungeon somewhere below the city."

"Fine!" Enkara met his stare and frowned at him. "I won't risk your safety by getting myself shut away somewhere, but if Ereshkigal manages to dig past my defenses and gets her claws into me, then you must tell your parents and let them deal with me."

Kuwari's expression still bordered on rebellious, but he nodded his agreement.

"We still need to learn more about the vision-dream and Ereshkigal's plans," Enkara said to redirect the topic to something more constructive. "The quickest way would be to ask High Priestess Kammani if something like this has ever happened before, but since we can't come straight out and ask, we'll have to find another way."

The prince nodded, his gaze turning thoughtful. "We could hunt through the city archive, look for any mention of previous attacks. I remember a few from my studies, but no exact details that match our present conditions. Unfortunately, accounts of a darker nature that might contain information dangerous to New Sumer are unlikely to be part of public record."

"At least it's a place to start."

"High Priestess Kammani keeps copies of all historical records back on Uruk." Kuwari rubbed his chin and compressed his lips. "I know for a fact she has scrolls in much greater number than what's here in Nineveh."

"Yes. She brought me some scrolls of our ancient kings and queens, and their Blades, when I was on New Assur training. Due to your vision, I would like to take a second look at some of them. And if we can learn more about the underworld anunnaki, all the better. But we can't just go off to Uruk without drawing suspicion."

"No, but we can start here, and if we find something in the public record, then we can say that it has caught your interest. And since we all know you're like a hyena with a bone when you've set your mind to something, it will look like natural curiosity as part of your Blade's training."

She wasn't entirely satisfied, but it was a place to start. Something better than having no direction at all.

CHAPTER ELEVEN

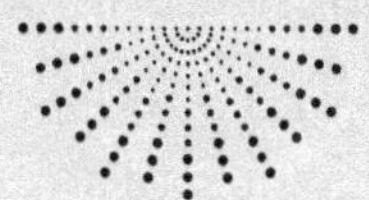

Kuwari ordered Enkara to her bed to rest and heal. Which she was fine with until he left without an explanation and only a vague promise to be back shortly. After the vicious vision-dream, she wanted to keep him in her sights. At least his father had doubled Kuwari's Shadow guard.

Unfortunately, the king had assigned a group to her as well, with the order that Enkara was to remain in bed until she healed. If it had been life or death, she would have fought the guards to reach Kuwari's side, but her gift didn't warn of any immediate danger to the prince, so she remained in her bed, belly down and bored out of her mind.

But I swear, as soon as the rebellious brat returns, she mused darkly, *I'll make him regret leaving without sharing his plans.*

After all, even though she could use their special link to track him, it was still common courtesy to notify his Blade.

Not long after she'd planned her revenge, the sound of the outer door opening announced his return. Soon he entered her room carrying a large armful of scrolls.

"Since we've been taken off active duty, I decided now is as good a time as any to start our research. These are the scrolls from the palace library that mention attacks against the throne. Most aren't detailed enough to offer much help, but if I remember correctly, a couple went into more detail."

Enkara nodded, her earlier annoyance forgotten.

"WELL, that was less useful than I'd hoped," Kuwari said with a tired sigh. He stopped and stretched. "We've been through all the scrolls and haven't found anything similar to the conundrum we find ourselves in."

Enkara wasn't so sure.

"Come read this. We may have gotten lucky," she said, walking the scroll she was reading over to Kuwari. "This one talks about one of your ancestors—Queen Asharru—and how she was the last of her line. It states that agents of Ereshkigal nearly managed to insert one of their number into her inner circle. She might actually have mated the male if her Blade hadn't intervened and saved her from her fate."

"Yes. Asharru and Tirigan. An unusual pairing. I remember their story now," Kuwari said, looking thoughtful. "I always wondered what my several-times-great grand-mother must have thought when she discovered the man she was expected to marry was actually there to destroy her, and that she had a stranger for a Blade. They didn't meet as children as is normal. That must have been a shock."

Kuwari took the scroll and reread the contents. After a moment he laughed. "While it doesn't directly pertain to our present concerns, it should be a good reminder why you have no need to be ashamed of your heritage. Not all Blades had privileged upbringings, some, like Blade Tirigan, had a horrific start to life."

Enkara wanted to say he was a pleasure slave, and while he had a terrible early life, Tirigan's parents weren't traitors to the throne but held her tongue. They had more important things to do. "Wasn't Tirigan the Blade who formed the Shadows as we know them now—giving them great power and authority to protect the royal line?"

"Yes," Kuwari agreed, his raised eyebrow saying he hadn't yet figured out where she was going with her line of thought.

"What if he did that because he knew Ereshkigal wasn't aiming to get someone close enough to assassinate Queen Asharru but instead looking to merge the two lines and use the child in some way? If a male child was born of that union, perhaps she planned to take that future king as her husband? By forming the Shadows, Blade Tirigan might have been trying to prevent future attempts of a similar nature."

"That's a lot of speculation."

"Yes, but why would Ereshkigal go to so much trouble to get a queen loyal to Ishtar to fall in love with one of the underworld's agents? It would take months or more likely years of planning, and every moment her agent was near the queen, he risked being found out and killed. A well-placed assassin would be much swifter and less likely to be discovered until too late." Enkara frowned at the scroll. "No, there had to be more to her plans than an assassination. You don't need the victim to love an assassin if you simply wish to eliminate a target."

"Ah," Kuwari said softly, deep in thought. "I hadn't thought of it in those terms. But, yes, Ereshkigal didn't want something to end, did she? She wanted it to begin."

"Yes. I think Ereshkigal wanted to somehow sow the seeds of her power into the royal line, but subtly so Ishtar wouldn't know what was afoot until too late. But Tirigan stopped her, so she's trying again. With us this time."

Kuwari rolled up the scroll and drummed his fingers along the storage cylinder. "I agree. But why would she wait so long to try again?"

"Perhaps she didn't. What's to say all the other assassination attempts stopped by Shadows and Blades throughout the centuries weren't part of a greater plan? Look at Ditanu. He was the only survivor out of all his siblings. What if he was always intended to survive and Ereshkigal was selecting the one best suited for her plans?"

Kuwari's brow furled. "That is a most disturbing thought, my Blade."

"If the Queen of the Underworld somehow managed to taint the sole remaining heir, then she could use the magic that links Royals and subjects, the very foundational magic that New Sumer is built on." Enkara frowned unhappily. "If that happened, then Ereshkigal could hold every gryphon hostage to her whim."

Kuwari's eyebrows drew further together at her ominous words. "We need to dig into this further. Unfortunately, we need to get to Uruk. And that might not be possible for a moon cycle or more, not with my upcoming name day celebration and then the spring rite festival."

CHAPTER TWELVE

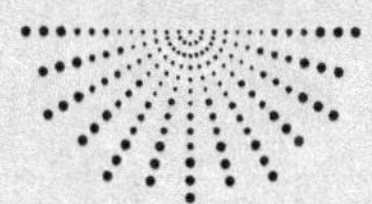

The fifth day of Enkara's convalescence dawned, and if they didn't give her leave to return to her training or some other duties, she was going to start raving at the walls. Being trapped inside—no matter how beautiful the space—and having nothing to do brought back memories of her time before she'd come to Nineveh, memories of hunger, cold, beatings, and great loneliness. Memories she'd done her best to bury.

But these few short days just told her how close to the surface they really were. They even haunted her dreams at night, transporting her back to a time when she was a frightened child, arms and legs curled tight around her body for comfort and warmth.

She'd taken to sitting next to Kuwari while he slept unaware of her. Actually, on some level he had to be aware because his sleeping mind still reached out to hers, wrapping around hers like a shield, keeping the dark memories at bay.

During the day, she didn't have that solace. She was just contemplating leaping out a window and escaping into the gardens when the outer door opened and by the sound of footsteps several people entered. Was Kuwari back early from his session with Burrukan?

But it wasn't Kuwari who stuck his head in.

Enkara jerked to attention and scrambled off her sleeping platform, sending scrolls rolling in all directions.

"Queen Iltani, forgive me. If I'd known you were coming, I would have been…ready," she ended a little lamely. Facing the queen in the practice ring was one thing—that was Blade training. Facing her as co-ruler of New Sumer always put Enkara on edge.

With a respectful bow and a belated, 'your majesty' Enkara straightened, already wondering what had brought the queen to her side.

"Oh, relax. I can see your trepidation clear across the room. You've known me for years. I'm just Iltani today."

"Yes…Blade Iltani."

The queen just sighed and rolled her eyes heavenward. "I've come to speak to you about a personal matter today."

Oh, Great Ishtar. Here it comes. The queen had at last picked up something in Enkara's nature and was here to discover what it was.

"If Kuwari asks you to accept his court again, please don't turn him down over some silly notion that you aren't good enough for him."

That wasn't anything like what Enkara had expected to hear. Floundering, she didn't know what to say. She knew her refusal had surprised everyone, but Kuwari was correct, she couldn't risk telling them why. Not even the woman standing before her now who had helped raise her. "Queen Iltani, please understand…"

"It's just Iltani. That's what you used to call me before you went to New Assur for training. I know it wasn't Burrukan who demanded formality. He hates titles even more than I do."

Everything she said was true, but it felt too informal now to call Kuwari's parents by their given names.

Iltani's brows scrunched together in frustration. "Fine, you don't have to talk, but please listen."

She put an arm around Enkara's shoulders and drew her back to the sleeping platform and sat.

"Of course."

"Good. I know you and Kuwari had some kind of falling out or misunderstanding, but after watching you these last few days, I know you don't love him any less. If anything, it seems your emotions have deepened and matured." Iltani drew a deep breath and then sighed. "And he still loves you more than his own life. While I didn't give birth to him, I love him as much as his siblings that I carried in my womb for months. Please don't crush his hope. If he asks you again, and he will, accept him."

Enkara swallowed hard and glanced down at her hands, then answered in a calm voice.

"I would never willingly hurt him."

"That's a start. But you could easily unwillingly hurt him with your rejection. I also felt your worries. You are afraid that somehow your love is dangerous to him. It isn't, you know. I can feel all dangers focused upon those of the Royal line and my power knows you would not harm him."

"I…"

"There is one more thing I need to say, and then I will leave you alone."

"I always value your advice."

"Kuwari told me he's seen future visions where you are more than just Blade and Prince," Iltani grinned. "I'm not asking you to roll over or do anything before you're ready. And accepting him as your betrothed in a trial year doesn't mean you have to give up who you are. Ditanu has an over-powering personality. I think it's a trait of the royal line. They all just need a firm hand."

Enkara felt a betraying smile tugging at her lips. "Over-powering is one way to describe it."

Iltani smiled. "But you are a strong, intelligent woman. You could temper his impulsiveness. When he was a child, you helped to guide his headstrong wildness into something constructive. You could still do that for him now that he is a man."

"I could do that as a friend."

The queen nodded her agreement. "Yes, you could. But there is also great passion shimming in Kuwari's soul. You could release it like no other woman."

Enkara cleared her throat, wondering if she could inter-rupt and redirect the conversation to less person topics.

But Queen Iltani ignored Enkara's nervousness. "On a more serious note, do you love Kuwari like he loves you? If the answer is yes, then please make both yourself and him happy by choosing a loving future together."

"Your words are wise," Enkara said as she glanced down at her hands. "I will dwell on them."

"Good." She patted Enkara's shoulder. "I suppose I should be getting back to my duties now."

Earlier, Enkara had wanted to get back to duties herself, but the queen's words had so startled her, the childhood memories which had been haunting her had gone into full retreat.

CHAPTER THIRTEEN

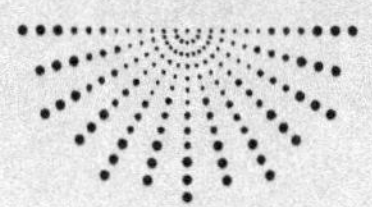

Seven mornings after the night of his vision, Kuwari again found himself given a reprieve from Councilor Nakurtum and final festival preparations. This time it was by the arrival of Burrukan. At first, he'd thought Enkara's mentor had come to see how her burn was healing, which he had, but ever a pragmatic warrior, Burrukan saw no reason not to attend to Kuwari's weapons training at the same time.

After Burrukan had checked over the burn running down Enkara's spine and seen for himself that it was indeed healing well and didn't restrict her movements, he'd ordered them into the practice ring.

They started out fighting hand-to-hand, then with knives, and now he was matching swords with his Blade.

He usually wasn't one to enjoy a good ass kicking, but it was much more enjoyable when it was Enkara and not

Burrukan doling out the punishment. He could typically hold his own, but this time he found he was easily distracted by the play of light on her sweat-slicked skin and the graceful motion of her body as she moved between the different sword forms.

"You're not paying attention again," Enkara said as she darted in close and gave him a love tap along his belly with the flat of her blade before sweeping his legs out from under him.

"Match over," Burrukan called, sounding entirely too underwhelmed.

Enkara reached down and offered him a hand up.

"By the way, I just gutted you and thrust my sword through your face if this had been a real fight," Enkara said with a smile as she began discarding her practice armor. "I was taking it easy on you too. You gave me at least ten opportunities to 'kill' you during the fight."

Kuwari scowled. She was probably correct though. If she'd been almost any other opponent, he'd have won the fight. In the past, only Burrukan and Queen Iltani had bested him so quickly.

"I'm ashamed to call either of you my apprentices," Burrukan growled out as he came stomping over. "Kuwari, if your eyes paid more attention to her feet than certain other body parts, she wouldn't have beaten you so easily. And Enkara, you were coddling him. An assassin won't be so forgiving of his faults. Remember that!"

"It won't happen again," Enkara said as she came to attention.

Burrukan grunted. "And get more sleep tonight."

"I'm fine," Enkara said, her tone guarded.

"A blind person could see the bags under your eyes. I don't know what you were doing last night, but it wasn't sleeping. Dulled reflexes will also get Kuwari killed."

Enkara jerked like Burrukan's words were a verbal slap. "After Kuwari's vision, I wanted to be alert for any reoccurrences."

Enkara had stayed up the entire night watching over him? He hadn't been aware of that. Hmm. He'd have to make sure she didn't attempt to do that again.

"You'll be useless to him without rest. Go take a nap once you are done here. That's an order."

"But Kuwari…"

"He's been without you for almost four years. He'll survive an afternoon by himself," Burrukan said and then pointed a finger at Enkara. "Go get some sleep. I'll stay with Kuwari the entire time."

She glanced at them and then gave her mentor a sharp nod. As she turned and bent to gather her discarded practice armor, Kuwari watched with more than a little appreciation of her feminine form.

"And you," Burrukan barked as the broad side of a wooden sword smacked against Kuwari shoulder. "If you hadn't been paying so much attention to Enkara's leather-clad assets, you would have won that shameful excuse of a fight."

Enkara jerked upright and spun to face Kuwari. He winked at her.

A moment later a wooden sword smacked against his bicep. "When you're in my training ring, your head better be in the fight. And I mean this head," the wooden sword slapped him along side of his ear, "Not the one below your belt."

Heat suffused Kuwari's cheeks, but he didn't deny Burrukan's words.

Once Enkara had stomped away, he chanced a glance at the older male. Burrukan was grinning. "Well, at least the Council should be happy you're a healthy young male ready to do your duty and beget the next generation of gryphon royalty."

Kuwari snorted with bitterness. "Thanks to the Council's interference they might have to wait over a year before there will be any 'getting of heirs' now."

"She's been back more than a week, and you still haven't convinced Enkara to be your future queen? I'm going to lose my bet with your father." Burrukan chuckled before his expression turned more serious. "Oh, by Ishtar's tits, here comes that infernal female."

Kuwari turned in the direction Burrukan was looking, then groaned when he saw Councilor Nakurtum striding toward them across the training field.

"I'm feeling rather tired suddenly. Perhaps I could use a nap as well," Kuwari said as he backed away from his mentor.

A hand slammed down on his shoulder before he'd taken two steps. A moment later he was being propelled forward by Burrukan, directly into Councilor Nakurtum's clutches.

"Ah, Prince Kuwari, good. I see you've just finished up with your lesson. I'm sure Regent Burrukan won't mind if I take you off his hands for a bit. We still have some items to go over and decisions to make before your name day celebration." Councilor Nakurtum smiled with genuine pleasure.

Damn. She knew she had him well and truly trapped.

"I'm sure the Prince is looking forward to it," Burrukan said trying and failing to keep a straight face.

Kuwari narrowed his eyes at his mentor. If the old goat thought *he* was going to escape unscathed...

"Councilor Nakurtum, you don't mind if Regent Burrukan joins us and gives his opinion on some of the plans, do you? He'll be accompanying me this afternoon." Kuwari smiled and put his hand on Burrukan's shoulder before he could make his escape.

Burrukan made a choking noise that was drowned out by Nakurtum's reply.

"Gladly. It never hurts to have additional male feedback on these kinds of things. I swear on Ishtar's name that King Ditanu goes out of his way to avoid planning festivals. I look forward to your input, Regent."

Burrukan made further strangled noises. Kuwari gave him a couple of thumps on the back.

"You going to survive, Regent?" Kuwari asked in his most innocent tone.

"I'm fine," he barked out. Though the look he gave Kuwari promised that the next match in the sand ring was going to hurt.

AFTER FAR LONGER THAN Kuwari wanted to spend in Nakurtum's company, she was at last satisfied with the final touches for the ceremony. At which point, both he and Burrukan bolted for the door and freedom at the same time. They made their escape and Burrukan left Kuwari at the entrance to his chambers.

Kuwari nodded to the guards stationed outside and entered his quarters on silent feet. If Enkara was still asleep, he didn't want to disturb her. Inside, he padded through the outer rooms and into his bedchamber, then stopped at the threshold to Enkara's room where he slowly brushed aside the fringed curtain.

Enkara was sprawled face down on her bed fully clothed and sound asleep. She even still wore her boots, although she'd removed her sword, harness, and outer leather vest. A glance at the wall rack confirmed she'd taken the time to put all her weapons in their proper places.

He reached for her boots and began to unlace them. At the disturbance, she muttered a sleepy question. "Shhh. Go back to sleep, I'm just removing your boots."

Showing the depth of her trust in him, she muttered his name and drifted back into a deeper sleep.

His poor Kara. She'd missed nearly two nights worth of sleep because of him. And her body was probably burning many of its resources healing the damaged skin running down her spine. When he'd applied the healing cream this morning, the skin had looked much improved compared to yesterday.

Though now, after their time in the ring, he should likely recheck it. He retrieved the small pot of cream from the table and returned to her side. After kneeling next to her, he untucked the linen shirt from the waist of her pants. Noting the shapely curve of her hips and backside encased in leather, he began to appreciate her training outfit as much as she did, if for different reasons.

He continued to drag her shirt higher up. She muttered a slurred 'go away' but allowed him to push the linen high enough to attend to his task. He spent a little longer than was strictly necessary gently working the cream into her skin, but he enjoyed being able to touch her too much to rush.

The gift which gave him the ability to see bits of the future also had another side. One he hadn't shared with a soul. Not even Enkara knew. But when he touched someone or was touched by them, he felt what they felt.

On occasion, it was very beneficial, like when someone had hostile intent toward him, or he wanted to get a read on one of the councilors during a meeting, but for the most part, it was just an uncomfortable ability to possess.

Sometimes when he touched Enkara, and she was having one of her rare unguarded moments, his gift allowed her warmth and love to wrap around him, and he could forget duty and scheming nobility for a time.

Like now. Her sleeping mind was open to him, and he basked in the fact that she loved him as a friend but was also starting to desire him as a man.

At last, he finished up and was just resealing the small pot of cream with its wax plug when Enkara rolled against him, seeking his warmth. As he caressed her hair away from one cheek, he knew he'd never do anything to betray the great gift of her love.

His gryphon nature, and the foreign power that his gifts

arose from, stirred and purred their agreement, saying in a wordless way that Enkara was theirs.

After basking in her love for that short time, it took a great deal of willpower to smooth down her shirt, tuck a blanket up to her shoulders and return to his own lonely chamber.

CHAPTER FOURTEEN

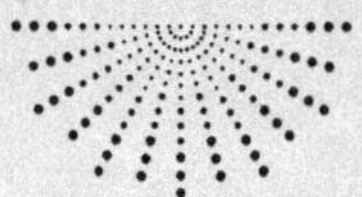

The day of the celebration officially naming Kuwari as Crown Prince dawned bright and warm. A breeze rolling in off the ocean carried the scent of brine and distant storms. But Enkara's instincts told her that the day was going to be free of rain, or at least of the wet variety.

Unfortunately, every member of the nobility was going to be descending upon Nineveh like rains during the monsoon season. Which might be the reason for Kuwari's foul mood. He'd always hated big gatherings for as long as she could remember.

"If you poke that pin into my head one more time," Kuwari growled, a sound that was more gryphon than human.

Enkara rolled her eyes at him and then shooed away the cluster of nervous servants. Kuwari's mood had only grown darker throughout the morning. She took up the spot the servants had vacated and began to fasten the gold beads into Kuwari's thick black braids.

"I feel like a male bird with all his plumage on display trying to attract a mate."

"An apt image. Though you forgot to mention the dancing and strutting that'll be expected later."

"Oh, Goddess. Let's run away now."

"And miss seeing your brothers and sister? No." It had been over three and a half years since she'd seen any of them and she missed them all terribly.

"Fine," Kuwari grunted unhappily.

"Just think," she said as she wove another of the gold beads into his hair. "By this time tomorrow, it will all be over."

"Ha. You know nothing. The nobles will still be drinking and partying tomorrow night."

"Then look on the bright side. Burrukan said he plans to have his usual training session tomorrow, bright and early, and he wants you there too."

"The man is evil. Who orders a training exercise the morning after a night-long celebration?"

It was Enkara's turn to laugh.

"Burrukan, of course. But don't worry, I'll keep you from having too much fun or drinking excessively. I remember your father's cautionary tale about his coronation night."

Kuwari glanced over his shoulder at her, disturbing the coil of hair she'd been working on, but that wasn't what halted her work. It was the thoughtful look he was giving her. A twinkle glinted in his eyes as a seductive smile crossed his face.

Enkara pinched and twisted some skin on the back of his bicep. He yelped and then tried to look all injured innocence again. Dropping her voice to a whisper, she leaned toward his ear. "Don't even think about ending your festival in the way Ditanu and Iltani ended his."

Kuwari smile grew bigger. "Too late."

While the thought of throttling some sense into him was tempting, she settled for giving his hair a firm tug.

"Ouch." He swatted her hands away.

At least his thoughts were focused back on something more appropriate than the king's coronation all those years ago when Ditanu and Iltani first became mates.

With a sigh, Enkara admitted that she'd have to watch out for more than physical dangers to his person. She'd have to protect him from himself. And if that included discipline to keep his mind from thoughts of bedding and mating his Blade, then she would be harsh.

Stepping back, she gestured for the servants to return and then she watched with folded arms and a stern expression as they put the finishing touches on his attire. Under her glower, he waited patiently as a servant applied kohl to his eyes. But she could see rebellion brewing as Kuwari tried to stare down a servant approaching with a small bowl of gold dust and a brush.

"Not on your life," he hissed at the servant who almost dropped the clay jar in her hurry to escape.

"My Prince," Enkara said with another roll of her eyes. "We are all well aware of how much you hate such refinements, but it is tradition, so there's no need to bite off the servant's head."

"You enjoy refinements?" His expression transformed, brightening into a delighted smile.

"I didn't say that."

He ignored her. "I need to show you what great aunt Kammani had made for you."

"What are you talking about?"

"I'll show you once the servants are finished with me."

Suppressing a groan, Enkara called back the servant and then marched over to stand against the wall. By the look in his eye, the Rebel Prince wasn't going to let her escape whatever he had planned. But maybe if she stayed quiet and pretended to be part of the wall, he'd forget his threat or get distracted or even run out of time.

Eventually, the servants finished up with Kuwari. Once they were gone, she allowed herself to look her fill. They'd done quite a remarkable job. Not that Kuwari needed any extra ornamentation to catch and hold the eye. But the luxurious fabric and jewels added to the exotic appeal.

Kohl darkened his eyes and matched the dark luster of his midnight hair. Gold beads and ornate combs held the many braids in place.

Goddess, Enkara was sure she was jealous of his hair. Even done up in braids, it was still thick, dark and lustrous like his father's. Her eyes followed the hair to where it brushed his broad shoulders. A hammered gold torc encircled his neck and draped down to cover his upper chest but left the rest of the muscular expanse bare.

Her eyes continued down his chest, appreciating muscles toned and sculpted by long sessions in the training ring. A wide gold belt, encrusted with amber and citrine jewels, encircled his waist. Below it, the fringed linen of his wrap circled his hips in several layers of artfully folded fabric that fell to his knee. Gold sandals covered his feet, the straps wrapping his calves.

Her gaze reversed and when she reached his face, that cursed smile was back in place, and her heart did an embarrassing little flip. She was still formulating some response when he beat her to it.

"That look on your face just made all of this worthwhile," Kuwari said with a gesture at his attire.

"Look?" She parroted stupidly, fearing her mind had turned to mush.

"Yes. That look of hunger you just raked over my body."

Heat burned her cheeks, but she refused to break eye contact. To her surprise and relief, he changed the subject. "Now come and see what Kammani had made for you."

He motioned her toward the large storage chest at the end of his bed where a garment had been laid out.

On first look, she spotted the familiar hammered gold, amber, and citrine. There was also a delicate belt and linen skirt with the same gold fringes. Unlike his, her outfit had an upper portion. The first item her gaze landed on was a torc similar to the one Kuwari wore. Though unlike his, this collar had a series of delicate golden chains suspended from it and they in turn attached to a portion of fabric that served the needs of modesty, if she wasn't expected to partake in any sword fighting.

Something else concerned her more. "If I wear that everyone will know I'm a Blade."

"That's why Kammani included this." He held out a shimmering golden veil that matched the other fabric of the outfit. "It attaches to the torc where it rests on your shoulders. Once in place, the long veil will hang down your back, obscuring your spine."

"It matches yours." Enkara frown unhappily. "It's a betrothal dress, isn't it?"

"Perhaps, but Kammani still wants you to wear it." Kuwari shrugged. "It's said Ishtar whispers things to her High Priestess. I think Kammani thought we would already be betrothed by the time of the celebration. I know that you still haven't agreed, but it would please me if you'd wear it. As a demonstration of our great and lasting friendship."

Tammuz's balls! Kuwari never played fair. He had her wrapped around his little finger and he knew it. She could never say no to him.

"Very well. Though people will get the wrong idea."

Kuwari shrugged. "I think that's why Kammani still wants you to wear it. If all the nobles think that I'm taken, they won't throw their daughters at me. My aunt is giving me a few more days of freedom and my father has convinced the Council to hold off on their announcement a little while longer."

"I'll wear it," she said as she started to gather up the pieces. "But only to give you a few more days' peace."

"Thank you."

She nodded, suddenly feeling awkward. "I'll go put this on."

He backed away, giving her room to step around him with her armful of dress and accessories. Once she reached her room, she fumbled with the outfit, but after a couple of false starts, she managed to get everything attached.

"Kuwari," she called plaintively. "I look absolutely ridiculous in this!"

He stuck his head in and grinned broadly at her. "Stop glowering. You look beautiful."

"I'm supposed to look fierce, not beautiful. Pretty isn't going to scare off the assassins."

Kuwari looked thoughtful for a moment. "I have something that might help with that.

He ducked through the archway and vanished into his chambers. She followed a moment later, more curious than annoyed. When she walked into his room, it was in time to see him toss back the lid of a storage chest and pull out a cloth-wrapped bundle. He brought it over to her and held it out.

"I was saving these for *your* name day, but I think you'd like them more now." He handed her the bundle and waited expectantly.

Feeling a hint of childlike joy, Enkara grinned as she unwrapped her gift.

Actually, it was two gifts. Matching daggers with golden hilts and amber stones set in the pommel.

"They're beautiful." She laid the bundle down on the table and then drew one of the blades. It had perfect balance like it had been forged for her hand.

"The sheaths are designed to be strapped to your thighs and are ornate enough to wear with your present attire."

Enkara practiced pulling the blade and was pleased with the smooth ease with which it came free. "Thank you."

"You might take that back in a moment." He held out a pot of kohl and the gold dust the servants had used on him earlier.

She scowled at him but allowed him to apply it with minimal complaints. Once that part was finished, he moved on to her hair, demonstrating a patience Enkara lacked.

When all was done Kuwari's grin broadened as he took in the full package. "Not half bad. Come and look in the mirror."

He pulled her into his chamber and over to where a highly polished mirror reflected their images back at them. A tall, solidly built woman stood to Kuwari's right. Her hair was done in artful braids and gold beads, kohl darkened her eyes, and gold dust shimmered on her brow and cheekbones.

She was an exotic beauty Enkara didn't recognize. The beautiful woman's lips twisted into a bitter smile. It was an illusion—painted on like the kohl around her eyes. Remove the dress, jewelry, and face paint and there was only a warrior, scarred by both her past and her training and often bruised and smudged with dirt.

Wanting to turn the topic away from herself, she glanced at him and asked, "When did you become so proficient with hair, kohl, and gold dust?"

Kuwari started to laugh. "My younger siblings. The servants never could pin them down long enough to make them civilized, so my father said if I wanted to one day learn to govern an empire, I should first be able to govern my siblings."

Enkara laughed. "I can imagine how that went."

"We all hated it at first, but they came around."

"And you learned the fine art of a beautician."

He snorted. "Goddess. Don't tell Burrukan."

She glanced away from Kuwari and studied the beautiful daggers he'd given her.

The blanket Enkara had made wasn't nearly as grand, but she'd been proud when she'd first finished it. Now she felt somewhat foolish at the thought of presenting her humble gift to the heir of the gryphon kingdom. Maybe he'd forgotten about the blanket. He hadn't mentioned it in the last few days.

"I haven't forgotten about the blanket, my lovely Kara." He ducked down and placed a kiss on her cheek. "I still expect to receive it later tonight after the celebration is over."

Damn him for being able to read her so easily! Time for some deflection. "If you don't hurry, you're going to be late for your own celebration."

"I'd be okay with that."

"Your parents won't be," Enkara said as she ushered him out of his chambers and into the hall.

"True," Kuwari sighed out his agreement as they walked. "But I'd happily trade all the parades, people, politics, rituals, food, drink, music and general revelry for a quiet day with just you and my family."

He wasn't the only one. But just then, Enkara's magical abilities thrilled in acknowledgment at the approach of more members of the gryphon royal line, saving her from having to respond directly to that emotionally loaded comment. "I doubt it will be quiet, but I think you're about to get part of your wish fulfilled."

A large company of Shadows marched around a corner

and into the hall. Walking just behind the row of Shadows, Kuwari's siblings were laughing and talking over each other in their excitement, or maybe that was an argument.

Kuwari planted his fists on his hips and sighed. "I honestly tried my best to train that rabble. I was even making headway, but our grandfather spoils them. Every time they return, I have to start fresh."

"You sound like their parent. You're only five years older than them."

"Different life experiences."

That was true Enkara admitted a little sadly. With his visions of the future, his special bond with her while she'd been a prisoner in a dank cell, assassins murdering his litter mates, and being raised as the heir to the kingdom, Kuwari hadn't really had a childhood.

Kuwari bumped shoulders with her. "Smile. This should be a time of happiness, not sadness."

She nodded but then was distracted when she got a good look at Kuwari's siblings. "Goddess! Look how much they've grown!"

Was that young woman Princess Alittum? Walking beside her had to be her brother, Akiya. He'd gotten so tall! And just behind them walked the identical twins of the litter, Etum and Eluti. She chuckled when she realized they were bickering. Some things never changed.

King Ditanu had named them after two of his own childhood friends who'd been killed in the invasion sixteen years ago because he said they shared the same warrior spirit as those other brave twins. While that might be true, Enkara had always thought the twin boys had shared a striking resemblance to Kuwari.

And now, after the last three and a half years, the youths had grown even more like their oldest brother, so much so, it was like looking at two slightly younger versions of Kuwari. It wouldn't be long before they were breaking hearts if they weren't already.

Behind the twins, the Shadows in the rear were herding the two youngest siblings. Erra, now that he was older, was starting to look more like his father, Burrukan. Though Enkara could still see a bit of Ahassunu in the shape of his eyes.

Walking sedately beside Erra was a beautiful little girl with Queen Iltani's rich sable hair and King Ditanu's dark eyes and luscious lashes.

"Is that Arwia?" Enkara asked, vocalizing her surprise, though her power as a Blade recognized her as a princess of royal blood. The last time she'd seen King Ditanu and Queen Iltani's daughter, she'd been a small fluffy cub.

"Yes. I'm certain I mentioned in one of my letters that she shifted to human form three seasons ago."

"You did…just seeing her this way for the first time is a bit of a surprise. When you wrote about your brothers and sisters, I always saw them as they were when I left for training. In my mind, I still saw Arwia as a little cub. I've missed so much."

Kuwari grinned. "Don't worry, you'll adapt. By the end of the day, they'll have chattered your ears right off your head, and you'll be wanting to return to the quiet of New Assur."

Princess Alittum noticed Kuwari first, then her eyes

landed on Enkara. A moment later she called out excitedly. The others all looked up and before Enkara could prepare herself, the six royal siblings broke free of their Shadow guards and raced straight toward her.

She was encircled on all sides by a wall of bodies and deafened by shouts and laughter. Hugs and tears came next, and Kuwari was unceremoniously shoved aside by his boisterous younger brothers and sisters.

"Order! Calm yourselves! Are you a bunch of savages?" Kuwari's shouted words were barely heard over the others all talking at once. His siblings ignored him. Enkara was helpless before the onslaught and could only hug them all in turn, tearing up as she told them how very much she'd missed them too.

Eventually, they did calm, but Enkara had to give them all repeated hugs, kisses and promises that she'd tell them everything they wanted to know about her training.

"We're going to be late for Kuwari's celebration if we don't hurry to the throne room."

"Do we really have to sit through the whole thing?" Akiya asked, sounding every bit the plaintive adolescent. His voice had deepened since the last time she'd seen him.

Akiya used to be the most like Kuwari in personality—a devilish little master of escape and manipulation. When they were younger, Kuwari and Akiya had planned many getaways that always ended with Enkara hunting them down.

"You should want to support Kuwari," Enkara reasoned with him. "He's always helped you with lessons and other less noble pursuits. You owe him."

"But it's going to be long and insufferable, full of adults chanting, praying and making speeches."

"I don't want to go either," Seven-year-old Erra whined and Arwia agreed.

Eluti and Etum added their voices to the choir of dissent.

"Quiet all of you!" Princess Alittum said, her tone reminding Enkara of King Ditanu when he called for order during an out of hand council session. "You will do nothing to bring shame to our brother this day! One day he will rule all New Sumer. This is the first step toward that. Both the occasion and our brother deserve our respect."

As the firstborn of the second royal litter, Alittum had adopted the role of Kuwari's second in command, and the others soon fell in line.

"Alittum is correct, you know," Enkara added. "By enduring things we'd rather not, we learn and grow."

A few groans answered her words, but they were quickly herded back into motion, and as a group, they continued to the already packed throne room. High Priestess Kammani arrived at the same time. After a quick exchange with Kuwari, congratulating him on his name day, Kammani volunteered to take his younger siblings into her care.

There was another chorus of moans and whining from his siblings, but Princess Alittum barked out an order to be silent. Enkara said her goodbyes, promising to see them later, and then she shooed them on into the hall.

Kuwari leaned on the grand double doors and glanced sidelong at her before whispering, "Are you ready for the nobility to attack like sharks with the scent of blood in the water?"

Enkara patted her new blades and smiled.

"Good. Later this evening, once the wine starts flowing, I want you to have them at the ready. You have my permission to lop off any hands that try to touch, squeeze, caress, or otherwise gain knowledge of my person."

"Of course, my Prince." Though she would be more concerned about assassins and would dispatch anyone with so much as a darkly ambitious thought.

CHAPTER FIFTEEN

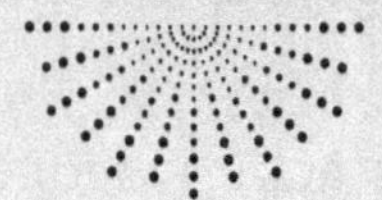

No assassins had appeared, and so far, the most exciting part of the day had been when she got to drive the three beautiful mares pulling Kuwari's chariot. The horses' manes and tails had been braided and bejeweled to match the same amber and citrine color scheme she and Kuwari wore.

King Ditanu and Queen Iltani led the way in their own chariot, their horses wearing silver and lapis lazuli. Regents Ahassunu and Burrukan followed behind Kuwari's chariot and wore emerald and malachite. Other chariots followed behind, carrying the rest of the royal family.

Overseeing everything was an army of watchful Shadows. Some were in human form while others were in their natural gryphon shape. Priests, priestesses, dancers, and nobles spilled out behind them, filling the streets of the city with singing and chanting.

That bit of enjoyment ended at the temple where yet

more priestesses and priests came forward to take the horses and lead the Royals up the outer steps of the ziggurat to begin the rituals.

As they climbed, priests and priestesses came forward to sprinkle the procession with purifying water and anoint them with sacred oil. At each landing, stone lamassu and anunnaki stood silent guard, carved into the walls of the ziggurat.

The stone guardians acknowledged each member of the royal line and the two Blades with small flares of magic. Her own power reverberated in answer, but otherwise, the spirit guardians showed no outward sign of disquiet.

The tension between her shoulder blades eased. Ever since she and Kuwari had been trapped in his vision-dream and they'd been confronted by Ereshkigal and her anunnaki, Enkara had been uneasy in the presence of the anunnaki protectors of the living world, as if she could no longer trust them.

But nothing untoward happened, and after a long ceremony, King Ditanu placed a crown upon his son's head just as the sun sank below the horizon. Enkara had started to wonder if she'd turned to stone like a Lamassu.

Finally, the sound of drums, lyres, reed pipes, and harps filled the air as musicians began to play and people started to dance. Servants came forward carrying food which novice priests and priestesses blessed to bring good luck to all those who partook.

The royal family then returned to their chariots and led the singing, dancing, and drinking procession back to the palace.

Enkara was certain more than a few of the nobles were drunk by the time they made it to the palace. Throughout the city, other celebrations would soon be in full swing in honor of Kuwari being anointed a ruling crown prince of New Sumer.

Once Kuwari and his parents were safely situated on their thrones, surrounded by watchful Shadows, Enkara took up her spot three strides behind Kuwari's new throne and allowed herself to disappear among the large potted plants like the other Shadows.

While she didn't relax her guard, she did sigh in silent relief. She wasn't comfortable with so many stares or speculative looks fixated on her. Oh, she knew Kuwari and his parents were the focus, but she'd been aware of whispers commenting on the similarity of hers and Kuwari's attire.

She wasn't given long to 'hide' in the plants. Nor were the whispers of speculation regarding her and the prince's relationship enough to dissuade some of the bolder nobles and soon the first of them were approaching Kuwari with their eligible daughters in tow.

At first, Kuwari diverted or waved them off as he and his family dined on the lavish dishes brought by servants, but as time passed and more drink flowed, nobles and governors alike grew bolder in their approaches.

Kuwari spoke and smiled and deflected as best he could, but eventually, priests and priestesses began to approach the royals in a swaying, shifting sensual dance. It was both ritualized and seductive at the same time. The Shadows let them dart up the dais stairs unhindered. Three priestesses broke away from the group of dancers and proceeded to seduce

Kuwari out of his throne and led him down among the throngs of revelers.

Enkara followed close at his heels, so too did a dozen other Shadows. This was one of the most nerve-racking parts of the festival. It was necessary to honor Ishtar with song, dance, and desire, but it was enough to earn more than one Shadow a few extra grey hairs.

Kuwari was already swaying and dancing among the other revelers, his movements slow and enticing to match the throb of the drums. Everyone around him began to mimic his actions until the entire floor of the great hall rolled with the motion of moving bodies.

Like a spell, the music and motion of swaying bodies spilled out into the surrounding hallways. Enkara wasn't immune to the power of the dance. Though she had no interest in the distractions of bodies brushing against each other in close proximity. Well, there was one body…

She gave herself a little shake and focused her mind, seeking any hint of danger that might want to touch Kuwari or a member of his family. She sensed nothing but instinctively followed close enough to intercede should she be needed.

Kuwari wove his way through the crowd, partaking in the dance while at the same time remaining somehow aloof, untouchable as if he wasn't penned in by bodies all around. It helped that other Shadows were running interference, doing their best to keep all but the most determined at bay.

But in time the crush of the crowd shoved Kuwari together with some partner or another. All skillfully put in his path by very sober and determined elders. Apparently, some of them saw the dance as a prelude to courtship.

Kuwari jerked away from his present partner with a glower over his shoulder at Enkara.

"Has my Blade forgotten her duty already?" Kuwari's thoughts were suddenly in her head.

"I'm scanning for danger. There is none."

"Perhaps not life or death danger, but if someone tries to rub their scent on me one more time..."

Enkara's instinctive grin melted away when she sensed the emotions accompanying his words. Annoyance. Anger. Indignation. And something darker and less clean —violation.

She might not know the exact cause or the source, but she began shoving bodies out of her path. Anyone who was too drunk or too stupid to get out of her way she threatened to carve up with her dagger. That got people moving.

When she reached his side, she put herself bodily between Kuwari and a gryphon woman. She didn't know this woman by name, but there was no doubt by her finery that she was from a noble house and had ambitions to increase her status.

Typically, when one of the Shadows glowered, it was enough to send people in the other direction. But these weren't normal circumstances. This was a high celebration with food and drink and close-packed bodies. Half as much stimulus was all it took for some gryphons to get their blood up, rousing instincts to hunt, claim territory, or seek out a potential mate and challenge for the right to court them.

More civilized behaviors tended to get kicked to the side by both sexes when that happened.

Enkara narrowed her eyes at the other woman. In her experience, the female of the gryphon species was actually the more volatile of the two sexes. "He's not interested. Move along."

"Why don't we let him decide that for himself?"

"He just did. That's why I'm here."

The other woman had the nerve to sniff at her as if she smelled something she didn't like. A moment later she looked away, dismissing Enkara as inferior and returned to dancing with the prince. This time she was more aggressive, brushing up against Kuwari in a suggestive way, even going so far as to press her hands against his chest.

The prince hissed and slapped the woman's hands away.

That's it. Time to teach the she-jackal a lesson.

Darting forward, Enkara used her strength, momentum, and the element of surprise to lock an arm around the woman's neck. After shoving her to her knees, she held the edge of her blade against the pulse pounding in her throat. In a very calm voice, modulated to carry over the music and noise of the celebration, she said, "He's not interested. Neither are you."

The female hissed in alarm or anger, but instincts won out, and she went limp in a showing of submission. Just like that, the minor challenge was over. Enkara released her. When the woman turned to study Enkara with a rebellious glint in her eye, a fierce grin and a wave of her dagger in time to the music was enough to send her rival into full retreat.

Rival? Where, by Ishtar, had that thought come from?

She wasn't given long to dwell on that disturbing thought before strong, long-fingered hands settled on her waist, thumbs sliding under the veil to caress the bare skin of her back. She had no trouble guessing the identity of the male, but Kuwari's purring voice only reinforced what she'd already known.

"You routed her good," Kuwari whispered as he ducked his head to nuzzle her neck. Soon he was pressing himself along her back and urging her into motion, his hands at her waist.

When she'd come to his rescue, she hadn't intended to become his next dance partner. She scanned the crowd, hoping another suitable partner would step in. None did. She'd done her job too well.

Her eyes sought out the nearest Shadow hoping for some form of aid, but only Uselli met her pleading gaze. He responded with a hearty laugh.

Damn. "Prince Kuwari, perhaps you'd like a refreshment?"

"No," he purred in her ear and pressed a kiss against her shoulder.

Enkara spun around to face the prince and aimed a stern look at him.

He smiled. "I'm good for a bit. Got a second wind as it were."

She'd just bet he did. Breaking his gaze, she renewed her hunt for his next dance partner. She was surprised to find a familiar face in the crowd. Lady Kullaa was dancing next to Uselli.

"Lady Kullaa, it's good to see you again." She grabbed the startled woman and dragged her forward, practically thrusting her into Kuwari's arms. "The Prince could use another partner."

When Kuwari looked over Kullaa's shoulder to meet Enkara's gaze, she wasn't expecting his brilliant smile or the light of challenge in his eyes.

Oh, that promised trouble later. But later was better than now with the entire crowded throne room looking on.

Thankfully Kuwari turned his attention back to his new partner, but Enkara knew he'd eventually return his focus to her—an event she dreaded but also, irrationally, looked forward to.

CHAPTER SIXTEEN

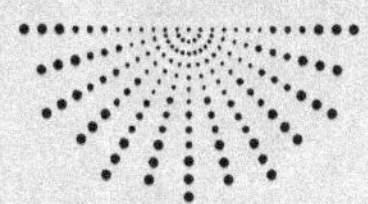

*E*ven after Kuwari had returned to the dais for refreshments and conversation with his father, Enkara could still feel the phantom weight of his hands on her skin and remember the soft caress of his breath across her neck.

She wanted to beat the silly memory right out of her head, but the disconcerting feelings were as stubborn as the one who'd triggered them. She was still scanning the crowd for danger and doing her best to ignore whatever spell the prince had woven over her when Queen Iltani joined her.

"Care if I hide in the plants with you?" Iltani asked with a grin. "Ditanu and Kuwari are having a father-son discussion about the best way to woo a woman. It seems Kuwari has already tried a few things with little luck. I figured I'd give them their privacy."

Enkara groaned and felt heat flush her cheeks. Damn it. Was she ever going to conquer this new weakness?

"What he and his father discuss is of no concern to me."

Iltani laughed. "Goodness. You're truly flustered when you completely forget that lying to me is pointless. Just what has that boy been up to?"

"That's not…I mean, we haven't…he's tried but I've been adamant."

"Kuwari hasn't made much progress with you then I take it?"

That at least she could answer truthfully. "Not as much as he'd like."

"Hmm, have you thought about what I said a few days ago?"

Enkara had been trying hard not to think about that.

"It's still true. What I said then. He loves you and you love him. Don't let fear of what others think dictate your own emotions."

"I won't. But I'm still wrestling with my own feelings," she admitted.

Queen Iltani gave her an affectionate pat on the shoulder. "Give yourself the time you need to understand your own emotions, and don't let outside forces urge you into anything that doesn't feel right. I suppose I must include myself in the 'outside forces' too."

"Thank you, Queen Iltani. I will think on your words."

Iltani snorted. "Don't overthink things, though."

Not knowing what else to say, Enkara mumbled an affirmative.

Queen Iltani merely smiled. "I suppose we should return to the males before they come up with something too outrageous even for a name day celebration."

"Oh, Goddess!" Iltani was right. Kuwari and King Ditanu were likely coming up with all kinds of creative and embarrassing scenarios. But as much as Enkara wanted to run right over and nip any of Kuwari's plans in the bud, she couldn't just wander back over there while they were still discussing her and how to improve Kuwari's chances.

"Don't worry," Queen Iltani said with another companionable pat on her shoulder. "I'll go over first and signal if it's safe for you to return."

Only after Iltani returned to King Ditanu's side and then gave Enkara a nod telling her it was all clear, did she make her way back to Kuwari.

"Oh, not again," Kuwari hissed under his breath.

Enkara knew it couldn't be in response to her return, but it still gave her pause. "That's not the most encouraging of greetings."

"Not you. Them." He jerked his chin in the direction of the priestesses and priests making their way to the front of the hall where the Royals sat.

Burrukan and Ahassunu had just returned from leading the dancing, and it now looked like it was Kuwari's turn again.

He grabbed her hand and leaned forward to whisper in her ear. "Just play along. I need more recovery time before I forge into the crowd again."

Waving one of the ever-present servants forward, he snatched up two goblets and then changed his mind and relieved the servant of his wine pitcher as well. The male bowed and backed away to go collect another pitcher from the kitchens. With his stolen goods, Kuwari circled around behind the dais into the somewhat secluded area ringed by screens and potted plants.

Presently, the alcove was empty. Instinctively Enkara scanned for any signs of danger among the shadowy corners where torchlight failed to fully penetrate. As expected, she found none. The other members of the King's Shadows were doing their duty, which allowed her to unearth whatever Kuwari was trying to hide from her.

"What did you mean by needing more time to recover from the crowd?" The way he'd said it was elusive. Kuwari didn't answer her right away. Instead, he downed an entire goblet of wine before he glanced at her.

"I just need to dull my senses a bit before venturing back into that seething pit."

She arched her brow wondering how to get the truth out of him before he changed topics.

"Go easy on the drink."

"Yes, Mother." Kuwari's smile grew into a grin, and he poured her a goblet.

Sighing, she took the offered goblet but set it aside for later. Crossing her arms, she cocked a hip and waited. "You going to tell me what you've been hiding?"

Kuwari glowered at her, but she stayed rooted in place. After a moment his glower turned into a frown and then a defeated sigh.

"Fine. But first, you need to promise that you won't change how you act around me once you hear the truth."

"No deal."

"Then I can't tell you."

Stubborn brat. "Fine. If I agree, will it have any kind of impact on your protection?"

"None in the least."

She'd been reading Kuwari's emotions all his life. He'd just spoken the truth.

"Fine. I promise not to tell anyone, but for the record, I'm aware you have some other agenda."

"Always," he chuckled.

Scowling, Enkara admitted the Rebel Prince had already won this round, and he hadn't even started talking yet. While she'd been away training, he'd been learning the brutal art of governing and swaying people to his will. The last was a natural talent which only made him more dangerous to free will everywhere.

"As you know, whatever power has gifted me with the visions to see the future has grown in strength since I became a man."

Enkara nodded, he'd alluded to such in his letters and when he'd visited her on New Assur.

"However, I never told you that I developed a second power after reaching adulthood."

"What? What happened to not keeping secrets and sharing everything with each other?"

Kuwari shrugged. "I was afraid you'd pull away once you learned the truth."

"Never." Enkara stepped closer and placed her hand on his shoulder and gave him a squeeze. When that didn't seem enough, she stepped closer and hugged him like she used to, wrapping him in a fierce embrace and allowing her love for him to flow across their special link. After too short a time, she pulled away and looked him in the eyes.

"I don't know what secret you've been hiding all these years, but it doesn't matter what it is. Nothing will ever drive me away. I'm your friend for life."

He reached out and took her hands in his. "That felt so good, a balm on my ragged senses after the day I've had." Kuwari took a deep breath, and the words just flowed out of him. "I think I've always had this ability to some extent. I just never understood it was unusual. But from my thirteenth year, I've been able to feel what another person feels when they touch me."

Enkara's mouth dropped open for a moment before she snapped it closed. He could feel what others felt when they touched him? No wonder she'd been picking up on his distress all evening. His deep dislike of social gatherings suddenly made sense.

"Can you read minds?"

"No. Just feel what they feel, but even that explanation is too simple. Sometimes it's almost like the two gifts work together and I get a glimpse of a vision accompanying the touch."

"That's terrible. So, you mean if..."

Her words failed her. She was still trying to understand the power.

"Hmmm. For example, if an assassin touched me in passing, I would sense the powerful feelings, and my vision might show me how the attack would come. It's always just a brief glance so I can continue to function without others knowing they betrayed something to me."

"That's a benefit at least, but the price is terribly high."

"Yes, if someone I touch feels hate, greed, or lust, I get the full effect." Kuwari winced. "At least I always know what a person thinks of me."

"You can't turn it off?" She glanced at her hand on his shoulder.

"It doesn't always happen with every touch, but no, I can't turn it off. And there are so many times when I wish I could. Like during festivals where drink flows too freely, and we gryphons get even more touchy-feely than normal." Kuwari rubbed his neck, working a kink out. "I suppose it's lucky I'm a prince and most don't dare touch me unless invited."

As he'd said, gryphons were naturally a very tactile species. Always having to hold back or guard himself against touch would be unnatural to him. And what about her touch? Could he read her as easily as all the others? Was it painful, disruptive, or disturbing to him?

What a terrible burden to carry in silence.

"Have you ever told anyone about this affliction?" she asked softly.

"No."

She pulled her hands from his and murmured an apology but swiftly he snatched up her hands again.

"See?" he said. "This is why I've never told anyone about the power. If I did, those I love would be more guarded. A hug, a pat, a reassuring squeeze—all those loving touches—I might risk losing them all if others found out about my power and tried to 'protect' me."

"What can I do to prevent the emotional bleed-through?"

How many times had she shared this emotional seepage

with him? What had he seen? Then she remembered how, even sleeping, his mind would wrap around hers and protect her from the nightmare memories from her childhood. Was he sucking all that darkness into himself?

"Calm, my beautiful Blade," he whispered in her ear. "Disciplined minds are far less likely to bombard me with emotion. And you have become much more disciplined in both body and mind during your training on New Assur."

She mulled over what he'd said. If she was careful to limit touch and to keep a tight rein on her emotions, she should be able to minimize the unwanted emotional transfers.

"Oh Enkara," he sighed and gave her hand a squeeze. "Are you forgetting your promise to me so soon?"

"I don't see how this—"

"You swore you wouldn't change how you treat me if I told you the truth."

"I know, but this changes things. It has to."

"Enkara, your touch, your emotions—I always look forward to them. When we touch, your love and friendship wraps around me and soothes away all the worries for a few precious moments. Please don't strip away my greatest source of solace."

"It really doesn't cause you distress?"

"No," he said and pulled her into a hug. "You give me peace."

That didn't sound so terrible.

"Very well, I'll try not to change how I treat you but explain the part about the drinking."

"When others start to drink, their minds become less disciplined. The more they drink, the more undisciplined they become and the greater the chance a simple touch will turn into a powerful emotional assault. But when I drink, it dulls whatever magical gift causes the visions."

"I'm sorry you have had to shoulder this burden alone for so long."

"While it can be annoying, there are times when I imagine the power will be more gift than curse."

She arched an eyebrow in question.

"Between lovers and mates," his eyes took on a heavy-lidded appearance, and his pupils dilated as he stepped closer. "I always liked what I felt when you touched me."

Another flush climbed up her cheeks. "I'm so sorry that I was…projecting that at you all those times."

"I'm not. Not when it's your emotions I'm feeling and your dreams and desires I see in my visions." He stroked her cheek. "You'll come to understand in your own time, but for now we have a celebration to get back to."

"I can't let you go back down there knowing what I know now."

"You must. There will be questions if I leave too early. This power is not one I want discovered. It also makes me vulnerable."

Enkara nodded, but she didn't like it. As Kuwari started to lead her from the shelter, something else occurred to her.

"Oh, Goddess. This is why you don't want to accept anyone else as your betrothed. They'd have open access to you and could bombard you with their untrained and unguarded mind day and night."

"There is that unpleasantness, but that's not why and you know it."

She didn't acknowledge the last part. "Now that I know why you don't want to betroth anyone else, I'll—"

"Don't." Kuwari's voice held fierce anger. "Don't say you'll agree to be my betrothed now just because you feel it's your duty. I've loved you all my life. I won't just be an obligation. I'll win your love through normal means."

He turned and started away, but she caught him by the hand before he'd made his escape. Kuwari glanced down at their joined hands, likely reading her emotions. Well, good. He'd know the truth.

"One day, when we get through whatever fate has planned for us," she gave his hands a squeeze, "I'll make sure you have no doubts about my love."

He nodded, looking solemn. "I can accept that."

"Good. Now about the crowd."

"Don't worry about me." He tugged her back onto the dais where the priests and priestesses were already waiting. "This is nothing new. I've survived this long, I'll survive this as well."

"I still don't like it."

He looked over his shoulder, his confident grin back in place. "Then stake your claim. You are, after all, half gryphon. The appropriate instincts must be buried somewhere inside."

Enkara snorted, though she was pleased to see the Rebel Prince was back, Kuwari's earlier vulnerabilities drawn back inside where the ruthless court couldn't detect them.

～

SOMETIME BETWEEN DUSK and dawn when many of the nobles had drank themselves into a stupor, Kuwari and his parents finally retired. Even then, Enkara had to glare down a few of the bolder females with plans to follow them to the royal wing.

All evening and well into the night, she'd kept circling back to how she could give him some semblance of peace from all this. But it wasn't until Kuwari returned to his own chambers and Enkara saw that her personal items had arrived from New Assur that she finally came to a decision.

Enkara followed Kuwari deeper into his suite all the way to his bedchamber. There, cursing under his breath, he began removing the gold ornaments from his hair.

With new purpose, she came up behind him. "Kuwari, there's something I need to say."

He turned to her with a guarded look. "If you wish to discuss which of the females I met tonight was the least leech-like and might make a passable betrothed, I'll skip the discussion until tomorrow or preferably never if it's all the same to you."

Before her courage failed, she stepped forward and pressed her lips against his.

He jerked in surprise but soon relaxed into the kiss. His lips were warm and firm under hers. Taking her time exploring, she nipped and caressed, learning him. Growing bolder, she flicked the tip of her tongue against the seam of his lips.

As if that was the signal he'd been waiting for, his arms came around her, and he was kissing her back with a passion to match what was rising within her. He made encouraging sounds when her hands began to run up and down his bare back. Sighing into her mouth, Kuwari drew her more tightly against him.

Then he broke the kiss and disappointment washed over her. It lasted only moments, then his lips found the lobe of her ear. Enkara fought back a surprised purr only to fail a moment later when he started raining kisses down her neck and shoulder, whispering of his love the entire time. She wrapped her arms around his neck and nuzzled the side of his face. Working the clasp of his torc, she freed him of the hefty chunk of gold.

She'd never thought that a simple set of broad shoulders could awaken desire, but she'd wanted to run her hands over his all evening. At last she did, caressing the firm muscle and nuzzling his warm skin, dragging in his wholesome male scent. Instincts roused. She worked harder to rub her scent into his skin.

Two large hands slid under the veil trailing down her back. His fingers caressed her spine, the pads brushing lightly down the newly-healed birthmark that would tell the world she was his Blade. His touch felt so good she nearly started purring again. He pressed closer until she could feel every flex and shift of his muscular body against hers.

It would be too easy to get lost in the warmth and passion —a part of her wanted to, but this was just supposed to be a promise of what would come later after they crushed whatever plans Ereshkigal had for them.

No longer returning his ardent caresses, she dipped her head to end the kiss. With a little shudder, she put some space between them.

"Did you understand my meaning from my emotions?" she asked a few moments later.

He pressed his forehead to hers and laughed softly, still breathing hard from earlier. "I might be a touch thick-headed at times, but even I didn't need my gift to understand what that was. You just agreed to be my betrothed in the most rewarding way, and now your emotions are telling me not to rush when I very much want to do exactly that."

"I'm sorry. My concerns about our future are still unchanged. If I'm Ereshkigal's Blade, I'm dangerous to you, but I also realize there are many dangers in your life. This is a promise that once we neutralize whatever threat Ereshkigal has planned, I'll accept your courtship and court you in return."

"What changed your mind?" he asked as he brushed a lock a hair from her cheek.

Enkara paused, not certain she could put a name to the emotions swirling through her mind. "Many things. While seeing others try to seduce you wasn't...pleasant, that's not what spurred me to act. It was watching as you were forced to hide your true self away from others so they couldn't use your emotions against you. I kept seeing more and more of the man I love disappear under the cold persona of a prince. I find the thought of losing my friend devastating."

"You'll never lose me. Nothing the court does could ever change that. For you, I'll always be Kuwari—just a man, not a prince."

"I am glad."

"Good, because you'll find I'm a selfish man. Is there a way I might persuade you for a little more?"

The grin accompanying his words was rakish.

"Actually, there *is* more to my gift." She leaned forward and pressed a quick kiss to his cheek and then turned and hurried into the outer chamber, leaving a clearly startled Kuwari behind.

She swiftly opened the travel bags containing her personal items. It took some hunting, but she found the blanket she'd made for him. When she turned and looked over her shoulder, Kuwari was leaning against the doorway between rooms, just watching her.

His gaze landed on the folded bundle she carried. The earlier questioning look melted into something with a bit more heat to it. She returned to him and silently presented the blanket.

Kuwari gazed down and then reached for it, slowly caressing the blanket reverently as if it was the greatest gift he'd ever received.

"It's beautiful."

Enkara snorted. "No, it's not. But I made it and promised myself I'd give it to you one day. At the time I don't think I intended it to be a courtship gift, not consciously."

"Beautiful or not," Kuwari stroked the blanket she'd given him, "this is the best name day gift I could have ever received because it is a gift for Kuwari the man, not Kuwari the Prince."

"I'll accept that." She returned his grin. "But we should go find our beds, because Burrukan will be banging on the door at dawn, shouting about lazy trainees."

Kuwari grimaced. "You're right. The old goat will be here at dawn. I suppose there is no need to rush things between us now that I know you've agreed to be mine like I knew you would."

"You saw this?"

"No, not this, but other things in the future."

His words did strange things to her heart.

"I might not have foreseen this night," he added, "but I feel a vision coming on."

"Really?" She couldn't hold back her grin.

"Why, yes. In it I see you helping me remove all these damned gold trinkets from my hair."

Laughing, Enkara helped him with that and then proceeded to shoo him off to bed. She didn't need the power of future-telling to know if she hadn't, Kuwari would have ended up following her to bed.

CHAPTER SEVENTEEN

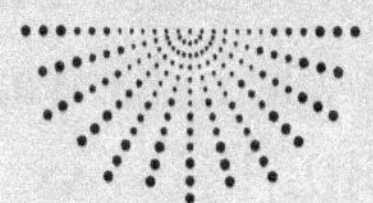

The day following the celebration, Kuwari awoke wrapped in Enkara's gift. The memory of her body pressed against his was still fresh in his mind. One long, beautiful dream had been born of those two things, and while the details of the dream had faded, the remnants were enough to stir his body even now. A fool's grin plastered itself on his face, but he couldn't stop.

Still grinning, he rolled over. An eagle-headed anunnaki stood at the side of his bed, reaching for him.

He screamed. Lashing out, his heart pounding, Kuwari knocked aside the outstretched hand. All thoughts of dreams and Enkara sank under a rising wave of adrenaline.

Rolling out of reach, he snatched up the dagger he kept under a pile of pillows at the side of his bed. Without hesitation, he continued off the bed and raced toward where his sword was hanging from the back of the chair next to the fireplace.

Halfway to his destination, he called a warning to Enkara. His concern ratcheted up another notch when she didn't respond out loud or mentally along their link. She slept lightly. If she didn't answer, it was because she couldn't.

Goddess, if they'd hurt her...

A second anunnaki stepped in his path, a glowing scepter held in his hands. The anunnaki swung the scepter like a club. It grazed his side when Kuwari sidestepped too late. Ropey magic pulsing with light wrapped him in a chilling power. Between one heartbeat and the next he no longer had control of his limbs and his dagger fell from his unfeeling fingers.

As his legs folded under him, only the sudden firm grip of the first anunnaki prevented Kuwari from crashing to the floor. The second one, joining the first, helped haul Kuwari's unresisting body over to the chair where his sword still hung.

Not that the sword would do him any good now. He couldn't move, couldn't form words, couldn't even raise his own head to glower at his enemies.

A moment later one of them grabbed a fistful of his hair and lifted his head.

"It would have been easier if you had stayed longer in the dream. I wasn't done speaking with my friend yet," the eagle-headed anunnaki said in a dry tone. "There is much we still need to discuss."

Kuwari reached for his gift, though this time he wasn't trying to speak with Enkara. He just needed to know her condition. Thankfully, his magic answered his need. From what he could tell, she was still deeply asleep, too deeply.

One of the anunnaki *had* done something to her. Though she wasn't physically hurt. Thank Tammuz.

Unable to help Enkara, he used the only defense left to him: his mind magic. Although, he wasn't sure if it would work with an anunnaki like it did with Enkara.

"What do you want? Why are you here?"

The anunnaki cocked his head in a bird-like manner. "To talk. Is that not what I already said?"

"There are better ways to open a conversation." Kuwari narrowed his eyes. *"Whatever your reasons, you're wasting your time. I'll not listen to lies."*

The feathers on the spirit guardian's head fluffed up before slicking down again. "Who said I wished to talk to *you*, young prince?"

What? But before Kuwari could decipher the anunnaki's meaning, the second one came forward and touched him with the scepter again. Darkness rushed in from all sides, stealing Kuwari's sight as well as his consciousness.

Kuwari moaned and thrashed in his bed, fighting his way free of the vision-dream. Sitting up, he tossed aside the blankets and looked around half expecting to see the two anunnaki, but it was Shadow Uselli his gaze landed on instead.

"Are you alright, Crown Prince Kuwari?" Uselli asked as he came to stand at the foot of the bed. "I heard you call out and was about to go wake Enkara. Was it another vision?"

"Thank you, but don't wake Enkara. I'm fine. It was just a nightmare."

The older Shadow gave him a searching look and then nodded. "I'll be in the outer chamber. Call if you have need of anything."

"I will."

The Shadow retreated and Kuwari sat on the edge of his bed and rested his head in his hands. Then feeling too restless to sit, he went over to one of the windows overlooking the gardens. Sweat covered his body and the cool night breeze struck his skin, raising gooseflesh and chilling him more as he shook from reaction.

Gods. One would think he'd be getting used to the damned visions by now, but they still shook him to the core. Even his head was pounding this time. Although that was more likely caused by thirst than the vision.

Feeling more disconcerted than normal at being jolted awake by a vision-dream, he returned to the bed and gathered up the blanket Enkara had made and pressed his face into the tight weave. Her scent soothed some of the tension and he felt calmer.

Sighing, he took in a few deeper breaths and then set Enkara's gift aside. Feeling somewhat more like himself, he stood and stretched, going through his morning warm up. While it was the last thing he wanted to do, Burrukan was likely going to show up soon to drag him off to the training fields for the promised early morning weapons practice. Afterward, Kuwari was determined to make some time for just himself and Enkara.

After he finished in the bathing chamber, he realized Enkara wasn't up yet. Usually, she'd be badgering him to get his lazy ass out of bed. Was he awake before her? That never happened.

His grin faded as he remembered the vision-dream. Rushing into her chamber, he skidded to a halt when he spotted her lying belly down on her bed, her face turned to the side, her expression peaceful. Sleeping. He reached for her mind with his gift just to confirm that. Just sleeping. Thank Tammuz. Sighing in relief, he walked the rest of the way to her bed and knelt next to her.

Briefly, he wondered what it would be like to wake next to her. The thought was pleasantly diverting. Enough that he found his fingers lifting the top edge of her blankets, ready to slide in beside her.

He froze, eyes widening in surprise. Her thick braid had fallen to the side and exposed the back of her neck. A glimmer of magic danced above Ishtar's mark. His heart pounded, blood surging in his veins. This was why he'd awoken early and severed the vision before he'd seen it to the end. Ishtar had just declared his Blade mature and ready to anoint with the blood of gryphon royalty.

He'd dwell on the meaning of the vision later. Now other priorities took precedence.

Twenty years he'd waited for this moment. Jerking at the neckline of her sleeping robe, he attempted to uncover more of the mark. Why wasn't she awake? She should be awake. This was momentous.

"What are you doing?" Enkara growled in a voice hoarse with sleep. "Are you trying to strangle me?"

She rolled over and slapped his hands away. Then glowered at him for good measure.

"Your mark is glowing."

Enkara's eyes widened. She jerked up so fast she narrowly missed cracking skulls with him. Only swift reflexes on his part saved both their heads. Unfortunately, the sudden motion set his to throbbing again. While he was busy holding his head, Enkara grabbed a hand mirror and pushed her robe down her arms, craning her neck so she could see the glowing tattoo for herself.

"Kuwari! Ishtar has finally summoned me to serve!"

The entire length of her spine glowed with power, telling all who saw it that this was one of Ishtar's chosen.

"We should share this with your parents and the high priestess." Excitement edged Enkara's voice.

He didn't respond. Instead, he forced his expression to remain neutral, but she must've seen something for she turned her head and stared him down with her best 'I'm going to pick your brain apart until I learn what you're hiding' look.

"You're thinking hard," she said instead.

"If we tell my parents, they'll report this to High Priestess Kammani, and she'll forbid us from completing the rite until the moon is in the correct phase and all the preparations are made."

Enkara looked both thoughtful and unhappy.

"I'm not sure if we should wait that long. The visions—the sooner Ishtar claims you as her Blade, the better."

To his relief, Enkara nodded agreement. "Don't we need certain items to appease the gods?"

"Normally, yes, but my father once told me that years ago one of his visions showed danger to Iltani, and he wanted to give her additional protection. They held their own small informal rite just between themselves and Ishtar."

"I say we don't wait to give our enemies time to act. We'll do our own ceremony now. There will be other ceremonies to appease Kammani."

"Yes." Kuwari agreed with growing excitement. Logically he knew Enkara was her own person, but a more primal part of his gryphon soul rejoiced that he'd be able to stamp his claim upon her at last. Once he anointed her tattoo with his blood, he would be giving her a part of his essence and she, in turn, would be branding herself on his heart and soul until their souls made the journey to the underworld.

Nothing could supersede that bond once formed.

"What do we need for this rite?" Enkara asked as she gathered up the daggers he'd given her as a gift.

"You, me, a sharp knife, and Ishtar's blessing."

Enkara nodded. "Then give me a few moments and I'll prepare."

She turned and left her room, heading for the bathing chamber. Uncertain and a little nervous, he returned to his own chamber to wait.

He knew what he was supposed to do. His father and great-Aunt Kammani had covered it as part of his education. But knowledge wasn't the same as experiencing a goddess's power for the first time.

"Kuwari?"

He nearly jumped out of his skin at the sound of his name.

"Sorry. I didn't mean to surprise you." Enkara stood on the threshold of the bathing chamber, belting on a new robe.

"You didn't surprise me."

"That's a lie," she said with a knowing smile.

"I was distracted, thinking of something else." Then he shook his head, and a rueful grin touched his lips as he realized something else. "Why am I trying to lie to you? I am nervous. I sometimes forget our gift runs two ways."

"I imagine being nervous is perfectly normal. You're going to summon a goddess." She looked over her shoulder. "If you're going to spill blood, we might as well do it in the bathing chamber where it will be easily cleaned up."

He nodded agreement and she turned and vanished within. Striding forward, he followed.

Inside he found her standing next to a stone bench, one of her daggers out of its sheath.

He unbuckled the belt around his waist and then stepped out of his robe, leaving him dressed only in his loincloth. Enkara watched him the whole time.

"Ishtar will be pleased."

This was the first time she'd ever vocalized an opinion about the two of them one day performing the Sacred Marriage for Ishtar and Tammuz. He might have attempted some small bit of flirting or innuendo, but Enkara shrugged off her own robe. He was suddenly speechless. As it slipped off her shoulders, he couldn't help but admire the expanse of luscious, warm brown skin and feminine curves.

When he made it back to her face, she met his gaze and then rolled her eyes and gestured at the bench. "Mind on the task."

But she moved with such easy confidence Kuwari

couldn't help but enjoy the beauty his Blade presented him. "The Harvest God will appreciate your beauty as well."

"I think the Harvest God isn't the only one." Enkara laughed, the sound full and rich and wrapping around him, making his body hurt in all the good ways.

"My Blade reads me too easily."

Enkara snorted. "It's really not that hard."

Then as she'd ordered, he turned his mind back to the task at hand, studying the dagger resting on the bench. "I never thought one of these would be used to shed my own blood."

Enkara shrugged. "It seems like something that would please the gods."

"Some more than others." Though in truth, he wasn't bothered by the thought of a little pain and blood if it made his Blade stronger and harder to kill. He'd probably donated more blood to the sands of the training ring than he'd shed for this ritual.

Enkara suddenly rested her hands on his shoulders and stepped closer. Knowing what she wanted, he bowed his head until their foreheads touched. Warm waves of love and determination rolled through her touch and into him.

His nerves now calmer, he straddled the bench and patted the area in front of him. After only the slightest hesitation Enkara settled, facing away from him, presenting her back.

As if his hand moved by some other will, his fingers splayed wide to stroke their way down Ishtar's mark. Enkara shuddered at his touch and glanced over her shoulder. "I don't mean to rush you, but Burrukan will likely be along soon."

As usual, Enkara was correct. Exhaling slowly, he brought the edge of the blade to his chest and made a swift slice over his right pectoral. The burning and warm wet sensation hadn't even fully registered to his senses before he'd switched hands and repeated the motion on the opposite side.

Soon two trails of blood were trickling their way down his chest, the slope of his muscles funneling it to the center. Shifting closer to Enkara, he wrapped an arm around her waist and pressed his chest to her back.

When his blood touched the tattoo, warm tingling magic sparked to life between them. The minor burning pain of the cuts faded as Enkara's magic reached for him. His own power answered, feeding more than just blood to her tattoo.

He used his weight to press her forward, leaning over her back to better seal them together.

"Ishtar, this night we come together to renew the pact between the gryphon kings and you, oh great Queen of Heaven. Your Blade has been anointed with royal blood as the ancient rites demand, bless her now with your power so that we may serve you to our fullest potential and never fail you."

Even before the last word was uttered, a stronger wave of magic stirred within him, and Enkara's magic answered his in sympathetic resonance.

A numbness spread from where his body pressed against her spine. Soon it rushed outward to every corner of his being until slowly the numbness receded, transforming into the tingle of returning feeling.

"This is the strangest sensation," Enkara whispered a little breathlessly.

Another wave of Ishtar's powerful magic rolled over him and sunk below his skin and Kuwari had to agree. It wasn't at all unpleasant though. In fact, the power was warmer now, more of a warm caress than an assault on the senses. He imagined this power could be very pleasant, but he held himself in check, unwilling to allow Ishtar to seduce him so easily, not when he'd been warned what would follow the first few pleasant waves.

Even though he was waiting for the next onslaught, the burning hot power surprised him, stealing his breath. He hissed in reaction. Under him Enkara tensed, sweat beginning to bead up on her skin.

Then as swiftly as it had come, the burning magic mellowed, settling into a pleasant warmth that made him think of other, more pleasant things that required such closeness.

"Kuwari! Mind on the task," Enkara barked out in a good imitation of Burrukan. It was almost enough to cool his ardor.

Closing his eyes, he sought to obey her but moments later an ancient presence manifested in the room with them, and ghostly fingers stroked across his shoulders, completely destroying his concentration. He jerked in surprise.

Ishtar stood next to them, just as glorious as her sister had been, but where Ereshkigal's power was cool, this goddess possessed a distinctly fiery power.

"So impatient," Ishtar said, her rich voice filling his mind. *"I see the son takes after his father. I wonder what other similarities you possess that I might enjoy."*

A seductive smile accompanied the words, and then the ghostly touch was back, stroking down his spine and over the curve of his backside, where she gave him a firm pinch.

Kuwari yelped in surprise and shifted closer to Enkara.

The goddess laughed. *"Alas, you're not yet ready to act as host for my Tammuz. One day you will. Behave yourself until then."*

With that, the goddess turned her attention to Enkara.

"Strong, beautiful Blade." Ishtar fingered one of Enkara's braids where it had fallen forward across her breast. *"If my sister thinks to have you without a fight, she is greatly mistaken. I have plans for you."*

Ishtar placed a hand on each of their shoulders, and a new wave of power swelled within them, rising up until it crested in a bright swirl of color, engulfing their bodies and even reflecting golden light upon the walls.

After a brief time, the power dimmed, and Ishtar removed her hands. It was like a great weight being lifted from his shoulders. He drew in a shuddering breath.

The goddess drifted a few steps away and then turned back to study them. "Be safe until we meet again and know you have our Blessing."

And then Ishtar's ancient presence was gone, taking all her warmth, passion, and power with her. Kuwari felt both bereft and relieved by the goddess's departure.

He was still shaking with reaction when Enkara stiffened in his arms.

"Something is wrong. I feel strange," Enkara's voice was calm, but he could feel the trembling in her body.

He grunted in surprise as another intense wave of emotions bled from Enkara and his gift drank it in, shaping the chaotic swirl into a vision. Feathered wings. A black-furred body. Oh.

"Enkara, do not be afraid. You're about to —"

Before he could finish his sentence, wings burst from her back as fur erupted across her skin and raced down her lower body. Moments later her hair vanished as a ruff of thick feathers took its place.

"Easy, beloved, we've awoken your gryphon." Kuwari tried to hold her until the disorientation that always plagued the first few shifts abated, but she twisted to the side, and they were both suddenly toppling off the bench.

One minute he was blinking up at the ceiling, the next he was looking into the face of a wild-eyed gryphon. She lowered her head, her beak wide, the deadly hooked tip descending toward his throat.

CHAPTER EIGHTEEN

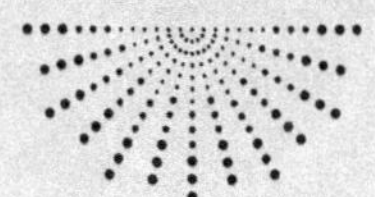

He held perfectly still. Gryphons were more volatile than humans by nature and sometimes during the first shift the powerful instincts overrode the human mind completely. She would never harm him but trapped deep within the palace, and unable to see the open sky, she might panic and hurt others in a blind rampage.

Opening his mind to her, he sent images of him leading her out of the palace to the gardens outside. The large gryphon merely blinked lazy eyes at him and began to purr.

Her beak lowered more, but she merely turned her head to rub her cheeks against his skin. She drew in a deep lungful of his scent, and her purring increased in volume.

Nuzzling and rubbing her face against every bit of exposed skin she could find, she worked her way down his neck and shoulders. When she reached the smear of blood on his newly healed chest, the thick wedge of her tongue darted out and cleaned away the traces before she continued her rubbing and purring. She worked her way down his chest and then back up his sides. He started twitching, and a shaky gasp escape him. "That tickles!"

Bracing a hand against her beak, he attempted to push her to a less ticklish region, but she planted a paw on the center of his chest and growled. When he stopped struggling, she returned to her scent marking.

"Fine, have your way with me." Kuwari reached out and ran his hand through the silky feathers covering her neck. The feathers were a glossy black that faded to a deep burgundy red at the tips. The largest feathers on her wings shared the same glossy blackness changing to burgundy two-thirds of the way down the shaft.

When she settled on her haunches, he was able to see a burgundy dorsal stripe contrasting nicely against her ebony fur. The strip followed her spine all the way to the muscular lion-like tail. Presently her tail was flicking, the burgundy tuft on the end swaying back and forth playfully.

"You could let me up now."

Enkara huffed out what sounded like a chuckle and rubbed a cheek against his abdomen. Kuwari was just resigning himself to the fact that the woman he loved wasn't finished with him when a shrill scream assaulted his hearing.

"Guards! Assassin!"

Shrieking a challenge, Enkara leaped off him and put herself between him and the servant. By the time he scrambled to his feet, she was already stalking the poor woman. He rushed to Enkara's side and placed a restraining hand on her shoulder, projecting contentment.

"She's no rival or threat. Enkara, listen to me. Focus on my voice. Come away now and we'll go hunting."

Enkara paused, lulled by his voice, but he wasn't sure if it would be enough to persuade her to ignore thousands of years of gryphon instinct that was telling her there was a rival female in her territory.

She stood on stiff legs, wings mantled in threat, but she looked away from the other female long enough to glance over her shoulder at him.

"That's it," he crooned. "That's my beautiful one. Come away."

In time, Enkara's human mind would fight its way free of the primal instincts ruling her, but he needed to keep her calm until then. Taking advantage of her temporary halt, he circled around in front, blocking her view of the panicked servant as well as the newly arrived Shadows.

"Crown Prince Kuwari, do you require assistance?"

It was Uselli again. Good. He was calm and capable.

"I'm fine, but if you could remove the servant and give Enkara and me some space, all will be well."

"First shift?" the Shadow asked.

"Yes. Unexpected. She had no time to prepare."

"We'll give you space but remain close enough should you require anything."

Once the others were gone, Enkara relaxed her guard. Reaching out, he caressed her cheeks and then massaged her upright tufted ears.

"It's good you're finally able to shift. We can go hunting together now."

He spoke mostly about inane things, merely wanting her to hear his voice and relax.

She was already calming when his father called to him from the outer chamber.

"Enter but come alone. Enkara has shifted and is ruled by her more primal instincts."

"That's what Uselli reported." Ditanu walked into the room and his nostrils immediately flared. "I smell blood. Yours?"

Ditanu homed in on the two pale scars on Kuwari's chest and one eyebrow arched with humor. "I see you take after me more than your mother. Ah, well, High Priestess Kammani should be getting used to Royals and Blades preempting the formal ritual."

Heat flushed Kuwari's cheeks. "I didn't realize exposing Enkara to my blood would trigger her change."

Ditanu chuckled. "That must've been a surprise. Did it happen during or after the Blooding Ceremony?"

"After."

That damned merry twinkle in his father's eyes grew brighter. "Somehow I imagine you envisioned a somewhat different ending to the ritual."

Kuwari grinned sheepishly. "Last night Enkara agreed to become my betrothed. I see no reason not to start the courtship before the official announcement."

Ditanu's expression relaxed, the fine lines around his mouth and between his brows smoothing. "I'm happy Enkara has finally admitted her feelings."

"As am I."

The merry light was back in his father's eyes a moment

later. "She couldn't stand aside and allow another female to claim you even if it was only going to be a false betrothal."

Ditanu held out his hand for Enkara to sniff. She gave it a good once over and then returned to rubbing her scent on the back of Kuwari's calves.

His father's look of humor grew as he took in Enkara's vigorous rubbing.

Kuwari scowled at his father, having a feeling this moment was going to be discussed with Burrukan later over a pitcher of wine and much laughter. "If you grin any harder, your face is going to split in two."

The king managed to choke back his laughter. "It's just that this type of scent marking often leads to other things."

"I have no intention of—"

"Enjoy your hunting trip, my son."

Damn! His father had seen a vision of this. That's how he'd gotten here so fast. Kuwari glowered at his father. "Enkara's human side will reassert itself shortly."

"Don't worry about your duties today," Ditanu said, completely ignoring his son's comment. "I'll see that everyone is made aware that you are taking a day for yourself."

"That isn't entirely necessary, I'm sure a morning hunt will be sufficient."

"Take the day, trust me." With that, his father left him standing there with Enkara half curled around him, and he didn't have the slightest idea how to bring her human mind to the forefront.

~

GATHERING her thoughts was like getting honey to flow from a clay jar on a cold morning. It would happen eventually but might take a long while. In the meantime, there were worse things than drawing in deep breaths of Kuwari's delectable scent.

Subtle variances in his scent markers told her many things. He was a male entering his prime breeding years. And his contentment over the fact she'd chosen him was a rich, warm scent suffusing the room.

What? Wait!

What had happened and why was she kneeling next to Kuwari?

Glancing down at herself, understanding struck. Ah! She'd finally shifted to gryphon form. A few other details snapped into place as well. She'd been scent marking Kuwari. While she'd likely find that embarrassing when she returned to human form, her gryphon mind thought it the most natural thing in the world.

"Come," Kuwari said as he looked down at her. "Hunt with me. It will help you become more accustomed to your new gryphon body."

Bobbing her head, she silently admitted she'd follow his delicious and entirely too appealing scent anywhere.

Gesturing her forward, he walked to the door and out into the corridor where he gave the guards new orders. As she followed, she discovered the spacious chambers and passageways now felt narrow and confining.

"We'll be out under the open sky shortly," Kuwari murmured in soothing tones, his fingers finding their way into her feathered ruff. After a few good scratches, she found herself purring.

She likely should feel somewhat more self-conscious than she did, but once they were outside, surrounded by the sky and the green scent of plants, her human concerns fell away. Her wings unfurled to cup the breeze.

"Soon," Kuwari promised. "Let me shift and I'll teach you the joys of flight."

As promised, he soon found a secluded part of the garden where he shed his clothing and shifted forms. Enkara sniffed as the handsome gryphon sidled up beside her playfully. He smelled even better as a gryphon and she liked the flex and ripple of muscles below his sleek fur. Purring, she decided her prince was a fine looking male in either shape.

He didn't give her long to admire him though, and soon he was touching her mind, showing her about the wind currents and the thermals rising from the ground and how to harness them to take command of the skies.

When she understood, he led her to a long flat bit of land where he put on a burst of speed, leaped up into the air and left the ground behind in a series of powerful wingbeats. He didn't go far. Circling back around, he slowed his airspeed and angled his wings to drop gracefully to the ground beside her.

He demonstrated twice more before urging her to run with him. Then with a mighty leap and a few beats of her wings, she was airborne, flying wingtip to wingtip with her chosen one.

CHAPTER NINETEEN

*L*ady Kullaa stood in the royal gardens, the flowers she'd been picking long forgotten, as five Shadows in gryphon form dropped out of the sky to land in a stretch of well-groomed grass surrounded by small, flowering trees. Moments later, Crown Prince Kuwari and an unknown female gryphon with glossy black feathers lightening to burgundy at the tips came in for a landing as well. The coloring was both rare and striking.

Kullaa felt a spike of guilt. She wasn't supposed to be here, and while she wasn't spying for her mother, she *was* curious which female had caught the prince's eye enough to share a flight with him.

Then the two shapeshifted and she realized the other female was Shadow Enkara. But that wasn't what shocked her. It was the tattoo running down Enkara's back that made Kullaa's eyes widen in surprise. Moments later Enkara pulled on her robe, hiding the mark of Ishtar.

Now it was apparent why Crown Prince Kuwari ignored every eligible female who crossed his path. They all paled in comparison to his goddess chosen Enkara.

Kullaa had once seen Queen Iltani's tattoo during the spring planting festival, so she knew the mark of a Blade when she saw one.

Enkara was Kuwari's Blade.

No one would ever have guessed. Never had two Blades been born at the same time. If her mother and the other council members had known this, they never would have interfered, no matter how much they wanted a pure-blooded gryphon lady sitting on the throne. None would be so arrogant as to go against Ishtar's wishes.

For some reason unknown to Kullaa, her mother, and the other council members, the Royals were keeping Enkara's title a secret. Assassination attempts were far from unusual. That must be the reason for the secrecy. And hadn't King Ditanu done something similar in his quest to protect Iltani?

Kullaa grinned as something else became clear. Her mother could do nothing to influence Crown Prince Kuwari's choice. Maybe now Kullaa would be permitted to court the male she fancied instead of being forced to appease her mother's wishes.

Excitement and hope flowed through her blood, and she waited impatiently for the prince and his escort to leave the gardens. Once they were gone, she squeezed out of her hiding spot. Well, she wasn't actually hiding. Not from the prince and Enkara. Her mother, that was another matter.

She'd been coming here every so often as an escape from her mother and the court. It was quiet here, and she'd found a broad flat rock overlooking the ocean at the edge of the garden that was perfect for sunning.

Sunning in the king's garden was the one bit of rebelliousness she allowed herself. She'd only been caught once, by Shadow Uselli. It had been her first meeting with the imposing Shadow. That first time she'd been terrified, thinking he was going to execute her for trespassing in the Royal Gardens.

Yet he only laughed and asked why she was there. Still too terrified to lie, she spilled the truth about her overbearing mother. Uselli had just laughed harder and told her she could continue to use the garden as long as the royal family wasn't present.

After that, she'd seen him in the garden a few times, and they'd always exchanged pleasantries before returning to their duties.

But now she'd gone and accidentally broken that rule. She'd be lucky if—

"Lady Kullaa," a deep, familiar male voice called from just behind her shoulder. "I thought I'd made myself clear about certain requirements."

Kullaa nearly jumped out of her skin but swallowed back her surprise and answered calmly. "Shadow Uselli, I'm so sorry. If I'd known the prince and Enkara had gone for a flight and would be coming back this way, I never would have stayed."

"All the same, you will accompany me back to my office for questioning." He said it with such a straight face, she began to fear he was in absolute earnest.

A blush climbed up her cheeks. She nodded her head, murmuring an apology.

Uselli maintained his serious expression for a good half of the trip to his office. Kullaa grew more and more nervous.

"Please don't tell my mother," she begged at last.

"What? Hold a conversation with that bloodthirsty jackal? Never." At which point, he doubled over laughing and told her he was looking for an excuse to avoid Burrukan in the practice ring.

After a long afternoon sitting across from Uselli, hunched over a plain, unadorned Ur board, losing round after round of the game to him, he took her last white square, winning again. But she'd never enjoyed losing a game as much as she did to the Shadow.

But eventually, he admitted he'd have to let her go or risk her mother calling for a hunt to look for her missing daughter.

She'd departed then, feeling ridiculously flustered and happy. At least until she reached her mother's chambers. Kullaa had barely closed the door behind her when she heard footsteps approaching.

"Where have you been?" Her mother growled.

"I went for a walk."

"For half the day?" she challenged in her best Council-woman tone.

"I... I sometimes walk in the garden reserved for the royal family. I know it's off-limits, but it's always so quiet there, and the king and his family almost never go there, and Shadow Uselli said it was all right as long as I'm not there when the Royals are using it."

Nakurtum's eyebrow nearly arched to her hairline. "You were caught and then given permission to return by the second in command of the Shadows? The king's oldest and closest friend?"

"Yes," Kullaa said in a meek voice, already knowing what her mother was thinking.

"That shows great favor. A Shadow wouldn't act without instruction. Either King Ditanu or Crown Prince Kuwari must favor you. And everyone saw how the prince selected you to dance with him three times during the night of the celebration."

Actually, Kullaa was pretty sure she'd been selected by Enkara because she'd been deemed safe and the least likely to assault the prince during the dance. "I can say with confidence that Kuwari and Enkara will be mated shortly."

"What? What are you talking about?"

"They love each other."

Nakurtum scoffed. "Enkara was raised with him like a sister."

"There is nothing brotherly and sisterly about their relationship."

"Be that as it may, Enkara is just an unknown half-breed orphan. Take away her upbringing, and she has no more social standing than a peasant or a servant. Prince Kuwari knows his duty. He'll pick a suitable mate to keep the magic of the gryphons strong."

Kullaa winced. "You may want to rethink your words, Mother. Even though she's an orphan and doesn't claim a tie to one of the noble houses, I think Enkara might be noble blood."

Her mother's eyes narrowed. "What makes you say that?"

"Her black and burgundy coloring is very unusual. When I was studying the heraldry lists during my education on Uruk, I read about the rare coloration. I just can't remember which line produces it."

"Black coloration? There hasn't been a black gryphon in several generations." Her mother looked thoughtful. "Enkara's heritage shouldn't be that difficult to track. And if she is noble blood and King Ditanu is hiding that fact, then there must be a reason."

"Mother! Just stop. It doesn't matter if Enkara is noble born or the daughter of a fishmonger, she's been chosen by Ishtar to be Kuwari's fated mate."

"Nonsense. The gods don't concern themselves with such insignificant mortal matters. Certainly not a half-breed gryphon like Enkara. But the council exists to make certain the royal line is protected from making bad decisions."

"Enkara is his Blade."

Kullaa savored the moment her mother understood her words.

Eyes widening, lips parting, Nakurtum mouthed the word "no." Then in a strangled voice, "That's not possible. There are never two."

"Until now, no," Kullaa agreed.

"But a second Blade!"

"I know it's hard to believe, but Enkara had been out flying with Kuwari, and when she shifted back to human form, I saw the tattoo. It was exactly like the one on Queen Iltani's spine."

For the first time in her life, Kullaa witnessed her mother

speechless. It was a new and rather enjoyable experience. "You see? Kuwari and Enkara are perfectly matched. No other female ever really had a chance with the prince." Kullaa squared her shoulders. "Given this new information, I would like to focus my courtship elsewhere."

Nakurtum's expression went from shocked to thoughtful. "You've done well my daughter, but don't start courting another male yet. There is still hope to land the prince."

"He loves Enkara. That was plain to see."

"Dear girl, have you not noticed that there are four thrones sitting at the front of the Great Hall?"

"Yes, of course —"

"King Ditanu has a queen to love and a consort to rule at his side."

"Two regents actually," Kullaa pointed out, feeling rebellious. "But that was just an elaborate ploy to protect Iltani when she was young and vulnerable. Ahassunu was never mated to King Ditanu."

"True, yet King Ditanu still shares the ruling of New Sumer with Regent Ahassunu even after he revealed to all that Iltani was his mated Blade and elevated her to Queen. Ditanu values Ahassunu for her wise guidance. Look at Enkara, training for war and protection, but she knows nothing about how to rule a kingdom."

"The situation with Enkara is nothing like Ditanu and Iltani. For one, Enkara is older and likely only a moon cycle or two away from completing the Blooding Ceremony. Once that happens there will be no need to hide what she is, and he'll be able to name her as his Blade and mate."

"Goddess, it will be a disaster. That girl is like a female

version of Burrukan—the least politically-minded man ever born."

"But it doesn't matter. Enkara is Ishtar's choice."

Nakurtum's eyes widened and she laughed. "Ishtar's choice for a Blade, yes, but many Blades never perform the Sacred Marriage or become mated to the monarch. Sometimes Ishtar simply wants the Blade to be a military leader to aid a young king or queen. For all we know, Ishtar fully plans for Kuwari to take a noblewoman as his mate for the good of all New Sumer."

"But Kuwari loves Enkara."

"Yes, yes, perhaps. But he's still unmated, and the gods haven't called on him and his Blade to perform the Sacred Marriage. It's likely they won't since they already have Ditanu and Iltani. And if the gods don't declare Enkara and Kuwari a pair, then that leaves you a wide, clear path to the throne."

"But Mother—"

"All I need is the correct leverage…and you may just have found that for me as well. I must arrange a trip to Uruk to view the heraldry scrolls."

Kullaa sank down in a nearby chair.

Oh, great goddess Ishtar, please strike me down for being so foolish as to think my mother and I could ever reach an understanding.

There would be no reasoning with her mother. Kullaa knew she needed to find a way to warn Crown Prince Kuwari and Shadow Enkara.

CHAPTER TWENTY

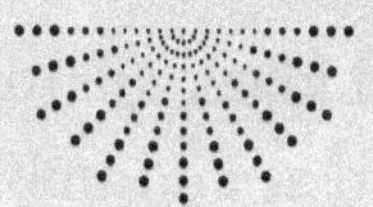

Priestess Enheduana placed a bowl of water on the altar. "Thus, do I honor Nammu of the primeval waters."

Balahu stepped forward and cupped his hands over the bowl, shaping the dome like-symbol for the heavens. "Thus, I do honor An of the Sky."

"And Ki of the earth." Enusat dropped a shard of volcanic rock into the small bowl.

Next Balathu placed a bloodied dagger and a stalk of diseased wheat upon the altar. "I honor slayed Nergal, God of Pestilence, War, and the killing high summer sun. May he soon be restored in all his glory."

Enheduana freed a tiny owl from his cage and gave him a gentle head scratch before setting him on a perch just above the altar. Reaching inside her robe's sleeve, she drew a dagger from a hidden sheath. The owl turned his wide, unblinking eyes upon her.

While he watched, she pressed the dagger's tip to her forearm, making a shallow cut. Once a few beads of crimson blood welled up, she raised her arm above the bowl. A few drops hit the water's surface, soon turning it a reddish-pink. While the wound was still bleeding freely, she smeared some on her fingers and anointed the tiny owl's head, beak, and chest.

"Thus, I honor Ereshkigal, guardian of souls, dweller in the land of Kur. Our great and noble Queen and Goddess, we honor you above all others."

"We honor Ereshkigal," Balathu and Enusat uttered in unison.

The little bird merely looked at the three robed figures with unblinking eyes. Though, soon he started to lick at the blood and then vigorously groomed himself.

Enheduana turned from the altar. The other two males followed close on her heels. Now that the ritual had been completed, they had business to attend to.

"Balathu, your message said you had some important news that couldn't wait." Enheduana hoped it was as vital as he claimed.

"I was attending to the offerings in the city temple when King Ditanu came to speak with High Priestess Kammani. From his expression, I knew it was something of importance, so when she led him out into the courtyard, I slipped up the stairs to the next level and waited by a window." Balathu paused as if to remember details.

Goddess give me patience. Was he going to tell her how many steps he took, too? "Go on?"

"They'd almost finished their conversation by the time I

reached a window overlooking the courtyard, but I was in time to hear Kammani mention that next time Kuwari and Enkara completed a Blooding Ceremony it would be a formal one, properly honoring Ishtar or they risked angering the gods."

This new development confirmed Enkara was Kuwari's Blade, which was good, but it was also bad news as well. "If they have already completed the first Blooding Ceremony, then we must enact our plans swiftly."

Enusat cleared his throat. "We can't be sure this is the first Blooding Ceremony. There might have been more. When I was in the palace kitchens earlier, I heard one of the servants speaking with another. Apparently, she walked in just after Enkara had shifted to gryphon form for the first time. Enkara almost killed the girl."

Enheduana compressed her lips. "Enkara hasn't even been back a moon cycle yet. I doubt they've had time to perform more than one Blooding Ceremony, but we need to intercede before there is a second or third. We can't allow Ishtar to steal back what rightfully belongs to Ereshkigal."

Enusat nodded agreement, though he looked concerned as well. "How are we going to stop the next ceremony?"

"We separate them."

"How? They are too well guarded."

"The same way we planned to deliver them to Ereshkigal in the first place."

"Our plans are nowhere near ready," Enusat stated, although his earlier expression of concern had transformed into something more purposeful.

He tucked his chin and stared unfocused at the floor, his

sharp mind likely playing through any number of scenarios. When he glanced up at her a short time later, Enheduana nodded. "You see that it's possible. We simply must accelerate our original plans."

"Simply accelerate? We'll need the aid of several anunnaki, and we haven't even summoned the first one yet." Balathu began wringing his hands. "If we summon too many, too quickly we risk a lamassu sensing the imbalance in the living world and notifying King Ditanu. If he and his Blade learn of us, we're dead and so too is the last hope of Ereshkigal reclaiming Nergal."

"Then we will just have to be very careful not to upset the balance," Enheduana said with growing conviction. "I'll summon the first of the anunnaki this night."

CHAPTER TWENTY-ONE

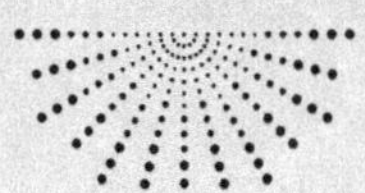

uwari stared down into his cup of tea and tried to bring into focus the blurry sense of unease that had been plaguing him for the last three days. It had started shortly after Enkara's first flight. He tried seeking out the cause but couldn't pin down what was amiss. For once he would have welcomed a vision, but none were forthcoming.

Though it might have had something to do with what his father had just revealed. Apparently, one or more of the councilors had gotten impatient and let slip that he would be entering into a betrothal with an as-yet-unnamed female.

While he'd known it would happen sooner or later, if it had been up to him, he would have held off to give Enkara a little more peace. Once others knew she was his choice, Enkara would suffer the full undivided attention of the court. Not something he'd wish on his darkest enemy.

"I would very much like to know which council member

slipped the news early," Kuwari told his father while half-consciously running his thumb over the jewel in his sword's pommel.

"I'm not sure knowing who did it changes much. The court was already speculating about you and Enkara after how you two danced the evening of your name day. It's clear who you favor. Your announcement will come as no real surprise."

"We didn't even dance together."

Ditanu chuckled. "You danced for her alone. Anyone with eyes could see that. Just make the announcement. Enkara will get used to the scrutiny in time."

Sighing, Kuwari stared down at his rapidly cooling tea. "Fine."

"You'll make the announcement?"

"Yes. Today. I'll do it over midday meal in the Great Hall when the council members and a large chunk of the nobility will be present for the afternoon petitions."

Ditanu stood and gave him a pat on the shoulder. "I can't believe you're old enough to be thinking of females, let alone old enough to soon be starting your own family. Not so long ago you were a fluffy little cub."

He grinned at his father's words. "What are you mumbling on about, old man? Enkara and I are already older than you and Iltani were the first time."

"Old? Watch your tongue, cub." Ditanu's tone lacked anger, and he was suspiciously holding a goblet in front of his mouth, likely to hide a grin. "All joking aside, I hope Enkara accepts you quickly. Once you form that bond, it's one less thing to worry over."

"On that topic, I do have one question."

Ditanu grinned. "What? Do you need another demonstration by a priest and priestess?"

Kuwari rolled his eyes. "No. It's about Enkara being half human. If she were pure gryphon, I'd wait for her to initiate the mating. If she were pure human, I'd make the first advance. But Enkara is both human and gryphon, and I don't know which way her nature runs."

Seeing his father was fighting back another gale of laughter, Kuwari stood and stomped across the room. "It's not like I was born knowing this pesky little detail."

"My son, you're overthinking things. Later, after you've retired for the night, go to Enkara and ask her. If she doesn't yet know, seduce each other and see what happens. If she welcomes you, enjoy the experience. Alternatively, if she kicks your ass halfway across the room, you'll know she's more gryphon than human in bed." Ditanu gave Kuwari another companionable pat. "For your sake, I hope she's more human than gryphon. Does that answer your questions? Or do you need more instructional details?"

"Gods no!" Kuwari winced. "The priest and priestess were detailed in the demonstrations. I get the basics."

"Good. Because if you need details, I was going to make Burrukan do the explaining just to watch him squirm. Did I tell you he beat me in the practice ring this morning? I'm not above revenge. So…if you need pointers?"

Kuwari thanked his father and left before he followed through on his threat about Burrukan. Though, later tonight he planned to apply his father's advice and see if Enkara would welcome him or kick him out into the corridor.

CHAPTER TWENTY-TWO

As Kuwari limped back to his chambers after a long and disastrous day, he decided that nothing could have gone worse even if a god of ill-luck came and sat on his shoulders. The first calamity had been his announcement that Enkara had agreed to become his betrothed.

Heartbeats after he'd uttered the words, he'd drawn Enkara close and kissed her as was tradition. She'd been so focused on the crowd, his kiss had startled her, and she'd jerked back and then froze like prey before a predator. He'd had to call her name three times before she'd stepped in beside him again and taken his outstretched hand.

He'd been so happy that Enkara was finally going to be his, he'd forgotten her aversion to public showings of emotion. The insecurity sprung from her childhood. She hadn't entirely gotten past it and large groups of people often still overwhelmed her.

Even after they'd sat down for the midday meal, she'd

remained stiff with embarrassment and nerves, nearly spilling a goblet of wine.

The court had broken out in boisterous chuckles. There'd even been a few shouted questions about if he'd forgotten to ask her first before announcing the betrothal.

He'd chuckled good-naturedly and steered the questions and well wishing to safer areas. As soon as the court had calmed, he'd immediately apologized to Enkara using their special link. Outwardly, she'd recovered her composure, smiling calmly and nodding to one noble or another as they came forward to personally wish them well, but all through the rest of the meal, Enkara had been more silent than usual.

After the meal, he'd wanted to apologize again and do something to make it up to her, but Burrukan had ambushed him and dragged him off to the practice ring while Queen Iltani had accompanied Enkara to the next ring over.

Distracted by earlier events, Burrukan had soundly thrashed Kuwari in the first fight and then ordered him to stay until he improved sufficiently. Unfortunately, it took the rest of the day and half the night to appease the evil old brute.

Last meal was long past and most of the palace, including the servants, were already asleep. He was too tired and sore to bother walking to the kitchens. He shuffled toward his own chambers in the hope that once he fell into bed, it would break the streak of evil luck plaguing him this day. Ahead, the Shadows standing guard saw his escort approaching and held open the doors.

Inside, the only light was from a fire burning in the hearth to stave off the ocean's chill. As he crossed into his own bedchamber, he glanced toward Enkara's with a small hope there'd be a bit of light to suggest she was still up. He wanted to talk to her after the day he'd had, but her chamber was dark and silent.

Brushing aside the fringed curtain, he peered into the darkness, merely needing to hear her soft breath, the sound of her heartbeat, the sweet aroma of her newly emerged gryphon nature.

Even the moon was against him, having already disappeared from the sky and offering no light. His eyes slowly picked out details in the shadows. Entering her chamber, he only managed six steps before the sharp edge of a table caught him precariously close to his groin.

Grunting in pained surprise, he halted.

"I suppose I should take pity on you," Enkara's voice reached out from somewhere in the darkness to wrap around his senses. "I had some time on my hands so had the servants help rearrange the room."

"Delightful use of your time," Kuwari said dryly as he rubbed at his abused flesh. "May I join you for a little while? I wanted to apologize for earlier, during mid-day meal—I should have realized—"

"There's a rug on the floor," Enkara said by way of reply. "Follow it to your right for about ten strides. That will bring you to the foot of the bed."

"Hmmm. Found the rug." He couldn't keep the purring tone out of his voice.

"Good, don't fall and break anything, I don't want to explain to the healers what you were doing stumbling around in my dark chamber."

"Your concern warms me," Kuwari echoed her sarcasm, but it was ruined by an undignified humph as he tripped over a stack of something on the floor.

"Be careful. I forgot to mention the stack of armor and weapons." Her voice held genuine concern this time. "We didn't get all the weapons racks put back up yet."

"It's fine. I just found them," he grumbled. "Are there any other items you forgot to mention?"

"No, nothing else that's in your path."

Kuwari continued forward, his hands outstretched before him until he found the edge of her sleeping platform. Carefully skirting it, he came along one side and began to undress.

He felt around blindly until he found the corner of her blanket.

"If that earlier rustle of fabric means you're now naked, I'd think hard before getting in this bed."

Enkara's voice was sleep-edged, and he didn't find it particularly threatening. Grinning in the darkness, he slid under the covers. "Who actually sleeps in clothing?"

"Not you I assume," Enkara said, but she merely reached out and took his hand, guiding him closer until he rolled up against her back. He wrapped one arm around her waist and burrowed the other underneath her pillows.

Grinning, he decided this was how he should always sleep. Nuzzling aside her braids and the neckline of her sleeping robe, he pressed a kiss to the skin of her tattoo, noting the slight roughness of Ishtar's mark.

"I know you have something on your mind." Enkara was

still sleepy sounding, but it didn't take much to figure out what he was thinking.

"I'm male," he said by way of reply, feeling humor and love mixing together in his heart.

She snorted and rolled onto her back so she could face him, though he didn't know how she could see anything in the absolute pitch darkness of her room.

"That's not what I was talking about. You're uneasy about something. I first noticed it the day of our Blooding Ceremony." He could hear the frown in her voice. "Does something about my gryphon form displease you?"

"No. Never that. I always knew you'd make a beautiful gryphon, but even if you had the narrowest rump in the history of our species, a bent spine, stunted wings and a club foot, I'd still love you." While that was true, she had picked up on the one thing he didn't want to speak about. Something he couldn't even put a name to yet. How was he ever going to explain it to her if he didn't know what this new itch beneath his skin was? All he knew was that it was both foreign and yet not. Something similar and yet different to the power of his visions.

Unfortunately, his visions didn't show him what it was. But whatever *it* was, he felt it stirring awake inside him and that scared him. Perhaps he could skirt this discussion altogether by steering it in another direction. "Earlier, when I announced we were betrothed, I'm sorry my public showing of affection embarrassed you before the court."

"Not a lie," she said and patted his hand. "But not the truth either."

"I..." Curse it! She'd always been able to sense his every

lie and evasion. When he'd been younger, that ability had spoiled more than one of his planned escapades. "I don't want to talk about it."

Beside him Enkara stiffened, then she tossed back the cover, stood and marched out of her room. While he was still fumbling in the darkness for the discarded blankets, she returned carrying a candle, the light enough to highlight her 'did you just dare to lie to me' look. He hadn't seen it since he was a child, but he admitted it still caused his heart to race a little.

She set the candle down on the table and kicked the blankets in his direction.

"Get dressed." Her glower never wavered. "What happened to 'we tell each other everything'? Because this, whatever this is, is definitely something."

Enkara was correct. He owed it to her to share this with her even if he didn't know exactly what *it* was. If it was something that could be dangerous to her, she deserved to know.

Sighing, he adjusted a blanket around his waist and sat heavily on her bed. Then he rubbed his face, trying to put the uneasy feeling into words. He began with the vision of the two anunnaki in his room and how they'd wanted to speak with him, but it wasn't really Kuwari they wanted to speak with.

"Even for a vision, that makes very little sense." Enkara stood with her back against the wall and her arms crossed.

"It does if I've been infected by something or someone."

Enkara pushed away from the wall, expression changing form annoyance to worry. "High Priestess Kammani once gave me a series of very old scrolls to read. One mentioned how an anunnaki can possess a human. But according to the scroll, they only do that to very dark souls, so they can drag the tainted soul into the underworld for judgment and stop it from doing greater damage to the mortal world."

"She ordered me to read the same one." Kuwari frowned down at his folded hands. Was there one of those guardians even now inside him? He'd sense it, wouldn't he?

"Still, that can't be what is causing this…" she shrugged, at a loss. "The scroll said it's a swift, clean death for the host."

"Only once the anunnaki abandons the body to take the soul to the underworld."

Enkara's lips parted, but no sound emerged. She tried a second time. "No."

He slumped his shoulders and rested his chin in his hand, not looking her in the eye when he said, "Since when has ignorant want ever changed the truth of something's nature?"

Her lips parted again, but she didn't deny his words. After a long, thoughtful pause she continued. "So, I might be Ereshkigal's Blade, and you might be possessed by one of the underworld anunnaki. Some pair we make."

"As much as I'd like it to be otherwise, I can't rule out that it's not an anunnaki."

Enkara sat next to him on the bed and bumped her shoulder against his. "Even if you have an anunnaki's spirit hidden somewhere inside and I can't feel it, then there must be something stopping it from taking your soul to the underworld. Otherwise, you'd already be there, and I would have destroyed every seal and layer of protection guarding the underworld to reach your side."

"Enkara, don't joke about such things—"

"Who says I'm joking?"

"Goddess, Enkara. I know you're not." He glanced up at the ceiling and then down at his hands. "All those years ago, when I first touched your mind, I simply wanted you, your love, the warmth of your soul. I didn't know better then. I do now, but I still can't let you go. Though if something were to happen to you because of me…"

"Kuwari, whatever fate has planned for us, it's not your fault." Enkara placed an arm around his shoulder.

At her urging, he turned his face to the side of her neck and wrapped an arm around her waist. "I've never seen a complete picture of our future. What I've seen has been a mixture of horror and hope."

"That is more than most people get." Her fingers were suddenly stroking the back of his neck and up into his hair. It was still in braids so she couldn't work her fingers through it like he wanted, but her hand soon stroked down his back in a caress that had a deep rumbling purr escaping him.

He leaned closer and Enkara smacked his shoulder. "Someone needs a bath before he attempts courtship."

"Goddess. I know I stink, but I'm too exhausted to get one at the moment. I'd likely fall asleep and drown."

"Well, I was going to suggest we share a bath and then afterward I could massage away the soreness from Burrukan's brutal training session, but if you prefer I don't —"

"Ignore me. I'm tired and mumbling," Kuwari said, unable

to keep the hint of humor out of his voice. "Though, I'm suddenly not as exhausted as I was before. I would love a bath."

"I thought as much." Flashing him a shy smile, she reached down and grabbed his hand, then dragged him from her room.

Grinning, he knew he'd follow his beloved Blade anywhere.

CHAPTER TWENTY-THREE

Several torches flickered and flared in a draft stirred by Enheduana's slow dance before the Queen of the Underworld's statue. The only witness to her summoning ritual was the tiny owl perched on the altar.

She ended the dance and spoke a prayer as she fed bits of a lion's heart to the sacred owl. When the owl took the offered tidbits, she sprinkled him with drops of wine mixed with her own blood.

She only hoped it was enough. After all, this was more than a simple offering, it was a proposition for aid. Now she hoped half a night's work was about to be rewarded. On the heels of her thought, a presence flared behind her, creeping down her spine in warning. She glanced over her shoulder in time to witness the anunnaki rising out of the ground, emerging from another realm entirely.

Turning slowly, she faced the newly arrived anunnaki. It was massive, towering over her. Though it made no outward sign of aggression, the anunnaki's sharp eyes tracked her every movement. His bird's head with its deadly hooked beak didn't show a hint of expression either. All she could ascertain was that this one was male to judge by his bare chest and large muscular figure. Not that it mattered, male or female, an anunnaki was a fierce guardian of the afterlife.

Flicking the feathers of his double set of wings, he tilted his head, studying her. "Why have you summoned me, gryphon?"

Enheduana bowed her head. "There is a task that needs performing."

"The gods always have tasks for their servants and guardians to perform. Speak your task and I shall decide if it is worthy."

"Kuwari and his Blade have already performed the first of the Blooding Ceremonies. If they complete another, we risk losing them to Ishtar and Tammuz. We must act swiftly to stop that from happening."

Enheduana waited for the anunnaki to make his decision. Surely, he would agree to act. They had to act, or everything they'd worked for would come to nothing.

The anunnaki turned from her to face the altar, and she was surprised to see him reach out to the tiny owl. He began ruffling the owl's head feathers to its utter delight. After a few moments of vigorous scratching, he placed the little owl on his shoulder. In turn, the owl stretched up to groom the anunnaki's feathers.

The guardian from the underworld proceeded to stroke the owl's feathers for long enough Enheduana had to repress the urge to pace. Showing impatience to an anunnaki was the best way to destroy any semblance of goodwill the creature might possess.

They were known to be stubborn and inclined to act as they saw fit. The older it was, the more likely it was to act in unexpected ways. At last, he finished scratching the owl's head feathers and placed the tiny bird back on his perch.

"I have spoken with Nergal. He wishes for the two younglings to learn the truth and choose for themselves. Force is never a good motivator."

"You risked speaking with Nergal?"

The anunnaki clacked his beak softly at the interruption and continued like she hadn't spoken. "However, he also agrees that Ishtar already has too great a hold on the Blade."

Isn't that what I said? Enheduana thought sourly but didn't let even a hint of her annoyance show on her face. Though the anunnaki clacked his beak and emitted at a throaty chuckle.

"Your plan would require us to abduct one of them. Separating them would severely limit the development of their powers. Nergal is attached to the pair and doesn't want to see either of them unduly distressed. He suggests we act to prevent Kuwari and Enkara from attending the next Sacred Marriage. The risk that Tammuz and Ishtar will claim them is too great."

Enheduana compressed her lips in thought. What the anunnaki said made sense. However, there was one problem. "Their presence will be expected."

"Then we make certain they are forbidden from attending."

"How? I don't have enough influence to sway enough of the Council to achieve such a thing."

"Then we create a situation that will make the King protective of his children."

"What do you have in mind?"

"An attempt upon a gryphon's cubs always stirs a parent's protective instincts."

Enheduana's eyes widened in surprise. While an anunnaki could be reasoned with if they deemed the cause worthy, having one take the initiative was very rare.

"As you say, that should work." She almost wished to ask this anunnaki his name, to figure out if he was one of the seven judges. But fear held her tongue. It was said an anunnaki only revealed his name to the soul he was transporting to the underworld.

"Do not take this action lightly. It may result in many, many unintended deaths. All the gods will be angry if we disturb the balance too greatly. Are you prepared for that, Priestess?"

Enheduana barked out a laugh. "The balance shifted millennia ago when Ishtar first tricked Nergal and trapped him in the world of the living."

"I know the history."

"Then how can you worry about a few lost lives when a god is held against his will, trapped to forever be reborn as a mortal, to never be able to rejoin his wife in the afterlife?"

The anunnaki ruffled his feathers and started to laugh. "Is that not exactly what Ereshkigal has forced Ishtar's husband to endure? The sisters could end this feud if they wanted."

"How can you say such a thing? Ereshkigal will hear of your insubordination."

"Insubordination?" Outwardly unflustered by her words, the anunnaki merely flattened his feathers back in place. "My duty is to protect all the souls in the land of the dead. Not to serve any one of the other gods. Remember that, Priestess."

A coil of fear stirred in her gut, but the need to know overrode it. "Who are you?"

"I am the first."

Enheduana's breath stilled in her lungs.

"Fear not, little Priestess, I will complete this task to help one whom I call a friend."

"Friend?" she dared question.

"Nergal is my friend. I would see him restored to his former self if that is his wish." The anunnaki speared her with a look. "We have much work to do if we don't want Ishtar to claim a second Blade."

"We must be meticulous in our planning and execution or one of the city's lamassu will sense your presence," Enheduana said, regaining her composure. "Will you be able to gather enough of your brethren?"

"Yes, even the threat of being ground beneath a Lamassu's hooves won't be enough to deter my kind. We so rarely get to play in the living realm since the sisters had their falling out."

"You will need to find suitable mortals to act as hosts. I have already spoken with the leader of the assassin's guild. He promised us aid as long as none of your anunnaki brethren take any of his people as hosts." She couldn't blame the guild master for that little stipulation since an anunnaki tended to take its host's soul with it when it returned to the underworld, leaving a lifeless husk behind.

"Fear not. I'm sure my fellows and I will find it no hardship seeking out a few other wicked mortals to take as hosts." He eyed her speculatively. "I do enjoy purifying a tainted soul, and if it is beyond healing, I'm not against consuming a little extra power."

Enheduana shuddered, and then the anunnaki fluffed his feathers, clacked his large beak as he laughed. "Yours isn't as dark as I prefer. Besides, I have a use for you. You can start by summoning three more of my brethren while I hunt for suitable hosts to hide us from the watchful Lamassu.

"Only three?"

"More will alert the lamassu of our presence no matter how carefully we hide."

Enheduana bowed her head. "I will see to the summoning immediately."

The anunnaki stepped back into the shadows and vanished. She might not be able to see him, but she could still feel his cold power prickling across her skin. It was an attempt to intimidate her. And it did, but she merely shook off the feeling of being watched and began preparations for summoning the next anunnaki.

CHAPTER TWENTY-FOUR

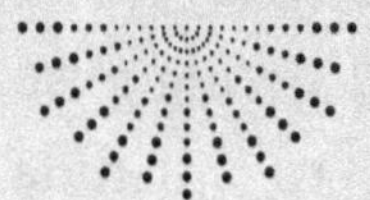

Kuwari's streak of ill luck hadn't abated. While it had taken the king and council much debating, they'd come to the unified consensus that the City-State of Nippur was the most deserving and the best place for him to settle into his role of Crown Prince of New Sumer. Nippur—Nakurtum's home territory.

While he'd always known Councilor Nakurtum had a great deal of power within the council, it had likely been noted that he and Lady Kullaa had struck up a friendship. Kuwari scowled. He liked Kullaa just fine, as a friend, but he very much wished she had any other female as a mother.

Now he and the rest of the royal family were getting relocated to Nippur where he'd be installed as ruling prince after much pomp and circumstance. Councilor Nakurtum and Lady Kullaa had left four days ago to begin preparations for the arrival of the court.

The only redeeming quality about the entire situation

was that Enkara would be at his side as his betrothed. Perhaps after all the festivities, they'd get some down time together.

Facing out to the vast ocean, Kuwari stretched his wings to catch the ocean breeze. Below, waves crashed against the cliff wall and sent salt spray high up into the air. Here at the top of the cliff, the royal party was mostly safe from the sea spray, but the occasional strong gust of wind still carried the fine mist high enough to sprinkle packs, harnesses, and feathers.

Shaking his wings, he displaced the fine droplets.

"Thanks," Enkara said with an accompanying glare as she wiped her face on her sleeve.

He gaped his beak at her and issued a hissing laugh. His beloved was in human form and unfortunately would remain in that form for the time being since her coloring was a little too noticeable and they didn't want a shrewd noble putting the pieces together until after Enkara's destiny as his Blade was revealed to the court. And that would only happen after she had full command of her power.

But that didn't mean he couldn't look forward to flying wing-tip to wing-tip with her again sometime soon. Though, it would have to wait until well after dark when all dark colors looked the same since her coloring was so rare.

In the meantime, Enkara would ride on his back.

She must have sensed his emotions because she was eyeing his naked back.

"I'd still prefer a saddle," Enkara said with an unhappy look between his naked back, the drop off to the ocean below, and then back to him again.

"A saddle would destroy my regal look." He sent a blast of humor down their link. *"The servants worked so very long and hard to make every feather gleam. They even applied a touch of oil to my beak. Makes me want to fly down to the beach and roll in the sand."*

He craned his head in Enkara's direction and found her admiring his powerful physique. When she realized she'd been discovered, she grinned. *"You already draw the eye of every female as it is. The servants' efforts are wasted on you."*

"You're the only female I care to have look. I'd even preen a little bit if I thought it might sway you toward my charms."

"You are a horrible flirt."

"Flirting implies a playfulness I lack. I am in deadly earnest. Haven't I convinced you of that yet?"

He liked the flush of pink that crawled up her otherwise calm expression. In the six nights since he'd announced their intention to formally become betrothed, he'd done his best to seduce his Blade, and while he hadn't yet succeeded, she hadn't tossed him out on his ass either.

"Mind on the task," Enkara said as she rapped him sharply on the shoulder.

Kuwari snapped his beak and grinned. She had a point, he supposed, but the court never did anything quickly, even getting ready for a royally decreed flight to Nippur.

"Do you think we'll be ready by sunset?" Enkara asked as she took in the sun still beginning its climb into the sky.

"Great goddess, we better or I'll be helping my father heave the worst of the culprits over the cliff," Kuwari said as he craned his neck again, hoping for a good scratch.

She smacked him on the shoulder again, so he just shifted

closer to her, urging her to mount up. Glowering, she did. Moments later King Ditanu gave the order to take flight.

Two companies of Shadows took to the air, the sound of their wing beats thunderous. His father and Iltani took to the air next, followed by Burrukan and Ahassunu.

Then it was Kuwari's turn, and Enkara grabbed handfuls of his fur. The air ruffled his feathers, and he joyfully stretched his wings wide. Each mighty down sweep powered him higher into the sky.

Kuwari's other siblings followed, fanning out behind him. On their heels flew close to two hundred accompanying Shadows. Well behind the guards, the rest of the court took to the air, over five hundred strong.

The sky was black with wings and the sound of thunderous flight. And this was just a pleasure flight. He briefly wondered what an army of gryphons on the wing might look like. Luckily, his visions had never shown him that possible future, and he hoped they never did.

AFTER AN UNEVENTFUL TRIP TO NIPPUR, the members of the royal party were shown to their quarters to rest up for the next day's celebration. Before long, Councilor Nakurtum and Lady Kullaa arrived to see that the Royals had everything they needed.

Kuwari had been hoping not to see the councilor so soon, but fate had different ideas.

"Crown Prince Kuwari, Nippur welcomes you,"

Nakurtum said and gestured for a servant to open the door. "I hope you like your quarters."

Kuwari nodded his head since he was still in gryphon form.

"The servants are here with your evening meal." She turned and nodded to the servant waiting at the door. Soon more entered carrying various trays of food.

Enkara carefully scanned the servants and the trays of food. When she deemed them safe, she chose a couple of pieces of fruit and began to eat them while she instructed the Shadows on guard duty for the night.

The councilor stepped closer while Enkara and the other Shadows were distracted by the servants.

"Crown Prince Kuwari, there is something of a delicate nature that we need to discuss, but it would be better spoken in privacy. At your earliest convenience, of course."

The councilor added the last part as an afterthought, he was sure. While he didn't know what game she was playing, she was a councilor, so it was a game with consequences. Best he learn what she planned as quickly as possible. He nodded his head again in agreement.

"Good. Simply send me word when you are ready." With that, she bowed and left.

CHAPTER TWENTY-FIVE

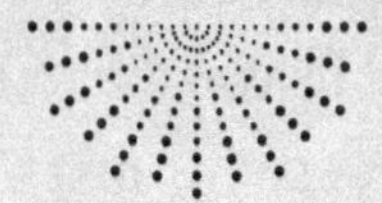

The next evening, Kuwari found himself surrounded by his younger siblings with Enkara herding them all toward Nippur's main hall.

"Get a move on, or we're going to be late," Enkara barked as she grabbed Prince Akiya by a shoulder and steered him in the right direction before he had a chance to escape.

"But it's going to be another long, boring formal dinner with the nobility. If we all bolted in different directions some of us surely would escape."

Eluti and Etum were bobbing their heads in agreement. At which point, seven-year-old Erra burst out crying because he was slower and would be the first one caught.

"Don't cry," Princess Alittum said, "While they're off making fools of themselves, we will be learning how to rule one of the other City-States."

"Alittum is correct," Kuwari said. "Besides, you have to

listen to Enkara. She outranks you now that she's my betrothed."

"What's betrothed?" Erra asked but seemed excited to stay and discover something new.

Kuwari sighed and explained while they walked. Soon the sixteen-year-old twins were laughing and making inappropriate comments. Akiya added a few more innuendos until even little Erra and Arwia were catching on. Kuwari glared at Etum and Eluti, but the twins just grinned back at him.

Meanwhile, Alittum merely pretended her four younger brothers didn't exist and grabbed Arwia's hand.

"Enough, all of you," Enkara said in a stern tone she was clearly having trouble maintaining. "We're nearly there. The entire court doesn't need to hear your thoughts."

"Crown Prince Kuwari," a familiar voice called from behind.

He sighed and then glanced over his shoulder to see Councilor Nakurtum approaching swiftly. The last day had been busy with moving into Nippur's palace and attending to a thousand little things. He hadn't had time to get back to the councilor to discover why she wanted to talk to him in private.

"I've been looking all over for you."

"I did mean to speak with you, but I became distracted with the move. My apologies. However, we were about to go in and sit. Why don't you join us?" *Because clearly, you're going to attach yourself to me like a leech.*

"Actually, what I need to discuss will only take a moment of your time. Can we do it here?"

Fine. Kuwari waved over one of the Shadows. "Can you please see my siblings safely to their seats?"

The Shadow bowed her head and then gathered a few of her brethren and started herding his unruly siblings.

"Can Enkara come with us?" Erra begged, but he'd already latched onto her with the grip of a starving crocodile.

Kuwari grinned at his youngest brother. "Very well. If Enkara doesn't mind."

He didn't miss how Enkara's gaze flicked over Councilor Nakurtum once before she nodded her agreement. "I won't be far should you need me for anything."

He translated that to mean 'If you need me to lop off her head, I'll be near.'

With that, she gathered together all six of his siblings and herded them in the direction of the Great Hall.

Once they were out of earshot, he whirled around to face the Councilor. "What do you want?"

"For you to set aside that woman and choose one not born of a traitorous line."

Nakurtum's words were like a kick to the gut—surprising, unpleasant and begging for a retaliatory strike, but he held his tongue, wondering how much she actually knew.

"Yes. I've heard about Enkara's unique coloration. It's rare and is only passed down through a few lines. Given where she was found, I did some looking in the heraldry lists on Uruk. I discovered she was the correct age to be one of Ziyatum's own grandchildren. One Zakiti, born of Ziyatum's oldest son and a human servant he fell in love with."

Kuwari clenched his jaws, refusing to confirm anything just yet.

"Zakiti's father was said to be lost in a storm, but I did some more digging while I was at Uruk, and I found a few of the servants that used to serve Ziyatum's house now serve High Priestess Kammani. They were a close-mouthed bunch, but I have my ways, and what interesting stories I heard."

Damn, she'd found something of substance. Kuwari's mind spun. He'd have to be quick to nip this in the bud. He just wondered what he'd have to trade for her silence.

Nakurtum continued her tale. "The servants told me of how Ziyatum was so enraged his first-born son would mate a human, a mere servant, that he had his own son killed and claimed it was an accident, that storm winds and the ocean took his son."

Nakurtum arched an eyebrow, waiting to see if he would confirm the tale. He didn't.

"The servants said there was more. Ziyatum imprisoned his son's human mate and daughter to hide the truth of his treachery, claiming they were lost alongside his son. But those servants knew differently since they were tasked with bringing food once a day to the dungeon below the palace."

"An interesting tale," Kuwari said at last.

"Oh, it's not a tale. I have proof." A delighted twinkle entered her eyes. "The heraldry lists had a description that sounds much like Enkara, but it also mentioned a small crescent scar on her shoulder. The servants said it happened during her birth when she was forcibly pulled from her mother's womb. It was a difficult birth, one that nearly claimed both mother and child. Does the scar sound familiar?"

Kuwari flared his nostrils but gave no other response, his mind already on what he'd have to do to bury the evidence Nakurtum had unearthed.

"If you're thinking of destroying the heraldry record or relocating the servants, don't bother. I've hidden the records in a safe place and the humans I've elevated as aids working for my household. I will bring them and the record to the Council and allow them to vote on what should be done with the daughter of a traitorous line. After all, those who weren't killed were to be sent into exile. I know we won't see your beloved Enkara suffer a similar fate because we both know she is no Shadow. She's something far more special."

How had she discovered Enkara was the granddaughter of Ziyatum? Worse, how had she learned Enkara was his Blade? Only the senior Shadows and his immediate family knew that detail. And what could he do to force the Councilor to hold her tongue?

"You don't know what you're talking about."

"Oh, I most certainly do. We both know it to be true. I'm not here to debate that with you. While I can only guess why you and your father have hidden who and what Enkara is from the Council, I assume it is only a temporary measure to protect her until she is fully trained."

Kuwari didn't respond verbally, but his body was betraying him, and he forced his fists to unclench and his shoulders to relax. "What do you want?"

"To give New Sumer the best protection it can get." Her voice lowered even more. "I know you love Enkara, and I don't expect you to set her aside. But even you must know she is a war leader at best. All I am suggesting is that you do as your father did. Name my daughter as your consort and allow her to rule at your side. It will be in name only, of course. Enkara shall be your true mate in secret."

"It isn't as simple as that," he said at last, knowing he had to say something or risk her going directly to the council with everything she knew.

"Yes, it is."

"I've already named Enkara as my intended betrothed."

"Yes, but the ceremonies have not yet been performed. There is still time to change your mind."

"People will grow suspicious if I suddenly just change my mind."

"Then let the rumors that Enkara doesn't love you in return flourish. That won't be hard for the court to believe. We've seen how she does her best to avoid your amorous attentions. It won't be difficult to make it believable."

"Enkara loves me!" Kuwari's nostrils flared with rage, and for the first time in years, he felt his gryphon stirring below his skin without him calling on it to shapeshift.

Nakurtum just shook her head at him. "Enkara serves you. I don't doubt that she loves you as well, but she serves you first."

A cold pit opened in Kuwari's stomach. *Nakurtum will do anything to get what she wants, remember that,* he reminded himself.

"I'm only asking you to postpone your official betrothal and allow my daughter closer. Over time, others will see what you want them to see, and they won't get suspicious when you name Kullaa as your betrothed and later consort."

"I'll think about your offer." *But only because I need time to figure out how to neutralize you.*

"I look forward to your decision."

He turned and walked away. Outwardly, he was cold and emotionless. Inwardly, he was seething with rage and the need to hunt and kill.

CHAPTER TWENTY-SIX

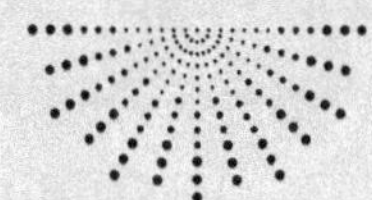

Enkara sat stiffly next to Kuwari, scanning the faces of the nobles sharing the table with the royal party. This dinner welcoming him to Nippur was no different than any other of the hundred such festivals held in honor of various religious rites. There was no reason to feel uneasy.

And yet she did.

She slid her hands up her robe's sleeves and wrapped her fingers around the hilts of the daggers Kuwari had gifted to her. No one else at the table noticed her small move, but the Shadows standing behind her did. The softest snick of sound marked when they drew their weapons and approached the high table.

Like a hazy gray fog at the peripheral of her vision, she sensed another power creeping into the room. It was like no threat she'd ever encountered before. While she might not be able to label it, she knew it *was* a threat. Enkara leaned close and whispered in Kuwari's ear. "I sense something. Have you had any visions that you haven't told me about?"

Kuwari arched his eyebrow. "No, but I take it this dreary dinner is about to change into something more interesting?"

King Ditanu leaned around Kuwari to meet Enkara's eyes. "From what direction is the danger coming?"

On his other side, Queen Iltani rose from her seat and stood with her hand resting on the hilt of her goddess-gifted crystalline sword of power. "It's coming from everywhere."

The Shadows along the walls converged on the high table, scanning the crowd around them as they moved.

"Clear the room," Iltani shouted suddenly.

Guards wearing the colors of Nippur's garrison jumped to obey the queen's command, but they were too late.

On the heels of the Queen's warning, a nobleman jumped up and managed to disarm a garrison guard in a blur of motion. Before anyone could stop him, he was rushing toward the royal family.

Some of the dining nobles screamed in fear while others stood as if to face the danger head-on. Neither activity was helpful. But Enkara didn't have time to worry; she was too busy leaping over the table to meet the oncoming threat.

Queen Iltani vaulted over the table a moment later. Together they faced the oncoming assassin only to realize a second assailant was running just steps behind the first. Enkara darted down the dais stairs to meet the first as Iltani engaged the second. All around them Shadows leaped forward forming two defensive lines between the high table and the enemy.

With the first strike of her sword against her opponent's,

Enkara assessed his skill level. He was good. Their blades blurred and danced, catching the light and flashing it back in strange glints. Though Enkara was more interested in her opponent's footwork than the pretty play of his blade.

Ah. There was the opening she'd been waiting for. He struck at her again. Shifting her weight, she dropped back on her left foot and then twisting to the side, her sword streaking toward the enemy. Surprise showed on his face the moment her sword buried its blade in his gut. Shoving him off, she whirled around to see Iltani had dispatched her opponent and was moving to the next.

She only had a moment to seek out Kuwari. He was still at the high table. Then her next opponent was upon her, and she met the descending blade that was meant to take her head. Deflecting the strike, she slammed her knee up into his groin and a dagger up under his chin.

A moment later, she ripped her dagger free and scanned the chaos. More Shadows and city guards rushed into the hall while panicked diners fled. Which was the natural order of things as far as Enkara was concerned. Anyone running toward the royal family who wasn't a Shadow was someone in need of killing.

A quick count showed thirteen revelers moving toward the high table. Goddess. Sixteen assassins in total. There hadn't been such a brazen attack since Kuwari was a cub.

As she moved to face the nearest of the assassins, she watched in horror as several Shadows fell before one particular adversary. This assassin didn't look like much. A man of medium height, build, and age. But the way he cut down fully trained Shadows was anything but ordinary.

Clearly, the hostiles had different levels of training. Hired mercenaries versus well-trained assassins? Enkara didn't have time to reason it out though. They were all just threats needing to be neutralized.

Queen Iltani intercepted the man Enkara had picked out as her next kill, so she glanced over her shoulder to make sure no enemy with equal skill was currently cutting their way toward the King or his family.

Ditanu and Burrukan were now in front of the table, shielding the younglings. Kuwari was absent. Cursing, Enkara swung around, seeking Kuwari, guided by her magic. She found him herding Lady Kullaa and Councilor Nakurtum toward the high table. Once all three were safe behind a line of Shadows, Enkara breathed a sigh of relief.

It didn't last long. Leaving the two women, he leaped down the stairs and halted at her side, his own sword smeared with blood.

"What do you think you're doing?" she shouted at him as she snatched up a second sword from the hand of a fallen Shadow. She didn't have time to hear Kuwari's answer. Leaping forward, she engaged three assassins who had gotten past the first line of Shadows.

Enkara met her new opponents, a man and two women, in a clash of steel on steel. She pivoted, cut, slashed and danced out of danger, all the time calmly keeping them all too busy to break away and engage Kuwari.

She landed a glancing blow to the thigh of the taller of the two female assassins. Long skirts hid how deep the wound went. It slowed the assassin, which was all Enkara needed. With a meaty sound and the crack and snap of bone, her sword thrust deep into the woman's ribcage.

Spinning away from the body, she parried her two remaining opponents.

Kuwari darted forward and thrust his sword into the other woman's gut. He flashed a grin at Enkara. "You were having all the fun. I felt left out."

The remaining assassin appeared unfazed by the death of his two cohorts and continued his attack. She and Kuwari worked like a well-oiled unit, and together they pushed back the third assassin.

"I really don't like assassins," Kuwari stated calmly a moment before the point of his sword erupted through the front of their opponent's chest.

"I had him," Enkara grumbled as she sidestepped and put her back to his.

"Learn to share." But the humor was missing from his voice. He saw the same thing as her. Dead Shadows.

The remaining assassins were engaged now. Two more were already dead at Queen Iltani's feet while Burrukan was finishing off his own opponent. A soundless warning urged Enkara into motion before she fully understood the danger.

All the remaining assassins broke away from their opponents and charged the line of Shadows protecting Kuwari's siblings. The two groups collided in the thunderous clash of steel, flashing blades and swiftly moving bodies. The Shadows held fast, giving her and Kuwari time to reach the battle before the last defensive line was broken.

She outpaced Kuwari as she bolted up the dais stairs at a diagonal, jumping fallen chairs, dishes, and injured and dying Shadows. There was nothing she could do for them except avenge their deaths. Burrukan and Iltani were sprinting toward her from the opposite direction. King Ditanu was positioned in the center of the defensive line, helping hold back the determined assassins.

Behind them, Regent Ahassunu stood with a sword in each hand. The twins, more skilled with the sword than their other brothers and sisters, flanked Ahassunu and together formed the final defensive line around the unarmed siblings.

Enkara roared in rage and slashed at the backs of the assassins. Burrukan and Iltani joined her moments later. Even outnumbered, the enemy put up a good fight, though no more Shadows fell to their blades.

"I want one of them alive for questioning!" Burrukan bellowed.

Carrying out his order proved difficult. Each time they managed to nearly disarm one of their foes, the enemy turned their daggers on themselves.

Shouting out a surprised curse, she watched helplessly as one of the assassins directly in front of her, reversed his hold on his sword and drove it into his own gut. As she kicked over the body slumped against her legs, she realized Kuwari wasn't at her side.

A quick glance around showed the room had emptied of both nobles and other citizens of Nippur. But there was one fight still going on.

Kuwari was facing off against a familiar assassin—the man of medium height and build and deadly sword skills. She'd thought Queen Iltani had finished him off, but apparently not.

Presently he was circling Kuwari, trying to find a way inside his defenses. But Burrukan had trained the prince, and he was holding his own, his sword a blur against his opponent's blade. Though, the assassin was skilled, matching Kuwari strike for strike. It wasn't until she ran closer that she heard the assassin speaking with her prince.

"It's good to cross swords with you again. It's been too long. You're rusty. Practice more or some assassin is going to send your soul spinning off into the next life." The male said with a grin of genuine warmth.

That's when Enkara's blood ran cold. This opponent was only toying with the prince.

Kuwari didn't rise to his opponent's verbal baiting though.

"Earlier, when you were protecting the two women, you should have let one of my brethren slip past your guard. We would have rid you of a couple thorns in your side."

"I think not," Kuwari's sword met the other male's in a shower of sparks, "Anunnaki."

"Ah, you know what I am." The anunnaki's sword struck Kuwari's and the prince nearly lost his grip, but Enkara stepped into the fight, her blade dancing with the anunnaki's sword.

"Ah, Blade. We meet again. As I said to Kuwari, you should let me kill the other girl. It will save you much trouble shortly."

Enkara laughed. "I think I'll skip taking advice from one of my sworn enemies."

"So misguided. I am not an enemy. Not to you or your prince."

"Don't think we need friends like you," Kuwari said as he lashed out at the anunnaki.

The anunnaki parried both hers and Kuwari's strikes, but her Blade's magic told her this creature was tiring and had already expended a great deal of power to take a host and hide from the Lamassu.

She and Kuwari renewed their assault upon the anunnaki.

"Ah. I see I'm out of time. Your Shadows and the other Blade just defeated the last of my brethren. My apologies. I must bow out of this fight now." In one swift motion, he drew a throwing knife and tossed it at the prince. Kuwari didn't deflect it in time, and it sliced a line high up on his thigh. Grunting in pain, he stumbled back but kept his sword at the ready.

"Didn't see that coming, did you, old friend?"

Shouting, Enkara lunged forward as Ishtar's fiery power boiled up from inside her. With a swift thrust, she impaled the anunnaki on her now flaming blade. The magic roared higher, and the host body burned to ash in heartbeats.

Even over the heat of Ishtar's magic, Enkara felt the anunnaki's cold power, a crisp chill in the center of the inferno. As it brushed past her, she swore she heard the anunnaki's laughter before he vanished, returning to the underworld, a dark soul in his grasp.

Shaking in reaction, Enkara could only stand there and watch the cloud of ash disperse as the fiery power vanished as quickly as the anunnaki. Gathering her thoughts, she turned to Kuwari.

Looking him over for other injuries, the only one she

spotted was the slice where the anunnaki's blade had grazed his thigh.

"You need to have that looked at," Enkara said as she set aside the sword she'd taken from the fallen Shadow. She wrapped her free arm around his waist, urging him to take some weight off his injured leg.

"I'm fine. It's just a minor wound. A healer will make short work of it. I want to see my family and then later you and I are going to discuss what we just heard."

"Fine. Healer first. It looks like your family made it through the battle unscathed. You're the only idiot who leaped past the defensive line and into the thick of battle." Enkara helped him limp toward where King Ditanu and the rest of Kuwari's siblings were gathered.

Her body was still primed for a fight, and even as she supported Kuwari, she scanned the area for any sign of the next attack.

"That was an anunnaki," Kuwari's lips brushed her ear as he spoke in a whisper. "The same one in my visions. Worse, he still seems to think he knows me."

Enkara frowned in thought. "This discussion needs to wait until we've alone."

"That's..." Kuwari stumbled. "I feel strange."

Sweat was beading on his skin where there had been only a slight sheen of moisture before. Even though her magic wasn't warning her of danger to Kuwari's life, it was clear he was in distress.

"The blade of the throwing knife. Poison!" Enkara shouted as she met his unfocused eyes. "Kuwari. Talk to me. Don't close your eyes."

She tightened her grip when he started to slump forward. "Help! Kuwari has been poisoned!"

Her shouts for help had others running toward her, but before even the first reached her, Kuwari slumped to the ground in the boneless manner of the dead.

Enkara's shouts for help changed to panicked screams for a healer. Then looking down at Kuwari's still form, she called on the cold power that lived within. It eagerly answered her call. She did not think or hesitate, begging Ereshkigal not to take Kuwari's soul to the underworld.

CHAPTER TWENTY-SEVEN

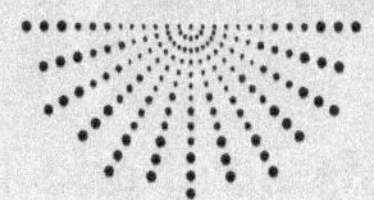

Drums pounded in his head and Kuwari wondered what he'd drank the night before and how much, so he wouldn't do it again. Strange, he didn't remember drinking, and since he preferred to remain alert for any and all chances to seduce Enkara, he couldn't dredge up a good reason why he'd overindulged.

Someone shifted positions next to him and he only then discovered Enkara was curled up next to him.

"Thank the Goddess you're awake."

He blinked open heavy-lidded eyes and slowly Enkara's face came into focus. The strange blurriness vanished after a couple more rapid blinks.

"What?" Flashes of memory returned even as he asked.

There had been an assassination attempt. Sword fights. Screaming and rushing people.

Hmm. Enkara was a warm weight pressed against the length of his body. So nice.

"Kuwari, can you talk?" Enkara's worried voice roused him enough that he grinned up at her foolishly. "Of course, anything for you."

"Do you remember what happened?"

She was too serious. He didn't like it. His mind and body were turning to less serious things.

"Kuwari?" Enkara leaned down until they were nearly nose to nose.

Grinning, he lifted his head and kissed her on the tip of her nose.

Enkara spoiled his fun by leaning back. "Priestess?"

At Enkara's call, Kuwari's great-aunt Kammani appeared in his field of vision. Damn. He'd much prefer to be alone with Enkara right now.

Maybe he could talk her into sending Kammani and the guards away.

"I know what you're thinking. Don't bother," Enkara snapped at him. "You're too weak from the poison."

"Poison? I feel fine."

"Well, you're not. At least you weren't when you first collapsed."

"Now that I think about it, there is something that would make me feel good." His suggestion was accompanied with a little wiggle of his fingers along her side.

"You said he'd be fine," Enkara's voice came out more accusation than statement. "What's wrong with him?"

"Nothing. I feel fine." It wasn't until both females turned to study him that he realized Enkara had been addressing Kammani.

"As I said earlier, the poison wasn't designed to kill. It was intended to incapacitate its victim, likely so the Prince could be more easily stolen away. This euphoria he's experiencing must be a side effect," Kammani said.

But it didn't look like the priestess's words reassured Enkara.

Then he remembered more about the attack. Some of the assassins had been anunnaki.

He needed to think, but his mind swung in a hundred different directions.

"Your parents are waiting in the outer chambers. I'll have one of the Shadows notify them that you're awake."

It took longer than it should for him to realize it was Kammani and not Enkara speaking to him.

As promised, his parents rushed into the room and were soon lavishing him with hugs and promises that they would hunt down those responsible for this latest atrocity. His father assured him none of their family had been hurt, but fourteen Shadows had been killed.

Fourteen deaths. He knew each and every one of them. Shadows were masters of their weapons. The number of deaths was shocking. He was still swallowing that bit of news when his father informed him that shortly after he'd lost consciousness, three lamassu had thundered into the hall and revealed the nature of the enemy.

Now his parents were aware something very serious was afoot if an anunnaki was involved. Instinctively, he wanted to guard his tongue, fearing even a hint of a half lie would have Iltani digging for the truth.

"Kuwari, they need to know," Enkara whispered along the link.

She was correct. Now that his sisters and brothers and other innocent lives were in peril, he needed to tell the truth. Or at least enough that his parents knew the true depth of danger.

Drawing in a deep breath, he told of his visions, how he'd first seen snippets but didn't understand their meaning. It wasn't until recently that everything came into focus. He told of how Ereshkigal wished to steal Enkara away from Ishtar and claim him in some perversion of the Sacred Marriage and how only Ishtar's protection had prevented that so far.

His parents were in an uproar for most of the afternoon. Angry at him for not speaking of what he knew earlier. Angry at Enkara for following his lead. Angry at the gods.

Eventually, his parents left him to rest and recover from the poison while they discussed this new danger in more detail. Once his parents were gone, he turned his thoughts toward Enkara, apologizing for the chastising she'd received for following his wishes.

Enkara dropped down onto his bed and then drew her legs up to sit cross-legged beside him.

"I knew what I was getting into when you asked for my silence. Besides, it's not like this is the first time you've gotten me in trouble." Enkara bumped her shoulder against his and Kuwari relaxed.

"Sleep now," he urged, sensing her exhaustion through the link they shared. He pulled her to his side. "I'm safe. We're surrounded by Shadows and defensive magic. I even saw a lamassu patrolling by the windows. There's probably more in the gardens. We're as safe now as we're ever likely to be."

He didn't think his reassurance would be enough but eventually, Enkara's eyelids drooped, and she slumped against his side, her breathing deepening in sleep.

CHAPTER TWENTY-EIGHT

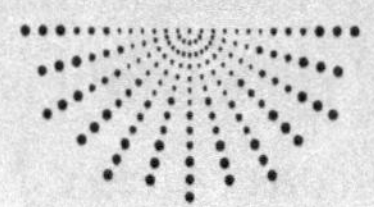

The day after the assassination attempt Kuwari and his siblings were bundled up and packed on the backs of Lamassu. The fierce and watchful behemoths were the only deterrent against another attack by an anunnaki.

King Ditanu wasn't taking any chances and wanted everyone back on Nineveh where they'd be safer with its greater layers of defensives spells. Kuwari had scowled and complained vocally, but for once he failed to sway his parents. Enkara was glad he lost that argument.

The flight was swift and brutal. From her seat behind Kuwari, she watched with tearing eyes as their Lamassu's vast wings ate up great distances with each flap. Below, the ocean sped by as wind tore at her hair, making speech almost impossible. Well, verbal speech.

Kuwari continued grumbling about being well enough to fly in gryphon form.

"No, you're not. Stop whining," Enkara mentally blasted

along their mental link. Ahead of her, Kuwari flinched, no doubt his 'mental' ears were ringing.

"You're correct," Kuwari countered, surprising her. *"It's not the lamassu that's bothering me. There's another problem that presented itself just before the start of the festivities yesterday."*

"What?! Why didn't you tell me?" Enkara fought the urge to grab his shoulders and give him a shake.

"I didn't have time and it certainly isn't something I'd consider life or death. More of an inconvenience I just haven't found a solution for yet."

Kuwari told her what Councilor Nakurtum had learned about her heritage and the ultimatum she'd issued.

"Ultimatum? It's blackmail and treason against the royal family! I will kill her," Enkara said in earnest.

"You won't." Kuwari's voice was calm. *"For now, I'll allow the Councilor to believe I'm willing to go along with her plan."*

"This is my fault."

Kuwari laughed. *"Hardly. We don't get to choose the family we're born into. It's not your fault that fate dropped your soul into a nest of treasonous snakes. Your heritage won't remain hidden forever. If not Nakurtum, someone else would have eventually unearthed the information."*

"I hate that she's using this against you."

"Can't say I'm happy about it either."

"And she's willing to use her own daughter horribly." Enkara scowled at his back. *"Are you sure I can't just kill Nakurtum?"*

"No killing." Kuwari twisted around to grin at her. *"My beautiful Blade is developing a bloodthirsty streak."*

"It's not bloodthirsty when it's a necessary duty." She

narrowed her eyes at him. *"You haven't told your parents yet, have you?"*

"No. They have enough to concern themselves with. This problem with Nakurtum is just an annoyance, not a deadly threat. If I can't handle one unruly councilor, then I'm not fit to rule one of the city-states, let alone all of New Sumer."

"Very well." But if Kuwari couldn't find a way to neutralize Nakurtum, she'd have a very firm word with the councilor, reminding her that a Blade's duty was to protect the crown from all threats. That included the Council.

CHAPTER TWENTY-NINE

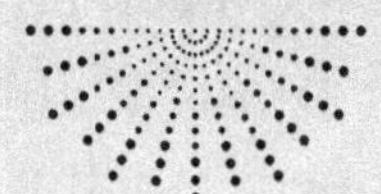

In the days following their arrival back on
Nineveh, routine slowly returned to the palace.
There were no more mysterious visitations by anunnaki,
assassination attempts, or councilors trying their hand at
blackmail. Kuwari hadn't had any visions either. Enkara was
grateful for the reprieve even if she was sure it was only
temporary.

The healers were still fussing over Kuwari, much to his
displeasure, but they assured his family he was healthy.
Though, they still wanted him to stay in bed for another day
to be certain there were no symptoms still to manifest from
the poison.

Even though everything seemed to be peaceful, Enkara
hadn't wanted to leave Kuwari's side for a moment. But
Burrukan and Iltani had insisted that she continue her training, saying it was now even more critical that she master all

forms of weapons and battle tactics. She couldn't disagree with that logic.

Shortly after noon both her instructors freed her from the morning-long training session since they had a council meeting to attend. Their slumped shoulders had said they would have much rather stayed and continue her lessons.

As Enkara made her way back to Kuwari's chambers, she hoped the healers' duties would pull them away elsewhere to give her some time alone with him. They still needed to concoct a plan to deal with Nakurtum.

She nodded to the guards outside Kuwari's suite and then proceeded within. Voices drifted from somewhere deeper in the chamber and Enkara followed the sound of conversation.

"What? Can't you smuggle me something more palatable than that weak broth the healer's keep shoving at me?" Kuwari's voice held more humorous affection than annoyance.

"If I tried to smuggle food, the Shadows would grow suspicious."

The feminine voice was familiar. Enkara halted outside Kuwari's bedchamber to observe. Lady Kullaa was perched in a chair with a scroll unrolled in her lap trying not to laugh, while Kuwari sat in his bed glowering down at the bowl of broth in his hands.

"One roll, that's all I asked for."

Lady Kullaa snorted. "And have them think I have nefarious plans in mind? No, thank you."

Kuwari grunted and sniffed at his broth. "The only nefarious plans are the ones your mother has set in motion."

Kullaa glanced down at her scroll, a stricken look on her

face. "I am so sorry about that. I can't express how much I wished I'd kept what I'd learned to myself. But I foolishly thought I could challenge my mother into allowing me to court...someone else."

"Oh, stop beating yourself up over that. Like I said earlier, even my father has lost a few rounds in the council chambers to Nakurtum."

"I should have found a way to get a warning to you before she spirited me away to Nippur."

"Things don't always happen as they should or how we'd wish. That's life."

Kullaa murmured her agreement and then returned to reading the scroll out loud. It was details taken from Nippur's ledgers. Not exactly a romantic ballot, but Enkara couldn't help but read more into it.

Kuwari and Kullaa would make a beautiful pair. If life had taken a different path and if Ishtar, or perhaps it was Ereshkigal, hadn't chosen Enkara as her Blade, would she ever have met the prince? Likely not. Or, at least, she wouldn't have known him as she did now—as a friend and the man she loved.

He would still be the Crown Prince of New Sumer, but she would be just another noble, one working to increase her house and personal status. Enkara could see how if she and Kuwari had never met, Lady Kullaa might have ended up mated to the prince.

The thought made Enkara infinitely sad. And yet it would be a happier outcome than if the Queen of the Underworld managed to spirit Kuwari off to her realm.

Enkara had no plans to become a tool for Ereshkigal, but

she wasn't so foolish to think it couldn't happen. Perhaps Nakurtum had the right of it all along.

Enkara took a step back, retreating the way she'd come.

"I know you're there," Kuwari called from his bed. "Don't you dare go sneaking away again. I've been waiting half the day to see you. Enkara!"

Groaning under her breath, she turned on her heels and crossed into Kuwari's sleeping chamber. Sometimes she forgot the deep soul tie that linked them flowed in both directions. He always knew where she was.

It was somewhat of a hindrance in this case.

"Ah. There is my betrothed," Kuwari said with a grin and then rolled his eyes toward Lady Kullaa. "She's been avoiding me since yesterday."

"I haven't been avoiding you." Enkara snorted and arched her brow. "Queen Iltani and Burrukan have been keeping me busy. They only now released me from weapons practice."

"What about this morning?"

He just wasn't letting it go. Well, maybe that shouldn't have been unexpected. She had left before he'd awoken this morning.

"Your father was questioning Queen Iltani and me earlier this morning. He wanted to go over every detail about the attack again. He was concerned that the Shadows and the lamassu didn't sense them until the attack was underway. He assumed it was a spell anchored to a medallion like what the enemy has used in the past."

Kuwari grunted in answer. Whether he was unhappy with her excuse or his broth, she wasn't sure.

"The Shadows looked over the bodies carefully. No medallions were found. High Priestess Kammani was there as well. She wasn't able to discern how the assassins hid their intent."

"That's easy to figure out." Kuwari smiled, though it was more a flash of white wolfish teeth against his brown skin than an expression of humor. "Certain anunnaki are more powerful than others. The seven judges of the underworld can hide their presence from even a lamassu for a short time if they are careful not to call on too much power while they are in the mortal world."

"How do you know that?"

Kuwari looked momentarily puzzled. "I must have read in somewhere in my studies. My tutors made me learn everything. I'm sure I've forgotten more than I remember."

Enkara frowned. "The ancient texts mention the seven judges of the underworld, but I don't remember reading anything about anunnaki with special powers."

"Perhaps we should travel to Uruk and see if the scrolls might give us other more useful clues," Kuwari suggested, a new purposeful look entering his eyes. "Besides, I still wanted to research Asharru and Tirigan more, to look for similarities with our…problem."

"Don't make any travel plans. You'll be lucky if your father lets us leave Nineveh anytime in the next hundred years."

Kuwari's happy look crumpled.

Lady Kullaa rolled up the scroll she'd been reading. "I'll leave you two to plan another escape, but I don't want to know anything about it. King Ditanu must already be greatly displeased with me for the role I played in my mother's plans."

"An escape! What a wonderful idea." Kuwari laughed, ignoring Kullaa's words.

Enkara groaned and then narrowed her eyes at Kuwari. *"Lady Kullaa thinks you've told your parents about what Nakurtum plans."*

"I saw no reason to let Lady Kullaa worry more than she already is. Thinking my parents are aware of the situation and working to counteract her mother's plans gives her comfort."

This once, she couldn't fault him for his little white lie. Lady Kullaa's only sin was naiveté. It wasn't her fault she had Nakurtum for a mother.

Remembering that Kullaa wasn't aware of their unspoken conversation, Enkara cleared her throat, folding her arms across her chest, and glowered at him. "There will be no escape attempts on my watch. And it's always my watch."

"See!" Kuwari crowed as he pointed at Enkara. "I can always get a rise out of her. She's just so much fun. I can't help myself."

Lady Kullaa politely agreed, and then after bobbing a curtsy in both their directions, retreated from the room.

"I didn't mean to chase away the poor woman," Enkara admitted a moment later.

"Kullaa already imparted the most important information when she first came. Apparently, the council convened earlier this morning while my parents were still hearing reports from Kammani and the Shadows. They are demanding that when my father and Iltani complete the Sacred Marriage, they want me and my younger siblings to stay here in Nineveh, citing that it's much more secure than Uruk. My father is likely going to agree."

"I think that's the wisest thing I've ever heard them utter."

He was in a malleable mood if he was willing to concede to the council's wishes so readily. Perhaps now was a good time to mention what she'd been stewing about since learning Nakurtum had discovered her true heritage.

"As much as I don't like Nakurtum's heavy-handedness, perhaps she is on to something. You and Lady Kullaa are well matched." Enkara rushed out the last before Kuwari could interrupt. "Perhaps we shouldn't be so hasty to go through with the formal betrothal rites."

She half expected an explosive verbal debate. Instead, he speared her with a calm, thoughtful look. After a few heart-beats of just staring, he huffed and tossed back the blankets to stand. It took him a moment to gain his balance, and Enkara stepped closer in case he needed her aid.

He took advantage and captured her arms. Leaning forward, he pressed their foreheads together and closed his eyes, drawing in slow, deep breaths. After a moment he opened his eyes and leaned back enough to look at her.

"You are the only woman I will ever love. You are my world. I would do anything for you. Give up my title. Surrender to Ereshkigal. Anything required to stay with you." The corner of his lip twitched. "Even though you are the densest woman in the land, you've captured my heart completely. I'll remind you of that fact as often as needed."

Great Ishtar, no. Enkara grabbed him by the shoulders and gave him one quick shake as if that would rattle some sense into him. "You can't mean that, not about Ereshkigal. Never—"

He cut her off. "I will have you at my side, in my bed, sharing my life. If not here in the mortal world, then in the underworld. I will not be separated from you."

Goddess save young fools!

She shoved him backward until he bumped into his bed and sat heavily. "I haven't survived all these years, enduring years of brutal training just so the Queen of the Underworld can win. Don't ever say such a thing again."

"I won't if you'll stop acting so foolishly. We haven't yet mated physically, but our hearts and souls already are. We are a pair. Tell me we aren't. Go on. Say it and see if your gift tells you it's a lie."

He fell silent and Enkara didn't speak. To deny his words would be a falsehood and she'd promised him she'd never lie. Unwilling to talk, she just stared at him in silence until Kuwari finally reached up and pulled her down on the bed next to him. He cupped her cheek and pressed a gentle kiss to her lips.

His lips were warm against hers, firm yet not dominating as he explored. It was shockingly pleasant.

He broke the kiss after a time. "You can't deny my words, can you?"

"No." Enkara's lips twisted in humor. "When have I ever been able to deny you anything?"

Kuwari snorted. "You've been doing a fine job every night since your return."

"And I'll continue to do a good job until you are well recovered. Perhaps we can discuss a compromise after that." She gave him a good-natured smack on his shoulder. "Now get some rest before the healers return."

His delighted laughter could probably be heard in the gardens.

CHAPTER THIRTY

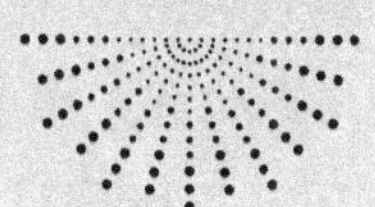

Kuwari leaned back in his chair and stretched his legs. Honestly, the council chambers needed more comfortable seating considering how long some of the councilors could tolerate their own voices. The meeting finally concluded, and now he needed to discuss plans for his and Enkara's next Blooding Ceremony with his great-aunt.

It had been eight days since the attack on Nippur. He was fully recovered and the sooner they could complete the next phase of the ceremony, the more at ease he'd feel.

Unfortunately, High Priestess Kammani was presently deep in discussion with Councilor Nakurtum about the upcoming Sacred Marriage, which would likely take precedence over a simple Blooding Ceremony, but if he turned his full persuasive charms upon his great-aunt, he might convince her of the importance and sway her into allowing a quick rite in the next day or two.

It would have to be soon, though, since it was only eleven days to the Spring Rites which culminated with the Sacred Marriage between Ishtar and Tammuz. All other rites were forbidden for a moon cycle afterward so they wouldn't interfere with Tammuz's great blessing during the planting season.

Final preparations were already being made, but this year, he and his siblings weren't going to be part of any of it. Unfortunately, that meant he hadn't had a reason to speak with High Priestess Kammani in the last few days.

Hence why he was still sitting in the most uncomfortable of chairs even after the meeting had officially ended.

A vision hinting at his chances of swaying Kammani would have been nice, but he'd only had one vision since the attack. He couldn't really complain. The vision had been an interesting one showing a possible resolution to his Enkara, Nakurtum, Lady Kullaa problem.

He hadn't yet told Enkara because she would act in defense of him and that might change the outcome. Besides, visions didn't always come to pass, or sometimes he misinterpreted them.

In this instance, it would be better to wait and see and hope.

Kuwari rolled his shoulders and rubbed the back of his neck. He used the motion to cast a glance behind him to where Enkara was standing along the wall with the other Shadows. She'd refused to sit at the council table even though it was her right now that she was his future betrothed.

She didn't acknowledge his look, outwardly, but he

sensed her mind brushing along his, her emotions flowing into him as she searched for what he was planning.

"I assure you," he said in their silent way, *"I have nothing wicked planned."*

She rolled her eyes at him before returning to scanning the room.

Eventually, Councilor Nakurtum and his great-aunt finished their discussion, and the priestess exited through the side door. Ha. She wasn't escaping him that easily.

He stood to follow Kammani, but Nakurtum laid her hand on his arm, forestalling him.

"You've been avoiding me." Her words held a sharp, displeased edge. "I need an answer about how you'd like me to handle the unfortunate lineage of your beloved. If you don't agree by the next council meeting, I shall reveal what I know. I am not bluffing."

"I have discussed it with Enkara." He responded with his best 'you're boring me' tone. "You may have noticed she wasn't sitting with me during Council."

Nakurtum's eyebrow arched. "You agree with my plan?"

"Yes."

"When can I expect the new…situation…to be made apparent to the citizens of New Sumer?"

Kuwari pretended to think about it for some moments. "It will be better if Enkara and I seem to rethink our relationship. Then I can make the announcement once the Spring Rites and the planting moon cycle has completed."

"That is longer than I'd hoped to wait."

Kuwari snorted. "And risk angering High Priestess Kammani? She's more fearsome than you."

Skepticism entered her expression. "I don't believe you. You have something else planned."

"For once I don't," Kuwari laughed. *At least it's no plan of my making.* "Accept my terms or not. It's up to you. But remember, I'm now a ruling prince. Nippur is mine to oversee, if you annoy me more than you already have, I'll see you removed from office and will install a new governor."

There was a long pause and a hardness about her gaze as she stared him down, but at last she nodded. "I find your terms acceptable."

"I thought you might," Kuwari said smoothly. "However, there is something I must discuss with my aunt. Good day, Councilor."

Without a backward glance, he turned and went in pursuit of Kammani.

KUWARI STOMPED toward the practice ring and brooded sourly.

"Pouting will give you wrinkles," Enkara said as she walked next to him.

"I'm not pouting."

Enkara grunted. Another snort of humor came from somewhere behind. Kuwari turned and glowered at Uselli, but the Shadow's expression had already returned to its usual placid appearance.

"I am not pouting!"

Enkara made a noncommittal noise in the back of her throat, drawing his attention back to her.

He glowered at Enkara. "You realize Kammani's denial affects you too, right?"

"We only have to wait a little over a moon's cycle and then she'll perform the ritual and appease all the gods."

He didn't want to wait for over a moon's cycle to complete the next Blooding Ceremony, but Kammani had been adamant. He'd still have been tempted to go behind his great-aunt's back, if there hadn't been the Nakurtum situation pending.

But if he'd pinned down the timing of what he'd seen in a vision, the problem would come to a resolution in eleven days, when most of the court was attending the Sacred Marriage rites.

"What are you smiling about," Enkara asked.

Kuwari's grin grew broader. "The future."

She groaned.

CHAPTER THIRTY-ONE

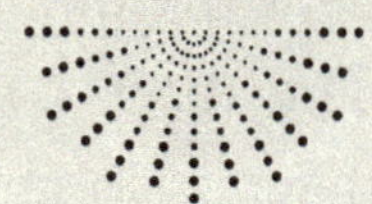

The day of the Sacred Marriage had dawned with the usual flurry of activity such vital rites inspired. After a hasty goodbye, the royals and most of the court had begun their flight to Uruk, leaving Kuwari and his younger siblings in the capable hands of Shadow Uselli and three council members. Not that Kuwari thought he needed help keeping his siblings in line, but it would free him up to keep a watchful eye on Nakurtum, one of the three councilors left behind.

Burrukan was anything but happy about separating the King from his children and dividing the Shadows, but his dark scowl wasn't enough to sway the Council or the King. Kuwari's father had held firm. Two-thirds of the Shadows had remained.

But Kuwari wasn't worried. His visions hadn't shown any danger coming for his family. He'd had to reassure Enkara of that fact more than once. Still, she remained more alert than usual. It likely had something to do with the temporarily abandoned city.

Every year, he was always surprised anew at how empty the palace and city looked with most of the inhabitants having flocked to Uruk for the ritual. The silence was eerie, but soon his siblings had dragged Enkara and him to the great hall where they spent the day with their Shadow and councilor nursemaids. The three councilors were there to ensure Kuwari's younger siblings were chaperoned adequately during their own smaller festival in honor of planting time.

Now all he had to do was wait a little longer for when his visions said the real entertainment would begin. Kuwari sipped his wine to hide his smirk.

"You're up to something," Enkara hissed at him from the corner of her mouth."

"I am," he agreed. "But it's nothing reprehensible, I promise."

She rumbled something about cunning rebel princes and then returned to her favorite position by the wall directly behind him. As usual, she'd refused to sit beside him, saying she needed to stay on guard since the Shadows were depleted until the royal party returned later tomorrow.

Further down the high table, a minor altercation drew his attention.

"Not too much to drink," Lady Kullaa warned Kuwari's twin brothers. Etum and Eluti looked rebellious, but a firm glower from him soon had them sullenly agreeing with Kullaa's suggestion.

The last thing he needed was for Burrukan to curtail his

little remaining freedom with more training sessions as punishment for allowing his siblings to run wild.

So, there was music, dance, food, and only enough wine to pacify his sixteen-year-old siblings without earning Kuwari extra early morning sessions in the practice ring. Erra and Arwia were easier to please. A game or two was all it took to make them go to bed happy.

Councilor Nakurtum and the other two councilors were never far, but he ignored them and simply enjoyed his time with Enkara and his siblings. By the end of the evening, he was even feeling generous enough to pacify Nakurtum by dancing with Lady Kullaa. Afterward, he dragged Enkara and his siblings onto the floor for more dancing.

Even Uselli was coaxed into joining the group with the siblings, a scowling Enkara, and a beaming Kullaa. Later he and Enkara returned to the high table for refreshments. After snatching up a plateful of his favorite sweetcakes, he popped a couple of the tiny honey-drenched seed patties in his mouth while he watched the small group still dancing. He noticed Lady Kullaa was swaying and twirling in time with the group, but her attention was all for Uselli.

Kuwari grinned and sipped his wine and ate another handful of the sweetcakes.

A long time later, when even the torches were burning down, Councilor Nakurtum appeared at his side. Behind her came servants bearing new pitchers of wine and more sweet treats. She gestured for a servant to refill his goblet.

Picking up his goblet, he smiled and thanked the servant and then pretended to sip at it. All the while he eyed

Nakurtum as she made her way down the table to refill Kullaa's goblet herself.

"*Oh, Nakurtum. Your plan is going to twist back on you and soundly bite you in the ass,*" Kuwari thought to himself as he watched the councilor walking back up the table toward his seat.

"Well, Crown Prince Kuwari, I must say this has been a bit of fun, but I do think it's time I see your younger siblings to bed." She bowed at the waist. "If you don't mind, I shall excuse myself to do just that."

"I'll stay up a bit longer and keep Kullaa and Enkara company." Kuwari smiled at her and then pretended to take another sip of his wine.

"Of course. Good evening, may you have good dreams." Councilor Nakurtum smiled at him and then turned to leave.

"She's up to something new." Enkara's voice held a hint of threat.

"When isn't she up to something?" Kuwari said innocently as he gathered up a few sweetcakes for later and placed them in a napkin, then tucked it into his robe.

"Never," Enkara said sourly, her expression turning nearly murderous now.

But before his beloved could storm off after her prey, Kuwari called over Uselli and Lady Kullaa.

"Lady Kullaa, I and my Shadow guard will leave you now. However, don't feel you need to retire yet. Councilors Pirhum and Ninsunu look to be in a debate that will surely go deep into the night. And the musicians and servants will be celebrating until dawn. I've instructed Uselli to remain with you as your chaperone."

She nodded politely. "Thank you, Prince Kuwari."

Rising, he prepared to leave. Enkara and several Shadows shifted closer to him, but his gaze was on Lady Kullaa. She didn't immediately return to the dance floor. Instead, she paused to drain her goblet in a few swallows.

As he walked from the hall, his conscience pricked at him, and he felt a small twinge of guilt. But he'd seen the outcome in a vision-dream and knew Kullaa would be well pleased. If he thought for a moment she would be unhappy, he would've intervened.

Outside in the hall, Enkara grabbed him and shoved him in the direction of the nearest seating alcove. When they were out of sight of any servant that might pass by, she leaned forward and then growled in his ear. "You! You're up to something. What game are you playing now?"

Goddess, she was beautiful when she was annoyed at him. She was so close he couldn't resist the opportunity and leaned forward until his lips brushed her ear. To prevent her from retreating, he cupped the back of her head with his hand.

She didn't struggle after the initial jolt of surprise at his unexpected touch. He trailed gentle kisses along her jaw until he made his way to her lips where he deepened the kiss.

To his delighted surprise, she melted against him and wrapped her arms around his waist. Eagerly he continued the kiss. It wasn't until her hands slid down and gave his backside a caressing squeeze that he grew suspicious.

Had Enkara drank the wine? No. He'd been watching for that. She never drank when on guard and she was never not on duty. Her caressing fingers stilled and then she gave him a savage twist and pinched. He broke the kiss with a startled yelp, pulling farther away.

"What was that for?" He asked as he rubbed his abused flesh.

"For your deception."

He shrugged. "Fine. I deserve that one. I have been keeping something from you, but if it makes you feel any better, I'll tell you about it later."

"Everything is always later with you," she grumbled.

He gave her his most innocent look. "You're the one who's making us wait. I'd be happy with *now* if you ever get tired of *later*."

Enkara snorted. "Do you stand in front of a mirror and practice that look?"

Before he could reply with a negative, she grabbed him by the shoulder and shoved him in the direction of his chambers. "Keep doing what you're doing, and you'll be waiting much longer. But who knows? If you're a good boy and go to bed when your elders say, perhaps tomorrow will bring better things."

It was Kuwari's turn to laugh.

Oh, my sweet Blade, you don't know how true your words are.

CHAPTER THIRTY-TWO

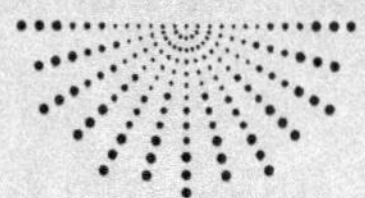

Distant pounding on the outer doors jolted Enkara out of sleep. She was already reaching for her clothing and weapons when a flurry of activity announced that several Shadows had entered the adjoining room. Enkara pulled on her shirt and practice leathers and had a dagger at the ready by the time she emerged into Kuwari's sleeping chamber.

Her eyebrow arched in surprise to see him already up and dressed like he was expecting this.

"Forgive me, my Prince, Blade Enkara. There is a situation that requires your attention," Shadow Kurumtum said as he straightened from a bow.

"Speak," Kuwari urged when Kurumtum hesitated too long.

Strangely, the older Shadow's gaze slid sideways to give Enkara a pitying look before returning to the prince. "Councilor Nakurtum requests that you come to Lady Kullaa's chambers. It seems she's entered her fertility cycle. The councilor is adamant she's responding to you."

"Lady Kullaa?" Enkara asked, her mind reeling from the information. Faced with this news, the sadness that engulfed her heart whenever her logical mind dwelled on how Kullaa would make Kuwari a good match reared to life far stronger than usual.

This time her logical mind was no comfort. But it didn't matter what she wanted if this was Ishtar's will.

Kuwari reached behind him and unerringly took her hand in his. Strangely he seemed unruffled by the news. Had he seen a vision of this moment? Was that what he'd wished to keep secret? If so, why was he so calm?

"We will come at once," Kuwari told Kurumtum and then began to walk, tugging Enkara along with him.

When gryphons entered their fertility cycle, either sex could be violent and territorial when ruled by instincts. While she didn't think Lady Kullaa would attempt to harm the prince, the danger was there if she'd shifted to gryphon form.

Enkara wasn't taking any chances. If need be, she and the other Shadows could run interference until the prince had time to shift to his own gryphon form. It wasn't until they were at Lady Kullaa's suites that Enkara realized she'd have to stay near during the mating to protect him from outside threats.

Her stomach plummeted. Kuwari must have sensed her hesitation for he gave her hand a squeeze as his mind touched hers.

"Beloved, I see now I should have shared what I have seen. I simply didn't want your reactions to change what might be the best outcome to all this. Lady Kullaa's fertility cycle is not natural. Council Nakurtum is behind it."

"Nakurtum? I'm going to kill her."

"Peace. Just allow events to unfold."

"No promises."

When they arrived, Uselli and five other Shadows were already outside the door leading to Lady Kullaa's chambers. Uselli informed Kuwari that Nakurtum was still inside with her daughter.

If Nakurtum was inside, it must mean Lady Kullaa was rational and in human form. If it had been otherwise, she would have run everyone out of her chambers since a female gryphon in the grip of her fertility cycle didn't tolerate anyone except the object of her desire.

That was a good sign. Rational was always beneficial.

"Shall we get this over with?" Kuwari asked Uselli.

The Shadow nodded but looked distressed. Enkara's one eyebrow arched as she remembered how much attention Lady Kullaa had been giving the Shadow earlier in the evening. She'd thought the lady might have feelings for the older male, but Enkara hadn't seen anything in Uselli's demeanor that suggested he returned the sentiment. Now she started to rethink that.

The Shadows were making ready to enter the chamber when the door banged open, and Councilor Nakurtum hastily exited a moment before a massive weight slammed into it. The door groaned under the impact but held.

Nakurtum looked up. Spotting Kuwari, a look of relief crossed her features.

"Ah. Thank the Goddess you're here. My daughter just shifted and is getting…agitated."

Kuwari snorted. "I don't doubt she is. Shall I go have a little chat with her?"

New suspicion bloomed in Nakurtum's eyes, but she didn't disagree with Kuwari. "Of course. How are you feeling yourself? I imagine you should be feeling some matching symptoms soon."

"I feel nothing yet, but it's early. And how can you be so certain I'm the match she's interested in?"

Nakurtum's lips compressed. "You're the only male she's been spending time with."

Kuwari laughed. "Half my Shadows are male in case you've never noticed. She could be responding to anyone of them."

"What? No, I'm certain it's you."

"I'll take Enkara and Uselli for protection and we'll go from there." Kuwari flashed his teeth at the councilor. "I think it's best if you stay here. Your daughter didn't seem very happy with you earlier."

"I think it's best—"

Kuwari turned to a nearby Shadow. "See that the councilor remains outside. I wouldn't want Lady Kullaa to have to live with the guilt of killing her own mother."

The Shadows moved to obey, and Kuwari pushed inside Lady Kullaa's chamber, forcing Enkara and a startled Uselli to quickly follow. Two steps in Kuwari raised his arm, holding her back while he faced a snarling gold and brown colored gryphon.

"Lady Kullaa, peace. I've brought the one you seek." Kuwari gave Uselli a shove toward the gryphon.

Kullaa's snarls halted, and she raised her head, sniffing deeply. A moment later she circled Uselli protectively and started purring.

"Shadow Uselli, unless I'm mistaken, you admire Lady Kullaa a great deal, and she admires you as well, even without the fertility drug her mother gave her." Kuwari tilted his head at the Shadow.

Uselli's expression showed shock for a few heartbeats, but it soon transformed into rage. "That devious harpy drugged her own daughter?"

"Yes. But as you can see, she miscalculated the outcome. I avoided the wine she'd tainted."

"You knew and did nothing to stop this?" Uselli's words held the snap of anger, but his expression softened when Kullaa bumped her head under his hand, looking for a scratch. He modulated his tone for his next statement. "I do not understand your reasoning, my prince. The Shadows would have acted to prevent this and Nakurtum would have been brought before her king and fellow councilors for punishment."

"Yes, but it isn't a crime punishable by death. Eventually, she'd be released back to Nippur where she would return to trying to find the best possible match for her daughter. If that happened, Lady Kullaa would miss out on getting to choose her own mate."

"How is this any better? She still doesn't get to choose."

"She's already chosen. You have been her choice since shortly after she arrived."

Uselli's stunned expression would have been entertaining under other circumstances, but Enkara understood his shock. She had been on the same end of some of Kuwari's elaborate plans a time or two herself.

"All you need to do is admit you share her feelings and I'll leave you two alone and ban Nakurtum from entering."

Uselli's internal battle was painful to see. Enkara wanted to pat him on the shoulder and tell him it was alright to reach for something he wanted if it was freely given.

"Lady Kullaa captured my heart shortly after I met her, but I'm old enough to be her father."

It was Enkara's turn to snort with laughter. "You're not yet even half a century old. You could easily live for two more. If I were Kullaa, I'd want you for however long I could have you."

"There," Kuwari said with a grin. "Don't argue with a woman's wisdom. You'll live in misery for the rest of your days if you do."

Uselli nodded and then squared his shoulders. "I will stay with Kullaa so that she knows I share her love, but I will only keep her company and help her through the worst of the symptoms. Then in the morning, if she truly wants me as her mate, I will be happy to oblige her with a proper courtship."

Kuwari's grin bloomed full force. "Good. I shall tell Nakurtum the happy news. The first part, not the bit about you being all noble."

Uselli nodded his thanks and then urged Kullaa deeper into the chambers. Kuwari and Enkara backed out of the room and closed the door softly behind them. Councilor Nakurtum was pacing outside.

When Enkara and Kuwari emerged without Uselli, the councilor's expression morphed from confident to horrified.

"What? What is going on? Did she attack the Shadow?"

"Not at all," Kuwari assured her. "Everything has turned out well and it was as I thought. Lady Kullaa responded to Shadow Uselli, and he returns her affections. They will make a very happy couple and produce beautiful cubs. In four seasons' time, you may be greeting your first grandchild."

The councilor shrieked in rage and tossed herself toward the door, but the Shadows blocked her.

Kuwari addressed Shadow Kurumtum. "Please see that Councilor Nakurtum is escorted to another set of guest quarters tonight."

"Of course, Prince Kuwari." Shadow Kurumtum locked a hand around the councilor's arm and half dragged her away.

"You've made an enemy of that one," Enkara said just above a whisper.

"She was an enemy the moment she decided she was going to defy Ishtar and place her own daughter in line for the throne."

Enkara couldn't fault Kuwari for his reasoning. "Can I kill her next time she crosses us?"

"Depends on the crime."

"What's to stop her from going to the council with what she knows about my heritage?"

Kuwari glanced over his shoulder at her, a wicked glint in his eye. "She knows I will retaliate. And add what she attempted tonight to her other efforts to force my hand, she has given me the means to destroy her."

"A knife through the ribs would be a swifter way to deal with the problem."

"You're sounding like Burrukan with breasts again."

Enkara couldn't help but roll her eyes and groan.

CHAPTER THIRTY-THREE

Kuwari was still chuckling as Enkara followed him across the expanse of the outer receiving chamber. When he settled in a chair by the fire, he glanced up at her. "Well, are you going to sit? Or stand there and glower all night?"

His words reinforced that she was tired. After all, she'd just been dragged out of bed by the arrival of Shadows with ill news. "Actually, I'm going to bed. You should too."

"I'm too restless. I'll go to bed in a bit."

"Alright. Goodnight then."

Kuwari's expression fell. "Fine. I'll just eat these by myself."

He preceded to pull out a napkin-wrapped package and revealed a dozen of his favorite sweet patties.

"Mmm, lint-covered sweet treats. No thanks."

Kuwari glanced down, examined them and then shrugged and popped one into his mouth.

"You're going to get fat."

He grinned at her between bites. "Not if Burrukan has anything to say about it. But if you're done insulting me and don't want to stay and talk, run along to bed."

As Enkara watched he popped two more of the tiny treats in his mouth and then made a shooing away gesture.

He popped another of the sweetcakes in his mouth and made a silly happy sound. "Too bad I didn't have a little wine to go with these."

"I think it would be wise to steer clear of wine for a while after what happened, don't you?"

Kuwari glanced around with a grin. "No. Not yet. I'm still not in your bed."

She rolled her eyes. "Why do you think getting drunk will improve your chances?"

Shrugging, he popped another treat in his mouth, chewing at length before swallowing and dignifying her question with an answer. "It worked for my father."

"You're an idiot, my prince."

"Only when it comes to you." His eyes had taken on the heavy-lidded look she was coming to know meant trouble. Time to make a hasty retreat.

"Fine. Good night. I'll see you in the morning. Don't forget the royal party will be returning and I'm sure Burrukan will be more than ready for another training session."

This time Kuwari rolled his eyes at her. "Yes, mother…"

He stopped midsentence, his eyes growing unfocused, the conversation, as well as the food in his hand, long forgotten as a vision gripped him.

Her exhaustion fell away. She was beside him a heartbeat later, waiting for the vision to release him from its clasp. After what felt like forever but was more likely only a few moments, Kuwari blinked up at her, awareness returning to his gaze.

He pushed the napkin containing the rest of the sweet patties off his lap and then bolted to his feet and rushed to their bathing chamber. Enkara was fast on his heels. Inside, Kuwari was bent over a bowl, forcing himself to throw up what he'd just eaten.

"What's wrong? Poison? More of the drug?"

He didn't answer her right away, taking a few moments to rinse his mouth and chew a few mint leaves. When he turned back to her, he looked much more flushed than he had earlier.

"I'm an idiot," Kuwari said, his earlier humor gone, replaced by worry in his eyes. "I...I missed something in my earlier vision. Nakurtum drugged more than just the wine, and I just saw the other half of my earlier vision."

Dammit!

She should have thought of that. It wasn't a secret that Kuwari had a weakness for sweet treats. "How bad is it?"

Kuwari didn't answer her right away, and she realized he was just standing next to her, leaning slightly into her. He dragged in a deep breath and exhaled a soft little purr at the end.

"Kuwari, I need you to focus."

He blinked his eyes open and took a step back.

"It's bad," he said at last. "What I ate earlier will already be in my bloodstream. I...I'll need to be sequestered away from you and any other females. Summon Uselli and tell him what's happened."

Kuwari gave himself a little shake and she could see him fighting to clear his thoughts enough to instruct her to his wishes. "No. Wait. Uselli is busy, isn't he? You must speak with Councilors Pirhum and Ninsunu and the next most senior Shadow. Goddess. I don't even remember who is still here."

"It's Old Kurumtum."

"I can't even think for the need raging through my bloodstream." He took a step back. "Enkara, I would never normally ask you to leave me, but I can't trust myself with you so close. And this is not how I want us to come together for the first time."

"Of course. I'll talk to Shadow Kurumtum and tell him what has happened."

"Make sure he understands that no females can come near me." He drew further from her. "Not even you, my beloved Blade."

The anguish in his gaze ate at Enkara's heart. "I won't allow anyone to steal your will or subvert your wishes. You have my word."

"Thank you, Enkara."

"Can you tell how bad this is going to be?"

"I don't know. Bad. I'm certain I've had a full dose, or perhaps even more than that. It hits the royal line harder than others."

"Hold on. I'll get help."

Enkara turned and ran out into the hall where she informed the Shadows on duty what had occurred. Then she went in pursuit of Shadow Kurumtum. He was always logical, calm and full of knowledge. He might know if there was anything that would help.

She eventually tracked Kurumtum to the kitchen, overseeing the disposal of the tainted wine.

"Kurumtum, I need to talk to you," she said in a rush.

Her sudden arrival drew the attention of the servants as well. Damnit. She wanted to tell Kurumtum what had happened in private. The fewer who knew, the better.

"Enkara, what's wrong?" But a moment later he must have read the truth in her face for his eyes widened in understanding and he swore. "Kuwari has been drugged, too, hasn't he?"

"Yes. It was in some of the food as well. Nakurtum was very busy."

Kurumtum nodded. "Walk with me."

Enkara did, but she couldn't stop thinking about the devious councilor.

"I know that look," Kurumtum said with a chuckle. "There will be no killing."

"I'll do what I must to protect Kuwari."

"Hah! Calm yourself. This is hardly life or death. Kuwari isn't physically or emotionally compromised. His gryphon nature has already picked out his mate. Even without intervention, he'd likely suffer no more than a case of aching nether regions come morning." Kurumtum slung an arm around Enkara's shoulder. "But having you near would soothe him through the worst of it."

"Kuwari doesn't want me near him either," Enkara said slowly.

"Only because the young cub's afraid he'll make a fool of himself and lose your respect. Don't worry about that." Kurumtum's merry expression faded. "You should worry about the other two council members. If given half a chance, they'll happily screw everything up. I saw Nakurtum with them earlier. After she was escorted from Lady Kullaa's chambers."

"You think they were a part of this?"

Kurumtum rubbed his chin. "Didn't say that. I just don't trust any council member that much."

"I trust the councilors to protect their own interests above all else."

"Exactly. Now, here's what you're going to do."

She stood and listened in disbelief as Kurumtum laid out his outrageous plan.

"You want me to abduct the prince and take him somewhere safe until he's free of the fertility drug," Enkara said just to clarify.

"Yes."

"But I can't just steal him away unnoticed." Though, she would find a way if forced.

"You can with the help of the Shadows. We'll lay down interference with the council members until you are safely away with the prince. And he'll be safe in the care of a Lamassu."

"Once I do, then what? He'll be difficult to...to..."

"Resist?" Kurumtum chuckled. "Refocus his attention. Sweat the fertility drug out of him."

"Pardon?"

"A sword fight." Kurumtum's grin grew broader. "Or

something else physical that will get his blood pumping without compromising your promise to him."

Enkara just stood there staring for a moment. She'd been going to say she couldn't risk Kuwari's life. But she wasn't really, was she? And this way she'd be able to stay close enough to comfort and protect him.

They were only halfway down the hall when voices shouted for them to halt. Enkara swung around to face the oncoming group. Nakurtum was in the company of Pirhum and Ninsunu, and they were surrounded by eight Shadows.

"Halt!" Ninsunu called. "We must speak. Councilor Nakurtum has brought something to our attention that is very disturbing."

Kurumtum laughed. "What? Did she tell you she drugged her own daughter and the prince?"

Councilor Ninsunu's expression shifted from concern to surprise to uncertainty. "No. The councilor's news is about Enkara's heritage. We have gone over the evidence and must request that she be placed under guard until the King and the rest of the council returns. You say Kuwari and Kullaa have been drugged?"

"Yes," Kurumtum said. "And I agree someone should be under guard until the King returns, but it's not Enkara. She's been in training to become a Shadow. She is one of us and can be trusted. Unlike Nakurtum."

Ninsunu arched one of her brows regally. "But she hasn't, in fact, finished her training and sworn under oath and spell to the King yet, has she?"

"No." Enkara bit out. "But I would die for Kuwari or any of his family."

Councilor Pirhum circled Enkara. "While both stories can't be true, and I am more inclined to believe Enkara, the fact remains if the prince received a large enough dose of the fertility drug, it could be lethal to one of the royal line. That must be our primary concern. Does he know how much he consumed? If it's a lower dose, he could endure it with help from one of the priestesses."

Enkara placed her hand on her sword's hilt. "Kuwari doesn't want any female around him until he's free of the drug."

"As much as we value the prince's opinion, we can't risk his life. A priestess will be summoned, and she will either ease him through the worst of the symptoms or take the drug herself and become his mate if the prince's condition worsens to the point of risking his death."

"I can't let you do that." Enkara clenched her other fist. "Kuwari doesn't want to have his choice taken away."

"Better his choice than his life."

Enkara's jaw dropped. The callousness of the councilors never failed to shock her. "Then please let me stay with him."

"Even if your heritage and motives were not presently in question, you still don't have a priestess's training."

It was true. All priests and priestesses were specially trained because no one ever knew when one of them might be called upon to perform the Sacred Marriage. Since Ditanu and Iltani had become mates, no priest or priestess had been called to perform the sacred marriage, but they still trained for it.

But that didn't matter. A priestess was only getting to Kuwari over her dead body. Enkara would honor her prince's request for as long as he wasn't in mortal danger. The moment it crossed over into that, she'd do what had to be done herself.

Pirhum continued, unaware of Enkara's decision. "I say we seek out a priestess and have her attend to the prince while Enkara and Nakurtum are held under guard. Ninsunu, what say you?"

The other councilor nodded. Enkara's hand tightened on her sword's hilt.

"I agree with Pirhum's council. Nakurtum and Enkara will both be held until the King's return, but for the safety of the prince a priestess must be selected." Ninsunu tilted her head toward Kurumtum. "See that Enkara is taken to a secure place and Nakurtum as well. For all we know they may be working together. Pirhum and I will go to the temple and speak with the priestesses on duty. With most away at the Spring Rites, finding a suitable female might be difficult. We will do our best. Once the two prisoners are secure, report to Crown Prince Kuwari's chambers and ensure that no other female goes near him."

Kurumtum muttered an affirmative and ordered four Shadows to secure Nakurtum while he and the rest would take Enkara into custody. At his nod, Enkara hesitantly unbuckled her weapons. If she hadn't known Kurumtum's words were a complete falsehood, she never would have surrendered, not even to her fellow Shadows. But the two councilors didn't have Enkara's gift and were so used to giving orders and having them obeyed, they didn't even hesitate to trust the Shadow's word.

Enkara allowed two of the other Shadows to come up and take her arms in a firm grip and lead her away.

Once they were out of earshot, Kurumtum whispered to her. "Just don't let him shift to gryphon form. If he does, you should as well and let nature take its course." He shrugged. "There are worse fates. He loves you. You love him. The council will have fits until they learn you're a Blade. All will fall into place."

"I…"

"Now, off you go while I see that Nakurtum is properly secured. I still have to pretend to follow the councilors' orders until the king returns." Kurumtum slowed his pace. "You and Kuwari better be gone by the time I reach his quarters."

When they turned a corner, the Shadows released her. Enkara nodded and then broke into a run.

CHAPTER THIRTY-FOUR

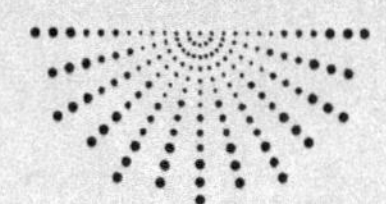

A disturbance in his outer chamber drew Kuwari out of the pounding misery assaulting his body. Moments later he heard a feminine voice converse with the male Shadows stationed throughout his chambers. Enkara was here.

He was on his feet and halfway across the room before the chair he'd been sitting in toppled to the floor. His beloved had returned.

Why, by Ishtar's great teats, was Enkara back? He'd ordered her away. Hadn't he? That had been one of his more foolish orders. But she'd left him like he'd asked.

A moment later the object of his thoughts rushed into his bedchamber. She grabbed his hand and then looking harried, scanned the room until she found his practice sword. Without a word, she snatched it up and then dragged him into her chamber where she lifted her own practice sword from the wall rack.

The strangeness of her behavior further helped him to focus on something other than what his body wanted to be doing.

She spun back to him and shoved his sword at him.

"We're going for a little trip," she said by way of explanation. "Kurumtum says the fertility drug can be sweated out since you're otherwise in fine form."

"That's—likely wholly true." He leaned forward and inhaled her scent. Smiling, he mumbled, "Why didn't I think of that?"

"Because neither of us ever thinks very clearly when the other is endangered. We just react."

"Oh." He wasn't sure if that was entirely true. His mind and body were both very clear about what they wanted to do with her.

"But there is the risk he could be wrong, too."

He?

"Do you trust me?"

That he could understand.

"Yes." It was a simple, beautiful truth.

"Come on. There isn't much time."

There wasn't much time for what, he wondered, his eyes sliding back toward Enkara's chamber. He'd rather stay than leave, but when Enkara started forward, he followed eagerly.

She led him out of his chambers, stopping only long enough to inform the assembled Shadows of Kurumtum's plan.

Kuwari narrowed his eyes, glowering at the circling Shadows. To a one, they were male and entirely too close to his future mate. He growled at those nearest and was rewarded by their retreat. It was only two body lengths worth of space, but it was enough to soothe his rising ire.

"Stop that! Don't you dare shift to gryphon form on me!" Enkara snapped at him, and he felt himself wilt slightly.

He'd displeased his beloved, but when he stepped closer to soothe her with caresses, she swatted his hands away. Huffing softly in annoyance, he turned his gaze back to the males. Perhaps if he challenged them, she'd be more impressed with him?

"Don't even think about that. You'll be fighting me and no one else. There will be no killing tonight."

He hissed his displeasure, but his beloved just ignored him.

They exited his chambers using the gilded door that led to the gardens. They wove their way through manicured pathways and neat flower beds. The ocean breeze blew stronger the closer to the cliffs they got.

Enkara hadn't explained what her plan was, but when she suddenly halted beside one of the towering Lamassu, even his lust-ravaged mind could comprehend her goal. "You're abducting me?"

"Yes, now get on." She vaulted up onto the leg and grasped the stone feathers of one wing to use as handholds. Swinging herself up onto the giant's back, she shouted at him to hurry and order the guardian to wake.

He settled in place on the Lamassu's back and then laid his hand against the cold stone.

"Wake, Ancient One. A prince of the royal blood has need."

Nothing was faster on the wing than a Lamassu. Beneath

his hand, the stone warmed as the guardian spirit responded to his summons.

"I sense no danger. What task does a Prince and his Blade require of me?"

"We need your powerful wings," Enkara urged. "And we need them now. I'll explain once we're in the air."

The Lamassu's powerful bull-like body lunged into motion, churning grass and crushing plants under his hooves. Then he gathered his mighty haunches and launched himself into the air. The thunder of his vast wings beating the air and propelling him higher would notify anyone who heard it that a lamassu had just taken wing.

Soon Nineveh fell away below them, and the lamassu circled the island in a lazy curve.

"Tell me more," the guardian said.

Kuwari wrapped his arms around Enkara's waist and dragged her back against his body. Content, he basked in her warmth and let her do the explaining, leaving him to revel in more pleasant concerns.

"Prince Kuwari was dosed with the sacred fertility potion against his will, and now the council fears for his life and wishes to match him with a trained priestess."

"Ah. A mortal affair."

"It is, and not something we'd normally bring to your attention. However, Kuwari has no wish to be mated to a stranger, and I gave him my word as his Blade that I'd protect him from such a fate."

"A noble act worthy of a Blade's great skill." The lamassu didn't even try to hide his amusement.

Dragging together his wayward thoughts, Kuwari cleared

his throat. "This is perhaps not the dire circumstances that would normally awaken one of your kind; however, it is Ishtar and Tammuz's right to determine the woman whom the future king of the gryphons should take to mate, not two mortal councilors."

"That is true. I offer my aid and will guard you and your Blade this night."

"Your aid is appreciated," Enkara whispered.

"Where would you have me take you?"

A long stretch of silence answered the Lamassu's question. Ah, his calm, rational Blade had panicked, not thinking beyond escape. Smiling, he nuzzled her hair out of the way and pressed a kiss to the back of her tattoo. Then before he got too distracted, he projected into the Lamassu's mind the image of a small island a day's flight from Nineveh. For the Lamassu's mighty wings, it would be a short trip. Which suited Kuwari just fine.

Before very long, they reached the small, isolated island. He dismounted first and Enkara was swift to follow. She scanned the area, no doubt looking for dangers.

"I shall patrol the island. Call me if you need me." With that last utterance, the lamassu trotted off, his massive strides carrying him far down the beach, heading south. He soon rounded an outcropping of rock fallen from the small cliffs that formed the southernmost point of the island.

When the lamassu was gone, he turned to Enkara.

"If there were danger here, he would have sensed it." Kuwari held out his hand. "Come. Let me show you a cavern I found a couple of years ago. It's sheltered. We'll be able to start a fire without it acting like a beacon for the Shadow guards Pirhum and Ninsunu will no doubt send after us the moment they realize Kurumtum tricked them."

"Don't worry. We won't need a fire to keep us warm." Enkara drew her wooden practice sword.

"Not the activity I was hoping for," he said, a slight purr in his voice.

"You'll thank me tomorrow once that cursed fertility drug works its way out of your system."

"Are you sure I can't persuade you?"

In answer, Enkara's wooden sword made a swipe at his head.

CHAPTER THIRTY-FIVE

Sweat rolled down Enkara's back, and her body was beginning to tire from the brutally long practice, but Kuwari still fought on with a dogged resolve she'd seen in him before when he was determined to win.

He wouldn't win this time. Burrukan and the other instructors on New Assur had trained her too well, but the idiot was too bull-headed to factor that in.

"Enough," she shouted as she struck, bringing her full momentum to bear. Their wooden swords came together in a heavy thwack and then she twisted, locking their cross pieces together. Another skilled twist with just the right amount of pressure sent Kuwari's sword flying across the sand.

His surprise lasted but a moment, and then he grinned, lunging forward to continue the fight using hand to hand.

"Goddess, Kuwari! Halt. We need to drink and replenish our reserves!"

Breathing hard, he grinned at her wordlessly until he got his breath back. Then sighing in disappointment, he straightened and rolled his shoulders. "Fine. We can stop if you need a break."

Enkara laughed and mock swung her sword at his backside. Kuwari leaped out of the way but returned to her side a moment later. "I yield!"

"Good. We'll take a quick break."

They'd already taken three other short breaks over the long night of practice. The first two times had ended with Enkara tossing his ass out of the cavern and renewing the sword fighting. During their last break, Kuwari had seemed more himself again, though his gaze spent more time below her neck than above it.

They'd both agreed he was over the worst of it. At least until Enkara built a small fire and sat by it to keep the chill from stiffening up well-used muscles. He'd settled far too close to her and soon tried to entice her into his lap.

That had begun round four of practice fighting.

As they made their way back to the small cavern where she'd left a fire burning, she hoped that this time Kuwari was truly himself again. He seemed like it. His skill level during their most recent practice bout had shown her his head was in the fight, but she'd have to wait and see what he was like in his 'down time' when his mind was allowed to wander to things other than where her next sword strike was coming from.

She ducked under the low entrance to the cavern and followed the glow from the dying embers to the center. After adding a couple of logs and stirring the embers back to life, she wandered over to the small trickle of fresh water running down the wall.

Kuwari knelt at the pool's edge and drank water from his cupped hands. Dropping to her knees next to him, she reached down and scooped up some of the cold water. After drinking as much as she dared, she splashed more onto her face and arms, trying to cool her overheated body.

"Too bad we didn't think to bring food with us," Kuwari said offhandedly.

"You're always hungry. Besides, food is what got you in trouble in the first place."

"At least I didn't drink the wine."

She glanced sidelong at him. He was splashing water on himself now, too. Completely ignoring her at the moment. That was a good sign. "How are you feeling?"

"Like a piece of meat that's been pounded on by the master cook." He rubbed at one dark bruise on his bicep. "You play rough."

"Your attention kept wandering." She shrugged. "Had to keep you focused on the fight."

He grunted and looked down in the pool, saying nothing. Enkara reached out and touched his shoulder.

"Are you back to yourself?" She cleared her throat. "No more unnatural urges?"

"No. Though they were not so very unnatural to me." He grimaced and looked at her. "I just normally have more control over them than that. I'm sorry. I know my behavior was unfitting many times."

"Most of the time," Enkara said with a chuckle. "But that's what I love about you too."

Kuwari's uncertain smile grew more confident. "Well, if this didn't damage my chances with you, I'll be happy to put it all behind me."

"It didn't," Enkara reassured him and leaned down to plant a kiss on his forehead. She wrinkled her nose. "But you'd stand a much better chance if you bathed. The sweat isn't so bad, but I can smell the bitter essence of the fertility drug mixed in. Go get cleaned up." *Before your hormones make me do something stupid.*

Kuwari sniffed at himself and then wrinkled his nose in turn. "As my lady commands."

He unfastened his belt and his scabbard. The practice sword landed with a thump against the rocky ground. Not even bothering to reprimand him for his ill treatment of the practice weapon, Enkara made her escape back to the fire before Kuwari could treat her to a distracting show.

"Gods! The water's colder than Ereshkigal's teats! Bah. And I don't even have soap." Kuwari hissed and moaned and then started cursing Councilor Nakurtum. There were further mumblings about the injustices he had suffered, but eventually, the sounds of splashing drowned out his mutterings.

After longer than she'd thought he'd last, he eventually returned to the fire, water dripping from his body. His linen wrap was again around his waist, though its golden fringes were a little worse for wear and the fabric wrinkled and damp, but he was blessedly dressed. Enkara wasn't ready to see him naked.

The long night had taken its toll upon her as well, his hormones seeming to reach into her body and stir her gryphon nature to full wakefulness. More than once she'd had to fight the powerful urge to shift to her gryphon form and roll in his delightful scent.

It was a mercy that she hadn't eaten any of the tainted food during the dinner.

But what was to stop this from happening again? Nakurtum wouldn't be given a second chance, but that didn't mean others wouldn't try something similar to achieve their own goals.

It was a distraction she and Kuwari couldn't risk. They had greater dangers on the horizon that needed their full attention. Her gaze cut away from the flames to study him.

He was sitting cross-legged beside her, his fingers working his damp braids back into order. A moment later he turned to study her. "What are you thinking so hard about? This close I can sense your worry. I don't even need to touch you to feel it."

"Nothing important." She looked away and gave the fire a savage poke. "I'm going to go wash up. Stay here and tend the fire."

She stood before Kuwari could question her further. Striding over to the small pool, she shed her clothing. The water was as cursedly cold as Kuwari had said, but she didn't care, and waded into the deepest point, which wasn't very deep. The water only came up to her waist, but it was enough to wash the sweat from her body and clear her mind.

Looking over her shoulder, she studied Kuwari as she bathed. He didn't turn away from the fire to catch glimpses of her nude form. He was behaving himself, which told her he was indeed free of the last vestiges of the fertility potion.

Otherwise, he would have been watching, or more than just watching.

Once she'd washed the sweat, sand, and other grime off her skin, she emerged from the water but didn't bother with her clothing. Walking forward, she came to a halt behind Kuwari.

"I see you behaved yourself."

He huffed but didn't take his eyes off the fire. "I figured you'd already been ogled enough by me tonight, likely more than any woman should have to suffer in her entire lifetime."

"It wasn't your fault." She touched his shoulder and then slowly came around to stand in front of him.

The fire's warm glow illuminated his startled expression.

"Ah, I managed to surprise my rebel prince, I see." Enkara lowered herself into his lap, straddling his thighs with her knees.

Shock only held him frozen for a heartbeat and then his hands came to rest on her hips, his warm fingers kneading her flesh. "Enkara, are you…"

"Yes." She leaned forward and pressed her lips to his in answer to his hesitant question. The kiss deepened and Kuwari moaned, his hands slowly exploring. She broke the kiss and pulled away enough to look him in the eye. "But only if it's what you want."

"I have always wanted you." And his caresses showed her just how much.

Sighing, Enkara allowed herself to touch him in turn, exploring and savoring every one of his contours and slopes. He was all hard muscle and hot, firm skin.

"So soft," he whispered in her ear as his caressing hands

slid up her sides and brushed feather-light over her ribcage. When he hesitated, she guided his hands up over her breasts. He chuckled. "And so demanding."

He didn't seem to mind, so she urged one of his hands lower. He needed no farther encouragement, and soon Enkara was arching her back and moaning out soft sounds of pleasure. She barely recognized her own voice. Surely that wasn't her?

But it was, and when Kuwari began kissing his way down her torso, pushing her back to the ground and parting her thighs, he showed her just what other sounds he could force from her mouth. Soon her gryphon nature rose, demanding more and she tugged him back up for a kiss, her own hands exploring him with determination. Stroking down his chest, her fingers fluttered against his abdomen, dragging a moan from deep in his chest. She discovered she liked the power she had over his body.

Emboldened, she reached down farther until she encountered the linen wrapping his waist and hips. It did little to block her fingers from finding what she sought and soon she was learning the shape and feel of him through the fabric. Kuwari groaned and thrust his hips forward.

Finding his belt, she made swift work of it, and then she was unwrapping what her hand had explored earlier.

Chuckling, Kuwari settled his hand over hers. "Not so fast, my eager one. I didn't just suffer through the longest ass-kicking of my life only to have you retake command so soon. I'm not done with you yet."

He clasped both her hands in one of his and then gently shoved her back with one hand pressed against her shoulder.

Enkara allowed herself to be pushed down. She could have broken his hold easily enough, but he did deserve a little sympathy after what she'd put him through to cleanse his system.

Surprisingly her back didn't hit the bare stone as she'd expected. Somehow, he'd maneuvered their clothing under her while she'd been distracted by his touch. He didn't give her long to contemplate how he'd managed it before he was settling down next to her, the warmth of his body delightful against her skin.

"I'm going to kiss every bit of that glorious expanse of body and only when you're begging me will I give you what you truly want."

"Is that a promise, a challenge, or a threat?" Enkara asked lazily as she pressed herself closer to him, rubbing up against him suggestively.

He hissed at the friction but continued to grin at her. "A promise. Nothing I do to you would ever be a threat."

"I know. Come here."

He did and they kissed for long moments before he broke away to place soft, barely felt brushes of his lips against her jaw. From there he moved down along her neck and over the curve of her shoulder before reversing course and nuzzling at her collarbone.

Enkara closed her eyes and sighed out in pleasure as he settled his weight more firmly on top of her. He licked, kissed and nipped a fiery trail down between her breasts, all the way to her belly button, then down and to the side to nibble at the protrusion of her hip. When he worked his way back up her side, her frustrated sigh soon turned to giggles.

"Stop!" she laughed and twisted in his embrace.

"Never," he replied and kissed his slow way up. "Rebel princes never do as we're told."

But his lips soon left the ticklish skin of her side and moved back up toward her breast. He nipped and teased all around her areola until at long last he took the nipple in his mouth.

She sighed out encouragements and arched her back. Once one was thoroughly ravaged, he moved on to the other. But Enkara grew frustrated with this slow, pleasurable torture and twisted her hands free of his clasp and moved them along his back, pressing and urging him closer.

When he still didn't get her meaning, she twisted one leg up over his hip and dug her heel into the fleshy muscle of his ass.

"Is my Blade really so very eager for her rebel prince?" he half purred, half laughed.

"Oh, Goddess. Shut up and get on with it or I'm going to flip you on your back and take what I want."

He settled between her thighs but kept his weight supported on one arm while the other stroked an errant lock of hair off her face. "Perhaps we can do it that way next time? I think I'd enjoy that very much."

Enkara only grimaced at his humor and drew him down to her for another kiss. This one was hotter and more urgent than the early, playful ones. Her prince was done being playful. So too was she. Reaching down, she grasped him and guided him to her entrance. As he slowly slid home, she stared into his eyes and reached out for his mind, enveloping him in her deep love.

"Goddess! Kara, you're so beautiful. Body, heart, and soul —each more beautiful than the last."

"My prince, my lover, my friend, I shall always be your solace in times of need."

And then he soon proved to her that he could soothe every one of her needs too.

NERGAL, God of war, plague, and the underworld, looked upon the two entwined lovers in what could only be a dream or a vision. They looked so peaceful and innocent. Well, perhaps not as innocent as they had been, he mused with a grin. The Blade had finally claimed her prince.

As was right and true. Blades were always supposed to claim their monarchs. Something that most mortals living in New Sumer misunderstood. Come to think about it, it was something most Blades did not understand either.

The monarch did not claim a Blade. The Blade claimed their monarch.

At least Enkara and Kuwari understood what Ishtar had intended when she created her Blades. Unfortunately, that wouldn't protect them from what Ereshkigal had planned.

The thought of Enkara and Kuwari coming to harm disturbed him.

He'd grown soft. Or, at least, Kuwari and Enkara had wormed their way into his heart without even trying. A rare thing indeed. But somehow it had become truth. He cared for these two young beings and now needed to find a way to protect them from what his beloved Ereshkigal had planned.

The irony wasn't lost on him. To protect them from his beloved was to continue his own peculiar enslavement. But somewhere in his last few hundred lives, he'd grown a conscience and couldn't stand aside and let innocent lives be ruined.

Of all the things he could have gained being reborn as a mortal repeatedly, he'd had to have gone and gained a conscience.

What a pesky thing for the King of the Underworld to acquire.

CHAPTER THIRTY-SIX

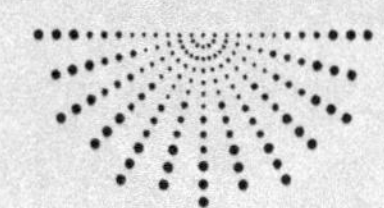

Of course, his Shadow guards had found him shortly after dawn, but at least the lamassu had warned him of their coming. That didn't mean he'd had his fill of Enkara. He'd have preferred more time alone with her.

He'd even come up with the idea to have the lamassu lead the Shadows off on another long chase, but Enkara had deflated his magnificent plans with the flat of a practice sword across his rump and an order to behave.

"Just so we're clear. It's really all your fault that we're here," he gestured broadly at the corridor around them as they walked toward the great hall. "Surrounded by grumpy, watchful Shadows instead of enjoying ourselves on a beach."

Enkara winced and he knew he'd struck a chord.

"Ah! You do regret your hasty decision to allow the Shadows to find us."

She scowled at him, which if he was honest wasn't the look he'd been hoping to receive.

"It looks bad."

Kuwari rubbed his chin. "What looks bad?"

"That I abducted you when you were under the influence of the fertility potion, and now we're mates." Enkara's look darkened farther. "I should have waited until after all the ruffled feathers had been smoothed before—"

"I don't care what others think. I know the truth and so do you. If Pirhum and Ninsunu don't believe us, it doesn't matter because Iltani and my father will know the truth."

Just then they walked into the great hall to discover it occupied by only six people: Pirhum, Ninsunu, Kurumtum, Uselli, Kullaa and most disturbing of all, Nakurtum was present and not bound in rope or chains. The group was too busy arguing amongst themselves to note his and Enkara's arrival.

"Why is Nakurtum free?" He bellowed as he entered. Then something else occurred to him. "Where is my father? The royal party should have returned by now."

Kuwari looked around the hall as a nagging sensation of dread coursed through his body. Something was wrong. Surely, he would have seen it in a vision if they had come under attack?

Councilor Pirhum recovered first. "Your father and the royal party have been delayed. A minor sickness broke out at the festival. I'm glad you've returned safely."

There was an unasked question at the end Kuwari decided to ignore. "A sickness? You're sure it wasn't poison?"

"The messenger informed us that the healers say it's nothing more than a natural illness. A fever, some dizziness. Your father is staying long enough for the healers to clear his party to return. He doesn't want to bring anything back to Nineveh."

Diseases were rare in the kingdom of New Sumer. Partly because of the isolation of the kingdom and partly because gryphons were not susceptible to many illnesses, and those they did contract were usually treated swiftly by the magic of the healers. In turn, benefiting the human population as well.

But a breakout, even a minor one, at the Spring Rite was not a good omen for the coming year.

"I don't care what lies she's been spinning since I've been gone. Have Nakurtum tossed in the dungeon. And summon me once my father returns. I would have a word with him."

"Have no fear," Ninsunu said with conviction in her voice and a dark look aimed at Enkara. "We will explain *all* that has happened while the King has been gone. As for Nakurtum, her warnings proved sound."

With a nod of her head, an aid waiting by the door scurried out into the hall, where the murmur of voices and the stomp of feet could be heard.

Now what, Kuwari wondered but was answered a moment later by the arrival of thirty of Nineveh's city garrison. They approached the Shadows with an alert caution but didn't back down when his escort of Shadows drew their blades.

"What's going on?" Kuwari snarled out, his hand going to the hilt of his own useless practice sword. Of all the times not to have a weapon.

"We are aware Shadow Enkara abducted you while you were under the influence of the fertility drug," Ninsunu explain. "And Shadow Kurumtum and a select few of the other Shadows went along with her plan. Kurumtum will not explain his reasoning and neither will the others with him. We can only assume they have thrown in their lot with Enkara."

"Enkara did nothing wrong. She acted to protect me."

Councilor Pirhum heaved his narrow and ancient frame off the bench where he had sat for the entire exchange so far. He cleared his throat and Kuwari hoped the oldest of the Council wasn't as easily fooled by Nakurtum's lies as the younger and more inexperienced Ninsunu.

"The timing of Nakurtum's 'newly' discovered information about Enkara's heritage is too thorough and too convenient to be a coincidence. She's likely been holding this over you both in the hope of securing a personal boon." Pirhum squinted his eyes at Nakurtum. "I can only guess that when Crown Prince Kuwari didn't agree, or things weren't progressing to Nakurtum's satisfaction, she used the fertility drug to hurry things along. That sound about right?"

Nakurtum's expression darkened, but she didn't respond with words.

Pirhum just chuckled. "Didn't work out so well, now did it? At least not for you." He glanced at Lady Kullaa. "And you, dear. Are you content with Uselli as your future mate?"

"I am most pleased." Lady Kullaa and Uselli shared a loving look before she turned to peer at Kuwari. "And I must thank the Crown Prince for being astute enough to know what my heart longed for even though I tried to hide my feelings. Thank you, my prince."

"You are most deserving of love, Lady Kullaa. May Ishtar and Tammuz bless your future union."

"Ah, I enjoy seeing young love." But Pirhum's grin vanished when he glanced at Enkara. "Unfortunately, it must now be overshadowed by a turn of unpleasantness. I do personally believe Enkara acted to protect Kuwari. And yet she went against the King's orders and put the prince's life at risk by taking him from the protection of Nineveh and your Shadow Guard. Enkara, do you deny this?"

Kuwari hissed in anger. "Wait one moment—"

"I don't deny it. I gave my word to him that I would protect him from getting mated to one he did not want." Enkara stepped forward to face the ancient councilor. "I answer only to him."

"I believe you. But the fact remains, by abducting Kuwari, you committed treason against the crown and broke your oath as a Shadow."

"She did no such thing," Kuwari snapped.

Ninsunu circled the table and came to stand directly in front of him. "Shadow Enkara convinced you to wake a lamassu so that none could track you down before she'd had her way. And in your befuddlement, you agreed. Your judgment was impaired. Do you deny any of what I said?"

"Befuddlement? Had her way with me?" Kuwari's voice grew louder until he was yelling at the woman. "Enkara was my choice! My betrothed!"

His outburst had her stepping back physically, but her narrowed eyes said she wasn't backing down. "Do you deny that you and Enkara are now mates?"

"Yes, she 'had her way with me' if by that you mean she kicked my ass in sword practice for most of the night. She knew that if she sweated the drug from my system, I would be well come morning and not mated to some random priestess you'd selected to be my queen."

Pirhum cleared his throat in a way that made Kuwari think the old male was trying to hold back a laugh. *Yes, old man, the situation was more a comedy of errors than a true danger to me. Now side with Enkara!*

Then Enkara started to laugh, startling them all. "None of you have the entire picture. Let me show it to you."

With that, she turned her back to the councilors and tugged her tunic up her back until she exposed a large portion of Ishtar's Mark.

While the two councilors were shocked speechless, the guards of the city garrison brought their spears against their chests and stamped their sandaled feet against the floor and then dropped into deep bows.

Enkara allowed her tunic to fall back in place and turned to face the councilors. "Only Ishtar may pass judgment on my actions. I will not apologize for what I do to protect my prince or uphold my oath as both Blade and Shadow. And part of that oath is to protect him from all threats, even misguided council members who would shackle him to a loveless match with whatever priestess you would have picked out to be his mate."

Pirhum bowed. "Forgive us. Had we been informed that there was a second Blade, we would never have questioned your actions."

Ninsunu followed a moment later with her own deep bow and muttered an apology.

"Hah, by that you mean, had I been a mere Shadow, I'd

even now be put to death for treason. I still would have done everything exactly the same."

Pirhum nodded and then turned to glare at Nakurtum. "If no one is against it, I'll have the city guard take Nakurtum into custody and once the king returns, I will inform him of what exactly has gone on and will suggest Lady Kullaa be elevated to her mother's seat in the council. If you are in agreement?" he asked Kuwari.

"I am."

"Good, now that we have that business out of the way," Pirhum grinned, his wrinkles becoming even more pronounced, "There's something else that needs to be mentioned. I might be old, but my eyesight and mind aren't so faded that I don't recognize a young strutting male when I see one. Should I organize a festival in honor of a newly mated couple?"

"I suppose that would be expected." Kuwari grinned. "Though curious minds should rest assured that Enkara and I waited until after the fertility drug ran its course. Now, if you are satisfied with our answers. I would like something to eat and a change of clothing." Kuwari placed an arm around Enkara's shoulders and guided her out of the Great Hall. His Shadow guard fell in around them.

ENKARA HAD BEEN nervous when King Ditanu and his co-rulers returned. If she'd just thought to tell the councilors that she was Kuwari's Blade, she never would have needed to abduct the prince in the first place. As a Blade, she outranked the council when it came to the safety of the kingdom or the royal line. But she'd been hiding her true nature for so long, it hadn't occurred to her to speak the truth until driven to it by the insufferable councilors.

In the end, she had nothing to worry about. King Ditanu had seen fragments of what would occur in a vision, but he'd been up at the top of a temple, moments away from Ishtar and Tammuz's arrival and hadn't had time to warn anyone.

Still, when he'd returned home later that day, he hugged his son and took Enkara in a strong embrace and welcomed her formally into his family. Burrukan clapped her on the shoulder and then took her aside while Kuwari was speaking with his father.

"It's about damn time you two sealed your bond. If you didn't do the deed soon, I was going to steal a bit of that fertility drug and dose you both myself. Then maybe you'd get over each other and could focus on your training."

Enkara laughed along with her mentor a little sheepishly since her gift told her his utterance was only half in jest. Next Queen Iltani took her into a fierce embrace, smiling and welcoming her into the family. "Although, you've always been part of this family from the moment Kuwari first touched your mind."

A warmth Enkara never remembered feeling bloomed in her chest. Belonging.

Even the standoffish Regent Ahassunu hugged her, seeming relieved that Kuwari was now safe from farther attempts by ambitious mothers seeking to align their house with the royal family through any means necessary.

Of course, she knew the relaxed, peaceful moment would

only last until word spread about her being a second Blade and newly mated to Crown Prince Kuwari. Then would begin the flurry of activity and well-wishing that went along with such things. She just hoped things calmed down in a few days and routine would return.

She could be happy with a few dull days free of gods, magic, oaths, and political intrigue.

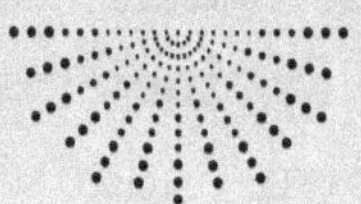

CHAPTER THIRTY-SEVEN

The days leading up to their first formal Blooding Ceremony sped by in a blur of training and activity. The news that Enkara was, in fact, his Blade soon leaked to the public. As promised, King Ditanu kept both Kuwari and Enkara under close guard, fearing to give their enemies targets until Enkara had full command of her power.

Kuwari was beginning to think he'd have preferred enemy assassins. With their freedom curtailed, for the time being, there was little official work for either he or Enkara to oversee. At first, he'd been delighted, thinking it would give them a great deal of personal time together.

And they did spend most every moment with each other. Unfortunately, Burrukan, Iltani, and Ahassunu were also present. When Burrukan and Iltani weren't attempting to pound them into the next life with all their training sessions, Ahassunu was drilling Enkara about statecraft.

Kuwari's one glimmer of hope lay in the formal Blooding Ceremony, where Ishtar would at last endow Enkara with, if not her full gifts, then at least enough that his parents would allow them their freedom again.

Anything to get him away from Burrukan for a time. He didn't know how Enkara had survived four years of his mentorship. Most nights Kuwari was too tired to seduce his lovely new mate. Luckily, she was half human, and her eagerness matched his own, and it was often she who pulled him down into bed for a session of love play before they both fell asleep in each other's arms.

But at last, the day of the Blooding Ceremony arrived, and Kuwari and Enkara found themselves on Uruk. This wasn't a secret ceremony. The entire court was in attendance to give their blessings and well wishes.

Kuwari really could have done without the nobles. But they were better than sword fights with Burrukan, so he graciously accepted their blessings.

The ceremony began in late afternoon, high up in the temple. The sun angled in through the wide arched windows to strike large, polished mirrors situated to carry the light deeper into the temple. His great aunt was overseeing everything, priests and priestesses efficiently carrying out her orders in preparation for the ritual.

The first order of business for the afternoon was a sacred cleansing overseen by acolytes and novices. Side by side, he and Enkara walked into the bathing chamber. Great archways opened out onto the wide blue sky, allowing a playful breeze to sweep in. Today the briny scent of the ocean was strong, and he could hear the calls of seabirds nesting along the cliffs and shore.

Beside him, Enkara drew in a deep breath. Even without the soul link they shared, he would have sensed her nervousness. "There's nothing to fear. We've done this same exact thing before. It's hardly new."

"Last time Ishtar appeared."

Kuwari shrugged. "That's nothing unheard of. She has appeared in many Blooding Ceremonies throughout history."

The approaching priests and priestesses interrupted their conversation, and Enkara didn't answer right away.

Enkara ignored the priestess who was undressing her and looked straight ahead, but her thoughts reached out to him. *"It's not Ishtar's appearance that I fear."*

"Ereshkigal wouldn't be so bold as to appear during such a public ceremony," he replied along their secret link.

"I know. It's just that disaster has dogged me most of my life. It makes seeing things in a positive light more difficult."

"If it gives you comfort, I see glimpses of darkness ahead but also a bright future. With you at my side, we will navigate those dangerous waters and come out on the other side with our love stronger than ever before."

When a priest cleared his throat, Kuwari's thoughts focused back on the ceremony, where it should have been all along, he chided himself. He knew what they were waiting for. He put a bit of space between them and shifted to gryphon form.

The priest approached and bowed once more but didn't

waste time selecting the first of several feathers that would later be woven into part of his Blade's ceremonial garb. Getting plucked was never something he'd considered fun, but at the same time, it pleased him to surrender several of his feathers for his mate.

It harkened back to a gryphon's nesting instinct, where a male would help build a nest and insulate it with his feathers. Yet the ritual spoke to his human side as well. There was something deeply intimate about the thought of her wearing something that had come from him. The next time she wore the ceremonial garb with his feathers sewn onto them would be during the Sacred Marriage.

The priests were particular, carefully selecting an even number of feathers from each wing before moving on to the thick ruff at his neck. They paused after pulling each feather, giving him time to alert them when he felt he'd surrendered enough for his Blade.

"If you keep letting them pluck you, you're never going to be able to get into the air and fly with me. I must confess, I like flying." At Enkara's words, a vision flared across his mind, one that depicted an aerial courtship that ended in a mating.

He twisted and snapped his beak at the priests to tell them he'd given enough feathers. Enkara's delighted laugh echoed across the sacred pool.

In total, the priests selected four of his long primaries, six of the secondary flight feathers and twelve shorter feathers from his neck ruff. The priests bowed and backed away with their prize.

Kuwari gave himself a shake and then groomed his

ruffled feathers back in place. When they were smooth, he shifted back to his human form.

He glanced at Enkara, where she stood waiting for him, a smile on her lips. Soon the priests and priestesses were ushering them into the large pool. He and Enkara walked side by side through the pool as prayers and chanting filled the chamber's high ceiling.

When they reached the other side, more priests and priestesses were waiting with scented oils and towels. Kuwari and Enkara allowed themselves to be buffed and primped and anointed with oils.

While Kuwari stood still and allowed them to tie on his ornate loincloth, he snuck glances at Enkara.

She held her arms out from her sides and allowed her attendants to fasten a golden chain around her waist, its many translucent veils fluttered in the breeze like streamers of light. She was the image of strength and power and feminine beauty. He allowed himself to drink in her exquisiteness.

Next, an ancient priestess wrapped a matching length of fabric around Enkara's breasts, hiding them from his view.

"You're pouting, my prince."

"No more than any male would seeing such beauty covered up."

Once he and Enkara were clothed, they were led out under one of the archways and up to the flat section at the top of the temple. Torches and cauldrons of burning oil offered light and heat as the sun began to sink into the ocean.

As his eyesight adjusted, he spotted his father and Iltani

standing to the right of High Priestess Kammani. They waited in the center of the space where a fire burned in a depression carved from the stone of the roof. Sitting next to the fire, a long bench-like altar occupied a good two body-lengths of space. As he approached it, he felt its power beating against his skin.

Here was a place kings, queens, princes, and princesses had shed blood to anoint each of Ishtar's Blades.

As he neared the high priestess, the lesser priests and priestesses joined their voices in a chant, calling down a blessing on a prince of the royal blood and his new Blade.

Enkara reached the narrow altar and calmly straddled it, but he could see the tension in her muscles. While he'd been studying his beloved, Priestess Kammani approached and handed him an ancient blade. Its bone hilt was smooth from hundreds of years of handling, and its blade was made of hammered copper.

The blade had its own magic, but that wasn't what drew his attention or made the fine dusting of hair on his arms stand to attention. No, there was another power, another presence on the roof with them. A banked, heated magic swirled through the air.

Ishtar was already here on the roof. Waiting. The most impatient of goddesses was here waiting. Enkara must have sensed her as well because her already tensed shoulders squared more.

Great Nammu of the primeval waters, mother of heaven and earth, please let everything go well here tonight.

When he realized he'd stood rooted in place longer than was seemly, he started forward. Only halting when he was at

Enkara's shoulder. Drawing in a deep, calming breath, he straddled the altar. Enkara reached behind her and freed the knot of fabric at the back of her neck, pulling the material away to expose the entire length of Ishtar's mark.

Drawing the blade down and across his right pectoral, he inhaled at the sharp pain. The coppery scent of blood coiled in his nose, stirring instincts and memories of their earlier blooding ceremony. Steeling himself, he drew the blade across the flesh of the opposite pectoral.

While the pain was swift and sharp, he was already focused on what was to come.

He shifted closer until his body was pressed against hers, then reaching around her waist, he dragged her back until the length of her spine was sealed to his chest. The warmth of his blood began to flow, trickling down his chest and dripping onto her spine. In its wake, he felt where her birthmark began to flare with magic, triggered by the presence of his blood.

Bracing one arm on the bench, he tightened the other around her waist, forcing her forward to better allow his blood to pool against her spine.

Goddess. It was glorious feeling his essence flow into her, strengthening her.

If he looked now, he knew he'd see the tattoo pulsing with power, echoing the beat of their hearts.

In turn, her power reached back into him and stamped her essence onto his soul. The mental link they shared flared with new power, growing stronger. Ishtar's greatest gift was an unseen one, but powerful all the same.

"Our hearts and souls have always been mated," he whispered into her mind. *"Our love will endure no matter what comes."*

"Always." Enkara tilted her head back toward him, but then the power rising within them both crested and suddenly that fierce magic was radiating off him. It was potent, breathtaking and a surprised grunt escaped him as he looked up to see clearly the powerful being now standing beside him.

Vast wings framed a naked and voluptuous feminine body. Her glorious power flowed from her in waves, caressing his skin and stirring him in ways that had him pressing closer to Enkara.

None of it was truly a surprise, though. He'd expected Ishtar to come and claim them from the moment he'd felt her presence on the temple roof.

Though she was here with them, and he could see the flames from the cauldrons through her shimmering form, he wasn't sure if anyone else could see her—not even his father or Iltani.

Then Ishtar dragged her hand slowly down his back, taking her time. Once she was satisfied that she had his full attention, she turned to Enkara and reached out with a heated caress that made his Blade jump.

With that touch, the goddess loosed a wild current of power into them both, claiming and blessing them as hers. It lasted only mere moments, but it felt like years, a glorious warmth surrounding and cocooning them both. His body shaking under the strain of a goddess's touch, he pressed his face into the curve of Enkara's neck. She, in turn, gripped his arms with bruising force. He wanted it to be over and yet he didn't, liking the way it fired his blood, making him feel alive and invincible.

Slowly the power and seductive warmth receded, and Kuwari's mind began to work again.

With a final caress and a sultry laugh, Ishtar withdrew her hands. "No wonder my sister is so eager to get her hands on you both. You," she stroked Enkara's bare shoulder, "would make her a lovely vessel to inhabit. And you," she caressed him from knee to hip, "would make her a virile husband."

Ereshkigal already had a husband. Was she planning to start a harem?

"Not a harem, my young prince. While Ereshkigal wants you as her husband, it's more than that. She wants you because you *are* her husband, and she will use Enkara's body to have you."

"What?" But her words just reinforced his visions and what the eagle-headed anunnaki had said.

"This situation came about because I made a mistake." The goddess looked chagrined. "It certainly wasn't my first and it won't be my last. But it is one of the ones that has come back to haunt me."

Kuwari remained silent. Not because he was speechless, but because one did not interrupt a goddess.

"Long after Tammuz traded himself to free me from my sister's domain, I still sought a way to strike back at Ereshkigal for the pain she caused us. Coming together once a year for the Spring Rites wasn't enough to satisfy me, so I hunted for ways to strike back at my sister, to make her feel the same pain I did, to force her to release Tammuz." The goddess turned fully to them, but her gaze was focused upon the stars, lost in thought or memory. "One day, long ago, I sent a lamassu to her husband, saying I wanted to mend my relationship with my sister, but that I could not step into her domain to tell her myself any more than she could venture into the living world."

Kuwari feared he knew where this was going. His earlier benediction to Nammu echoed in his mind. It might take the primordial mother to solve this mess.

"When Nergal came to my palace, I slew him, but instead of letting him return to the underworld, I locked his soul into an endless cycle of rebirths. Each time his host body died, he would be reborn into a new body instead of returning to the Underworld and his beloved."

Ishtar sighed, surprising him. It somehow made her more personable.

"I thought this would make her surrender my Tammuz to me if I held her own husband hostage. But Ereshkigal's distrust of me ran even deeper than I realized. She did not trust me to uphold the bargain. Instead, she sent her anunnaki to begin the hunt for Nergal, thinking they would be able to find his host body and drag the soul back to the underworld."

Ishtar turned her gaze from the stars to look again upon Kuwari and Enkara. "They were swift to learn that as soon as they dragged her husband back to the underworld, he'd vanish a moment later, reborn into a new body. Each time, they would start the hunt again. But I learned to hide him well so that even the anunnaki couldn't find him without searching for years and years."

Enkara shifted in his arms, and he sensed she wanted to speak but held back. Likely wise since the goddess wasn't yet done her tale.

"But one of the anunnaki, the oldest of the seven judges, did find Nergal's soul and while the guardian couldn't hold my sister's husband in the underworld, he was able to direct where Nergal was reborn." The goddess paused in her tale and looked directly at Kuwari. "Nergal lives within you."

Kuwari rocked back hearing the truth spelled out clearly. Even though he'd been piecing it together on his own, the news still came as a shock. The god of war, plague, and death lived within him.

Enkara straightened and faced down the goddess. "Now Ereshkigal wishes to reclaim her husband by having us perform some strange version of the Sacred Marriage?"

"Yes. But Ereshkigal doesn't plan for it to be one day out of the year. She wants to bring you both there and use an anunnaki's power to tie you to the Kur, so she and her husband can use you and Kuwari as often as they wish."

"She wants us to be slaves," Enkara whispered to herself in thought. "But slaves can rebel and fight for their freedom."

Ishtar barked out a harsh laugh. "Yes. But my sister knows this as well. That's why I think she's planning to endow you and Kuwari with a large portion of her power. Once she does, you will be unable to return to the world of the living, and Nergal will grow stronger with each feeding until he wakes and takes over Kuwari's body."

Enkara made an angry sound of denial. "But surely there is something we can do to rid Kuwari of Nergal's presence."

The goddess gave her a sad look. "Not even I can remove

Nergal without killing Kuwari. Nergal is where he wants to be, and he will remain with Kuwari until death, but that doesn't mean you must be his slave. If Ereshkigal can't reach him, he will never grow in power and take control of Kuwari. Guard against that if you love your prince at all."

"I shall protect him with my life."

"Do that. For I can't venture back to my sister's domain to rescue you should you become prisoners there. Life and death exist in a balance but the two cannot inhabit the same place at the same time, or all creation begins to fray, as we found out when I was trapped in my sister's domain. That's the only reason Tammuz was able to negotiate for my release."

"A bitter way to learn that lesson," Kuwari said softly.

The goddess looked at him, pain visible in her eyes. "Indeed, it is, young one. I hope you must never endure such bitterness."

"Armed with your warning and your grace, we will seek to remain clear of your sister's clutches."

"See that you do, for all our sakes," Ishtar agreed. "But that doesn't mean you or I are helpless against my sister's plans. Remember, you are my gryphon and his fierce Blade. If the worst comes to pass and one of you finds yourself in Ereshkigal's domain, the other must make swift to their side. And remember my sister cannot tolerate my power in her realm." A mysterious little smile crossed the goddess's lips. "The act of creation is painful for her. And the Sacred Marriage is nothing if not an act of creation, making fertile all the surrounding land and everyone in it."

Kuwari bowed his head in understanding. "As my

goddess commands. I will heed your wise words and call for my beloved should I ever find myself in the underworld before my proper time."

"Do that, young one, but always be on guard for dangers here as well. Enkara, you must master the new gifts I've bestowed upon you as my Avenging Blade, else Ereshkigal will attempt to make you hers. Iltani will be able to guide you; though, only you can conquer the wild power and harness it to your will. But this," she paused and spread her hands wide as a bright light flashed into being and transformed into the length of a long, crystalline sword, "should help you focus your power."

Enkara reverently took the weapon. "I shall not disappoint you!"

Ishtar smiled at Enkara's fervor. "And both of you beware, for my sister's hatred runs deep. If she can't find a way to seduce you into her arms, she will do it by other, less wholesome, means: dark deeds that even I at my worst would not use."

"I will do all in my power to keep Kuwari safe." Enkara's words were full of determination, but he tasted the fear in her thoughts.

At last, the power flowing off the goddess slowed and finally stopped. Her appearance faded, growing blurry and then two heartbeats later, she vanished from his sight.

Ishtar might be gone, but her words of warning still rang in his ears. He would heed them.

Enkara shifted, turning to look over her shoulder at him. *I will not let Ereshkigal have you. My word of honor.*

Kuwari bowed his head and pressed a kiss to her shoulder. *"And I will not let her have you either."*

All around them, the priests and priestesses continued to chant, never knowing that their goddess had been standing in their midst and divulged such disturbing tidings to their Crown Prince.

CHAPTER THIRTY-EIGHT

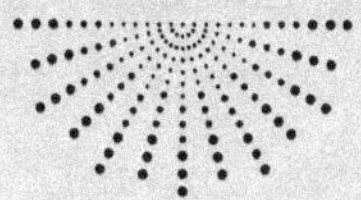

$\mathcal{A}$ few days passed and Enkara saw no evidence that Ereshkigal was ready to implement her plan. She didn't doubt Ishtar's warning, but perchance they would be lucky and get a few moons grace. Time enough to master her new powers.

Not that that was likely to happen, but Enkara could wish.

Kuwari shared with his parents some of Ishtar's warning. Though he downplayed the bit about how Ereshkigal might attempt to claim Enkara as her Blade and how he was host to a god. Both situations were unchangeable and would needlessly worry his parents.

Even without the worst bits, his parents were still duly concerned and doubled the guard on them both. Queen Iltani set aside her other duties to join Burrukan during Enkara's daily training lesson.

Today she was once again in the outdoor practice ring, its sands warm under her feet. She used the soothing, ever-present power thrumming in the ground beneath her feet to help balance the wild energy within herself. The crystalline sword helped her channel some of the new power, but it was still unwieldy.

All heat and fire and distraction, just waiting for her to shape it into some purpose or let it slip her control. Since the time of her childhood, she'd thought of Ishtar as a goddess of fertility and life, not a deity of vengeance and destruction.

But the power in the sword firmly reminded Enkara that the creator of the gryphons was a multi-faceted goddess. Though Ereshkigal, Queen of the Underworld, always seemed so much more frightening and deadly, her sister was equal or perhaps greater in power.

And Enkara couldn't forget for one minute that she and Kuwari were currently at the heart of the contention between these two powerful deities. She pushed that thought away for later and faced Iltani across the sand.

"Ah, good," Iltani said as she glanced over Enkara's shoulder. "Here comes Kuwari."

Burrukan had suggested Kuwari take part in Enkara's training session to 'make it real' and he'd agreed. Enkara felt a smile tugging at her lips and she turned toward Kuwari. Earlier they'd walked to the practice grounds together, but he'd said he wanted to grab something to help with her training.

Curious, she'd only nodded and watched him hurry away. Now he returned, and Enkara's earlier confidence deflated when she saw what he carried awkwardly in his arms.

It was an archery target, which wasn't so strange. But Kuwari had had entirely too much fun dressing up the wooden target until it was vaguely man-shaped. He'd clothed it in one of his old outfits and then stuffed it with straw. He'd even gone so far as to place a braided wig upon the wooden stump that doubled as the target's head.

After jamming it firmly into the sand, he turned and walked over to her. Her expression must have given something away for he stopped before her and pressed a kiss to her forehead.

"I love you and trust you with my life, but your powers are new and much greater than even you or Iltani realize."

Enkara nodded at the wisdom in that.

A short time later, Iltani joined them and patted Enkara on the shoulder. "I will form a defensive shield around 'the prince' and you will try to breach it without harming your beloved." Iltani's instructions were delivered with a straight face.

Enkara snorted and looked at 'the prince' with a raised eyebrow. "As you wish."

Kuwari patted her on the back and then moved off to stand and watch from the sidelines.

"I'll begin slowly so you can feel and see what I do," Iltani said. "Once you've mastered the power, you'll be able to summon a shield into place fast as a thought."

The crystalline sword in Enkara's hands throbbed in response to Iltani's rising power. A glow illuminated the Queen's skin, then a moment later, golden light, like tiny licks of flame shimmered across her body.

She shaped the power, ordering it to heel, and soon the

magic was leaping out from her body to dance and flare brightly like flames in a breeze. Iltani gestured with her hands, fingers making small swirling motions.

In answer, the power grew brighter and flowed outward and surrounded the archery target.

"There. Now the trick for you will be to attempt to study my work, looking for weaknesses."

Enkara drew in a deep breath and summoned the power simmering in her blood. It leaped to her call, flowing out along her skin, and soon it danced in the air like tiny flames. Not for the first time, Enkara was relieved to see her power looking the same as Iltani's. She'd always half expected something about the color or texture to betray her dual nature to others.

At least, for now, Ereshkigal's power remained dormant.

The power shifted and twisted back upon itself, coiling and quivering in the air. She imposed her will upon it, and the magic calmed by small degrees, but stray tendrils broke away from the mass, fighting to be free of her will.

She let none of it escape. Once she had the fiery ball under control, she consciously directed it toward the archery target. The power streaked through the air, and Enkara shaped it with her mind until it expanded as it flew before colliding with Iltani's sphere of power.

And absolutely nothing happened.

Kuwari cleared his throat. "I believe you actually have to direct it to do something."

"Thanks." She sent a dark glower in his direction. "I hadn't thought of that."

Queen Iltani coughed into her hand and then walked

over to Enkara. "Truthfully, you already have more control of the power than I did after twice as many Blooding Ceremonies. In the beginning, I was all instinct and emotion and only managed to vanquish our enemies because of Ishtar's control and guidance."

Enkara gave her a doubtful look.

"I'm not lying. You'd sense it if I was."

While the Queen's words were obviously true, they still didn't help Enkara much. She needed to master these powers before a goddess took the choice from her. She feared it would be Ereshkigal who would be doing the taking, especially now that she knew what the Queen of the Underworld truly sought.

Iltani stood at Enkara's shoulder and gestured for her to copy her moves. When the Queen held out her arm, Enkara did the same. "Strong emotion is good for calling the power and weaponizing it, but a clear, calm mind is best for more intricate spell work. Brute force only gets you so far."

To demonstrate, Iltani waved her fingers, and a small webbing of magic appeared between them. With a flick of her wrist, it spun out longer, weaving itself into a length of shimmering rope. Then she snapped her fingers closed, and the rope and glowing power vanished.

"The destructive side of the power always came easier for me. It likely will for you as well, but in some instances, like if someone is holding your beloved prisoner, brute force might kill him instead of freeing him."

Which, again, didn't help Enkara understand how to control her magic, but she tried.

Closing her eyes, she channeled the magic through her

crystalline sword. The power came swiftly to her call, but it wasn't interested in performing delicate spell work. Predictably, it tried to slip her control.

Curse it! You will obey me!

She mentally hauled back on the obnoxiously willful power and then flung it at the archery target protected by Queen Iltani's spell.

The second spell flew as true as the first had, slamming into the glowing sphere, but this time her magic sunk below the surface of the protective sphere, flowing through a hundred thousand unseen tiny pores in the smooth surface.

Excitement fluttered in Enkara's stomach. Perhaps this wouldn't be as difficult as she'd thought.

Then the protective sphere cracked, loosing a sound like a scream. Enkara jerked in surprise, and even Iltani flinched at the sudden noise. The sphere shattered, sending hundreds of small shards streaking in all directions. Including into the straw man.

Only Iltani's hastily raised shield protected them from the bright little pulses of light and fiery magic. The straw prince didn't fare so well. Hungry shards of power bit into the straw and cloth, savaging it and destroying all it touched. Burning bits of straw and splinters of wood flew in all directions. Moments later only a smoldering pit remained.

"Goddess," Iltani said a little breathlessly, and then left Enkara to go investigate the pit.

Kuwari sauntered over to the smoking ruin and gave it a once-over. "Ah. I think you might have used a touch too much power."

The corner of his lip quirked up, but otherwise, he kept a straight face.

Right around then Enkara wanted the ground to swallow her. But something else became obvious. Giving Kuwari an accusing glare, she said. "You saw this. You knew it was going to happen. Why didn't you say something?"

"And miss all the fun? Never." But Kuwari walked over to her and wrapped her in a strong embrace. The urge to strangle him subsided.

"You still could have told me."

"Yes. But what would you have learned? This fearsome power is something you will need to master on your own through trial and error." He pressed a kiss to her forehead.

"Fine. I forgive you. And I don't blame you for keeping well back."

"Do you know what else my visions show me?"

"Do I want to know?" Though she did. She always wanted to know what his visions showed him since they often hinted at unseen dangers to come.

"I see you mastering this power to become one of the most powerful Blades ever born." Kuwari placed a finger to her lips. "But don't tell my parents. My father would be swift to defend Iltani's title as greatest Blade ever."

"I'm more than happy to let her keep the title." And that was true. The strength of her own power scared Enkara.

Iltani had finished her walk around the pit and now was approaching them again.

"While that was impressive in a brutal sort of way, let's see if you can breach a second sphere without obliterating everything inside."

Kuwari laughed. "Don't look at me. I'm not volunteering to play 'helpless victim' for several days yet."

Enkara groaned and somehow knew her mate was going to be telling this tale around the high table later tonight at dinner.

Great Ishtar grant her patience.

CHAPTER THIRTY-NINE

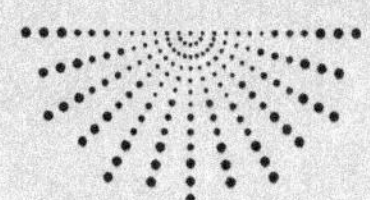

Time continued its steady march and as Kuwari had promised, Enkara gained greater mastery of her new power. She was just starting to allow herself to believe all would be well when the first deaths were reported.

She and Kuwari were just returning to the palace from the outdoor training field when a Shadow rushed up to them.

"Crown Prince Kuwari, Blade Enkara, the King requires you to attend to him at once in the council chambers." The Shadow, a short woman by the name of Amata, didn't tell them what was going on. It wasn't until they reached King Ditanu and High Priestess Kammani in the great hall that they learned the dire news. The first to have taken sick just after the Spring Rites had since died mysteriously.

"Didn't the healers say they thought it only a minor illness, just one they hadn't seen before? I thought the first to show signs of sickness were already better?" Kuwari directed his questions at his father.

Ditanu looked up from a report he held in one hand. "That is what I thought as well."

Kuwari leaned over his father's shoulder to read the missive for himself. Enkara hung back and waited for either king, prince, or priestess to fill in the details.

Finally, King Ditanu spoke. "The early symptoms are just that. Premature and not indicative of the full illness. After the first wave of chills and headache, the disease goes into a quiescent stage where it silently grows within the host body. Once the illness has a strong enough foothold, it reappears with a new set of symptoms. A high fever with uncontrolled sweating, followed by violent shaking and difficulty breathing. Later the sweating turns to bleeding from the pores of the skin and then from the eyes, ears, nose, and mouth. The only mercy is that the victim loses consciousness long before they drown in their own blood."

"The news grows worse," High Priestess Kammani said softly.

"None who came down with the illness have survived its final phase." Ditanu crumpled up the report. "Princess Arwia and Prince Erra both came down with a fever today."

"Goddess," Enkara whispered, horrified.

"A Goddess indeed," Ditanu said darkly. "I fear this must be a plague sent by Ereshkigal."

High Priestess Kammani nodded as she came to stand next to the king. "We will discover how this is spreading to stop others from falling ill. We will find a cure. We must. We can't allow Ereshkigal to take souls before their time."

"We will fight this," King Ditanu agreed. "Summon Iltani and the Regents, the rest of the council, too. I want the most senior healers brought in as well. I don't care where they are or what they're doing, gather them all."

Queen Iltani and Burrukan were the first to arrive, followed by a worried Regent Ahassunu. Soon more councilors came, answering the summons by their king. Not long after, the healers arrived. King Ditanu laid out plans that might help slow the spread of the disease to uninfected city-states and then requested a list of anything and everything the healers might need.

"I'll get the herbs and other supplies even if I have to hunt for them myself," Ditanu said, his king's mask falling away, showing a glimpse of the worried father beneath the calm exterior.

THE MEETING WENT LONG into the night and when it concluded each councilor, healer, priest, and priestess was assigned a work detail comprised of servants and nobles alike. When New Sumer was threatened all became equals.

Kuwari and Enkara had been assigned the task of hauling emergency sleeping pallets from storage in the lower levels of the palace. They were generally reserved for coronations when the entire population of New Sumer descended upon Nineveh, he reflected, far outstripping the capacity of available lodgings.

Now the pallets would be used for the sick as they were brought to the healer's quarters. From the dark glimpses of his visions, he saw how the sick would overflow out into the halls around the healers' quarters and later, further still, filling the great hall, council chambers, courtyards, gardens and any bit of available space.

Presently, he was standing shoulder to shoulder with Councilor Enheduana and a priest named Balathu. Enheduana was a pleasant sort of woman, hardworking and not given to chattiness outside of the council chambers. Unfortunately, the priest was in love with his own voice.

Though that might just have been nerves. Some people didn't handle stress well.

Knowing hundreds of their people were even now falling ill tended to do that. He was just reaching up to remove a stack of the wood pallet frames from the shelf in the far back corner of the storage room when Enheduana placed a hand on his arm and then held out a cloth-wrapped bundle.

At the touch of her skin to his, the gift and curse that allowed him to read others flared to life. He felt her true allegiances and they were not to Ishtar. He stepped back and instinctively drew a dagger.

"You won't be needing that. I am no threat to you as you already know. Otherwise, your Blade would be leaping across the chamber to gut me where I stand." Enheduana thrust the package at him again. "Take this and use it if you don't want to see your younger siblings die. When I was 'blessing' them earlier, I delivered a more potent version of my Lady's plague to them. They won't have days like the other victims."

Kuwari's nostrils flared as he fought to stop himself from reaching across the distance and wrapping his fingers around her treacherous throat. "Why have you betrayed your king and your people?"

"I have not betrayed my king. I serve my queen. Ereshkigal, Queen of the Underworld. Her bidding I carry out and no other's."

Rage continued to build inside him, but he fought it down. High emotion wouldn't help his younger siblings.

"What must I do?" he said at last.

"Negotiate with my queen and learn what she wants. I'm sure you can both come to a resolution."

"I already know what she wants."

"Ah," Enheduana said. "Ishtar has been whispering in your ear. It matters not. Only your cooperation can save your innocent sisters and brothers now."

"I could kill you where you stand and still negotiate later."

"My life belongs to Queen Ereshkigal. I would gladly die to further her wishes." Enheduana placed the small cloth bundle down on the shelf next to the pallet frames.

"While killing you would make me feel better, it would also alert my Blade, and she would stop me from contacting Ereshkigal and possibly saving my siblings. Circumstances outside of your control are the only reason you will survive this day. Remember that, Enheduana."

Kuwari snatched up the bundle and then shoved it under his belt.

Once his business with the Queen of the Underworld was done, he'd be certain to clean house and send the souls of all Ereshkigal's faithful servants back to her side.

He spun and walked away from the traitorous viper.

Enkara, sensing his mood, stopped what she was doing and came to his side.

"What's going on?"

"My siblings have been exposed to a more potent version of this disease. They don't have much time."

"What?" Enkara placed her hand on his shoulder and forced him to look at her. "You had a vision, didn't you?"

If he lied, she'd sense it. He said nothing, letting her come to her own conclusions.

"Goddess, it must be bad if you're not willing to talk about it."

"I need to see them, to confirm this news."

Enkara frowned unhappily but nodded and led him out of the storage levels. Once they reached the nursery, Shadows bowed but blocked the way.

"I'm sorry my Prince, but King Ditanu doesn't want you exposed to the sickness." A female Shadow explained in an apologetic tone. "Only the healers and their helpers are allowed beyond."

"I've had a vision, seen danger to my siblings. Move! Now!" Kuwari's barked command made the Shadows stiffen, but they held their ground.

Rage swept through Kuwari. Why must everything go badly?

"Get. Out. Of. My. Way!"

Still, the guards stood firm. It was Enkara who came to his rescue, stopping him from attacking one of his own Shadow guards.

"This new danger is to more than just his little sister and brothers. I feel new danger to Kuwari as well. I am

Ishtar's Blade! You will move and allow me to do what I must!"

This time the guards bowed and moved.

Enkara led the way, and he followed close on her heels. Inside, they made their way deeper into the nursery. He came upon his little sister first. A healer with a headscarf was tending to her, dipping a rag that might once have been white into a bowl of steaming herb-scented water. She wrung it out and used it to wipe away the sheen of bloody sweat from his sister's face.

More welled up within moments. A trickle of red seeped from the corner of her eye and rolled down her cheek to disappear into her hair. The healer looked up at his approach.

"My Prince, you shouldn't be here," she said, her voice muffled by the thick scarf.

Kuwari ignored the woman.

Just this morning he'd seen his sister at first meal, laughing and playing with his brothers. Now she might be dead by moonrise.

Great Goddess Ishtar, please protect my family.

But he already knew she couldn't, not without confronting her sister.

So be it. He'd deal with this himself.

Ereshkigal might think she'd set the perfect trap for him, but he, in turn, was going to trap her and force her to call back her sickness and swear never to harm his family or his people again.

And then he was going to force her into a deal she couldn't break, not in his lifetime at least.

He saw it now, a vision snapping clear. It was the only way to save lives and create a truce between these two warring goddesses. Enkara would be livid, but it was sacrifice himself or watch all New Sumer fall.

Unwrapping the bundle, a small medallion fell into his hand. Its metal was dark and unnaturally cold.

"What is that thing?" She leaned closer for a better look. Then she stiffened. "Where did you get that thing?"

Before Enkara could stop him, he looped the heavy chain over his head.

"No!"

As the medallion came to rest upon his chest, its magic flared to life, expanding out, racing down his extremities. With a loud roaring like that of a great ocean storm, everything shifted around him, and he was swept far from where he'd been.

When the world righted itself, Enkara was far-off, but distantly he could still feel her fear.

Blinking, he realized he was staring at a mural depicting Ereshkigal and Nergal sitting upon their thrones, overseeing the afterlife. In the forefront of the painting, the seven anunnaki judges were weighing the deeds of a newly arrived soul, determining if it was pure enough to join the other souls floating about their existence under a vast, star-speckled sky.

Spinning around to face the room, he came nose to beak with a now familiar eagle-headed anunnaki.

"Welcome home, King Nergal. We have long awaited your return."

CHAPTER FORTY

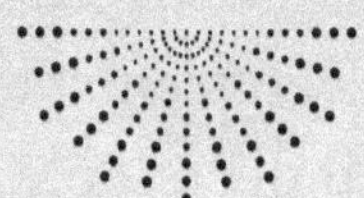

One moment Kuwari had been standing directly before her, almost within touching distance. Then he'd pulled out a medallion that gave off that familiar dark power she remembered too well from her childhood. Even though she was standing so close, she wasn't fast enough to stop him from swiftly looping the chain around his neck.

Faster than a blink of an eye, he was gone in a rush of cold power.

Enkara screamed her rage. Shadows came running, but there was nothing they could do to help. The Crown Prince was far beyond their ability to reach. Only she could aid her beloved now, but she needed Ishtar's help to reach the underworld.

She broke into a run, darting up through the halls of the palace, making her way to the outside. Shadows raced after her, knowing something had happened to the prince, but not what. There was no time to explain.

With her new powers strengthening her, she outpaced even the fastest of the Shadows, at least those on two legs. Her expanded awareness told her several had halted to take on gryphon form. But the moments it took them to shift forms was all she needed.

The temple loomed in front of her, and she darted up the stairs. Racing past the line of columns, she entered the temple itself. She wove between startled priests and priestesses to move deeper into the temple.

When she reached the altar room, a foreign magic greeted her. Skidding to a halt, she drew her crystalline blade and scanned the circular room. Torches and copper mirrors delivered ample light. There were no shadows where an assailant could hide. And yet something was here.

It felt powerful and old. Like a Lamassu, but not.

There was only one creature that felt like that.

"I know you're here." How it was here, she didn't know. One of its kind should not have been able to reside in Ishtar's own temple.

"Ah, you've come far if you can sense me in my natural form," the anunnaki said as he appeared before her.

Its body was that of a well-built man in his prime, but the rest of it—him—was far less human looking. A noble desert eagle's head sat atop a thick neck. And framing his wide shoulders were two sets of massive wings. He was dressed like the carving of the anunnaki she'd seen in the temple and palace, with a fringed, knee-length tunic. Overlaying that was a sash of rich golden fabric. An ornate headdress with a golden diadem rested on top of his feathered head. Large, penetrating black eyes watched her every move.

She knew from legend that some of the anunnaki could appear more human if they wished. That this one did not, suggested he was looking to inspire fear or reverence.

"I appear in my true form out of respect to the temple of Ishtar."

The legends and sacred texts also said the anunnaki could read a mortal's mind as easily as a person could read an unrolled scroll. Since the scrolls were correct about that, she could only assume they were correct about an anunnaki's more formidable abilities.

And here he stood in Ishtar's temple, at her very altar.

Whatever his reason for being here, it couldn't be good.

"You wonder how and why I'm here." The anunnaki sidestepped her and slowly paced around the altar piled high with offerings. His body language was non-threatening. And why shouldn't it be? He didn't have to threaten at all. If he wanted, he could harvest souls like a farmer scything his wheat field.

For all he looked solidly flesh and blood, she knew she was looking at a spirit. A powerful spirit that purified souls before they descended to the underworld. But his powers ran deeper than that. Like all anunnaki, he could battle demons and other dark spirits, rendering them impotent.

Enkara's hand tightened on the hilt of her crystalline sword. It might be the only weapon that could harm such a powerful guardian spirit.

"Yes, Blade. That sword could send me back to the underworld to lick my wounds, but if you love your people, you'll hear what I have to offer."

"Speak then." While he did, Enkara would attempt to figure out his real purpose.

"I bring with me the means to heal the sick and stop the spread of the disease." He stepped back and for the first time, she spotted a simple wooden bucket like a servant would use to hold water for cleaning. Except this one had rosettes carved into the wood and beside it lay a large pinecone.

Neither item was as ordinary as it looked. The anunnaki were known to use everyday items from the living world and imbue them with great power. Those deceptively normal looking tools were then used for purification and blessing.

"They can heal the sickness spreading through your people as easily as purifying a darkened soul," he offered.

"The illness you started?"

"I? No, this was not my doing. And none of the other anunnaki were involved with this particular event. Our role is to protect, bless, and drive away evil. Plagues are not our domain."

"And yet you allowed it to happen."

"I control the sisters no more than you control one of the great ocean storms that blow and rage across the islands." The anunnaki actually chuckled at the thought. "However, you are correct. The sisters' war has caused much grief. But perhaps with proper guidance from me, you, and Prince Kuwari we can get them to bury their animosity for a little while."

"Is that why you're here? Kuwari traded his life for his family and his people."

"That is not why I'm here, but Kuwari did trade himself in the hope that his sacrifice will be enough to save all those he loves and prevent the Queen of the Underworld from striking out again later."

"Ishtar will not stand for it. Nor will I. Together we are strong enough to rescue Kuwari."

"Ah. I see you came to the temple hoping to gain the aid of a goddess, but they are fickle creatures. She is not here and has allowed one of the anunnaki into her domain for the first time in thousands of years. Why do you think that is?"

Enkara's mind whirled, not liking what his words implied. Yet he was here, and Ishtar was not answering her silent prayers.

"I have spoken with your great Ishtar, and she has listened to my advice. She will sacrifice Crown Prince Kuwari to save the rest of her gryphons."

Enkara was speechless. Never had she felt so betrayed before. All Ishtar's words of honor, and her pleas to her Avenging Blade to always guard Kuwari, it was all for nothing.

And, yet, Enkara realized, if someone had offered her and Kuwari an ultimatum of sacrificing themselves for the good of their people, they both would have agreed without question. She drew in deep, calming breaths.

Ishtar might have abandoned Kuwari, but Enkara never would. "Your plan for a treaty between the sisters requires more than just Kuwari, though, doesn't it? Ishtar told me how Ereshkigal can't touch Kuwari directly without killing him. If she does, the soul of her beloved husband will vanish again, beyond her reach."

"Yes."

"You need me to come with you."

"Yes, brave Blade."

"How do I know you haven't been sent by Ereshkigal?"

"You don't," the anunnaki said simply. "But I could have come with my six brothers and taken you by surprise. I came alone, with honesty in my heart."

Enkara looked back at the altar of Ishtar and stared at the deceptively simple bucket and cone. "I will go with you after I've seen your 'cure' at work. You will start with Kuwari's siblings since they have a more virulent version."

"Very well. I shall heal them now and while I prove to you that my words are true, others of my kind will arrive and tend every human and gryphon struck down by this disease." He reached out and reclaimed his tools and then gestured for Enkara to lead the way.

She did. There was no other choice. It was either accept his help and surrender her freedom or watch an entire kingdom fall.

When they left the altar room, Enkara understood why no Shadows had interrupted her conversation with the anunnaki. The guards were trapped outside, prevented from entering the heart of the temple by a shimmering shield.

The anunnaki waved a hand and the shield blocking their way vanished.

A few tense moments followed while she explained to the Shadows and newly arriving city guards what was going on. The tension was further eased by the arrival of a lamassu who greeted the anunnaki and assured him there would be peace before returning to his post.

Had the anunnaki truly meant to harm anyone, the lamassu would have known and reacted accordingly.

Together they made their way back to the palace and the nursery. The anunnaki faded from view, but she could still feel his ancient presence. He must know enough about the living world and mortals to hide his presence. If others saw him and guessed his purpose here, they would be mobbed, impeding their progress.

"All anunnaki once aided the lamassu in guarding and protecting this world. I know the ways of mortals."

"Must you read every thought?"

"You are projecting them." The anunnaki said in a matter-of-fact tone.

Well…curse it. "I'm sorry."

"It is the special bond you share with your gryphon prince. The magic you both used to forge it comes from Nergal. As an anunnaki of the underworld, I'm sensitive to it, allowing me to easily read you even though you are also a Blade. With more training, you should be able to control it better."

If Enkara lived long enough, she would strive to master that skill.

When they at last reached the nursery, the guards on duty allowed Enkara and her escort to pass without question because they were unaware of the invisible anunnaki pacing alongside her. She continued deeper into the nursery until she heard the familiar voice of the senior healer.

"I'm sorry, she is beyond my ability to help."

The healer's words were met with a broken sob.

Heart pounding and dread curling in her stomach, Enkara continued in. Were they already too late? Horror swamped her. Her throat tightened in dread as she braced for what she'd find inside.

Crossing the threshold from the play area into the sleeping chambers, Enkara's gaze landed on King Ditanu where he sat on the edge of the bed and held a small body in his arms. Tears coursed down his face. Queen Iltani was next to him, sobbing against his shoulder.

The senior healer was standing at the foot of the bed with two other aids flanking her. Her eyes were ringed by dark shadows, and her face etched with grief—the countenance of one who had seen too much sadness already. "It is only a matter of time. I'm sorry."

Slowly, Enkara dragged herself forward and peered down at the child. She caught her breath, almost not recognizing little Arwia. Her skin was gray, the only color the bright blood weeping from the corners of her eyes and mouth. Her chest still labored to draw breath, the sound wet and heavy.

"There is still life," the anunnaki said as he became visible.

Healers, servants, and royals all jerked with surprise. The healers recoiled, the servants fell to the ground in silent homage, and Ditanu and Iltani both drew their blades. The guards raced forward, instinctively prepared to attack the intruder, not having processed that their weapons would be ineffective against an opponent such as this.

"Wait!" Enkara shouted. "He's here to heal the sick. A lamassu confirmed it."

The anunnaki bowed to King Ditanu and Queen Iltani. "My brothers and I come to restore the balance. Ereshkigal and her servants have overstepped their authority."

King Ditanu recovered faster than his guards. He ordered

them out of the way, allowing the anunnaki to approach unhindered. Once the winged being was at the side of the bed, he dipped the long, ordinary looking pinecone into his small bucket.

When he lifted the cone from the water, Enkara realized that what was in the wooden vessel wasn't water at all. Bright magic dripped from the individual scales of the cone. Where drops fell to splash against Arwia's pallid skin, the divine magic flared brighter, enveloping the child.

The anunnaki chanted an ancient blessing and then stepped back. The bright healing light faded, and Enkara found herself holding her breath. Then the small body on the bed moved, and Arwia pushed back the blankets covering her and looked around shyly. Other than her messy hair, she looked completely healthy. No trace of blood or sickness remained.

When the child's eyes landed on the anunnaki, they grew wide, and Arwia smiled, reaching out for the guardian spirit.

The anunnaki moved close enough so the child's reaching fingers could touch the feathers of his double set of wings. Enkara noted the softening and rounding of the eyes in the anunnaki's eagle-like head. This creature, though capable of killing any mortal and purifying or even eating the soul if it was incurable, had a gentle streak as well.

Arwia giggled in delight. "An anunnaki!"

"Thank you, ancient one," King Ditanu said, giving the creature a deep bow.

Enkara had only ever seen the king bow to a lamassu before.

"I am in your debt for healing my child, but there are many more innocents struck down by this illness."

"I know. It is why I have come. More of my brethren are waiting as we speak. I feared to bring the numbers needed until I had a chance to speak with you, lest you think we were an invading force."

"You may call the rest. I will not turn away your aid." Ditanu gave Arwia a firm hug and then set her back on the bed. The healers came forward to examine the girl while the king gestured for the anunnaki to follow. "There are many other innocent cubs struck down by this illness. I would trade my own life to save them all."

"I do not require payment to right a wrong."

In the next chamber, they found Regents Ahassunu and Burrukan kneeling by a large bed. Erra looked to be little better than Arwia had been.

The anunnaki projected calm and shortly after the swift blessing and purification ritual, the boy regained consciousness and blinked open his eyes. He was healed and healthy, just like Arwia.

Wordlessly, the anunnaki moved out into the hall, showering all the mortals as he went. Once outside, Enkara saw that the other anunnaki had arrived as promised and were healing the sick.

After that, the ancient one—Enkara had resorted to giving him that label since he hadn't shared his name—turned to look at her.

"My brethren will stay and heal all those who have been struck down by this illness, but it is time for us to leave."

"Leave?" Only then did King Ditanu scan the crowd

around him. His ever-present king's mask cracking and falling away. "Where is my oldest son? Where is Kuwari?"

The anunnaki bowed. "Your son has gone to the underworld to negotiate with Queen Ereshkigal to prevent this from happening again."

"No." The king's denial reopened Enkara's own fears for her beloved prince.

"Your son knows that Ereshkigal will never rest. She will always seek to make others feel what she herself felt at the loss of her beloved. An accord must be reached, a treaty drawn up between the two goddesses. Crown Prince Kuwari is key to that."

"I failed him." Queen Iltani said as tears flowed from her red-rimmed eyes. "He always knew this dark future was coming for him and yet he never complained or deviated from his moral code. Our beautiful boy. How can Ishtar allow this?"

"A sacrifice is sometimes needed to bring about peace." The anunnaki looked to Enkara again. "And other times a compromise like the Sacred Marriage will do well enough. Are you ready young Blade?"

King Ditanu drew his sword. "What are you—"

"Yes," Enkara said, cutting off the king for the first time in her life. But she was too focused on what the guardian spirit had just said. The ancient one had just given her the seeds of a plan that might free Kuwari. "I am ready to go now."

The anunnaki nodded and then raised his hand and brought it down upon her head. Magic surged, dancing all around her in vivid hues, shimmering brighter until all the colors were burned away, leaving only a blinding white glow in its wake.

Then solid blackness snuffed out the light. A moment later, she felt the world shift as she fell through the layers of the mortal world.

CHAPTER FORTY-ONE

The temple he found himself in was familiar to Kuwari. After all, he'd been here before in his visions. Now he stood looking out over a stone balcony, a beautiful city spreading out below him. This one easily rivaled the splendor of Nineveh. And the sky! Never had he seen such stars. They expanded across the sky in ribbons of glorious color, so bright he needed no other light to see the city below.

As spectacular as it was, its beauty didn't touch him.

Anunnaki patrolled the pristine streets. People, or perhaps he should call them what they truly were, spirits of the dead, moved around below, attending to whatever spirits did in the underworld, he supposed.

"Once you agree to my terms, you will grow accustomed to your new home, and soon your Blade will join you here. My husband and I can make you happy."

Kuwari doubted that. He turned to glance sidelong at

Ereshkigal where she stood at his shoulder, overlooking the capital of her domain.

She was every bit the regal queen and goddess rolled into one glorious package. Great beauty forged with fearsome power. He didn't doubt her husband would be eager to again hold her in his embrace. Kuwari just wished Nergal wouldn't be using his arms to do it.

None of this was what he would have chosen, but fate seldom delivered the outcome of one's desire. And the twenty anunnaki lining the walls of the chamber behind him were there to ensure he didn't try to trick his way free of this fate.

Turning, he smiled at Ereshkigal, completely catching the goddess off guard. She drew in a sharp breath before recovering enough to speak. "You are my sister's greatest gift to the world was the gryphons and the men and women of the royal line."

"And what is yours?"

"Creating my own perfect Blade to match you in every way."

"Creation isn't your gift. You can't claim any part of Enkara's greatness."

"No? Perhaps not. But I shaped her, and she will become my Blade in time."

"Only if you can convince her."

Ereshkigal's expression twisted into something dark and filled with rage. Oh, she was still annoyed with him for discovering that little tidbit of news. But he'd gladly use it to save his beloved.

The moment the medallion had brought him to the land

of Kur, his gift of visions had latched upon Ereshkigal and showed him many interesting things. One of the most beneficial was the knowledge that the Queen of the Underworld couldn't force Enkara to act as her host without first gaining her permission.

Being half-human, Enkara was under the protection of Enki, creator god of the first humans. It hadn't taken Kuwari long to figure out that he was also protected to some small degree since Ishtar had blended the lines of humans and gryphons long ago to tame the wildness of the winged predators. That had been a handy bit of knowledge.

After Ereshkigal mastered her rage, she stared out at the city below them again. "Have you come to a decision?"

"I have," Kuwari agreed. "If you promise to call back your disease and refrain from launching further attacks against New Sumer and its people, I will willingly surrender my body to Nergal."

"You know I want more."

"We all want more. Sometimes it's denied, and we must settle for crumbs."

"I cannot touch my husband without killing you and sending his spirit spinning away to be reborn."

"Then I suggest being careful not to touch. Isn't having your husband as a companion better than nothing at all? If I don't surrender to him and allow his power to adapt my body to survive here, I won't live long, and you will lose your chance." Kuwari arched an eyebrow at Ereshkigal. "And next time Ishtar will be ready to stop even your cleverest anunnaki from slipping Nergal's soul into one of her gryphon royals."

"How do I know you'll hold up your end of the bargain if I send my anunnaki to cure the disease?"

Kuwari grinned. "I'll swear to a god I hold in high esteem."

It was Ereshkigal's turn to arch an eyebrow. "If you think to trick me into allowing one of Ishtar's agents here…"

"No. But Tammuz is trapped here, is he not?" Kuwari looked out over the balcony again. "I will swear my word to him that I will uphold any agreement forged between you and me."

"Very well." Ereshkigal suspicious expression relaxed somewhat, which probably meant there was nothing that the god of agriculture could do for him. "I will have him summoned."

"No one summons me. Ereshkigal, sometimes I think you forget it isn't your power that holds me here," a new voice said directly behind them, "Death is no barrier to the god of renewal. Only my oath keeps me here. I gave my word so that my beloved Ishtar could be free."

Kuwari spun and laid his eyes on a tall male approaching them from the chamber's opposite entrance. He looked young, barely more than an adolescent, with a wild mop of black hair and dusty olive skin, but the power rolling off him was much more ancient than his appearance would suggest.

Dropping to his knees, Kuwari prostrated himself on the polished stone floor. "I am honored."

Tammuz sighed wearily. "It would have pleased me better if we'd met under different circumstances. I grow tired of this manipulation and backstabbing among my fellow gods. We've lost our integrity somewhere along the path."

Kuwari glanced up at the god of shepherds and green things. "Your words are wise. Please know that if events had progressed as I wished, I would have been honored to be your host for the Sacred Marriage."

"I can see that in your soul."

Tammuz's expression was unworried, almost relaxed. Kuwari wished his own soul shared that same deep calm.

And then Tammuz's voice was in his mind. *"Fear not, young gryphon prince, if my plans come to fruition, you may yet have the chance to act as my host one day."*

Only training from an earlier age to mask his thoughts, expression, and emotions allowed Kuwari to keep a neutral expression in place at the harvest god's words. But for all that control, renewed hope still blossomed in his heart.

"Enough talk," Ereshkigal said and five anunnaki stepped forward from the others lining the edge of the room. "You five and Tammuz shall bear witness to this oath between the gryphon prince and myself."

With nods and muttered agreements, the anunnaki drew closer, circling Kuwari.

Seeing no point in putting it off, he swore upon is life, soul and love of his kingdom that he would surrender himself to Nergal's control if the Queen of the Underworld spared New Sumer from the current disease ravaging its shores and all future attempts.

In turn, Ereshkigal swore to end her war upon the gryphon kingdom, its people, and those of the royal line.

"We witness this," the five anunnaki said in unison.

"As do I," Tammuz said softly.

Kuwari was still coming to terms with his new existence

when a disturbance drew his attention to the ranks of anunnaki standing behind the four judges. Weaving his way out from behind others of his kind, a tall, powerfully built eagled-headed male stepped forward. The essence of his power was familiar.

But Kuwari barely noticed the new anunnaki, his eyes only for the woman who walked beside him with her hands bound in front of her. Enkara. His bravely irrational Blade had come to set him free, but only managed to get caught herself. If he'd had the strength to communicate over the vast distance between the underworld and the mortal world, he would have warned her not to come. There would be no freedom for him now, not after he'd sworn an oath to Ereshkigal.

CHAPTER FORTY-TWO

Enkara kept her head up proudly as she walked next to the anunnaki. He was a strangely calming presence. Otherwise, Enkara would have been clenching her hands into fists if they weren't already tied so tightly she couldn't move them.

"Ah. The first Judge has returned from a successful hunt. Come forward Blade where I can get a better look at you." With a regal nod of her head, Ereshkigal indicated a spot two paces in front of her.

Enkara marched forward. There would be no fighting this goddess. At least not yet. When she'd cleared the small crowd of anunnaki standing guard, she studied Ereshkigal. The Queen of the Underworld was equally as stunning to behold as her fierier sister. But that was the only thing they shared.

Where Ishtar's magic was all passion and fire, Ereshkigal's was like a vast, ice-covered mountain lake. Deep and cold and ready to suck you under and never let you surface again once that power had you in its grip.

Enkara tried to suppress a shudder but failed. Concentrating on Kuwari, she drew strength and warmth from him instead.

"Beloved," he whispered in her mind. *"As much as I have always wanted you near me, this one time I would have preferred you had stayed away."*

"We promised to follow where the other went. This is me keeping that oath."

Kuwari visibly winced at the word oath. *"You shouldn't have come, no matter what Ishtar said. You'll be a slave alongside me now. I'm sorry, but there was no other way to safeguard the kingdom."*

"Who said anything about being a slave? I came willingly, of my own choice."

"You are crazier than me." His soft mental touch filled her with his love.

"Kuwari, much has already happened since you came here. Our eagle-headed friend who accompanied me healed your siblings and called others of his kind to purify the rest of Nineveh's sick and dying. He promised to see that all the city-states are cured."

"Do you trust him?"

"Yes. After a fashion. The lamassu did not see him or his brothers as a threat. Even if he is not a friend, at least he isn't our enemy either."

A third mind brushed against their private link before invading it far too easily, startling Enkara until Kuwari showed her it was Tammuz.

"The Anunnaki are ancient and have their own honor code," Tammuz said, *"Once one offers you his aid, he will carry out whatever task set him so long as it doesn't conflict with his own duties."*

Feeling foolish for not recognizing the harvest god, she rectified her social blunder by swiftly dropping to her knees and then bowing her forehead to the floor.

"That is not necessary, Blade Enkara," Tammuz said with a hint of humor before his tone turned serious once more. *"This anunnaki is also my friend. You can trust him."*

When Enkara straightened, Ereshkigal was standing nearer, studying her with a critical eye. "You're pleasing to the eye. A good fit never goes amiss."

"You must be willing," Kuwari interjected. "She can't force you to act as host, or she risks angering Enki."

"True. But I shall enjoy bargaining to gain your agreement, Blade. There are many things I can offer, but likely only one you'd compromise your morals to have." She suggestively ran her gaze over Kuwari. "I look forward to the negotiating, but first I must attend to Crown Prince Kuwari so that my husband's spirit may awaken. The prince has a very powerful mind and will need help learning to surrender, but I believe my husband will wish to be part of these discussions."

A look of mild revulsion crossed Kuwari's features but by the time the queen looked at him he had his emotionless mask back in place.

"Take Blade Enkara and have her fed, bathed and dressed so that she is ready when I call."

Enkara was somewhat surprised that there was food and

water and such in the underworld. What need did spirits have for such things?

"Your expression is so open. Nothing like your prince." Smiling in delight, Ereshkigal explained. "While this is the underworld, I have mortal servants as well. Priests and priestesses who live here with me, safely away from the other gods who might try to poach them from me. And what do you think happens to all that food left on altars throughout the kingdom of New Sumer?"

Enkara knew the teachings, that the food was for those in the afterlife, but secretly she'd always just assumed it was eaten by the temple servants or was discarded once the altars were cleaned. She'd never thought it made its way to the afterlife or that mortals were living here.

"I will summon you when I am ready. And destroy that crystalline sword she was wearing when you captured her. I can feel it tainting my realm with my sister's power." Ereshkigal shuddered. "It offends my senses."

With that the Queen of the Underworld dismissed Enkara. At a silent signal from the goddess, a priest came forward carrying long gloves made of tanned animal skin. Ereshkigal pulled on the soft leather gloves as she turned her attention entirely upon Kuwari.

The prince stood his ground as Ereshkigal walked a slow circle around him and then stopped directly in front of him to press her palm against his chest. She whispered something to him below Enkara's hearing, but she could guess the type of conversation by the flare of a blush upon Kuwari's cheeks.

"You might as well tell me what that whore is whispering to you, so I know how much revenge I have to exact later." Enkara

didn't care if various gods and goddesses overheard their conversation.

"You can look in my head if you wish. I'm not giving her words more power by repeating them."

Enkara restrained herself. Barely. *"I'm half-gryphon. I will make her pay for touching what is rightfully mine."*

"I imagine the goddess will have something to say to that."

"Let her."

The anunnaki ushered her away, but every twenty paces, she glanced back at Kuwari until she walked under an archway and out into a hall. She did not have to like this situation, she only had to endure it for a short while until she managed to bargain for their freedom. She hoped.

CHAPTER FORTY-THREE

The anunnaki led her lower into the temple until they eventually came to a hall with several curtained alcoves. When they entered one, she discovered they were personal chambers, likely belonging to the priests, priestesses, and servants Ereshkigal had mentioned.

"If you plan to free Kuwari," the anunnaki spoke suddenly, "you will have to do it swiftly, before she attempts to wake the spirit of her husband and discovers something I'd rather she not know about until after you've rejoined your prince."

"Tell me now if it is a danger I should know about."

"It is a long story and there's no time. You'll understand shortly." The anunnaki waved his hand in the air, and suddenly he was holding a garment comprised of many veils. "I believe this is appropriate attire for the role you are about to play."

When he shook out the skirt, she recognized the many veils as the ceremonial garb worn by Ishtar's Blade during various rites and ceremonies, but most notably during the Sacred Marriage.

The anunnaki must have stolen it from the mortal world. Enkara reached out a hand and took what he offered. Kuwari's feathers, removed during the formal blooding ceremony had been beautifully stitched into the waist of the skirt as well as falling from the back of the diadem.

She stroked the feathers and felt that much closer to Kuwari. "Thank you for this."

"Ishtar also said you'd want this," he said as he returned her harness, scabbard and the hefty weight of the crystalline sword he'd taken from her earlier.

She glanced up in surprise but accepted the sword from him. Then she retreated behind a screen and shed her training tunic and donned the battle dress of Ishtar's Avenging Blade.

The sword warmed in her hands and Ishtar whispered into her mind. *"I am proud of you. Do not falter and you will again have your freedom and Kuwari at your side."*

"Forgive me for doubting you. I shouldn't have lost faith, not even when you wouldn't answer me."

The goddess's warm humor danced across Enkara's mind. *"I had to make my sister believe I'd sacrificed you and Kuwari for the sake of my other gryphons. But you are a true Blade in all ways. I will never abandon you."*

When she was ready, the anunnaki led her back out into the hall. This time they headed farther down instead of back up. Enkara arched an eyebrow and the anunnaki explained.

"While the negotiations will be held on the roof for all to see, Ereshkigal has sent Kuwari down to the lower levels of the temple where she plans to wake Nergal and begin altering the prince so that he can reside here permanently." The anunnaki increased his pace. "Once she completes that, there will be no going home for either you or your prince."

"We must hurry." Enkara broke into a run and the anunnaki glided along beside her.

They halted four levels down from where they'd started and Enkara's magic told her Kuwari was here, just a few chambers worth of space between them. She would relax once she had his back and he had hers again.

As they hurried down a corridor, she felt as the anunnaki called power. One moment his hands were empty, the next he was holding Kuwari's favorite sword and set of daggers.

Mild envy of the anunnaki's power was quickly pushed aside for the more immediate concern of how dangerous their plan was and how quickly it could go wrong. For it to even work, Enkara would need to be touching Kuwari before the Queen of the Underworld knew what she was about.

The anunnaki led her farther down a narrow corridor but held his hand up signaling that they should stop. He listened—at least she thought he listened, his head turning this way and that—and then he urged her into motion again.

They ghosted through the archway on silent feet. Enkara slid sideways and put her back to the wall and held her sword at the ready. But there was no attack. Her eyes narrowed. The room was silent but not empty. Kuwari and

Tammuz were standing beside an altar in the center of the room.

When the anunnaki started forward again, the two males looked in their direction.

"Ah, the young Blade has come for her beloved," Kuwari said, his speech patterns nothing like she was used to hearing.

Enkara skidded to a halt and raised the tip of her crystalline sword higher in readiness to do battle. What she would fight, she didn't know.

"Easy, Enkara," Tammuz said. "Don't call power yet. We don't want Ereshkigal to know that we are defying her. It's a miracle she hasn't yet sensed our manipulation."

"Ereshkigal is the lawmaker here. She'd never expect anyone would be capable of defying her in her own realm," said Kuwari who wasn't her Kuwari at all.

"Who are you?" Though she knew this must be Nergal, Ereshkigal's husband, the god of war and pestilence, a bringer of death. She was too late? Ereshkigal had already awakened her husband.

"I am the one you name in your mind," he murmured along their mental link. *"Nergal. Though, those other titles were applied to me by mortals. Humans don't need encouragement to war. They seem to do that readily enough on their own."*

"What about the 'pestilence' and the 'bringer of death' parts?"

He shrugged. "I am a bringer of death and a balancer. I free souls from dying flesh and help them cross over into the afterlife."

Enkara edged closer. "What has become of Kuwari?"

"He is still here with me. Unharmed."

"Is he now a slave to you?" Her eyes worked fine, but she had to hear the words to confirm what her heart and mind already dreaded.

"No. I have no interest in a slave, but Tammuz and I needed to talk. This was the fastest way. Kuwari willingly surrendered but do not fear. You will get your prince back shortly. In the meantime, we'd like to discuss an amendment to the anunnaki's original plan with Ishtar." Nergal gestured for Enkara to join them.

She was reluctant, but in the end, she joined them and listened as they laid out their plan.

After hearing it in its fullness, she shook her head doubtfully. "I don't know. This plan sounds like it could enrage both goddesses instead of just one if it goes badly."

"Leave it to us to soothe our queens," Tammuz said. "But you are correct. There is great risk to our plan. It might fail completely and ruin any chance you have of negotiating with Ereshkigal."

"But with your plan, I might get Ereshkigal to release Kuwari from the underworld."

"That is the hope," Nergal said.

"And you'll just agree to give up your chance to return to your queen's side?"

"I've grown to care for you and Kuwari as well. And if it works out like I hope, I'll still get to be with my queen."

"But you must agree to this," Tammuz interjected. "We will not force you."

"If Kuwari agrees, then I will gladly follow."

Nergal nodded and then said his goodbyes to Tammuz. A short time later, he surrendered control back to Kuwari.

Enkara held herself back only long enough to use their mental link to confirm it really was him and then she was dragging him into an embrace.

"You idiot. Give me some warning next time you decide to let a god borrow your body."

"I'm sorry." Kuwari brushed back her hair so he could press a kiss to her shoulder. "Time was short, and we needed to hammer out the bones of a plan. It was easier if Nergal and Tammuz could talk directly."

"Do you really think this will work? That it's not suicide? Neither Ereshkigal nor Ishtar are known for their calm and controlled responses."

"No risks, no rewards," Kuwari said with a chuckle.

Enkara muttered a prayer to Anu, hoping the father of the gods might be swayed into intervening should two of his granddaughters go to war.

"How can an Avenging Blade of a goddess have so little faith?" Kuwari's grin was back in place.

"Oh, I have faith. Lots of faith that if something can go wrong, it usually does."

"You're terrible."

Enkara rolled her eyes and then turned serious. "I know we don't have much time, that Ereshkigal will be here soon, but seeing Nergal in control of your body really drove something home. Has he been there the whole time watching? Or has he been unaware, asleep and dreaming?"

Kuwari's expression turned thoughtful. "I think he's been aware of his surroundings. It may even go deeper than that.

He might share my emotions, experiencing some or all of what I have experienced. It's also why my visions are so much stronger than my father's, whose gift is no small thing."

Nergal might have been spying on them? That was a disconcerting thought.

CHAPTER FORTY-FOUR

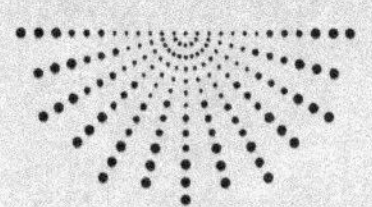

Outside in the hall, Enkara heard the approach of many people. Moments later, Ereshkigal entered with a horde of chanting, dancing, and praying priests and priestesses. The group halted, their surprise evident by the sudden cessation of sound.

"What is going on here?" Ereshkigal shouted.

"A rebellion," Tammuz said calmly, taking hold of Enkara's arm and then a moment later, Kuwari's.

Enkara reached for her power the same moment Tammuz summoned his. Ishtar's warm magic flooded out, eager to reunite with the harvest god's, but they didn't stop there and included Kuwari and Nergal in their net of building magic.

"Stop!" Ereshkigal screamed as she summoned her own power and shouted for the anunnaki to separate them. "Ishtar can't perform the Sacred Marriage within the Kur. They are contrary powers! It will rip the realms apart!"

The eagle-headed anunnaki paced forward to face Ereshkigal. "I and my brethren will not serve you in this endeavor."

"What?" Ereshkigal's shock flicked to rage and then back to fear as the power continued to pour off Enkara and Tammuz. "You knew about this? Are you a part of this?"

"This is a deviation from my plan, but yes, I was aware no party was pleased with the way things were, so it was time for a change. Though this is a little livelier than I'd envisioned," the anunnaki's beak clacked in humor.

Enkara found nothing humorous about the situation. Drawing on such great amounts of power without Ishtar's guidance was taxing her. She'd never mastered this level of magic in training yet. Only with Tammuz and Nergal's aid was she able to rein back the great power they'd summoned.

Though for how much longer, she didn't know. Given half a chance, it felt like the power wanted to burst forth from the depths of her bones and incinerate her and everyone in the immediate area.

Just hold on for a little longer, Kuwari-Nergal whispered into her mind.

"Have you all lost your minds?" Ereshkigal shrieked. "It will destroy the Kur!"

"Actually," the anunnaki continued, tilting his head one way and then another, "Without Tammuz merged with Kuwari, they can't draw enough power to destroy the Kur, but that's not their intention. Though it will certainly bring life to the land of the dead. We'll be sorting out the mess for eons. Your priestesses will likely all end up with child and will need time to raise them. Babies in the underworld. Pure chaos."

"Go!" Ereshkigal yelled, her rage and torment etched clearly upon her face. "I free Kuwari from his oath. I decree it void. All anunnaki shall witness it."

Enkara swallowed back the power she'd been keeping in check, an act much harder than the actual summoning. Sweat poured down her skin, and her arms and legs shook with the force of exerting her will upon Ishtar's fractious power.

When she at last had it under control, Tammuz released his hold on her arm. Kuwari did the same a moment later.

"It is witnessed," Tammuz said.

"Just go before you upset the balance greater than you already have!" Ereshkigal stumbled back, her wings sweeping a priest out of her way as she turned to leave.

The anunnaki overtook her and placed a hand on her shoulder. "You are out of balance. Bitterness holds sway over your heart and mind. It taints all within the underworld. You used to value honor and integrity. I am sorry if you see my actions as a betrayal, but I had to act."

"If you seek forgiveness, you will not get it."

"Then it is good I do not seek that," the anunnaki said. "But if you are willing to listen—"

"I am not. I have agreed to their terms. They are free to go. Their kingdom is safe from me. I want them gone."

"There is something else—"

"What more do you want from me? What more do you dare ask?" Ereshkigal advanced upon the other winged being, her eyes sparkling with rage and rising confrontation.

"It was Ishtar who, in her naïve arrogance, crossed into my domain, breaking all the seals placed there to warn mortals and foolish gods away, but she was so focused on demanding I take back my gifts of death and renewal she didn't know she'd inadvertently allowed the Kur to trap her."

Ereshkigal's voice edged higher, in step with her rising rage. "Finally understanding what she'd done, she cried out to Tammuz for aid. He did the only thing he could and surrendered his life force to her so that she could return to the living world and make it fertile once more. With that act, he trapped himself here for eternity. Then do you know what my wise and most beloved sister did? She blamed me! Then she stole my husband, so I would know her pain. A pain she brought upon herself."

Kuwari-Nergal stepped forward, his hands outstretched before him, beseeching her to listen. "Beloved, it is not that we are asking for something else. The young prince and his Blade are offering you a gift. Please do not turn it down out of spite and misplaced pride."

Ereshkigal looked genuinely baffled for a moment. "Nergal? How?"

"I have been awake for many years, watching as my host and his Blade grew. Their love is so pure and all-encompassing even I find myself touched by it and will not willingly let harm come to them if it is in my power to prevent."

New pain and horror transformed Ereshkigal's expression. "Oh, my Nergal. I have given Kuwari back his freedom. I had to save the Kur and all the souls within its domain."

Enkara felt a tiny welling of pity for what the Queen of the Underworld must now be feeling.

"Shhh, my love. I know and would have done the same."

Ereshkigal stepped closer, her wings folding down as she unconsciously sought to protect herself from a trap. "My Nergal, to have you so close at last…only to lose you."

"You do not have to lose him, not completely," Enkara joined in at last, seeing the opportunity Nergal had said to watch for. She sheathed her crystalline blade, unbuckled the harness and laid it aside. Then with hands outstretched before her, she dropped to her knees and closed her eyes. In a graceful move, she prostrated herself before Ereshkigal.

"Great Queen, I know you have been wronged and have wronged in turn, but if it is in my power to stop that vicious cycle, I gladly will. I humbly offer myself for your use as a host during a Sacred Marriage. Tammuz and Nergal suggested we create a new ritual, one that takes place during the dying season to balance the one between Ishtar and Tammuz in the Spring."

Enkara remained bowed down, but she expanded her senses to follow every sound and movement in the room. "I would be a willing host so that you and your husband could be together again."

"I do not need your pity, mortal."

"It's not pity," Enkara countered, fighting down the annoyance she felt rising within her at the goddess's attitude. "It's righting an injustice. For one night a year, you can be with your beloved, just as Ishtar can have her Tammuz. It is symmetry and balance. I assure you, while I might once have pitied you, all I need to do to vanquish it is remember what you attempted to do to Kuwari's younger brothers and sisters and every other soul in New Sumer."

Kuwari-Nergal stepped closer to Ereshkigal. "Will you accept this gift? For me, if you are too proud to accept it for yourself? I have missed you."

The goddess drew back as if his nearness somehow weakened her. She spun on her heels and then marched away to stand beside a carved and painted column. She leaned against the stone, one arm bracing her weight and then to the surprise of Enkara and perhaps every other person in the room, her shoulders began to shake.

Soft sobs reached their ears, and then Kuwari-Nergal walked over and took Ereshkigal in his arms.

Enkara held her breath, afraid of what any accidental skin contact would do to Kuwari. But Nergal was cautious as he bent down to place a kiss on the top of Ereshkigal's headdress and then he murmured soft words, rocking her gently in his arms.

Eventually, he guided her over to a bench and sat her down upon it. Ereshkigal's weakness lasted only a few moments more and then she dried her tears—one's of joy, Enkara realized.

The Queen of the Underworld turned to look up at Enkara. "Come forward, Blade."

Enkara obeyed but held her breath, not knowing what this goddess would do. Though she hoped for all concerned that Ereshkigal would agree to the terms. New Sumer and its people needed a rest from the feud between the two sister goddesses.

"I want two nights and two days a year. The solstices. Tammuz and Ishtar can have the equinoxes. Then I will accept your gift," Ereshkigal said, and she stood, coming to circle Enkara.

"I believe I can speak for Kuwari as well when I say we are willing. As for Tammuz and Ishtar," she glanced over her shoulder at the harvest god. He nodded his head and grinned. "I would guess they would not be against such an arrangement. Although perhaps I would not be the best one to mention it to Ishtar. I am certain she did not intend for Kuwari and me to become your Monarch and Blade."

Ereshkigal inclined her head. "That would be her loss but doesn't affect the agreement we make here today."

"No," Enkara agreed. "I will honor your request for the solstices."

Ereshkigal glanced from her to look upon Kuwari, a clear look of longing in her eyes. "I have one other request to ask as well." She hesitated then added, "Though you don't have to agree to this one."

"I would be honored to hear it."

"I want to spend the rest of tonight with my husband."

For two beats of her heart, Enkara was certain her mask of neutrality cracked and showed how much that disturbed her. This goddess wanted to spend the night with Enkara's mate. It took several more heartbeats before she could form a non-fiery response. "Do you mean you wish for us to perform a Sacred Marriage ritual this night?"

That was mildly better than what Enkara thought the goddess truly meant. Please, let the fates not ask her to stand aside while another woman, goddess though she might be, made love to Kuwari.

"No. Neither of you are physically or mentally prepared to act as hosts during that rite, and there is much ritual and magic which needs to be performed beforehand. We'll save that for the summer solstice." Ereshkigal held out her gloved hand for Kuwari. He took it.

What, by great Anu, was going on? Enkara wasn't the adventurous type.

"I have missed my king. I simply want to sit and talk with my husband, to know what it was like living all those lives only to die and be reborn to start fresh." With a gloved hand, Ereshkigal brushed a caress along Kuwari's jawline. "While I look forward to a more intimate time with my husband, I cannot do that tonight without killing Kuwari, and that would start the cycle anew."

"If Kuwari is willing, so am I." Enkara understood Ereshkigal in that moment. If she'd been separated from Kuwari for thousands of years and she was at last given a chance to see and talk to him again, but nothing more physical, she would take what was offered even if she did want so much more.

"I am in your debt." There was a depth of emotion in those simple two words.

The Queen of the Underworld's thanks came as a surprise, making her seem more compassionate than she'd appeared at first.

When Ereshkigal tugged on Kuwari's hand, he allowed her to pull him along. They were almost to one of the archways leading to the stone stairs when the queen glanced over her shoulder. "Blade, attend us." Her gaze landed on Tammuz next. "Even you, my troublesome trickster brother-by-marriage, are welcome to join us. I'm feeling rather benevolent tonight. I might even forgive betrayal by a certain anunnaki judge."

With that, she turned and continued to walk. Enkara and the anunnaki glided along behind. The Queen of the Underworld toured her city, showing Nergal some of what had changed since he'd last been here. He in turn shared some of the stories he'd gained from hundreds of lifetimes.

"I have learned what it is to be mortal and fear death, to dread the loss of what we know and value. It gave me a different outlook," Nergal said as they walked under the star-filled sky. "I would like to share that with you one day if you'll allow."

Ereshkigal looked surprised. "I will happily accept anything you want to share with me, my beloved."

He nodded and the tension in his shoulders relaxed.

Soon Tammuz was telling Enkara stories of his and Ishtar's first meeting and how she'd not been that impressed with him, that a simple human farmer had almost won her hand in marriage, but with much courtship, he swayed her.

"Your Kuwari reminds me a little of myself when I was younger. Stubborn and bull-headed to a fault. It's likely why I feel a kinship with him after only knowing him such a short time. He's a determined sort."

Enkara laughed and agreed wholeheartedly. Soon she relaxed and enjoyed the strange tour of the underworld. The stars were brighter and filled the sky with more glorious color than what resided in the living world.

Everything seemed just a little more beautiful and peaceful here than back home. But for all that she could admire the beauty of the underworld for what it was, when Ereshkigal said the sun would be rising on New Sumer and it was time to return to the living world, Enkara was more than ready to go home.

With a final kiss to the top of her head, Nergal said goodbye to his wife and then released his hold upon Kuwari to return to his state of half-slumber until he was called during the solstice rite.

Kuwari swayed on his feet and Enkara stepped forward to steady him.

"Are you all right?" she asked using their mental link.

"Yes. I'm tired and have the mother of all headaches, but I'm me again, and we managed what I think could have been classified as a small miracle."

Ereshkigal turned her gaze upon them both. "Now that you are ours, at least two days out of each year, I will expect to see you guarded by an appropriate number of anunnaki befitting your new status."

The eagle-headed anunnaki's beak gaped open in avian humor. "I shall see that it's done, my Queen."

"Good." She turned and walked away.

Once she was gone from sight and presumably out of earshot as well, the anunnaki clicked his beak. "I will see them returned home as well, apparently."

"Thank you," Kuwari said, an answering grin on his lips. "For I haven't a clue how to return to the living world and my visions never showed me that detail either."

As it turned out, the trip to the living world was easy. The anunnaki placed a hand on each of their shoulders, called power, and in the next moment Enkara and Kuwari were no longer in the Underworld. Instead, they were once again standing on the black-sand beaches of Nineveh.

"Be well, Blade and Prince. And expect the arrival of your anunnaki guard shortly. Until we meet again." The anunnaki bowed then and left them standing there on the beach, within easy walking distance of Ishtar's Gate and the processional way.

"Let's walk slowly," Kuwari said. "I need time to think of something to calm my parents so they don't imprison me in the nursery after what I did and what we've agreed to."

Enkara bumped shoulders with him. "Has the silver-tongued prince run out of persuasive words? That's a first. Should I be concerned?"

"No. I just need to think of something really, really good. Getting banished back to the nursery with all my younger brothers and sisters would curtail certain...er...fun activities I intend to partake in with my Blade later tonight."

"Hmmm, what about the traitors that released the plague and delivered you to the underworld. The anunnaki told me about them."

"Ah! That's something I can work with. It was councilor Enheduana. She isn't a councilor at all, but one of Ereshkigal's priestesses. With a little swift talking, I should be able to nicely redirect my father's anger toward hunting down Enheduana and her collaborators."

"Well, you're about to get your chance to prove just how good your persuasive skills are, because I think someone had a vision of our arrival." She pointed to where the gate was opening, and a horde of Shadows were even now making their swift way forward. They were soon outdistanced by King Ditanu and Queen Iltani.

"Damn it, I'm not ready yet." Kuwari wasn't given long to worry though. Ditanu reached his son and wrapped him in his arms. A moment later a powerful arm snaked out and hooked Enkara into a bone crushing hug as well.

"My idiot son and his equally foolhardy Blade, I swear you scared forty years off my life." Ditanu gave them two more powerful squeezes and then released them. "The youthful escapades Iltani and I undertook pale in comparison to what my visions say you just lived through."

Iltani was steps behind Ditanu, and she grabbed Kuwari and Enkara before either of them could formulate a response to his father's comment. After another series of crushing hugs, they were released into Burrukan and Ahassunu's care.

Everyone babbled at once, demanding to know about everything that had occurred. Kuwari winced at the noise.

"Peace! I'll tell you everything, but merciful goddess Ishtar, please just stop all the shouting."

"Fine. We'll be silent if you start talking faster," Ditanu said with a grumble.

Enkara bumped shoulders with her prince and grinned. *"Shall I start?"*

"Please, goddess, yes." He laughed ruefully. *"It will give me more time to work on my defense."*

Chuckling, Enkara started their tale. It took the entire walk home and most of the rest of the day to finally satisfy everyone's questions, but she didn't mind.

She and Kuwari now had their entire lives before them, minus two days spent in the underworld each year. As far as possible futures that might have unfolded, she thought they had done alright, all other possibilities considered.

THE END

THANK you for reading Blade's Honor. For more in the same world, you can continue by reading Blade's Destiny.

BOOKS BY LISA BLACKWOOD

Gargoyle & Sorceress

Dawn of the Sorceress

Sorceress Awakening

Sorceress Rising

Sorceress Hunting

Sorceress at War

Sorceress Enraged

Legacy of the Sorceress

Sorcery & Firedrakes

Scion of the Sorceress

Sorceress Eternal

In Deception's Shadow Series (Epic Fantasy Romance)

Betrayal's Price

Herd Mistress

Maiden's Wolf

Death's Queen

The Prince's Gryphon (forthcoming)

Ishtar's Legacy Series (Epic Fantasy Romance)

Ishtar's Blade

The Blade's Beginning (short story)

Blade's Honor

Blade's Destiny

The Blade's Shadow

First Queen of the Gryphons

The King of the Anunnaki (forthcoming)

The Anunnaki's Blade (forthcoming)

Huntress vs Huntsman (Epic Fantasy Romance)

Master of the Hunt

Night Huntress

Dragon Archer

Soul Mage